The Three Loves OF CHARLIE DELANEY

BOOK TWO

JOEY W. KISER

iUniverse®

CHARLIE DELANEY
BOOK TWO

iUniverse books may be ordered through booksellers or by contacting:
iUniverse
1663 Liberty Drive
Bloomington, IN 47403
www.iuniverse.com
1-800-Authors (1-800-288-4677)

ISBN: 978-1-4917-7740-4 (sc)
ISBN: 978-1-4917-8628-4 (hc)
ISBN: 978-1-4917-7739-8 (e)

Library of Congress Control Number: 2015917891

Print information available on the last page.

iUniverse rev. date: 1/08/2016

CONTENTS

Chapter 1
CHARLIE'S SECOND LOVE

It is one cold Monday morning in the northern part of North Carolina, January 1987, Charlie Delaney rides down the road in his truck. The previous week, he turned twenty-six. He has just started a new year that will transform his normal existence into a life of purpose, meaning, and fulfillment.

As Charlie drives down the road, he gets a strong urge for a pizza. He has just gotten off work, and he doesn't want to go home and cook anything. While passing a shopping center, he sees a Little Tony's Pizza. When the stoplight turns green, he whips his truck into the parking lot and parks. He eagerly proceeds to walk toward the little restaurant.

Charlie has never been to this particular pizza place before but is eager to try it out. He is so hungry he could eat a horse. As he reaches the restaurant and opens the door, he finds the place deserted but hears people in the back.

"Hello! Is anyone here?" Charlie calls out, waiting for someone to come out from the back. He is pleasantly surprised when a cute little redhead appears.

Looking at Charlie with a sweet, innocent smile, she says, "Hello, sir. May I help you?"

Charlie looks at her, dumbfounded. He just can't get over how beautiful she is. "Yeah, you sure can. If you are on the menu, I'll take you as an order to go."

The girl blushes a little and says, "No, I am not on the menu, but I'll be glad to fix you a pizza."

"What's your name?"

With the same shy, innocent smile, the girl replies, "Karen. Karen Thomas."

"Charlie. Charlie Delaney. You sure are real pretty."

Karen continues to smile. "Thank you, sir."

Charlie notices that even her voice is soft and heavenly.

"Please, don't call me sir; call me Charlie."

"Okay, Charlie. What can I get for you today?"

Charlie glances at the menu. "What do you recommend, Karen?" Not waiting for her reply, Charlie adds, "You sure have the prettiest red hair and the most radiant blue eyes I have ever seen."

Ignoring Charlie's last remark, Karen says, "The special today is, buy one pizza with eight toppings at the regular price and get the second one free."

"Well, if I order that, I am going to need help eating the second one. If I order the two pizzas, will you help me eat them?"

Karen looks at Charlie and says bluntly, "No. My boss won't let me eat here with any of the customers. Besides, customers don't eat here; it's takeout only."

Charlie smiles pleasantly. "What time do you get off? I'll save the pizzas for then. We could go over to my house and have dinner together."

She responds flatly, "No thanks, Mr. Delaney. I have a boyfriend, and I don't think he would like that."

"What he doesn't know won't hurt him."

"No, thank you. I'm not that kind of girl."

Realizing that she took it the wrong way, Charlie replies, "I'm sorry. I didn't mean to come on so strong. Since this is the first time I have met you, I shouldn't behave so boldly. It's just that you are so pretty."

Karen smiles. "Well, have you made up your mind what you want?"

"Yes, I'll have a medium pepperoni pizza with mushrooms, onions, and green peppers, please."

"Okay. That will take about fifteen minutes."

"Oh boy! I get to talk to you for fifteen whole minutes."

"Not quite. I have work to do in the back when there aren't any customers to wait on."

"What do I look like, a scarecrow?"

"But you have already been waited on, sir."

"What's this 'sir' talk? Please call me Charlie."

Charlie's sad expression draws Karen's attention.

"Okay, Charlie. Sorry … I forgot. My boss likes me to stay busy."

"I understand. Could you tell me something before you leave, Karen?"

"Yes."

"How old are you?"

"I'm nineteen."

"I am twenty-six. Matter of fact, I turned twenty-six just last week."

Karen turns around and goes into the back without giving Charlie a response. He finds a seat and sits down. About five minutes later, Karen walks to the front again. Her eyes meet Charlie's, and they smile at each other. Karen shyly turns away, returning to the back again. Charlie continues to stare at the scrumptious teenager. He can't get over how beautiful she is.

"So, if you're nineteen, you must have just graduated from high school."

Still in the back, Karen answers, "Yes, that's right. I graduated last summer."

"Are you going to college anywhere?"

"No. The main reason I'm not going to college is the money; besides, I don't know what I want to be anyway."

Charlie, staring at her large, full breasts, says, "Yeah, I know. It's a big decision."

"I'll probably have decided by this time next year. Maybe I'll have enough money saved up by then."

"Don't your folks help out any?"

"My mama can't help out much. It takes all she makes to pay the bills."

"What about your father?"

"My father is dead. He died in Vietnam when I was a little girl."

"I'm sorry to hear that."

"Yeah … that's the way it goes." Karen returns to the front as she says this, her young happy face now looking sad and depressed.

Charlie notices this and doesn't say anything else in response.

As Charlie and Karen continue to talk, customers start coming in the door. Charlie doesn't get to talk to Karen for much longer because of the other people. Before long, Charlie's pizza is ready.

Karen takes it from the back counter and gets Charlie's attention with her sweet-sounding voice. "Charlie, your pizza is ready."

He gets up, walks over to the cash register, and pays for the pizza. Giving Karen a wink, he says, "See you later, Cubby."

"Why did you call me that?"

Charlie grins sweetly. "You just look like a Cubby, so I thought I would start calling you that."

She just shakes her head, a puzzled look on her face. "Bye-bye."

Charlie looks at her with admiration. "See you tomorrow, Karen. Same time, same place." He winks at her again, takes his pizza, and leaves the place happily, with a big cheerful grin on his face.

As Charlie gets to his truck, he realizes something wonderful has happened. Cupid has shot another arrow at him. It was love at first sight. Charlie just can't get over how pretty Karen is. She is young and sexy and has the voice of an angel. She is as pretty as a girl could possibly be. Charlie can't believe how attracted he is to this girl. He can't seem to get her out of his mind.

When he gets home, he takes the pizza inside the house and begins to eat it. He finishes half of it and then puts the rest in the freezer.

Charlie tells himself, *When Karen and I get married and have a few kids, I'll have something to show them: the very first pizza she brought to me.* While Charlie relaxes in his living room, he continues to think about Karen. The more he thinks about her, the fonder he becomes of her. *I wonder if she will go out with me. She mentioned a boyfriend. I wonder if it is a serious relationship. When I go by there tomorrow, I'll have to find out how serious she is about him. He is the only thing in my way.*

Charlie thinks more about what he wants to say to his redheaded sweetheart tomorrow. He is somewhat controlled by this girl. She has a special mysterious something about her that pulls at him with a strange magnetic force. His mind seems to be filled with a special joy and happiness. He realizes that she is someone very special, not just another attractive girl that he has found but someone with a purpose for him.

While lying in bed, Charlie says out loud, "She has the smile of an angel. Her eyes are as radiant as two blue sapphires glistening with innocence. Her sweetness could only belong to a virgin. Oh, how wonderful it would be if she were a virgin, pure as snow on a mountaintop. Maybe that is why she has taken over my heart so easily and so soon. I wonder how I could find out if she is one without asking her. Maybe I could lead up to it gradually so it won't look so obvious. I don't know … she is so beautiful. I hope she will go out with me. It will break my heart if she doesn't. All I know is I will have to wait till tomorrow to find out."

Charlie looks up to the ceiling and says a little prayer. "Dear God in heaven, if it be your will, please let our relationship develop into a true and long-lasting one. Let her see me as the new love in her life. Give me the strength and the knowledge to say the right things to her. I know I haven't prayed to you in a long time; therefore, please, if it be your will, grant me this request. Amen."

Charlie rolls over and goes to sleep. But he doesn't sleep very well at all. He keeps tossing and turning and waking up all through the night. He has brief dreams of his new redheaded love.

The night goes by slowly, but the sun finally comes up. Charlie feels tired and run-down when he gets up in the morning. He decides not to go to work, so he calls in to take a vacation day.

This is no big deal for Charlie's employer, who just says, "Okay. See you tomorrow morning."

After hanging up the phone, Charlie is glad he decided not to go to work today. "Boy, if I went to work today, I don't think I could make it through the day." He decides to lie back down and sleep a few more hours before doing anything.

Soon, Charlie wakes up from his nap, feeling much more rested. He is eager to get started on his new and exciting endeavor: to find out more about this compelling red-haired girl. He opens the phone book and looks up all the people with the last name Thomas. As Charlie writes these names down, he remembers Karen telling him that her father died in Vietnam. He writes this information down also. He thinks about all the important information he wants to know about her so that when he speaks to her, he'll know what to ask.

At about four o'clock, Charlie gets into his truck and nervously makes his way to the little pizza place. He parks his truck close to the restaurant, gets out, and proceeds to walk inside. As Karen comes out from the back, he realizes that he is the only customer.

Karen sees Charlie and smiles innocently at him. She throws up her hand and says happily, "Hello again. Back for another pizza, Mr. Charlie?"

Charlie smiles. "Yes, ma'am! I'm back for another one of your delicious pizzas, Miss Karen."

"Tell me what you want on it."

"I'll take a medium pepperoni pizza with mushrooms, onions, and green peppers, please."

Karen writes down the order and takes it to the back. In a few minutes, she comes to the front again. "So how's everything going today, Charlie?"

Charlie is happy that she has remembered to call him by his first name. So happy in fact that he forgets about the things he wanted to talk to her about.

"Oh, everything is going just fine. I'm glad you are working today. I had a bad feeling you might not be here today."

Karen just smiles her sweet, innocent smile.

"By the way, how often do you work here anyway?

"I work here five days a week, ten to five, and every other Saturday."

Seeing an opening and without any further delay, Charlie asks her if she'll be working this coming Saturday.

Karen shows a reluctant smile. "No, not this week. I had last Saturday off, so this week is my time to work."

"I'm sorry to hear that. I was hoping you and I could go out for dinner this weekend."

"Even if I were off, I wouldn't go out with you. I told you yesterday that I have a boyfriend, a very serious boyfriend. He and I have been going together since ninth grade."

Charlie's hopes of going out with her shatter like a piece of glass thrown against a brick wall. He looks as sad as a basset hound when he hears these words.

Seeing this look on Charlie's face, Karen says, "Don't look so sad,

Charlie. There are plenty of girls who would like to go out with a handsome guy like you."

These words lift Charlie's spirit somewhat, but he still feels down.

"So you have been going with this guy since the ninth grade?" he asks.

"That's right," Karen says. "He and I have been through some rough times these last five years."

"Do you love him?"

Karen blushes a little. "Well … I think so. I mean, sometimes I love him to death, but then there are times I don't want to be around him at all."

Charlie's eyes brighten. "So you don't know for sure if you really love him?"

Showing a determined look, Karen speaks with a clear voice. "Let me put it this way, Charlie. I love him enough not to go out with anyone else."

Charlie realizes that she doesn't want to keep talking about this, so he decides to change the subject. "Oh, I understand. You said yesterday that you just graduated from high school."

"That's right. Last summer."

Charlie grins. "Well, if you ever do decide to go to college, you ought to take up drama; you sure would make a pretty actress. All you would have to do is smile and say a few lines, and you would be making millions of dollars a year."

This seems to be just what Karen wanted to hear.

With an excited grin, she says, "Really! You think I would make a good actress?"

"Sure do. If I knew you were going to be in a movie, I'd come and see you."

"Well … thank you, Charlie. You know something—I always wanted to be an actress."

Charlie sees how happy he has made her, so he decides to lay on a few more compliments.

"Can you sing?"

"A little bit but not much. I'm kinda shy when it comes to singing in front of people."

Charlie gazes into her enticing blue eyes. "I bet you can sing real well. You have a pleasant-sounding voice. Who knows—one day you might even be a star."

Karen smiles joyfully, blushes a little, and says, "I doubt that, Charlie."

"You might even drive one of those fancy, expensive cars one day."

"Oh, I don't know about that."

"What kind of car do you drive now?"

"Oh, just a simple little red Mustang." She points outside at the little red car parked two cars down from where his truck is parked. Charlie smiles gladly as he sees the red automobile out in the parking lot. He had gotten what he wanted: to know which car was Karen's.

Before long, Charlie's pizza is done. As he pays Karen for it, he smiles at her sweet face. He doesn't go on again about taking her out.

"Would it be all right if I come by and talk to you some more sometime?"

"Yes, that will be all right with me, Charlie."

So Charlie leaves the establishment, with pizza in hand and ideas in mind.

Charlie walks toward his truck while casually looking at Karen's little red Mustang. He puts his pizza inside his truck, starts it up, and drives around the parking lot of the shopping center, circling back around to where Karen's car is. Taking out a pen, he writes down her license plate number. He now has all the information about Karen that he needs.

As he drives home, all kinds of ideas flood Charlie's mind. First of all, he needs to find out where Karen lives and who her boyfriend is. Now that he has her license plate number, it will be only a matter of time before he gets the other information. Until now, Charlie's life has seemed dull and simple. He needs a little more excitement and a rousing new adventure. Knowing anything worth having won't be easy to get, he is determined to win over Karen and gain her affection. Charlie wouldn't care if Karen had been going with her boyfriend since kindergarten. He wants her so badly that he isn't going to let anything interfere with his objective, and that is to have Karen as his girlfriend.

As Charlie pulls up to his driveway, he wonders how to go about getting the information about Karen. He thinks for a moment and then unlocks his front door and walks inside his house. He walks straight to the phone book, setting the pizza on the counter as he turns the pages. He looks in the yellow pages for a private investigator, one that looks very professional. He then calls the number. The first time he calls, the number is busy. In a few minutes, Charlie tries again.

This time, a woman answers. “Hello. Bowman Investigations. May I help you?”

Charlie’s mind goes blank but only for a few seconds.

“Hello. My name is Charlie Delaney. I was wondering if you could help me find some information on someone.”

“You called the right place, Mr. Delaney. That’s just what we do.”

Charlie starts to relax as the woman continues to speak.

“Would you like to come in and talk with Mr. Bowman? He would be glad to help you, sir.”

Charlie shyly replies, “I sure would, Miss … Miss … oh, by the way, who am I speaking with?”

“My name is Nancy Walker. I’m Mr. Bowman’s secretary and special assistant.”

Charlie pauses for a few seconds while deciding what to do.

“Yes, I would like to talk to Mr. Bowman personally, if it wouldn’t be much trouble.”

“When would you like to come in, Mr. Delaney?”

“Oh, sometime late in the day tomorrow.”

“I’ll put you down for tomorrow afternoon at four-thirty.”

“Fine. I’ll see you then. Oh, by the way, how much does Mr. Bowman charge for his services?”

“Mr. Bowman charges about the same as most other investigation agencies. He would have to talk to you first before he could quote you a specific price.”

“Okay, but could you give me a general idea on something very simple?”

“Well, I believe his standard fee is two hundred dollars a day, plus expenses.”

Charlie’s heart suddenly stops beating. “Two hundred dollars a day!

Gosh, that seems to me to be a whole lot. Does he work by the hour? What I have in mind might not take a whole day."

"Oh no, Mr. Bowman works strictly by the day. There is a minimum of one day. No matter how long he has to work on that day, he gets compensation for the whole day."

Charlie is bewildered, wondering if it will be worth it. But then he just thinks about how beautiful Karen is, with those radiant blue eyes and long luscious red hair.

"Do you still want to talk with Mr. Bowman tomorrow, sir?"

Charlie comes out of his trance and says, "Yes, ma'am. I still want to talk with Mr. Bowman. I'll be there tomorrow at four-thirty sharp."

"We will be looking for you tomorrow, Mr. Delaney. Mr. Bowman is a very qualified investigator. He has been in the business for twenty years."

"Okay, I'll see him then."

"We will be expecting you tomorrow at four-thirty, Mr. Delaney. Thank you so much for calling."

"Thank you, Mrs. Walker."

After making the arrangements to see the private investigator, Charlie realizes that this little venture isn't going to be cheap. He accepts what he has to do with a positive frame of mind, prepared to pay for it at any cost.

The next day, as Charlie gets ready for work, he has a few second thoughts about going to see the investigator. He doesn't want to get his hopes up too high, but a voice deep down keeps pushing him on. He thinks to himself that he doesn't have anything else to live for. Karen means more to him than anything else, so Charlie talks himself into going.

After work, Charlie rushes to his truck and makes his way to the investigator's office. On the way, he stops at the bank to withdraw a few hundred dollars from his savings account. As Charlie walks up to the investigator's office, he begins to feel quite silly about the whole thing, but since he has gone this far, and just to satisfy his curiosity about Karen, he works up his courage and walks into the office.

Nancy Walker greets him as he walks through the door. "Hello. May I help you, sir?"

"Yes, my name is Charlie Delaney. I have an appointment to see Mr. Bowman."

"Yes, Mr. Delaney. Mr. Bowman will be right with you. Please have a seat, and I'll see if he is ready."

"Thank you."

As Charlie takes a seat in the waiting room, he has more negative feelings about the whole matter. Before too long, Nancy comes back and escorts Charlie to Mr. Bowman's office. Charlie reluctantly follows her, now feeling quite timid.

"Hello. You must be Mr. Delaney," says Mr. Bowman, greeting Charlie at the door to his office. "How do you do, sir?"

"Oh, pretty good. How about yourself?"

"Fine, just fine. I couldn't be better." Mr. Bowman offers Charlie a seat, and Nancy exits, closing the door behind her as Charlie sits down.

Mr. Bowman sits down behind his desk.

"My secretary has told me you want me to investigate a certain matter for you."

"That's right. There is a certain girl I want to know a little more about, if it wouldn't be much trouble."

"No trouble at all. Please tell me all about it."

"I want to know more about a young lady named Karen Thomas. All I know about her is that she is nineteen years old, has gorgeous red hair and radiant blue eyes, works at Little Tony's Pizza, and drives a red Mustang. Also, I happen to be madly in love with her."

Showing a concerned look, Mr. Bowman says, "You happen to be in love with her, you say."

"Yes, sir. There's just something about her … she has completely taken over my heart. I can't seem to get her out of my mind. All I know is I must find out all I can about her."

"How long have you known this girl, Mr. Delaney?"

"Please call me Charlie. You make me nervous calling me Mr. Delaney."

"Fine. How long have you known Miss or Mrs. Thomas?"

"It's Miss Karen Thomas. I met her only two days ago. She has a boyfriend, a very serious boyfriend. I want to know who he is and as much as possible about him."

"What is the reason for all this, if you don't mind me asking?"

"Like I told you earlier, I can't explain it. I met her the day before yesterday, and I have really fallen for this girl something awful, sir. I must find out all about her so I can try to develop some type of relationship with her before her boyfriend marries her."

Nodding his head, Mr. Bowman replies, "Oh, I see. You just want to know about her background."

"Right. Simple stuff: just about where she lives, who her mother is—you know, general information. I have written down all the information I want to know." Charlie hands Mr. Bowman a sheet of paper with the notes he's written. "But most of all, I want to know who her boyfriend is. Where he works, how much he earns, the places he goes—everything you can possibly find out."

"What you are asking me to do might take a little time. It also might be a little expensive."

Charlie scratches his head, "How little are you talking about?"

"I don't know how long it will take for me to gather this information, Charlie. My rate is two hundred dollars a day, plus expenses."

"That's what your secretary told me yesterday. I don't want to sink much more than three or four hundred, at the most."

"I see. What do you say I work on the case for a day or two and see what I come up with? If you want me to pursue the matter in greater detail, we can talk some more."

Charlie responds with a joyous smile. "That sounds pretty good, Mr. Bowman. When can you start on the case?"

"I can start on the case tomorrow, if that will be all right with you."

"That sounds just fine."

Now Mr. Bowman smiles too.

"I have been doing this work for twenty years. It shouldn't take me too long to find out the information you want to know."

Mr. Bowman stands up and walks around his desk, and Charlie stands up too. The two men move closer together and shake hands.

"Mr. Delaney … I'm sorry, Charlie … don't get your hopes up on finding everything you want to know. Just be patient; I'll do the best job I can for you."

"That's all I can ask, sir. That's all I can ask. Just do the best you can and I will surely and certainly appreciate it."

Mr. Bowman smiles again and says, "Thank you, Charlie."

"All the information I know about Miss Thomas is on that paper, even her license plate number. As I mentioned, she drives a red Mustang."

Mr. Bowman shows some interest. "Fine. This will help a great deal. I have a buddy who works at the police department. He can find out where she lives and a whole bunch of other things."

"I thought it might help. I'm glad she told me what kind of car she drives."

"Oh yes. I'm glad she told you too, Charlie."

Just before Charlie leaves the office, Mr. Bowman says, "Oh, by the way, I need to be paid for the first two days in advance."

"Oh, I guess I should have known that." He reaches in his billfold, takes out four hundred-dollar bills, and hands the money to Mr. Bowman.

Mr. Bowman takes the money, writes out a receipt for four hundred dollars, and hands it to Charlie.

Charlie writes his name, address, and phone number on a piece of paper and hands it to Mr. Bowman. "Here you go, Mr. Bowman. Give me a call when everything is in."

"I sure will, Charlie. It sure is good doing business with you. Just wait a few days for my phone call."

"Yes, sir. I will be waiting for my phone to ring."

Charlie departs Mr. Bowman's office, saying good-bye to Nancy on his way out. He gets in his truck and drives home. Knowing it's too close to the dinner rush to get to talk to Karen, he just sets his sights on seeing her tomorrow.

After work Thursday afternoon, Charlie drives over to the little pizza place once again. He spots Karen's little red Mustang in the parking lot and pulls into a spot nearby. Not wasting any time, he anxiously walks up to the door of the restaurant, walks in, and spots his luscious little redhead right behind the counter.

"Hi, Karen. How are you doing today?"

"Just fine, Charlie. How are you doing?"

"Life couldn't be any better now that I have seen you again."

"Oh, I wouldn't go that far. I didn't see you yesterday, so I thought you wouldn't be back."

Charlie is glad to hear that Karen missed him and has been thinking about him. He grins from ear to ear. "Yeah, I missed you yesterday too. I'll have to stay twice as long today to make up for it."

Karen smiles intriguingly when she hears Charlie's words. She looks so breathtaking today. Her long red hair is styled just right. Her luminous blue eyes sparkle as her cute smile floods the room with a sweet array of beauty. She is a picture of loveliness.

Charlie can't believe that there is such a beautiful girl in the whole world. His heart is full of joy and happiness as he gazes at the young damsel. Karen seems to like him a whole lot. He can tell by just looking into her tender and caring eyes.

Charlie steps right up to the counter, and without another second passing, tells her exactly what he is thinking. This is the first time he's ever done this with a girl.

"You know, Karen, you have the most beautiful eyes I have ever seen in my entire life." His voice is soft, and his words are true.

"Thank you, Charlie."

"Your long red hair is so silky and straight. No woman on earth has the same spectacular style as you have. It highlights your entire face with a beauty I have never seen before."

Karen blushes. "Well, thank you again, Charlie. You keep this up, and I'll have to give my boyfriend his walking papers."

Charlie's heart grows three inches as her words reach his ears. He responds with enthusiasm and fervor. "Really! Do you really mean that, Karen?"

Realizing that Charlie took her seriously, Karen quickly replies, "I was just kidding, Charlie. I would never do that to him."

Charlie's hopes rush back down, but he has reason to believe that she has her doubts about this boyfriend.

"You told me you have been going with him since the ninth grade," he says.

"That's right, Charlie. It has been over five years now."

"Haven't you ever thought about dating anybody else? Just to see if you really love him, I mean."

Karen looks down at the floor as she speaks. "Well … maybe … I don't know. Maybe … Sometimes … I don't know."

Charlie smiles. "Sounds like you're not certain on that subject."

"Well, we talked about it, but we have agreed that neither one of us will start seeing anyone else."

"So, if you see him with another girl, you might dump him?"

"Now wait a minute! I didn't say that. That's enough about that now."

Charlie gazes into Karen's eyes, realizing once again that she doesn't want to keep talking about this subject. He understands; however, her words and actions tell him that if she ever caught her boyfriend out with another girl, she might just cut him loose. Charlie thinks that this might be the way to get him out of Karen's life. The way Karen pushed her lips out when Charlie brought up the subject of seeing her boyfriend with another girl gives him the impression she wouldn't stand for that.

"You know, Karen, I find it easy to talk to you. I mean, I can open up to you a lot easier than I can with any other girl I've ever known."

"You know something, Charlie, I find it easy to talk to you also."

"I'm glad I met you. You really seem to be a sweet girl."

"Well, thank you, Charlie. I'm glad I met you too."

Customers start to come into the restaurant, so Charlie doesn't get to talk to Karen for too much longer. He wishes he could talk to her without any interruptions or interference.

As Karen finishes with her last customer, she asks, "Oh, by the way, Charlie, do you want anything to eat?"

Although not really hungry, Charlie answers, "Yes, I'll take my usual: a medium pepperoni pizza with mushrooms, onions and green peppers."

"You sure like pizza, Charlie."

Customers start rolling in, two and three at a time. Karen focuses on taking orders from the customers. Charlie just gets to look at her until his pizza is ready.

"Charlie, your pizza is done."

He walks over to the counter, pays Karen, and then whispers to her, "I wish everyone would decide to eat at Pizza Hut so I could talk to you more."

Karen grins as she gives him his change. "If they all did that, Charlie, I wouldn't have a job for very long."

"Yeah, I guess you are right. See you tomorrow, Karen."

"So long, Charlie. You behave yourself."

"I will. You do the same."

As Charlie carries his pizza out to his truck, he feels happy and content, even though he wishes he could have talked to Karen a little longer. He drives home, thinking to himself, *You know, Charlie ole' boy, trying to talk to Karen at the pizza place is becoming very frustrating. Every time we start talking, a customer walks in and gets in the way. I'm going to have to ask her if I could start calling her at home. I know she'll say no; but, then again, she might say yes. It will be worth a try anyway. And if she does say no, I'm going to have to find some other way to talk to her without all those interruptions.*

Charlie goes home and devours the whole pizza in a very short time. For someone who said he wasn't very hungry, he sure ate as if he was. He has begun to like eating pizza every day. He doesn't have much choice; that is, if he wants to keep seeing Karen.

He has started to believe that Karen is beginning to like him more and more. *She is coming around quite nicely. I wonder if she really is in love with her boyfriend. I wonder what she would do if she caught him with another girl. I bet she would hit the roof. I bet she would dump him cold.*

With that thought, Charlie begins to plot how he could make that happen without Karen knowing that he had arranged it. He thinks over in his mind the things he wants to say to her when he sees her tomorrow, and he doesn't waste any unnecessary time. He understands plainly that he hasn't much time to talk to her, so he must have quality conversations ready when he arrives. The main objective is to tell her everything she wants to hear.

In the meantime, Charlie he decides to do all those things he has been putting off: doing laundry, opening his mail, sending off all those bills, washing the dishes, and completing all his normal household chores. This keeps Charlie busy. With his mind occupied, Karen doesn't become an obsession for him.

That's something he hopes doesn't happen. He loves her and he wants to have her, but if it's not in the stars, then Charlie doesn't want to set himself up for a big disappointment. He says aloud to himself, "I must accept what happens and not let my emotions ruin my life. If worse comes to worst, I must accept that. If she chooses someone else, I must be man enough to take it in stride and not let it get me down. I haven't always gotten what I want in life, so I should accept whatever happens. Karen will decide what she wants."

Before long, Charlie feels tired and gets ready for bed, worn out from all of the work he has done. He soon falls asleep and begins to dream a very strange dream.

In the dream, Charlie is walking down a long, black, dreary road. He sees Karen smiling and waving at him. Beside Karen is her boyfriend. He is laughing at Charlie. As Charlie keeps walking, he spots Mr. Bowman hiding behind a bush and writing something in his notepad. Charlie hears Karen's boyfriend laugh louder and louder. All of a sudden, Karen starts to scream hysterically. Charlie looks at her boyfriend and realizes that he is dead.

Mr. Bowman shot Karen's boyfriend in the back. Mr. Bowman runs over to Charlie and asks him for four hundred dollars. Charlie hands the money to Mr. Bowman who then departs the scene.

Karen runs over to Charlie.

"Charlie, come quick! He's dead … he's dead. My boyfriend is dead! Please come!"

Charlie follows Karen.

She points to where her boyfriend lies in a pool of blood. "Charlie! Who could have done this?" Karen screams. "Who would ever do this to my boyfriend? Who, Charlie? Who could do such a thing!"

Karen starts to cry, and then she gives Charlie a horrified look.

Confused, Charlie stares at Karen's frightened face. "I don't know, Karen. I don't know who would do such a thing."

Just then, Karen's boyfriend jumps up. "You killed me, Charlie," he says in a scary way. "You killed me."

This gives Charlie a fright. He feels his hair standing on end.

He looks at the scary-looking guy and cries out, "Go away! Go away! Stay away from me! Go away!" Charlie sees that Karen's boyfriend keeps walking toward him anyway. The man's facial expression is full of evil and ugliness.

The scary sight of the man's face wakes Charlie with a fright.

"Leave me alone!" Charlie cries out, now awake and in a cold sweat. His breathing is fast and uncontrolled. He now realizes he has had a terrible nightmare. The clock on the bedside table registers 3:00 a.m. It takes Charlie a while to settle down from his fright, but he soon he gets control of himself. He hasn't had a nightmare like that one in a long time. Charlie lies awake for a long time. He thinks about what happened in the dream, but then, like everyone who has ever had a nightmare, he soon forgets all about it and what it was about. About an hour later, Charlie falls back to sleep; he doesn't wake up until his alarm goes off at 6:30 a.m. It is time to start another day.

In the morning, Charlie tries to remember what the nightmare was about, but he soon forgets it—except the part that scared the hell out of him. He remembers how Karen's boyfriend got up from the ground and looked at him with that evil, sinister expression. Charlie doesn't have to think hard to remember him saying, "You killed me, Charlie. You killed me."

Soon Charlie is dressed and on his way to work. It doesn't take him long to get there. As he pulls into his parking space, he thinks, *I wonder how Mr. Bowman is doing. I sure hope he finds some information I can use.*

Charlie then hurries inside, feeling a peculiar sort of nervousness. Before he knows it, it's time to go home. Charlie waits for the whistle to sound, and then he rushes out to his truck.

He gets in, and without even thinking twice about where he's going, starts driving toward Little Tony's Pizza. Arriving quickly, he parks his truck in the usual area and happily spots Karen's red Mustang. Without any delay, Charlie walks into the restaurant, excited and enthusiastic.

There are several customers sitting and waiting for their orders. This makes it more difficult for Charlie to talk openly and freely to Karen. He spots her at the cash register, taking a customer's money.

As Karen looks up and sees Charlie, she gives him a warm, happy smile. She waves and mouths hello.

After the customer walks away, Charlie walks over to Karen, feeling extremely nervous. "Hey, Karen. How are you doing today?

Karen smiles sweetly. "I'm pretty tired today, Charlie. It has been busy all day long."

"I know how you feel. It was a busy day at work for me also."

"Where do you work, Charlie? You've never told me."

"Steven's Knitting Inc. You know … the plant over on Broad Street."

"Oh yeah, I think I know where you are talking about." Karen doesn't know where the place is, but she goes along like she does.

Charlie starts to look at the menu. "I believe I will have something different today, Karen. What do you recommend?"

"Well … the meatball sandwich is pretty good."

"That's what I'll have. I'm glad I asked you, Karen."

Karen smiles and shakes her head at Charlie. She writes down the order and takes it to the back.

She is only gone a few seconds, and then she returns to the counter, where Charlie stands waiting for her. Charlie looks at Karen as though she just came down from heaven. Her beauty is breathtaking. Her skin is whiter than an ivory statue. She is neither too short nor too tall, but just the right height. Her hair is long and silky and red. Her breasts are unusually large and full. They push out her shirt with great abundance. Her facial features are simply glorious. It's like looking at an angel. Her lustrous blue eyes are soft, but they sparkle like jewels in the sun. The combination of her luscious long red hair, white skin, and radiant blue eyes makes Charlie's head spin.

Staring at Karen with wonder, Charlie says softly, "Karen, I just can't get over how white your skin is."

She looks at Charlie shyly. "Yeah, I try to stay out of the sun as much as I can."

"Don't you ever go to the beach or to swimming pools?"

"No, not really, Charlie. The times I have gone to the beach I got sunburned badly. My skin burns real easily, and that's a terrible feeling."

"Yes, I know what you mean there. I sure have been burned pretty badly in my life too."

"Not as bad as I do, I'll bet. I get as red as my hair, and I don't have to stay out very long to get burned that way either."

"You don't?"

"No, not long at all. Once, several years ago, I was out on the beach for only thirty minutes. When I stood up from the sand, I was blistered all over. Mama had to take me to the hospital."

"You had to go to the hospital!"

"Yes, Charlie. I was in real bad shape. The doctors told me I had second-degree burns."

"Really? Did they put something on your skin?"

"Yes, they sure did, but it made it hurt even more. I cried a whole lot."

Charlie looks at Karen sadly when she tells him this. "How long did you have to stay at the hospital?"

"Oh, several hours I guess. It hurt so badly that I told myself I would never lie in the sun again, and I haven't."

"I don't blame you one bit."

"And besides, I like my skin white."

"Me too, Karen. I mean, your white skin highlights your red hair, and your red hair highlights your blue eyes, and your blue eyes highlight your white skin. The three-part combination makes you look like something that has just come down from heaven."

"Well, Charlie, you sure know the right things to say to a girl. I bet you talk like that to all the girls you meet, don't you, Charlie?"

Charlie gives Karen a very serious look. In a soft voice he says, "There are no other girls in my life, Karen. I don't have a girlfriend. I have never been married. And ever since I met you, I don't want to even look at another girl."

Karen blushes a little, seeming to try to handle his compliments as best she can.

"I mean it, Karen. You have got to be the prettiest and the sweetest and the cutest girl I have ever met."

Karen looks around and then says softly, "Charlie, people are listening. Let me go see if your sandwich is ready."

Karen walks to the back and slowly looks for Charlie's order. She knows it's not ready, but she takes her time because Charlie is making her nervous in front of the other customers. She soon comes back to the front.

Charlie stares at her with warm, loving eyes. He smiles tenderly at her innocent face. His shining eyes begin to pull at hers like two magnets that have come close together.

"I know you told me you have a boyfriend, Karen, so I won't keep asking you out. However, I was just wondering if you would give me your phone number so I can talk to you at home. I don't want you to be embarrassed by my words when all these other people listen to us."

"Put yourself in my place, Charlie. What if you were my boyfriend, and a good-looking guy came in here, asked for my phone number, and I gave it to him. How would you feel?"

Charlie's loving gaze turns into a confused and uncomfortable expression. He pauses for a moment and then quickly replies. "Well, Karen, if you were my girlfriend, and you didn't love me and wanted to see someone else, if I loved you, truly loved you, I would want you to be happy. And if I weren't the one who made you happy, I would want you to find someone who did make you happy. So if that were the case, I would want you to sit down with me and tell me you wanted to start dating other people. And then, after you sat down with me and discussed this out in the open, when this guy came in here and asked for your phone number, I would probably understand if you gave it to him."

Karen looks at Charlie, her face glowing with a happy expression. "You know what, Charlie?"

"What?"

Karen grins and then looks at the floor. "Why don't you ask me what my phone number is on Monday? Maybe I will have an answer for you then."

Charlie grins, very excited but controlled. "All right. I sure will, Karen, I sure will!"

A voice then calls out from the back. "Meatball sandwich coming up!"

Karen walks over and gets it. She walks back to Charlie and gives him the sandwich.

Charlie pays Karen for the sandwich, happily tells her good-bye, and then walks out the door as if he has conquered the world. Charlie eats the sandwich as he drives home. He is content with what he has accomplished. He begins to believe that Karen is starting to come around. She seems to like him as he is. He thinks about how silly it was to hire a PI when, in time, he will have Karen telling him everything he wants to know. He wishes now that he had saved that four hundred dollars for a nice going-steady ring, but deep down, he is eager to hear what Mr. Bowman has found out about this red-haired beauty.

As Charlie pulls into his driveway, he notices a car parked there.

Charlie begins to feel uneasy. As he slowly approaches the car, he sees someone sitting in it, and that someone happens to be Mr. Bowman.

Charlie gets out of his truck and walks over to Mr. Bowman's car. Mr. Bowman remains in his car, but he rolls down the window. Noticing a mysterious look on Mr. Bowman's face, Charlie wonders what is wrong.

"Hello, Mr. Bowman. I thought you were going to call me."

Mr. Bowman looks at Charlie with concern. "Charlie, I have some information for you pertaining to Miss Karen Thomas, but there is something very important I must talk to you about first."

Charlie, now also showing a look of concern, says, "You looked very upset when you said that, Mr. Bowman."

Mr. Bowman holds Charlie gaze. "Oh, I am, Charlie. I am very upset. What I have to say is so important that I didn't want to tell it to you over the phone. That is why I thought I would drive over to see you in person. I believe it's something you should know today."

Charlie's look of concern deepens into worry, and he asks Mr. Bowman to come into the house. Mr. Bowman and Charlie walk toward the house. As they walk, Mr. Bowman glances around, as if looking for something. He seems very suspiciousness.

Charlie walks up to his front door, unlocks it, and proceeds to go in. Mr. Bowman quickly follows Charlie inside. Charlie shuts the door and locks it. He turns on the lights and walks into the kitchen, where he and Mr. Bowman sit down at the breakfast table.

Mr. Bowman then begins to tell Charlie what is bothering him. "Charlie, let me get straight to the point." He puts a large envelope on the table. "First of all, do you have anything you want to tell me, Charlie?"

Puzzled, Charlie just looks at Mr. Bowman. "No, nothing that I know of. What do you mean?"

"You know, like who you are working for."

Charlie begins to feel uneasy. He stares at Mr. Bowman. "What are you talking about?"

Looking directly at Charlie, Mr. Bowman says, "When I started calling my resources to find the information you wanted, something happened: I got an unexpected visit from someone who works for our government." Charlie listens with intense fascination as Mr. Bowman continues. "He came by my office about three hours ago. He and I had a very loud and very unpleasant conversation about someone I was trying to find out about for you."

Charlie gives Mr. Bowman a scared look. "Keep talking, sir."

With a mysterious look on his face, Mr. Bowman continues. "All right, Charlie. But before I tell you what that conversation was about, let me tell you a little bit about Miss Karen Thomas's family."

The atmosphere in the room takes on a whole new momentum of intrigue and appeal. The tension is so thick, you could cut it with a knife.

"First of all, Charlie, Miss Karen Thomas's complete file is in this envelope. It contains all the basic information you wanted to know."

Charlie reaches over to open it, but Mr. Bowman takes the envelope before Charlie gets his hands on it. "Before I let you have this envelope, Charlie, I want to tell you a few things."

Charlie gives Mr. Bowman his complete and undivided attention, not uttering a sound.

"Charlie, while doing my research on Miss Thomas, I started to do a background check on her family. This is something I do with all my clients, and it was something you also specifically requested."

Charlie's eyes remain focused on the mysterious investigator.

"When I called my buddy in Chicago to run her name through his computer, he told me all about her family's past. After he faxed the information to me, I started to get curious about her father."

Charlie still doesn't say a word. He keeps listening, intrigued.

"When his name went through the computer, all that came out was that he was an air force colonel who had died in Vietnam. I wanted to know more, so I went back and pressured my colleagues to pursue the matter further."

"What did you find out, Mr. Bowman?"

"That's what I'm about to tell you, Charlie. His air force record was closed. So I called up my buddy in Washington, DC, and told him to open it up and fax me all the information in his file. My buddy in Washington has ways to get in and find out things that nobody else can."

"Well, what was in it?"

Mr. Bowman begins to unravel the mystery. "What was in it was strange and bizarre, Charlie." He opens the envelope he brought with him, takes out all the documents, and spreads them across the table. Selecting one of the papers, he starts to tell Charlie about a secret file. "You see, Charlie, Miss Thomas's father was a very important man in the air force. He served three tours in Vietnam. He made more than two hundred sorties. He was shot down three times but was never a prisoner of war. He was never even captured all the time he was in the service. His military career would make John Wayne look like a Cub Scout."

"So what seems to be wrong? If his career was so good, why are you giving me all these negative vibrations?" asks Charlie.

"That's what I'm trying to lead up to Charlie; there is nothing wrong with his career. That's the problem. If there is nothing wrong with the statistical reports about his record, then why has it been classified and kept a secret for such a long time? This doesn't add up."

"Oh, I see. You think the air force might be trying to cover up something."

"I don't *think* there might be a cover-up; I *know* there is a cover-up. Three hours ago, a two-star general from the Pentagon paid me a little visit."

"Well, what did he have to say?"

"He wanted to know why I wanted Colonel Thomas's file, and also for whom I was working."

"You didn't tell him my name, did you?"

"No, Charlie, I didn't tell him your name. I'm just wondering if you wanted this information so you could pass it along to Mrs. Thomas or Miss Karen Thomas."

"No, sir, I just wanted to know a little bit about Karen so I could try to develop some kind of relationship with her. I don't work for her. That's for sure."

Mr. Bowman smiles, seemingly relieved. "That's what I wanted to hear you say, Charlie, because if you're working for Mrs. Thomas, or for someone else, I will have to tell that general all about you. You see, Charlie, Mrs. Thomas tried to find out about her husband some time ago. She started messing around and almost stirred up a hornet's nest. Mrs. Thomas's husband, Colonel Alan S. Thomas, was killed in

South Vietnam on July 17, 1970. He died under what the air force calls 'friendly fire.' But the family thinks he was shot down by enemy fire."

"Why doesn't the air force tell them how he really died?"

"You see, Charlie, it's not that easy. It becomes quite complicated from here on."

"Try to tell me the whole story."

"Okay, Charlie, I'll try. The air force told the family about Colonel Thomas's death while we were still fighting in Vietnam. They covered up the truth because of morale, pride, and other things—all stupid reasons beyond my understanding. You see, there were a lot of people protesting against the war back then. If word got out that we killed one of our best soldiers, one as highly decorated as Colonel Thomas, the CIA and the Pentagon and the other government organizations would have taken a lot of heat because of it."

"Hmm … yes, I am beginning to understand," says Charlie.

"If the air force tells a family that one of their members has died because of enemy fire, then that individual better have died of enemy fire, because if the truth is revealed later that the government, our government, didn't tell the truth, they might get sued for millions and millions of dollars, plus go through a lot of shame and aggravation."

"So the government is just trying to cover its ass."

"That's about the size of it, Charlie."

"Here I am … I don't even know much about a girl I happen to be in love with, but I know secrets about her family that she doesn't know."

Mr. Bowman gives Charlie a very stern look. "You must make sure make damn sure that you don't ever tell Miss Thomas about this. And, most especially, don't ever tell her mother, Mrs. Elizabeth Thomas. They should never be told about what I have just told you. You don't know how much trouble you will start if you tell them."

"I understand what you are saying, Mr. Bowman, but I was brought up to think that honesty is the best policy."

"Charlie, I was brought up the same way, but sometimes you have to have a little vision of what would happen if the truth were to be out in the open."

"What do you mean, Mr. Bowman?"

"I mean, how much heartache do you think Miss Thomas and her mother would have to go through if the truth came out? Would it bring back Karen's father and Mrs. Thomas's husband?"

"I guess not."

"Miss Karen Thomas was only two years old, nearly three, when her father died in Vietnam. She didn't even know him. She thinks that he died fighting for his country and was killed by the enemy. What do you think she would go through if she found out that he died because of some incompetent idiot on our side who launched some weapon that killed him? Do you think the truth would be of any help to her, Charlie?"

"I guess not, Mr. Bowman, I guess not. I understand what you mean about keeping this a secret. If they ever found out the truth, it would hurt Karen and her mother a great deal. You won't have to worry about me, Mr. Bowman. I will keep this under my hat."

Mr. Bowman smiles with obvious relief. "Very good, Charlie, very good. I'm glad you understand the situation."

As Charlie and Mr. Bowman sit at the table, the phone rings. Scared as a rabbit, Charlie just looks at Mr. Bowman.

"Go ahead, Charlie, answer it. No one knows you know anything about this but me."

Charlie walks over to the phone and picks it up. "Hello. This is Charlie Delaney's residence." He hears a familiar voice on the other end of the line.

"Hello. Is that you, Charlie?"

Charlie immediately knows who it is, but he can't believe it. It's Karen! He is so surprised that he drops the phone on the floor. He picks it up and says, "Karen, is that you?"

"Yes, Charlie, it's me. I hope you don't mind if I call you."

"No, I don't mind at all. How in the world did you know my phone number?"

"Haven't you ever heard of a phone book?"

"Oh yeah … there's nothing like a good old phone book to help you find someone's phone number." Charlie hears Karen laughing on the other end of the line. He waits patiently for her to speak.

"Charlie, could I ask you something?"

"Sure! You can ask me anything you want to."

"I can't talk long. I was just wondering if you go to church."

"Uh ... well ... um ... sure! I mean ... I have been to church before."

"Oh good. I want to invite you to come to church with my mama and me on Sunday."

Charlie cannot believe his ears. He has not been to church in years.

"Sure, Karen. That will be great."

"Fine. When you come to Little Tony's tomorrow, I will have a map already drawn out for you so you'll know exactly where the church is. You are coming over to see me at work tomorrow, aren't you?"

"Sure, Karen. I'll be there."

"I can't talk any longer. I will be looking for you tomorrow, Charlie."

"I'll be there."

"Remember—I get off at five, so don't be late."

"I won't. I'll come over there sometime around three o'clock. Okay, Karen?"

"Okay, Charlie. Bye-bye, now," Karen says and then hangs up.

As Charlie puts the phone down, he thinks to himself, *I can't believe it! I just can't believe it! She called me. She actually called me at my house. She really called me! Here I was, wondering if I would ever get the chance to call her, and she looks up my number and calls me! I just can't get over it.*

Charlie walks back into the kitchen, where Mr. Bowman is still sitting.

"Anything wrong, Charlie?"

Charlie realizes Mr. Bowman couldn't hear his end of the conversation, so he doesn't know who Charlie was talking with on the phone.

"Nothing is wrong, Mr. Bowman. Matter of fact, everything is just lovely."

"All right. I'm going to leave you all this information I have gathered."

"That will be just fine."

"Oh yeah, before I forget, I couldn't find out anything about Miss Thomas's boyfriend. It's pretty hard to find out about someone without at least having a name to go on."

"Yes, I guess it is very difficult without a name."

Mr. Bowman crushes out one cigarette and begins to smoke another one. "I parked my car up the street from Miss Thomas's house and waited for two hours after she arrived home from work yesterday. I was hoping he would drive up so I could get his license plate number, but he never came by. It got dark, so I went home."

Charlie looks at Mr. Bowman with disappointment. "I was hoping you would find out who he is."

"Remember what I told you the other day: I will do the best I can; that's all I can do."

"I understand, Mr. Bowman. I realize that it was a difficult task to ask, but it is important that I find out about this man."

"I will be glad to pursue the matter in more detail. I can't promise you anything, though. But if you give me his name, or his license plate number, I could find out a lot about him."

Charlie thinks to himself for a few moments and then says, "I'll tell you what: wait until I find out a little bit about him, then I'll give you a ring and maybe you could gather some information for me."

"Sounds like a good idea, Charlie. Just let me know when you want me to help you."

Charlie pauses and then asks, "I know this isn't a good thing to ask, but how much will this type of investigating cost me?"

"Same as the last time: two hundred a day, plus expenses."

"Oh … I thought it might be a little bit less since it's just routine information."

"No, it's the same. And, just as before, I have to have the money in advance before I go to work. I incurred about a hundred dollars in expenses working on this case, Charlie."

"Oh … I thought the four hundred would take care of everything. But since you worked hard and got more than I expected, I will be glad to pay you the extra hundred." Charlie reaches into his billfold, pulls out five twenty-dollar bills, and hands the money to Mr. Bowman. The PI takes the money, thanks Charlie, and stuffs the bills in his shirt.

"Oh, by the way, Mr. Bowman, what else did that two-star general say?"

With a big grin, Mr. Bowman crushes out his cigarette, sits back, and gives Charlie an intriguing look.

"Well, Charlie, you should have seen this guy. He was as big as a moose. He looked like somebody shot him in the face with a submachine gun." They both laugh, and then Mr. Bowman continues. "He had the personality of a crow, but he was strictly a military man."

Charlie sits back and relaxes as Mr. Bowman describes his interaction with the general. "He got right to the point—no how are you, no foreplay, no leading up to what he wanted to say. He walked right into my office and said, 'Why are you trying to find out about Colonel Alan Thomas?'"

"You mean he came all the way from Washington, DC, just to find out why you are asking questions about Karen's father?"

"Yes, he came all that way just to find out who wanted to know about Colonel Thomas, and why. But I didn't tell him anything about you, Charlie. It was really none of his big, fat-ass business anyway."

"Sounds like you handled yourself pretty well."

"Yes, Charlie, I handled myself as well as could be expected. A lot of private investigators would have cracked when they saw those two stars. Most would have told him everything he wanted to know. But when that lard ass started raising his voice at me, I answered back that he could cram those stars up his ass."

Charlie and Mr. Bowman start to laugh out loud, uncontrollably and without holding anything back.

"You mean you actually said that to a two-star general?"

Mr. Bowman lights another cigarette and takes a drag. Exhaling, he says, "Yeah, Charlie, that's the way you have to talk to military men: loud and harsh. It seemed scary then, but now I wish I had ordered him to give me ten push-ups for cursing a civilian. You see, Charlie, I've been in the military."

"Really? How long were you in for?"

"I was in the Marine Corps for twelve long, hard years, Charlie. Twelve of the roughest, most difficult years of my life, I guess."

"Why do you say that, Mr. Bowman?"

"Because, Charlie, I don't like anyone talking mean to me about anything. If there's one thing I can't stand, it's someone yelling and screaming at me."

"I guess they did that a lot."

"Charlie, they did that from the moment you woke up in the morning until you went to bed. Those sergeants were the worst. They called my mother a whore, my father a whore-hopping pimp, and my grandmother a prehistoric slut."

Charlie listens, giving Mr. Bowman his complete attention.

"Charlie, they didn't care how they talked to you," says Mr. Bowman. "That reminds me of a story about a particular sergeant I knew. Would you like to hear it?"

"Heck, yeah! Please tell me, Mr. Bowman."

The PI puts out his cigarette. "Okay. One day, a sergeant jumped on my shit for not being ready on time. He started to call my mother every name in the book, at the top of his voice. I looked at him and told him, 'If you say one more thing about my mother, I'm going to beat the goddamn hell out of you.'"

Charlie's eyes open wide with excitement. "What did you do to him?"

"Let's just say that he didn't say anything more about my mother or anyone else in my family. A few minutes later, that ugly gorilla ordered me to strip down to my underwear, right there in front of the other men outside the barracks. He looked at me, and then he told the other men that this was what happened to men who threatened their commanding officers. After that, he ordered me to stand on one foot, so I stood on that one foot. He then told me if that foot I had in the air touched the ground, even one time, he would throw me in the brig for a month for being out of uniform. I'll never forget that."

"What happened next?"

"Well, Charlie, all of the other men in formation looked at me, hoping I wouldn't put my foot down. I stood there, I guess for about an hour, and then the sergeant told me to put my clothes back on and get into line."

"You mean the whole group of men stood there for an hour and watched you stand half naked with one foot in the air!"

"That's right, Charlie. That sergeant wanted to show everyone he was in control of things."

Shaking his head in admiration Charlie says, "So you were a marine."

"Yes, Charlie, and I still am a marine. I will always be a marine. That's why I talked to that fat-ass two-star general of the air force the way I did. He is just a goddamn air force general. I was a second lieutenant in the United States Marine Corps."

Charlie is impressed and continues to look at Mr. Bowman with admiration.

Mr. Bowman seems to appreciate the admiration, and he speaks with authority. "Charlie, back then the Marine Corps had to do things like that in order to create discipline. The sergeant had to make the men show complete obedience to him."

"I guess so."

"They are not as rough today as they were then, but they are still very strict. They have to be, or they aren't doing their jobs correctly. I just didn't like being made a fool of out in the open like that. And calling members of my family names was the worst part."

"It sounds like something I wouldn't want to get into either. I'm like you in a way, Mr. Bowman: I couldn't stand anybody talking to me as if I were a piece of dirt, and I especially wouldn't tolerate anyone talking that way to or about my family."

Charlie then offers Mr. Bowman something to drink.

"No, Charlie, I must be going now. I have a few things to do before I go home, but thanks anyway."

"Well, I'm glad you came over and told me all this. When I get the name of Karen's boyfriend, I will give you a call."

"I will be glad to help you out all I can. I hope the information I have gathered for you does some good."

"Thank you, sir, I believe it will. At least I hope it does."

Mr. Bowman starts to walk toward the door. Charlie walks behind him.

As they reach the door, Charlie says, "Thank you again for all you have done for me."

"You're welcome again, Charlie. You have a nice rest of the day."

Mr. Bowman departs the house.

Charlie watches through the doorway as the PI gets into his car and drives away. He then shuts the door and locks it, and quickly walks back into the kitchen. Sitting at the table, he begins to look over the information in the envelope, reading the reports multiple times. He studies the papers as if preparing for a major college exam. As he reads the material, the volume of information amazes him, and he is fascinated by how well it is organized. He soon knows all about Karen and her family.

Mr. Bowman sure did a good job on this. Everything, and I mean everything, I wanted to know about Karen is here—except who her boyfriend is, of course.

Charlie spends the rest of the evening poring over the information. At eleven-thirty, he puts aside his reading materials, takes a shower, and goes to bed.

As he lies in his bed, he thinks to himself, *Everything seems to be going smoothly, Charlie ole boy. I hope that continues. I hope Karen and I soon develop a long and lasting relationship. I hope her mother likes me, and I hope her boyfriend gets hit by a car.* He snickers at the last part, begins to drift off, and soon falls into a deep and peaceful sleep.

Charlie wakes the next morning, well rested after sleeping late. It's Saturday, so he doesn't have to go to work.

After he gets up, he puts on some clothes, walks into the kitchen, and he fixes himself a bowl of cereal. As he eats his cereal, he looks over at Karen's dossier once again. He tries to remember all he can about his new love, and then puts the information back into the envelope and looks around to see where would be a good place to keep it. He decides to place it in the closet in his bedroom, which he does after he finishes his breakfast.

While Charlie reads the newspaper, the phone rings. He walks over to the phone and answers it.

A female voice says, "Hello. Is this Mr. Charlie Delaney's residence?"

"Yes. This is Charlie Delaney. Who am I speaking with, please?"

"Hello, Mr. Delaney. This is Elizabeth Thomas."

Charlie can't believe his ears! He tries to contain his excitement.

Elizabeth Thomas says, "I'm calling you about my daughter, Karen. She has been talking to me about you, Mr. Delaney."

"Yes, ma'am. I met her at Little Tony's Pizza, the place where she works."

Mrs. Thomas says, "Yes, she has told me about you somewhat. I hope you don't get the wrong opinion of me, but I'm calling to tell you that I want you to stay away from my daughter."

Charlie nearly falls down when he hears these horrible words. Trying to get control of himself, he sits down on the sofa.

"I beg your pardon, Mrs. Thomas."

"Let me try to explain the situation to you a little more clearly. My daughter has been seeing a young man for over six years now. She and he will eventually get married if nothing comes between them."

Charlie listens to her words with complete comprehension. His heart beats a thousand times a minute as he absorbs her words.

"Mr. Delaney, I was going to wait to tell you this after I met you, but I believed it would be better if I told you now, before Karen gets any more deeply involved with you."

Charlie's shock begins to turn to anger. Keeping his tone firm, he says, "Mrs. Thomas, I believe you are too late to stop what has already started. I like Karen a whole lot. I think she is the nicest and the sweetest and the most beautiful girl I have ever met. She likes me, and I like her. I don't think there is anything wrong with trying to develop a relationship with somebody I care a great deal about!"

"Young man, you listen here! This is my daughter we are talking about. Karen is the only child I have. She means more to me than anything in this world, and I don't want her to mess up and start a problem with Steve."

"Steve? Who is Steve?"

"Steve is the young man my daughter happens to be in love with. He happens to be my future son-in-law, and he is also someone I love."

Charlie tries to stay calm so he won't say anything he might regret later, but he stands up to Karen's mother. "Mrs. Thomas, if you really love your daughter you should let her make up her own mind. I don't think your daughter is in love with this Steve. If she were, I don't think she would call me up and ask me to go to church with you and her on Sunday."

"She told me last night that she'd asked you, but that doesn't mean anything. She loves Steve."

"Mrs. Thomas, I'm not trying to make your life miserable or Karen's life unhappy. What would you think about yourself if Karen does marry this Steve character and realizes later that she doesn't love him? How would you feel then?" Charlie pauses for a moment as he waits for Mrs.

Thomas to think about what he just said, and then he continues. "You see, Mrs. Thomas, Karen hasn't seen all the different types of men in this world. She might not know who she wants. When you date one person, and one person only, for such a long time, that person becomes an obligation. Karen might want to get out of this relationship but doesn't know how to."

Mrs. Thomas listens in silence.

Barely pausing, Charlie goes on. "Wouldn't it be better for Karen to look around new territories, just to see what's on the other side, than to get married and later wish she never did?"

Obviously not buying Charlie's philosophy, Mrs. Thomas replies, "Mr. Delaney, I thought you were going to cooperate with me and stop seeing my daughter, but after hearing you talk, I don't think you are going to cooperate with me at all."

"I think you should meet me first, Mrs. Thomas, and then you should try to put what Karen wants before what you want."

"You listen to me, young man, and you listen to me good! I have always put Karen first, and I will continue to put her first. She is happy with Steve, and that's what's important to me: Karen's happiness. And I don't want some interfering man like you telling me otherwise."

"Hey, I'm not interfering. Karen called me, or have you forgotten that?"

Charlie begins to get very disturbed by Karen's mother's hostility. He loses his head for a moment and says, "I think you should butt out of this situation until you understand Karen's feelings a little more clearly."

"Okay, young man, I tried to be as nice about this as I could possibly be, but it looks like you are going to be a little difficult. I just want you to know you are not welcome to sit with us in church on Sunday. I want you to know I am going to make your life as miserable as I can until you leave my daughter alone. You take that for what it's worth!"

Mrs. Thomas slams the phone down, and Charlie is left with only a dial tone and some very hurt feelings.

As the day goes by, Charlie wonders if he handled Mrs. Thomas in the best way. He begins to worry about how he is going to deal with her. She made it perfectly clear what will happen if he and Karen start to date or to see each other in a steady way. Charlie doesn't know how to handle this situation.

Later in the day, Charlie is nervous about seeing Karen. He realizes he has to go over to Little Tony's to pick up the map Karen talked about giving him. Knowing that, he doesn't have to think any more about the subject. He has gone too far to develop something with Karen to back out now. So he just hopes for the best, preparing to deal with the situation as it develops.

Charlie starts to drive toward the little pizza shop, thinking about what he wants to say to Karen before he arrives. He has a hard time keeping his mind on Karen after learning what her mother thinks about him. But Charlie tries to keep a positive attitude about it.

Maybe Karen's mother will learn to love me after she meets me, Sunday, Charlie tells himself.

Charlie arrives at the shopping center where Little Tony's is located. He scans the parking lot, searching for Karen's car. Spotting it close to the restaurant, he feels content to see that she is at work. Not wasting any time, he gets out of his truck and walks through the parking lot. He opens the door to the pizza place, walks in, and sees a happy, smiling Karen looking over in his direction.

"Hello, Charlie. How are you?"

"I'm doing fine now that I am looking at you."

Karen gives him a girlish grin. "I hope you didn't mind my calling you yesterday."

"Not at all. I was glad to hear from you. Really! You can call me anytime you want to. I really like hearing your voice."

Karen smiles flirtatiously at Charlie and then reaches into her purse. She pulls out a piece of paper and hands it to him. "Here you go, Charlie," she says softly. "Here is the map I told you about. It shows you exactly where my church is located."

Charlie takes the map from Karen and looks it over.

"Karen, you are going to have to go over it with me. It looks like it is located somewhere I have never been."

"Sure, Charlie. I will be glad to explain it to you."

Karen then tells Charlie how to read the map, where to go, where to turn, and what landmarks to look for. After Karen goes over the map with Charlie, he understands how to get there.

"It shouldn't be hard to find it now, Karen. Although it would be easier if I just came over to your house and went with you and your mother. How does that sound?"

"I don't think that would be a very good idea right now, Charlie. I told my mama about you, and she wasn't too hip on the idea that you should come over to the house yet. Don't get her wrong, Charlie. It's just that I have a boyfriend I've been seeing for a long time now, and my mama doesn't want me to start bringing home other boys—even if it's to go to church. She is old-fashioned."

Charlie wonders if he should tell Karen about her mother's phone call this morning. He decides not to, as bringing it up would take away Karen's cheerfulness.

"Oh, I guess I can kinda understand what she thinks, Karen. I'm sure she just wants you to be happy, and she probably thinks you should have only one guy."

"Yeah ... something like that. I wish she would take my side on things and not try to get me to do things just because she is looking out for my best interest. Sometimes those best interests are her best interest, not mine."

"Mothers will be mothers. You must try to get along with them the best way you can."

"Charlie, do you have that problem with your mama?"

Charlie pauses before answering. "No. You see, Karen, my mother and father are both dead. They both died a long time ago."

"I'm sorry to hear that, Charlie. I already told you my father died in Vietnam. I was only two years old, so I never got to know him. I don't know what I would do if something ever happened to my mama."

"You love your mother a whole lot, don't you?"

"I sure do. I don't know what I would do if she weren't there when I need her. She never remarried after my father died. I'm all she has in this world, and she is all I have in this world also."

"That's good, that you and your mother get along so well."

"I didn't say we get along so well; I love her a whole lot, but we have our disagreements."

"Oh yeah ... what kind of disagreements?"

"Oh, nothing big ... just a lot of little things."

Seeing Karen's expression turn sour, Charlie realizes that she doesn't want to get into a long discussion on this matter. He wittily changes tacks. "I hope when I meet your mother tomorrow she takes a liking to me, because I want her to like me."

A big, happy smile spreads across Karen's face. Her eyes light up when she hears these words. "Charlie, I hope she takes a liking to you too, but if she says something that bothers you, try not to let it."

Charlie grins at Karen and says, "I hope when she meets me she takes a liking to me in the same way I took a liking to you, but if she does say something out of the way, I'll try to overlook it."

Karen's facial expression shows that she and her mother have already had a few words on this matter. Charlie knows firsthand how her mother feels about him, but he doesn't let on to Karen. He looks at the menu on the wall and then orders his usual medium pepperoni pizza with mushrooms, onions, and green peppers.

Karen writes down the order and takes it to the back.

When she returns to the counter, Charlie says, "Do you think your mother will feel it's all right if I take you two out for lunch after church services?"

Karen looks at Charlie. "Maybe, Charlie. I'll ask her, but I don't think she will."

"Fine. I hope she says it will be all right. It would mean a whole lot to me."

"Don't get your hopes up, Charlie, but I'll put in a good word for you."

"Good! I think that will help. Try to put several good words in for me."

Karen smiles.

Charlie now brings up the subject he has wanted to bring up for quite some time now: his rival, Steve.

"Is what's-his-name going to attend Sunday services?"

Karen looks at Charlie, confused. "What's-his-name? Who are you talking about, Charlie?"

"You know, your so-called boyfriend, what's-his-name."

"His name is Steve, Charlie. I don't know if he'll be there. He comes to church sometimes, but not every Sunday. I'll ask him to if you would like me to."

"No! I mean … don't ask him specifically on my account. I would rather just sit with you and your mother, if that's all right with you."

Karen laughs a little feminine laugh. "Well, I won't ask him specifically, but if he shows up, try not to let him upset you any. He and my mama are as close as two peas in a pod. She might be the one who makes you feel a little uncomfortable; she thinks that you are coming between me Steve and me. Isn't that silly?"

Charlie puts on a funny grin. "Yeah, that's silly. Ha, ha, ha!"

"But remember—if my mama does say something to you, just try to not let it bother you. My mama sometimes can be a little hard to understand, so please try to keep that in mind beforehand."

"Yes, ma'am! I will try not to let anything your mother says bother me or upset me."

"Good. I don't think she will say anything real bad, since we will be in church, but try to get on her good side. Like you've done with me." Karen laughs that little feminine laugh again.

This sweet, innocent laugh has captured Charlie's attention. "Do that again, Karen."

"Do what again?"

"That laugh. Make that laugh again."

"What laugh are you talking about?"

"You know, the way you just laughed. That laugh of yours just sounds so pleasant. I have never heard a laugh so pleasant and joyful in my life."

Karen laughs again, making the sound Charlie loves without even thinking about it.

Charlie looks at Karen with love in his eyes. In a very soft and caring way, he says, "Karen, I know I shouldn't say this but … I made a mistake earlier in my life by not telling someone how I felt. This happened a long time ago, and I don't want to make the same mistake twice. I just want you to know … and I know I haven't known you for long, but I want you to know …"

Charlie's voice trails off, and for a while, he doesn't say anything.

Finally, Karen says, "Yes, Charlie? What did you want to tell me?"

Charlie reaches over, gently takes Karen's hand, and gazes into her attentive blue eyes. His voice is very gentle, warm, and caring when he says, "Karen, I love you with all my heart."

Karen looks at Charlie, her eyes moist, and says, "Charlie, I think I love you the same way." A tear then slowly makes its way down Karen's soft white cheek.

Charlie leans over and gently presses his eager, passionate lips against Karen's soft, innocent mouth. It is a soft, tender kiss.

Charlie gazes intently at Karen. "That's enough for today, my love," he says. "We should proceed at a very slow and gentle pace. I will see you tomorrow. My heart will ache until I see your tender, loving face again, but for now I must go."

Charlie presses his lips once more against Karen's innocent ruby ones. And then he steps away and walks backward to the door. Karen doesn't say a thing. She just stares at Charlie in a paralyzed stupor. Charlie continues to gaze at Karen, both of them silent in the emotional atmosphere. After a few moments pass, Charlie slowly opens the door, and without uttering a sound, departs from the little pizza shop.

Karen, still gazing at the door, finally comes to from her tranquil trance. Tears of joy trickle down her milky white complexion. She still stands in the same place and doesn't move, as if her feet were glued to the floor.

She puts on a cheerful happy grin and whispers to the empty room, "Charlie Delaney, I love you. I love you, Charlie Delaney."

Charlie goes to his truck, without stopping, and heads straight home. He realizes that his dream has come true. His prayer has been answered.

"Thank you, Lord! Thank you, Almighty God! Thank you, thank you, and thank you again!" he says aloud while driving.

Charlie arrives home with tears of joy in his eyes. He goes straight inside his house, walks into his bedroom, and collapses on his bed. He still can't believe Karen said she loves him. Charlie stays in his bedroom for hours, reminiscing about what has taken place today. He is so happy. He is as happy as he has ever been in his entire life. Love has finally brought him the full understanding of what life is all about.

After a few hours pass, Charlie begins to feel a little hungry. He then realizes he forgot his pizza at Little Tony's. He laughs to himself because of why he forgot. He walks into the kitchen happily and begins to fix himself a sandwich, bringing it with him into the living room, where he turns on the TV, sits down on the couch, and starts to eat. After Charlie finishes his sandwich, he walks back into the kitchen, throws away his paper plate, and proceeds to go back into the living room. Just as he sits down, the phone rings. He gets up, walks quickly to the phone, and picks it up.

"Hello."

"Charlie? Is that you?" says a familiar female voice.

"Karen? Is that you?"

"Yes, Charlie, it's me. Are you busy?"

"Oh no. I was just sitting here, watching TV and thinking of you."

"I thought I would call you and see how you were doing."

"I'm doing better than I have in a long, long time. It's so good to pick up the phone and hear your lovely voice."

"Well, Charlie, that's what I want to talk to you about. It's not ladylike for the girl to have to call the guy. I was just wondering if you still wanted my phone number. Then you can call me."

Charlie practically falls to the floor. "Yes, Karen, I sure would like your number!"

Charlie already has Karen's phone number, thanks to Mr. Bowman, but isn't about to tell her that. Besides, he would much rather have Karen give it to him.

"Have you got a pencil and something to write on?"

"Hold the phone while I run get one." Charlie makes a mad dash to the kitchen, finds a pencil and notepad in a drawer, takes them, and runs back into the living room. Grabbing the phone again, he says, "I'm back, Karen. You can give me your number now."

"Okay, Charlie. It's 555-3221."

"Okay. I have your phone number now, and I will guard it with my life. I'll place it under my pillow so I will have it close to me when I dream of you."

Karen laughs. "You know something, Charlie?"

"What?"

"I still can't believe what happened at Little Tony's today. I have never felt so wonderful in my entire life."

Charlie moves the phone closer to the couch, lying down on it and stretching out.

"I can't believe it, Karen. It was one of the most wonderful days in my life. I just had to tell you how I felt, and I'm glad I did."

"I'm glad you did too, Charlie. I am glad you said what you said, but I'm still going with Steve for right now."

"Haven't you told him about wanting to start dating other people yet?"

"Kinda. Charlie, I have talked to him about it, but he didn't think it was a good idea. As a matter of fact, when I told him I wanted to have the freedom of dating other guys, he started to laugh like I'd said something funny."

"Maybe I should meet with him and straighten his ass out." Karen gets very upset when she hears this.

"Oh no, Charlie, I don't like you talking like that. It's something I will handle, and I want you to promise me you won't do anything like what you are thinking about doing."

"I wouldn't hurt him … too much. I would simply explain to him that you and I are in love with each other and that he is getting in the way. And then, if he couldn't accept that, I would just slap him around a few times."

"Charlie Delaney! You will do no such thing! Promise me that you and Steve will never use force upon each other. Promise me."

"Well … I promise not to hurt him too much if he tries to start something."

"Now that's not what I said, young man. You promise me you won't fight with him, or you can just give me back my phone number."

"Oh no, not that. Sure, I promi—" Charlie stops suddenly and then says, "Oh, by the way, Cubby, what did you do with my pepperoni pizza?"

Karen seems to forget about the promise for the moment. She happily replies, "I ate it, Charlie."

Before Karen has a chance to think about the promise again, Charlie says, "I was only kidding when I said what I did about slapping him around anyway." However, he wasn't picking; he meant it! He just didn't want to make Karen that promise.

"Charlie, you're not a violent person, are you?"

Charlie smiles as he says, "Me? Oh no, I wouldn't hurt a fly. I'm just your normal, everyday, lovable kind of guy."

Karen laughs. "Oh good, Charlie. I don't want to start seeing someone who has a violent temper."

"You don't have to worry about that, Karen. Love is what's on my mind, not violence and anger."

"You don't mind if I ask a few questions about you, do you, Charlie? I mean, I don't really know much about you, and I would like to find out a few things."

"Sure, you can ask me anything you want to. I don't have any secrets to keep from you."

"Good. I was wondering if you drink. I don't like someone who drinks too much."

"Oh no, not really … just on special occasions. It's not something I do on a daily or weekly basis."

"Good, Charlie. That is one of the things Steve does that I don't like very much. At first, I didn't mind it so much, but as time went on, and with his drinking buddies putting dirty ideas in his mind, it has become somewhat of a problem."

"You don't have to be concerned about me having any problem with that. I guess I haven't had a beer in over three months now, Cubby."

"I'm glad to hear that, Charlie. That puts my mind at ease."

Now feeling very happy, Charlie says, "Now can I ask a question about you?"

"You sure can. I would be glad to answer anything you have to ask. I don't have any secrets either."

Charlie works up his courage and asks, "Who is this Steve? I mean, what is his last name? What does he do for a living? How old is he?"

"Hold it, Charlie! One question at a time. A girl has got to have time to think about what she is going to say."

"Oh, I'm sorry, Cubby. I didn't mean to go so fast."

"That's a good one, Charlie. I haven't known you a week yet, and you have already told me that you love me. If you were any faster, the world would have to speed up some just to keep up with you."

Charlie begins to laugh, and Karen does too.

"First of all, Steve's last name is Johnson. He and I have been seeing each other since ninth grade, like I told you when you and I first met. We've been going together for about five years now."

Without thinking, interjects, "Your mother told me you have been going together for about six years … uh-oh."

"Huh? My mama told you what? When did you speak to my mama?"

Now that the cat is out of the bag, Charlie decides to tell Karen about her mother's phone call.

"Oh, didn't I tell you that your mother called me today?"

"No! I don't recollect you did. What did she say to you, Charlie?"

"Oh, nothing worth mentioning; she just wanted to find out about me and to tell me to stay away from you."

Karen becomes very agitated when she hears this. "She told you *what!*"

"She told me it would not be a good idea if I kept seeing you. She also said if I continue to see you, she will make my life miserable."

"She didn't say that to you. Please, Charlie, tell me she didn't tell you that."

"Karen, I wouldn't dare say something like that if it weren't the truth."

"Charlie, I'm glad you told me this. I am going to have a little talk with that mother of mine. She has gone just a little bit too far this time. She told me she wouldn't say anything to you until she met you, so she lied to me. Charlie, that mother of mine lied to me."

"Now Karen, calm down. Remember she is your mother, so don't be mean or say anything ugly to her about this. I want you *and* your mother to like me. I don't want you two at each other's throats."

"Charlie, it's so good to hear you talk this way. But that mother of mine has got to be told that she hasn't any right to interfere. I can decide whom I want to see."

Wisely, Charlie changes the subject, because Karen might want to go and talk to her mother now, but Charlie wants her to stay on the line and talk to him as long as she will. He loves to hear her voice.

"I'm glad you called, Cubby. It makes me so happy to hear your voice again."

"I'm glad I called you too, Charlie. I haven't ever met a guy quite like you. You are so mature and so easy to talk to and so good-looking."

"Oh, I don't know about that, but it's good to know you think so."

"Why is such a good-looking guy like you not married?"

"I don't know. I guess I have been waiting for a girl like you to come into my life and make it worthwhile."

Karen blushes. "Oh, Charlie, you always know just the right thing to say."

Charlie shyly says, "Another reason I'm not married is because I haven't been on a date in over six years."

"How come so long, Charlie?"

"I don't know, Cubby. Women have been quite rude to me. They talk mean without ever considering that they might be hurting my feelings." Karen listens quietly as Charlie talks. "That's the one thing in my life that I can't tolerate: someone talking mean to me. I guess that's why I like you so much, Karen. You are so nice and so sweet. I don't think you have ever said a mean thing in your entire life."

This sinks right into Karen's heart.

"Charlie, that is the sweetest thing anybody has ever said to me." Karen pauses for a moment and then asks, "Charlie, do you mean you haven't been out on a date in six years? Don't you get lonely?"

"I sure do, Karen. I guess I get lonelier than anybody in the whole world sometimes. It's something I have gotten used to."

"How does anybody get used to being lonely?"

"I don't know how, Karen. It's just something you have to get used to. It's not all that bad, though. I have the freedom to go and do anything I want to. I don't have anyone to talk mean to me if I don't straighten up my room. It has its good points; of course, it has its bad points also."

"You sound like you like your freedom more than anything else."

"That's right, Cubby. My freedom is the most important thing in my life. To have the freedom to go where I want to; the freedom to think about what I want to think about without anyone putting hate into me; the freedom to live without other people trying to arrange my life to suit theirs. It is something I can't completely explain in words. It's something you have to feel in your heart and soul. It is a wonderful feeling to be out of everyone's control."

"That was beautiful, Charlie. That was the most beautiful thing I have ever heard in my life."

"Stick around then, because I am just full of things like that, Cubby."

"I'll bet you are, Charlie, I'll bet you are."

Changing the subject, Charlie asks, "Have you told Steve about us, Karen? Or should I say, are you going to tell Steve about us?"

"Charlie, I have told Steve that I was thinking about seeing other people. I guess I wasn't firm enough. But I haven't told him about you. You know, I really haven't had time. Everything has gone so fast that I really haven't had time to think, let alone tell him about us."

"When are you going to tell him about us?"

"I don't know, Charlie. I am supposed to go out with him tonight. I will talk to him, but I think it is too soon to tell him about you. It will be hard, Charlie, because I am still fond of him. But, Charlie, I don't love him; I know that now. I have known it for quite some time, but didn't know how to convince myself to finally acknowledge it."

Charlie smiles, and his eyes twinkle. "I understand, Karen. It's hard to tell someone something like this when you have been with him for so long."

"Yeah, that's true, Charlie. It's not something I am looking forward to, but it's something I know I need to do."

"I hope you don't back out at the last moment. I know from past experience that when you want to say something that's on your mind, it's even harder when the time to say it arrives."

"Charlie, has anybody ever told you that you're real smart?"

Hearing the smile in her voice, Charlie laughs softly. "No, not really, Karen, but I have had some people look at me like they wanted to."

"Charlie, when I tell Steve, I know how he is going to take it, so I hope you will understand and be patient with what his response will be."

"I don't quite understand what you are trying to say, Karen."

"I am going to tell him just what I told him earlier: I want the freedom to start seeing other guys. I'm not going to tell him anything else for the time being. I don't want to hurt him. If I tell him that he and I are through, it will hurt him a great deal, and I'm not ready for that. I hope you understand."

Charlie's satisfied smile diminishes somewhat. "You mean, if he asks you out, you will still go out with him?"

Karen's voice is nervous when she replies. "For the time being, I will. Time has a way of resolving things that nothing else will. He'll soon start to see other girls, and then, later on, we will agree to stop seeing each other. I hope you will be patient with my decision on how to deal with this."

"I will agree to anything you ask, Karen. I love you. I mean it. I love you. I want you to handle this situation as you think best. I just want to hold you in my arms without knowing you are still attached to someone else. It sounds like a selfish thing to ask, but when you are in love with someone, nothing else seems to matter."

"Charlie, I think you are the most understanding guy I have ever known. Steve would never be talking like this. All he cares about is drinking with his friends and playing golf."

Charlie, hearing this, charmingly replies, "Playing golf? Huh! A gorgeous thing like you, and he would rather go chasing after a little ball hundreds of yards away. It would seem he'd rather spend time with you. It sounds like the guy must not like you as much as he loves booze and golf."

"Sometimes I wonder myself, Charlie. He took me out to a bar. You know the type that sells liquor. He took me there one time and got drunk as a skunk. All he talked about while we were there and on the way home was golf. Golf, golf, golf! How many birdies he got, how many bogeys he got, how many pars he got. He was on the green one time and almost hit a poor little eagle."

Charlie laughs out loud with a roar while listening attentively.

Karen doesn't seem to understand why he is laughing, and she continues. "I can't stand to hear about golf. I don't mind if he plays it, but it has gotten to be an obsession with him. It means more to him than me. Nothing should come between two people who have been going together as long as we have, you know. Am I right, Charlie?"

"Yes, you are, Karen. I agree with you 100 percent. Nothing will ever come between you and me, Cubby. I will always put you first in my life. I have never felt like this in all my life. You have done something to me no other girl has ever done. I hope and pray that one day you will feel this wonderful feeling that I am feeling now."

"Charlie, what I told you in the pizza shop is how I feel about you. I think I love you too, Charlie."

Charlie then hears nothing but silence. After the long pause, he says, "Karen, are you all right?"

"Yes, Charlie. Everything is all right. It's just that I never said those words to anyone before, and when I did just now, a strange and wonderful thing happened. It was exactly what you said a while ago: a wonderful and beautiful feeling. The more times I say it, the more frightened I get, though. I'm not used to feeling this way. I must go now, Charlie."

"Must you? I want to talk to you a little more."

"Charlie, I think it would be better if I go now. I need to try to comprehend these strange new feelings. Please understand that, Charlie."

"Okay, Cubby. I understand."

"Charlie, I think that's what I love about you—the way you understand things so well. The way you know how to come up with a solution to situations is something I wish I could do better."

"I am a good teacher. I will be glad to teach you all the tricks I know. You have the rest of your life to learn them, Cubby."

Instead of hanging up, Karen is drawn to Charlie, to open up and talk some more. For the first time, she has experienced telling someone that she loves him. This first-time feeling compels Karen to stay on the line and talk to Charlie a little longer.

Karen opens up and says, "Charlie, I wish you and I could be together without all the problems that lie ahead for me. I will be glad when all my negative feelings and all my problems are finally dealt with."

"Don't worry, Cubby. I will help you through them, and I will be there when the going gets tough. That's what a true boyfriend is supposed to do. He is supposed to put into the relationship, not just see what he can get out of it."

"The more I talk to you, Charlie, the more I want to …" Her voice trails off into another long pause.

Charlie finally breaks the silence. "Yes, Karen, the more you want to … what?"

"I can't tell you any more than what I have already told you, Charlie. I must be by myself now, alone, so I can try to comprehend my feelings. I need to understand how to deal with this in a more mature way. All I want to say for now is that I love you, Charlie. So just please be patient with me in the days that follow."

"Sure, Cubby, I will try to understand as best as I can, but I still—"

"Charlie, please don't be angry with me, but I really must go now. Bye-bye, Charlie."

After Karen hangs up, Charlie sits up on the couch, with the phone still in his hand. He tries to put what just happened into perspective.

He thinks to himself, *This can't be happening to me. She has called me twice now. She has told me she loves me. I just can't believe it. There is only one thing in my way now … No, two things: Steve, and Karen's mother. I don't think I will have too much of a problem with Karen's mother; she'll come around in time. It's that Steve who'll be a problem.*

And then Charlie remembers what Karen told him. "Johnson," he says aloud. "Steve Johnson. I have his last name now."

Charlie gets the phone book, opens it, and finds about a dozen Steve Johnsons. *He probably still lives with his parents, if he's only nineteen,* Charlie reasons. *So it's still going to be a problem to find out about this guy. If only I knew where he lived.*

Charlie considers the matter over and over in his head until he grows tired, and then he goes to bed.

For a while, he just tosses and turns, but then he finally falls asleep.

Charlie soon has another strange dream. He and Karen are at the altar in a small white church. Karen wears a beautiful white gown, and tears of happiness fill her eyes. The organist plays "Here Comes the Bride" in a very small, white church. Charlie wears a white tuxedo. Standing next to Karen, he gazes at her in all her loveliness. She is frightened as she looks back at him. There is an eerie feeling in the church. A strong wind soon starts to blow everything around. As the wind increases and grows stronger, Charlie hears a wicked, horrifying laugh. He looks up and sees a witch riding a broom. The witch keeps flying above the ceremony, shrieking. Charlie remembers that voice: it belongs to Karen's mother. He sees the witch land her broom right in front of him.

The witch stares at him. "Charlie Delaney, I told you to stay away from my daughter. Now I must destroy you."

When Charlie hears these startling words, he freaks out.

He watches Karen walk toward the witch. "Mama, you will do no such thing. I love Charlie. You must accept this and leave us alone."

The witch turns to Charlie and says, "Charlie, I will give you one more opportunity to stay away from my daughter. If you marry her, you will have to answer grave consequences." The witch gets back on her broom and starts to fly off. She flies around and around inside the church. She laughs a terrifying laugh as she flies.

Charlie then hears a man's voice saying, "Karen. Karen, I love you. Please take me back. Please take me back. Don't you know that I love you?"

When Charlie turns around, he sees exactly the same character he saw in the dream he had earlier in the week: Karen's boyfriend, Steve Johnson. He still has that evil look in his eyes. He stares at Charlie with a death glare.

Charlie runs over to Karen, takes her by the hand, and starts to run out of the church. Once outside, he sees a lot of people waiting and staring at them. Mr. Bowman is there; so is his secretary, Nancy Walker. The witch is there, along with a bunch of other people.

Steve comes running out of the church, screaming, "Karen! Karen! Take me back! Take me back! I love you, Karen. Please take me back. You belong to me."

Charlie wakes up then, with a violent thrust upward. He looks around and realizes he just had another nightmare. His heart is beating fast, hammering in his chest. His face is covered in a cold sweat. He looks at the clock, which once again registers 3:00 a.m. It takes him a little while to calm down, but he finally gets control of himself.

He finally falls asleep. It is Sunday morning, so he sleeps late and doesn't wake up until after nine o'clock. He thinks about the nightmare he had. After mulling it over for a while, he can't seem to figure out what is causing these dreams. This puzzles him immensely. Charlie tries to think about them in detail, but, like all of his dreams, he soon forgets them. He soon realizes they are about his new love, and all the stress that he has been through because of it. He tries to remember what he dreamed, but once he is fully awake, he can't remember all the details of the nightmare.

Charlie gets up and makes his way to the kitchen to fix himself something to eat. He thinks to himself, *I'll bet I'm having these nightmares because I'm eating all those pizzas. Maybe I should stop eating so many and start eating something else.*

So Charlie fixes himself an egg and cheese sandwich. As Charlie is eating his sandwich he gets a great idea.

I think I will join a health club so I can work off all this nervous energy. Yeah, maybe if I work out, these dreams will stop.

Charlie walks over to where he left the phone book, turns the pages to the listings for local health clubs, and decides which one he will go to. He wants these dreams to stop.

Chapter 2
THE PLOT TO WIN HER OVER

Charlie goes upstairs to his bedroom and puts his suit on. He then nervously drives over to Karen's church, arriving at about ten-thirty and waiting until he sees Karen and her mother drive up.

As the two ladies drive into the church parking lot, Karen immediately spots Charlie. Karen and her mother get out of Mrs. Thomas's car and begin to walk over to Charlie's truck.

Charlie watches nervously as they approach him, getting out of his truck just as they reach it.

Charlie smiles at Karen, and she smiles back.

Mrs. Thomas has a stern expression as she looks at Charlie. Karen introduces Charlie to her mother, who greets him but doesn't say much to him after that.

Charlie doesn't say much to Mrs. Thomas either.

The three of them walk into the crowded church and find seats in the balcony.

Karen sits down first.

"Charlie, come sit beside me." She takes his hand and guides him to sit next to her on her left.

Mrs. Thomas walks over and sits next to Karen on her right.

Karen leans over and whispers to her mother, "Why don't you sit next to Charlie?"

Mrs. Thomas seems a little reluctant at first, but then, without saying anything, she gets up, steps past Karen, and sits down beside Charlie.

Now Charlie is in between Karen and Mrs. Thomas.

Mrs. Thomas looks over at Charlie. "Is it all right if I sit next to you, Charlie?"

"If you want to, it's fine with me." He still shows a bit of nervousness and shyness toward Mrs. Thomas.

Mrs. Thomas seems to interpret this as a sign that Charlie has sensitive feelings toward her.

The choir emerges, and each member takes a seat behind the pulpit. The reverend and the choir director come out and sit down in their own chairs. The church is nearly full, and the well-dressed people all wait patiently for the reverend to make his opening statement.

Charlie looks around and marvels at the grand appearance of the church. He hasn't been in a church since his mother died. Like everyone else, he is also eager to hear the sermon.

The choir director gets up, walks over to the podium, and says, "All stand. Turn to page 1, and sing 'Holy, Holy, Holy.'"

The entire congregation stands. Karen and Mrs. Thomas each open a hymnal and begin to sing. Karen holds her hymnal at an angle so that Charlie can read the words. Charlie isn't much of a singer, so he softly sings the song to himself as the others sing openly. Karen and her mother sing in full voice.

After the congregation finishes the song, the choir director says to the assemblage, "Remain standing, turn in your hymnals to page 158, and sing all four stanzas of 'The Old Rugged Cross.'"

Karen and her mother quickly turn the pages to where the song is located. As soon as they find it, they join in with the other people. Charlie again reads the words from Karen's hymnal and softly sings to himself.

After the song is finished the choir director announces, "You may all be seated."

The entire congregation sits down. As the reverend remains sitting in his chair, the choir director walks over and sits down in his own chair. The reverend still remains seated. A quiet stillness fills the inside of the church. The people eagerly and attentively wait for the reverend to begin his sermon.

At last, the reverend gets up and walks over to the podium.

He looks out at his congregation, and with a smile on his face, announces, "Good morning! I am glad you are all here, and I hope today's sermon is a blessing to you all."

Charlie reaches over and takes Karen's hand.

Karen whispers in Charlie's ear, "I don't think it's proper for you to hold my hand with my mama sitting next to you."

Charlie looks over at Mrs. Thomas. She looks back at him as if to say that she doesn't approve of his holding her daughter's hand. Charlie releases Karen's hand, and they all focus their attention on the reverend.

"I want to begin my sermon today on a subject that we can all relate to. This is a subject that every man, woman, and child will have to deal with in their lives. Something most people don't think is evil. Something that people think is good and right. It is something that gets into the human heart. It can set the stage for self-destructing the soul if not taken seriously. That's why I want to preach about this particular thing today."

Charlie looks around, noticing that the entire congregation is listening with rapt attention. They all have serious expressions on their faces.

The reverend says, "But before I tell you what this wicked thing is, I would first like to tell you what this thing has done."

The reverend pauses before continuing. "It has turned ordinary men into monsters. It blocks truth and honesty. It puts barriers between man and God. And once something comes between you and God, you set yourself up for the deceptions and manipulations of the devil. Once this awful thing takes hold of you, it won't let you look at yourself as who and what you really and truly are. It will lie to you, and it will make you lie to yourself. It will control every part of you. And, because of it, you will spend eternity denying you ever did anything wrong in your life. It will lie to you so effectively that you will never ask for forgiveness for any wrongdoing in your life; in fact, it will tell you that you have never done anything wrong that you need to be forgiven for. It will tell you that you are better than everyone else. It lives and grows more facile in the most righteous of men."

As he listens with great curiosity, Charlie wonders what this thing could be. He hardly breathes as he listens.

"Those who possess this thing are the ones who will deny it more than those who don't have it. Because of its power, it is the foundation of the destruction of the soul. But the individuals who possess it welcomes it more than any other human emotion, because of the power it makes them feel. Once this thing gets into your heart, nothing will make it leave, because you won't want it to leave—ever! That's why it is so self-destructive, because you won't admit its presence!"

The rapt congregation just looks wordlessly at the reverend. The silence in the church is deafening.

The reverend breaks the silence. "It will grow in you so slowly that you won't even know where it came from. But it will take a long time for it to develop to the degree where it will harm you. It will only grow in you if you allow it to grow—and you will allow it to grow, because of the power it will make you feel. You will be the one who allows it to develop into something destructive. Remember this: you and you only will be the one who allows it to develop into something destructive."

The reverend walks around the stage and looks at his congregation sternly. He walks back to the podium, takes out a white handkerchief, and wipes his sweaty forehead.

He speaks again in a calm and gentle voice. "Ladies and gentlemen, I am telling you all this so you will look at yourselves and try to prevent this thing from ever keeping you out of heaven. I want you to take what I am telling you seriously, because when I tell you what this thing is, you will look up at me and tell me with your eyes, 'Not me, Reverend, not me. It won't keep me out of heaven. I won't let it.' Let me tell you something right now!"

The reverend pauses for a moment. When he continues, his voice is loud and full of emotion. With his hands in the air, he declares, "This thing got into the heart of God's most favorite and most obedient angel. This thing turned this angel into the most evil of all creations. It made this angel the devil!"

The congregation remains silent, but their eyes show great emotion as they continue to listen.

"If this thing can turn one of God's most faithful angels into an evil being, it can turn any one of you into a monster also. That is why I think it is very important to warn you of this thing … because no creature is immune to it. From this moment forward, you must always be on the lookout so this thing doesn't ever destroy you as it will destroy this angel I have talked about."

Intrigued, Charlie keeps looking at the reverend.

The reverend continues. "I want you all to know what this thing is so that you will also know what it can do to you."

Charlie holds his breath as the reverend captures the attention of the entire congregation. An aura of mystery and intrigue fill the church, and the momentum the reverend has built is palpable.

The reverend clears his throat and then announces with authority, "Pride! Pride is what I have been telling you people about!"

The people in the church look around in amazement and shock. The reverend pauses until the church is quiet. His stern expression and unflinching gaze rivet the congregation, captivating the interest of one and all.

"The pride I am talking about is self-pride. Now I want to tell you of the two types of pride. One type of pride is the good pride: the pride of anything except yourself. You know, the pride that we have for our children, and the pride we have for our country. That is the good pride, because this kind of pride is not self-destructive. As men and women, we do need to have some pride."

The eyes of the members of the congregation show a little understanding and wonder.

The reverend continues. "Without the good type of pride, we would not have the self-respect or self-esteem to be good and righteous people. But—" The reverend interrupts himself, directing a stern and harsh expression toward the center of his congregation. He raises his hand and points it at them. "But … be very, very careful of not becoming self-righteous."

His voice gets louder as he continues. "I want you never to become so self-righteous that you think you are always right. This will be a sign to watch out for, because when you become self-righteous, you have already got this thing in your heart. So try to always keep this self-pride out of your heart."

Charlie turns to see Mrs. Thomas listening to the reverend with deep concentration.

The reverend adds, "You stand up when you hear the national

anthem, and you place your hand over your heart. Do you know why you do this?"

Some of the people begin to smile, as if knowing what the reverend is going to say.

He smiles back at them and then speaks in a normal tone. "You do this in order to prevent pride from getting into your heart. When you hear the words of the national anthem, you feel pride. Not self-pride, but pride in our nation and what our nation went through when this song was written. You place your hand over your heart to shield it from pride."

The congregation smiles at the reverend as he transforms his calm demeanor into a very emotional reaction.

"Therefore, I want you to always be ready to put this shield into place when pride is around so that it won't get into your heart. When it does get into your heart, it will block the way of asking forgiveness for your sins. It won't let you admit your sins. It will tell you that you aren't sinning at all, and if you never admit your sins, you will continue to practice them until your soul is black and wicked. And then, you will do evil things and tell yourself at the same time that you are doing nothing wrong, and in fact, that there is nothing bad you can do. It will progress until you become as evil as the devil himself. You see, self-pride will stop you from admitting any bad things, and by doing so, it will eventually turn you into a monster without a conscience."

The reverend walks back to the podium, reviews some of his notes, and then starts to walk freely around the stage.

He casually looks at the choir. "You know, a little while ago, when you all sang that lovely and inspirational song, I must admit I felt a little pride when I heard you singing."

He walks around and looks at the congregation. "You see, even I can feel pride. Everybody feels pride, so you must always be on the lookout for it so that it won't get into your heart."

Charlie looks over at Karen and smiles at her. Karen looks at Charlie and smiles back. Mrs. Thomas doesn't take her eyes off the reverend.

The reverend continues. "I hope everyone here understands why self-pride is such a terrible thing to deal with. Once you have pride in your heart, asking for forgiveness of your sins becomes a thing of the past. How many people think they haven't done anything wrong this month?"

He looks around and notices many people looking away from him. He starts to walk around again, as the church is filled with a restless quiet. And then the reverend says, "Well, if you said to yourself that you haven't done anything wrong this month, I just want you to know that the pride in your heart has just blocked your sense of reality. You can see how important it is for each one of us to acknowledge our faults before they become bigger than ourselves."

The reverend walks around and begins to smile at his congregation.

"You see, without asking for forgiveness, you can't be forgiven. That is the whole thesis of why Jesus died on the cross: so all our sins will be forgiven. If we never ask for our sins to be forgiven, they won't be forgiven. And then, we will continue to sin more and more and more, until we sin so many times that our own souls become lost. The biggest road block to asking for forgiveness is our own self-pride."

The reverend takes a breath, and then he continues in a provocative tone. "How long will we sin before we ask for forgiveness?"

After a long pause, the reverend speaks in a calm and gentle voice. "We will sin forever, until we ask for forgiveness! The devil today hasn't asked for forgiveness, and he never will. That's why he will end up in an eternal lake of fire. And everyone who doesn't ask for forgiveness will join him. So many people end up in hell because they won't ask for forgiveness. They don't acknowledge that they have done wrong, so they continue to do wrong. Why do they continue to do wrong?"

There is a short pause as the reverend looks out at his congregation.

"I'll tell you why: it's because the self-pride in their hearts won't let them repent. Remember: if you end up in hell, it will be because you choose to be there—because of the pride in your heart."

Charlie looks around and notices everyone in the church is listening to the reverend with complete attention. Their eyes show great consideration and involvement.

The reverend continues. "Here is another thing self-pride will do to you: it will make you hate. That's right, it will make you hate, because it will make you feel you are better than anyone else. Once you start to feel that you are better than someone else, you will hate anybody who threatens your way of thinking, and that is everybody else in the world. That's why there is so much hate in the world, because there are so many people who think they are better than someone else. Just because somebody might act differently, or worship God in a different way, or look a little different, doesn't mean that person is a lesser human being than you are. All these things can be blamed on the pride that is in our hearts. How many people now can admit that sometime this month they did or said something wrong, and now wish they could ask forgiveness from the person they wronged?"

Mrs. Thomas looks over at Charlie, and Charlie looks back at Mrs. Thomas, his face and eyes humble and shy. She looks at Charlie with a little remorse. Charlie doesn't look at her long, soon turning his attention back to the reverend.

Karen then looks at her mother, gazing at her in a similar way to the way Charlie did. Mrs. Thomas doesn't say anything, but she looks at her daughter with compassion and remorsefulness.

The reverend continues. "I see that a lot of you are looking down at the floor as if it were covered with hundred-dollar bills."

Some of the people begin to laugh. Others remain silent, with sad, remorseful looks on their faces, including Mrs. Thomas.

"You see what happens when you don't ask for forgiveness?" the reverend asks. "Just look at you. Look at the misery you feel right now because of what you have done or what you have said. It's something that makes you feel as low as a jackrabbit in high grass. You don't want to come out because you are afraid something might get you. But if you just put your pride on a shelf somewhere and admit your mistakes, you will feel as good as anyone can feel. In other words, all you have to do is repent for what you have done wrong, and your sins will be washed away and forgotten forever. You don't have to feel that guilty feeling that about half of you are feeling right now, and I can tell that you're feeling it by your sad eyes and faces."

Some members of the congregation, after hearing the reverend's words, break the silence with some more soft laughter. They all seem to have enjoyed the reverend's sermon today.

Charlie turns toward Mrs. Thomas and notices she is looking at him. Charlie doesn't look at her for very long, once again returning his focus to the reverend.

Looking at his congregation, the reverend smiles compassionately and says in a gentle voice, "I hope you all have learned something about yourselves today. I also hope you will put into practice what I have preached today."

He then walks to the podium, reviews his notes, resumes walking around the stage.

"I want to invite any of you who don't know Christ as their personal savior to come forward and accept him into your lives today, because forgiveness begins with Christ. You will never have any guilt on your conscience if you will let Christ wash your sins away. He suffered long nailed to a cross so that our sins will be forgiven. All we have to do is ask him to come into our lives, ask him to forgive us for our sins. That's all there is to it. Just ask him today to come into your life and cleanse your soul."

The reverend pauses and then says, "I'm going to ask the choir to sing 'Just As I Am' as I wait for you to come up here, as I offer this personal invitation to invite Christ into your life today." The choir begins to sing as the reverend walks down to the front of the podium to receive the people for this invitation.

Charlie sees several people come up to the front to talk with the reverend. As the choir sings the last verse of the hymn, the reverend holds up his hands, and the choir stops singing.

The reverend concludes his sermon by making a few announcements, and then he ends the service with a prayer. He walks toward the front door as the choir sings for the last time.

Everyone begins to walk toward the door to exit the church.

Charlie looks over at Karen and says, "That sure was a good sermon!"

Karen replies, "Yes! I believe that was one of the best sermons I have ever heard him preach. Well, mama, how did you like the reverend's sermon?"

Mrs. Thomas doesn't show much emotion as she says, "I think it was a very worthwhile sermon."

"Well, I hope you'll do what Reverend Heath said, mama, and put into practice what he preached in his sermon today."

Mrs. Thomas gives Karen a stern look. “Don’t worry about me, young lady.”

The three of them follow the crowd of people toward the door, waiting patiently to shake hands with the reverend.

Afterward, they walk out of the church with happy expressions on their faces.

“Mama, do you want to eat with Charlie and me, or do you want to go home?”

Mrs. Thomas looks at Karen, surprised. “I am hungry too. I will eat out with you two, as long as Charlie doesn’t mind.”

“It will be fine with me if you want to join Karen and me, Mrs. Thomas.”

“Well, what are we waiting for? Let’s go!”

They arrange to meet at a familiar steak house nearby. Mrs. Thomas drives her car, and Karen rides with Charlie. All three of them soon arrive at the steak house. Charlie holds the door open for the ladies, and then enters the restaurant behind them.

Charlie looks up at the menu on the wall, easily deciding on what he wants to eat.

Both Mrs. Thomas and Karen seem to find it hard to choose, but, eventually, they decide, and all three of them place their orders.

Finding a nice, quiet booth near a window, they sit down. Charlie and Karen sit on one side, and Mrs. Thomas sits opposite them. They enjoy some small talk as they wait for their steaks. The atmosphere is pleasant and tranquil.

Mrs. Thomas looks over at Charlie and Karen. “Reverend Heath did preach a good sermon this morning.”

Karen looks at her mother. “Yes. I think that was one of his best sermons ever.”

Looking at Charlie, Mrs. Thomas asks, “How did you like the sermon today, Charlie?”

Charlie looks at Mrs. Thomas shyly and then says softly, “I thought it was a very good sermon indeed.”

Karen says, “Reverend Heath has been preaching for a long time. I am glad he is happy here. I hope he never moves away or leaves our church.”

Mrs. Thomas remarks, "If he ever did move away, I believe I would attend another church. He is the main reason I have attended church there all these years. If he ever did leave, the whole church would probably fall apart. It's hard to find someone like Reverend Heath."

Agreeing with her mother, Karen says, "Yeah, it would be difficult to replace him. That's for sure."

Just then, Charlie decides to go to the restroom. "Will you two ladies please excuse me for a minute? I must go to the men's room." He gets up and leaves the table.

Karen looks at her mother impatiently, as if waiting for her to say something.

Mrs. Thomas glances over at her daughter. "You know, Reverend Heath's sermon today did have something important in it."

"Yes, I think it was just what you needed."

"Something I needed? What makes you say that, dear? There is something important in it for you too, young lady."

"Don't worry about me, mama. Don't you think you need to apologize to Charlie for calling him up the other day and telling him to stay away from me?"

"Well … maybe I will apologize. I am still thinking about it."

"Maybe? When Charlie gets back from the restroom, I will go to the ladies' room, mama. When I get back, you had better have apologized to him."

"Young lady, I don't need you to tell me when I should apologize to someone for something I have done. I will talk to him when I am ready."

"The sooner you apologize to him, the better off you and I will be. I can't believe you called and talked to him without talking to me first."

"Now let's not get into that. I thought I was only doing what any mother would do for her only daughter."

"I hope you have had a change of heart now, mama, because what you did was wrong. If you don't apologize to Charlie, he might not like you. Have you ever thought of that?"

"Yes, I have thought about that a great deal. I don't think he likes me very much anyway."

"Can you blame him for that?"

"I guess not, dear. I will have a little talk with him."

"Fine. I am glad you finally see it my way."

"Your way? I am going to talk to him my way, not just because you think I should, but because it is something I think I should do."

"Mama! As long as you apologize to him, that's all that matters."

Charlie approaches the table and sits back down beside Karen.

Karen, Charlie, and Mrs. Thomas talk for only a short time before Karen announces, "I believe I will go to the little girls' room before our food arrives."

Hearing these words, Charlie gets up so that Karen can go to the restroom.

As soon as Karen departs the table, Mrs. Thomas smiles at Charlie. "Karen sure does look nice today, doesn't she, Charlie?"

Charlie looks at Mrs. Thomas nervously. "Yes, ma'am, she sure does. She looks pretty every day."

"Charlie, I agree with you completely. She sure is a real pretty girl."

"Yes, ma'am, she sure is that."

Mrs. Thomas looks at Charlie, her eyes filled with guilt. She stares at him until his eyes meet hers.

"You know, Charlie, Karen is my only child. She is all I have. She is my life."

"Yes, ma'am, I know that."

"Ever since her father died in Vietnam, I have become as close to her one person could possibly be to another. As the years have gone by, I have been overprotective of her. You see, Charlie, she is my baby."

"Yes, ma'am, I understand."

"Whenever I think she is going to make a mistake in her life, something deep within me automatically steps in to try to prevent her from making it. I just don't want her to make any mistakes that she will be sorry for later."

Charlie fixes his eyes on her mouth, giving her a very sad and innocent expression.

Mrs. Thomas smiles tenderly at Charlie. "The other day when I called you and told you to stay away from my daughter, I thought I was doing the right thing. Now that I have listened to Karen tell me about how much she likes you—and now that I have met you—I realize what a mistake I made by calling and telling you to stay away from her."

Charlie continues to look shyly at Mrs. Thomas. He doesn't say anything, but his eyes communicate the sincerity in his heart.

"After hearing Reverend Heath's sermon today, I came to realize that I had no right to call you up and talk to you in that way. Charlie, I just want you to know ... I am very sorry about what I said to you. I hope you will forgive me for the way I behaved."

Charlie looks at Mrs. Thomas with compassionate eyes. "Yes, ma'am, I forgive you. I am glad I came to church with you and Karen. I have learned a great deal today. I am glad you and I won't be enemies anymore."

"Me too, Charlie. Me too."

Before long, Karen comes walking back to the table. She sits down beside Charlie and gives her mother a concerned look.

Charlie says, "I'm glad you're back."

Karen smiles at Charlie. "Well, did you and mama talk about anything worthwhile while I was gone?"

"Yes, dear. Charlie and I had a nice little chat while you were gone."

Just as Mrs. Thomas finishes her statement, a young lady arrives at the table with a large tray of food. Setting the tray down at the table beside them, she places a plate in front of each of them.

After the waitress finishes serving the three platters, she says, "I will be right back with your iced tea."

Charlie looks up at the waitress and asks, "May I have some steak sauce?"

The waitress looks at Charlie and says, "Yes, sir. I will bring you some right away."

She looks at Karen and Mrs. Thomas. "Is there anything else you would like?"

Mrs. Thomas kindly replies, "No thank you. That will be all."

As the waitress departs the table, Charlie says, "Boy, does this look good!"

Karen says, "It sure does. I will never be able to eat all of this."

Mrs. Thomas says, "Whatever you don't finish you can take home, dear."

As the three begin to eat their lunch, conversation doesn't develop into anything important. The setting is pleasant and nice. The waitress soon returns with their tea. She also places a pitcher of it on the table so that they will have plenty. She asks one more time if she can get them anything else.

Charlie says softly, "Can I still have some steak sauce?"

The waitress hits her head with her palm. "Yes, sir. I'm so sorry. I forgot it, but I will be right back with some."

The waitress quickly departs their table.

Karen looks over at Charlie, perplexed, and says, "It would be a sin to put steak sauce on such a beautiful steak, Charlie."

"That is the only way I can eat a steak, Karen."

Mrs. Thomas nods her head. "He is right, Karen. The only way to eat a steak is with a taste of steak sauce on it."

"Well, you both can ruin your steaks if you want to, but I'm not going to."

The waitress soon returns with the steak sauce. Charlie pours a heap on his steak. He passes the sauce to Mrs. Thomas, who pours a great deal on her steak too.

Karen, eating her steak, looks over and says, "If both of you would just take a bite of your steaks without anything on them, you would see what I mean."

Charlie cuts off a piece of his steak without any steak sauce on it and places it in his mouth. The two ladies watch him chew it until he swallows. He looks first at Mrs. Thomas and then at Karen. After a short pause, he announces, "Just what I thought: it definitely needs steak sauce."

Mrs. Thomas laughs as Karen just shakes her head in disbelief.

Before long, the three finish their meal. Charlie reaches over to fill everyone's glass with tea one last time.

The waitress returns, places the check facedown on the table, and asks if there is anything else they would like. They all say no, and she leaves the table.

Charlie reaches over, takes the check, and puts it in his front pocket. "How was everything, ladies?"

"I believe that was the best steak I have ever had," says Mrs. Thomas.

Karen adds, "I believe you are right, mama. It was cooked just the way I like it."

Charlie looks over at Karen's plate. "I thought you said there was no way you could eat all of it. It sure looks to me like you ate it all."

"Yes, dear, it looks like you did a very good job of eating everything."

"It was so good, I just didn't want to have to throw it away."

Mrs. Thomas says, "Believe me, it wouldn't have been thrown away. I would have taken it home and eaten it later, because I wouldn't have let a steak this good go to waste."

"You never did tell me what you two talked about while I went to the ladies' room earlier. You two seem to be getting along a lot better since then."

"I guess you could say we buried the hatchet, dear," Mrs. Thomas politely replies.

"Yes, Karen. Your mother and I had a very nice talk while you were gone." Charlie looks over at Mrs. Thomas and smiles at her.

"Okay. What exactly did you two talk about?"

This forces Mrs. Thomas to tell Karen the truth. "Dear, if you must know, I simply apologized to Charlie for calling him the other day and speaking to him the way I did."

Karen's face shows she is surprised but happy. "Well, I am glad you two have come to terms with each other. I am glad Reverend Heath decided to preach that particular sermon today. It made the whole day turn out right."

Charlie replies, "I believe you are right about that, Karen. I believe you are right."

Charlie, Karen, and Mrs. Thomas get up and exit the booth. While the ladies walk to the front, Charlie reaches into his pocket, pulls out three one-dollar bills, and lays them on the table. He then walks up to the front and pays for the meal, politely holding the door open as the two ladies walk out. All three depart from the restaurant and walk over to Mrs. Thomas's car. She takes out her keys, unlocks the door, gets in the car, and drives off. Charlie walks Karen to his truck. They get in and proceed to drive to Karen's house, following Mrs. Thomas.

When Charlie enters the house, he notices several pictures of a man hanging on the wall. He has bright-red hair and blues eyes. In one of the pictures the man is in a military uniform. He notices how much Karen resembles the man. Mrs. Thomas disappears into another room in the house, while Karen stays close to Charlie. Charlie continues to study the pictures carefully.

"That's my daddy, Charlie."

"Really! You look a great deal like him. I see where you get your blue eyes and rich red hair from now."

Karen takes Charlie into the living room, and the two sit down on the couch.

Mrs. Thomas comes out of the kitchen, enters the living room, and sits down on a chair. She looks at Charlie in a curious way.

Mrs. Thomas begins to ask Charlie questions. "So tell me, Mr. Delaney—"

"Please call me Charlie."

"Okay. Charlie, have you ever been married before?"

Charlie looks straight at Mrs. Thomas and speaks in a clear voice. "No, ma'am. I have never been married."

"How old are you, Charlie?"

Charlie hesitates for a second before answering. "I am twenty-six years old, Mrs. Thomas."

She smiles as she replies. "You are still young, Charlie. You still have plenty of time."

Karen joins the conversation, and the three talk about small matters, nothing too serious or personal. Charlie keeps looking at a picture of Karen's father.

"You keep staring at my husband's picture. Is there anything wrong?"

"No, ma'am. It's just that Karen looks just like him."

"Yes, she is the spitting image of her daddy. She takes after him more than she takes after me. I mean her personality, that is."

Charlie continues to look at the picture, thinking, *I know more about him than I wish to know.*

Karen interjects, "You remember my telling you that I never got to know my daddy, Charlie. He died in Vietnam when I was only two."

Charlie nods, looking at Karen with compassion.

Mrs. Thomas says, "Yes, that's right, Charlie. Karen never got to know her father. That stupid war took away my husband and Karen's daddy."

After hearing her mother's words, Karen's mood changes, and she becomes very upset. She looks at Charlie and then at the picture. When she speaks, she is distraught, and there are tears in her eyes.

"Yeah, that stupid war took away my daddy. If that damn war had never started, my daddy would have watched me grow up and been here to take care of us."

Karen gets up and walks into the kitchen.

Mrs. Thomas gazes over at Charlie and softly says to him, "Charlie, whenever Karen starts to talk about her father, she always gets upset. When she comes back, please don't talk about Alan or Vietnam."

"Yes, ma'am. I will not talk about it anymore."

Just then, the phone rings.

Karen calls out from the kitchen, "I have it." She reaches out and picks up the phone hanging on the wall between the kitchen and the living room. "Hello, Steve. What are you calling me for?" She takes the phone as far as it can reach into the kitchen.

Charlie, like Mrs. Thomas, quietly listens.

Karen lowers her voice. "You know I told you not to call me … I don't want to hear your excuses!" Karen listens as Steve talks to her anyway.

Mrs. Thomas and Charlie sit quietly as they wait to hear Karen's voice.

"No, you listen here, young man! Don't you dare come over here. You heard what I said. If you dare come over here, then we are through. I told you last night that I don't want you calling me all the time."

Mrs. Thomas interrupts Charlie's listening as Karen's voice grows softer.

"You know, Charlie, if you hadn't gotten involved with my daughter, she might have married Steve."

Charlie gazes at Mrs. Thomas's content expression. "Listen to how she is talking to him. Do you think they would be a happy couple?"

"Charlie, I thought they were happy together all of these years."

"Sometimes when two people seem to be happy, they are really just pretending to be. You see, Mrs. Thomas, Karen has been dating this guy for so long that she hasn't really seen what else is out there in the world."

"It's just fine with me if she never sees what's out there. You see,

Charlie, there are a lot of mean people out there. I just want her to find someone she can love and settle down with and live a quiet, happy life."

Charlie shows some compassion as he speaks. "I want Karen to find the same thing, Mrs. Thomas."

Karen's voice interrupts Charlie and Mrs. Thomas's conversation.

"I told you no! Listen here, Steve, you are getting me pissed off. I am not going to change my mind … I can see this conversation is going nowhere. Let me spell it out for you. I need time to think about us. I need time to think about what I want to do, and you're not letting me do that."

There is a long silence as Karen listens to Steve.

Mrs. Thomas, seeming to be uncomfortable that they are listening to Karen's conversation, says to Charlie, "So tell me, Charlie, how long have you been seeing Karen?"

Charlie reluctantly looks at Mrs. Thomas and says, "Not long, Mrs. Thomas. Just a week."

Mrs. Thomas flashes him a wry grin, asking bluntly, "Are you going out with my daughter just so you can sleep with her?"

Charlie suddenly shows a surprised and disappointed expression. He angrily replies, "Mrs. Thomas! I don't think that was a very proper thing to ask."

"Well, Charlie, you are a lot older than Karen. And most men your age are usually after only one thing."

Charlie begins to get very agitated. "Mrs. Thomas, I have never met anyone in my life whom I care about as much as I care about Karen. I have not dated or seen anyone on a regular basis in over six years. Mrs. Thomas, I have lived my life celibate, and I want to tell you right now that my intentions with Karen are promiscuous ones!"

"Well, Charlie, I am delighted to hear this. You mean you have never known a woman intimately?"

Charlie realizes how open the conversation has become. His eyes bashfully gaze at Mrs. Thomas as he nods. And then, in a soft voice he says, "Yes, ma'am, that's right. I have never known a woman that way."

Intrigued, she replies, "Well, Charlie, I'm glad you told me this."

Charlie smiles, and a bit of redness shows in his cheeks.

They gaze at each other in wonder and amazement.

"To tell the truth, Charlie, I am proud of you. In this world where sex is such a complex problem, it is nice to know someone who has a little bit of self-control."

"Thank you, Mrs. Thomas. I appreciate your saying that."

"Does Karen know this?"

Charlie looks at her excitedly. "No, ma'am. I have told no one of this, and I would hope you wouldn't tell anyone either."

Mrs. Thomas smiles a pleasant smile and shows him a look of admiration. "You should tell Karen. She would probably admire you if you told her."

"Oh no, Mrs. Thomas! I don't feel comfortable talking about things like this."

"You are talking about it to me, aren't you?"

"Yes, ma'am, but … I don't think I would feel comfortable talking about it to anyone else." Charlie blushes as he says this.

Mrs. Thomas smiles at him. "Okay, Charlie, it will be our little secret."

"Thank you, Mrs. Thomas. I sure do appreciate it."

Charlie and Mrs. Thomas then sit quietly as they hear Karen slam the phone down in the kitchen.

Karen comes back into the living room and sits down on the couch next to Charlie.

"What is the matter, dear?" asks Mrs. Thomas.

Although her face still shows her emotional distress, Karen's voice is calm when she answers. "Oh, it's nothing, mama. Just something I will have to deal with in my own way."

Charlie, not knowing what to say, just sits quietly beside Karen. He reaches over and takes her hand.

"Well, I have housework to do. Would you both please excuse me?"

Charlie smiles, half rising as Mrs. Thomas gets up.

Before she leaves the room, Mrs. Thomas looks over at Charlie. "It sure has been nice talking to you, Charlie. Maybe we can get Karen to stay on the phone a little longer next time."

Karen shoots her mother a surprised and curious look, and Mrs. Thomas exits the living room.

Karen then gives Charlie the same surprised, curious look. "So what did you and my mama talk about, Charlie?"

"Oh, nothing much. We just talked about you and me and small matters."

"Mama sure has changed her attitude about you since this morning."

"Yes, Karen, she sure has. I think she likes me now."

"I'm glad! I'm really glad she has taken a liking to you, Charlie. I knew once she met you, she would come to like you. I'm so happy how everything has turned out. This has been a real good day."

Charlie and Karen sit on the couch and talk for an hour or two, until Charlie has to go. He leans over and gives Karen a nice, soft kiss. She responds very affectionately. They get up and walk over to the door, with Karen holding Charlie's hand.

When they reach the door, Karen looks at him sadly. "I wish you wouldn't go, Charlie. Please stay on and have dinner with mama and me."

Charlie gazes into Karen's big blue eyes, marveling at her beautiful face and innocent expression. "No, Karen, I must go now. I had the best time I have had in a long time, but I must go now."

Karen moves closer, puts her arms around Charlie's neck, and hugs him.

"I'm glad you got to meet my mama. I'm also glad you both are getting along so well. It's important to me that you and mama like each other."

"Me too, Karen, me too. I believe I will grow to like your mother as if she were my own."

Karen again tries to get Charlie to stay a little longer, but he seems to have something else on his mind, something mysterious. He kisses her softly one more time. She tries to make the kiss longer, but Charlie pulls away.

"Come on, big guy, you can kiss me better than that. Mama ain't watching us."

Charlie smiles, enchanted. His voice is soft and pure as he says, "You look too innocent for me to start kissing you any stronger. I want to remember the sweet, virtuous look in your eyes as long as I possibly can. I like to see you wanting me as I leave, and that magnetic pull will want me to come back."

Karen looks at Charlie as if hypnotized. The look in his eyes overwhelms her young, innocent heart. She smiles with a look of desire as her shining eyes begin to water.

Gazing down at the young redheaded virgin, Charlie says, "I will come by and see you at work on Wednesday."

"Wednesday? Why so long, Charlie?"

"We must not see each other too much at first, because we may get tired of each other."

Karen looks at Charlie sadly once again. "I don't think I will ever feel that way, Charlie."

Charlie kisses Karen on the cheek, says good-bye one more time, and then turns and walks out the door. He walks to his truck, turns, and looks back at Karen. He waves good-bye, and she waves back.

Charlie gets into his truck and drives away. He does have someone on his mind: Steve. Now knowing that Karen needs a little help in ridding herself of this man, Charlie studies—or, rather, schemes on—ways to shake off this male nuisance so that he, Charlie, can have Karen all to himself.

As Charlie drives, he gets an idea. *Hmm … I think I will drive over to the bookstore.* So he drives to a shopping center with a bookstore, parks his truck, gets out, and walks into the store. He looks around and notices a few people in the store, standing and reading. He goes over to the sports section and begins to look for something feverishly. He picks up a book, looks it over, and then puts it back. He picks up another one, reads a little, and then puts it back. Charlie does this several times until he finds a book he is particularly interested in. Holding the book, he flashes a devious little grin and walks up to the front to pay for his mysterious little treasure. Charlie smiles at the cashier with a look of strength as he receives his change.

The cashier looks at Charlie and says, "That is a very good and informative book, sir. It should teach you everything you want to know."

Charlie smiles gladly and says, "Thank you. It does look like a very educational book. Thank you again, and have a nice day."

"You too, sir, and please come back."

Charlie happily walks out of the store, gets into his truck, and drives home.

As soon as Charlie gets home, he rushes into his house and begins to read the book he has just purchased. As he reads, he takes out a notepad and begins to make notes. Charlie stays up late, reading until he finishes the book. He then crawls into bed and falls asleep.

After work the next afternoon, Charlie drives straight home. He walks into his house in a very anxious manner. His mind seems to be occupied with something important. He doesn't waste any time picking up the phone and calling Mr. Bowman.

The phone rings a few times, and then Nancy Walker answers. "Hello. Bowman Investigations. May I help you?"

"Yes, this is Charlie Delaney. I was wondering if I could speak to Mr. Bowman."

"Hello, Mr. Delaney. I'll see if he is free."

Charlie eagerly waits, holding on for a few minutes.

"Hello, Charlie. What can I do for you?" asks Mr. Bowman.

"I found out the name of Karen's boyfriend. I want you to find out all you can about him, if it wouldn't be too much trouble."

"No trouble at all, Charlie. What is this man's name?"

"His name is Steve Johnson. He should be about twenty years old. All I know about him is that he likes to play golf. See what you can find out about him."

"Sure thing, Charlie. How many days would you like for me to spend on the case?"

Charlie pauses for a moment. "Oh, about two days should do it; four hundred dollars' worth."

"Fine, Charlie. I'll get on it tomorrow. Don't worry about paying me up front. You are a good customer. You have established credit with me. I'll just send you a bill when the tab reaches four bills."

"Sounds like a winner. I will be waiting for your call sometime later this week."

"Okay, Charlie. I have gotta run now. I'll talk with you later in the week."

After Charlie hangs up the phone, he gets an idea for how to break up Karen and Steve. *I've been going about this situation all wrong. What*

I need to do is find this guy Steve and become his friend, for a short while anyway. Then, when the moment, is right I will pounce on him when he is at his weakest point, after he has said things he will regret … things that he will be ashamed of. Then I will strike like a bolt of lightning. But first, I must get him to know me. Let him get to like me, to be his friend, because friends say things other people never hear. That's what I'll do: I will be his friend.

So Charlie starts to work on his secret plan.

Before long, Wednesday arrives; Charlie is eager to see Karen. After work, he drives straight over to Little Tony's Pizza and casually walks into the establishment. He sees Karen behind the counter, waiting on the customers. He stands, motionless, until Karen glances over and sees his happy face smiling at her. She tries not to let Charlie's presence interrupt her job performance, but she waves at him.

Charlie walks over to Karen. "Hello there, beautiful. What's the special for today?"

Karen looks at Charlie, and a flash of anger sparks in her eyes. "The special today is, why haven't you called me?!"

Charlie, detecting her hostility, says, "Why haven't I called you? Was I supposed to?"

She stares at him, then looks away. As she looks back at him, she says in a ticked-off manner, "No, Charlie, you weren't supposed to, but I thought you would anyway."

Charlie gives Karen a puzzled look, asking in a soft voice, "Are you mad at me?"

Karen looks at him, curiosity showing in her eyes. "Charlie, look at me."

Charlie looks at Karen like a basset hound that has just disobeyed its master.

"Charlie, are you seeing someone else?"

"No! No, Karen, I am not seeing anyone else."

"Would you tell me if you were?"

"Karen, if I were seeing someone else, I would not keep it from you. I would tell you flat out, but I am not seeing anyone else. I don't want to see anyone else. I love you and only you."

Karen beams at Charlie with a big happy smile. "Charlie, I am glad you said that. You have put my mind at ease."

Charlie smiles back and says, "I am sorry for not calling you Monday or Tuesday. I will make it up to you by taking you out to the nicest place in town for dinner on Saturday night."

Karen looks at Charlie with a little reluctance in her eyes. "I'm sorry, Charlie, but I can't go out with you Saturday night."

With a confused look on his face, Charlie says, "Why not?"

"Well, Charlie, I am going out with Steve Saturday night."

"Huh?"

"You see, Charlie … Steve asked me out for Saturday night. I told him yes."

"I thought you told him not to call you anymore for a while."

"When did you hear me say that?"

"Sunday, when I was in the living room talking with your mother. We both heard you say that you didn't want him to be calling you for a while."

"You mean you were listening in on my conversation with Steve?"

"No! We were not listening in on your conversation. We just overheard what you were talking about."

"Then you were listening in on my conversation!"

"I was not! Well, I was not listening in *too* much."

A customer is now waiting for service.

Karen looks at Charlie and says in an angry tone, "If you would please excuse me, I have a customer waiting."

Charlie just stands there as Karen walks away to wait on the customer. She takes his order and then walks back over to Charlie, who eagerly waits for her to return.

Showing a peeved expression, Karen says, "Well?"

Confused, Charlie says, "Well, what?"

"Well, are you going to apologize to me for listening in on my conversation with Steve?"

"Apologize?! Apologize for what?"

"What do you mean for what?" Karen doesn't wait for Charlie's reply. "Either you apologize for listening in, or you can just go home."

Now quite surprised, Charlie says, "Okay, Karen. I am sorry for listening in on your phone call."

Not satisfied, Karen replies, "That's not good enough, Charlie. You didn't say it like you meant it."

Charlie, now completely dumbfounded, looks directly at Karen, reaches over, and takes her hand in his. He speaks in a very soft and compassionate way. "I'm sorry, Cubby. I won't ever do it again. Will you forgive me this time?"

Karen smiles with joy, saying sweetly, "Yes, Charlie, I forgive you."

Charlie then leans over and lightly kisses her on her innocent-looking lips.

Customers begin to roll into the pizza establishment in great numbers.

"I have got to go back to work now, Charlie."

"How about going out to dinner with me tonight?"

"Not tonight, Charlie. I need to talk to Steve a little more. After I talk with him Saturday night, then you and I can start dating."

With a puzzled look, Charlie says, "I thought you had already talked to Steve about that matter."

"I talked to him, Charlie, but I didn't break everything to him at once. I thought it would be better if I did it in stages. I have got to go back to work now, Charlie."

Karen walks over and begins waiting on the customers.

Charlie just sits down and waits until Karen has a free moment, and then, with a humble expression on his face, he looks at Karen and says, "How about I pick you up at seven o'clock Sunday night?"

"Well, Charlie, let me talk to Steve before I make any plans with you. Call me on Sunday afternoon, and I will tell you then. How does that sound?"

Charlie just looks sad as he nods his head. He waves good-bye, leaving without ordering anything to eat.

Feeling depressed, Charlie walks out to his truck and drives home. When he arrives, he walks into his house and goes directly to his bedroom. He locates his secret little book, flips through the pages, and continues working on his plan once more.

By Friday morning, Charlie is eager to learn what Mr. Bowman has found out. During his lunch hour, Charlie dials the PI's number.

Once again, Charlie hears Nancy Walker's voice over the line. "Hello. Bowman Investigations. May I help you?"

Charlie eagerly replies, "Hello, Nancy. This is Charlie Delaney. Is Mr. Bowman free?"

"Hello, Mr. Delaney. Mr. Bowman was just talking about you. He has some information for you. Just a minute and I'll see if he is free."

Charlie waits expectantly.

"Hello, Charlie," Mr. Bowman says when he gets on the phone. "I have some information for you."

"Great! What is it?"

"This Steve Johnson is a member of the South Park Country Club."

"Yeah? I know where that is."

"Good. They have a very nice golf course there; I have played there many times."

"You have?"

"Yes, Charlie. Many times."

"Don't you have to be a member to play golf there?"

"Oh no, Charlie. Anybody can play golf there. It's just that if you are a member, you don't have to pay the greens fee. Plus, there is a tennis court, a swimming pool, and a special clubhouse, all for members only. But anybody can play golf there."

"I'm glad you told me that, Mr. Bowman."

"But, Charlie, listen to this. Steve Johnson has a few honey pies he spends time with over at the tennis courts. I know there are two: a blonde and a brunette. And from what I have gathered, they are doing more than just playing tennis."

"Excellent, Mr. Bowman! Excellent! Anything else?"

"Johnson lives with his parents, and he drives a blue Chevelle. I also prepared a complete general informational report on him: where he went to school, where he lives, and things like that."

"Excellent! Right after I get off work, I'll stop by to pick it up."

"Okay, Charlie. I'll see you then, but I have got to run now."

"Okay, Mr. Bowman. I will be there at around four-thirty. See you then."

After work, Charlie stops by Mr. Bowman's office to retrieve the report. He gives the PI another four hundred dollars, goes home, and reads the report thoroughly. Charlie learns a great deal about Steve Johnson, and is now satisfied that he knows who he is up against. He goes to bed with a sense of accomplishment.

Saturday morning soon arrives. Charlie gets up early and looks through his secret book one more time. While fixing his breakfast, he thinks about his plan one last time. As soon as he finishes eating, he puts the dishes in the sink, goes to his bedroom, and gets dressed.

It is now time to put his plan into action!

Charlie gets a sensational idea. *I believe I will play a game of golf today. I haven't played in nearly a year. Yes, indeed, I think I will play a game today. I hope I will find this Steve and play a round with him. He might even take a liking to me. I will get him to say something that will make his pride burn up his integrity. And then, I will finish him off with a little fear, pain, and intimidation.*

With a delighted grin, Charlie feels that he has now perfected the details of his plan. All he has to do is put his plan into action and make it a reality.

It's still a little cold outside this early in the morning, so Charlie decides to wait a little. At around one o'clock, Charlie gets into his truck and drives to the South Park Country Club. As he nears the golf course he wonders aloud, "Why on earth would a man want to mess around with another girl when he has someone like Karen Thomas? I just can't understand that."

Charlie drives past the last hole and sees a few golfers hitting away at their golf balls. It's just before two o'clock. As Charlie parks his truck at the country club, he feels a sense of remorse, but he gets out and proceeds to walk toward the clubhouse anyway. He opens the door and walks inside. Several men are sitting in the room, watching TV. Charlie walks to the counter up front.

He addresses the man behind the counter. "Hello. I would like to rent a set of golf clubs and play nine holes."

The man says, "Okay. Do you want to ride or walk?"

"I would like to ride."

"Are you by yourself, or are you with someone?"

"Oh, I'm by myself."

"You need to have someone to play with if you want to ride. We don't have enough carts to go around just for a single."

Charlie just looks at the man, disappointed. Just then, they both hear laughter in the background.

A voice says, "Can you believe he missed that shot!"

Everyone looks at the TV, which shows some professionals playing golf.

Someone else yells, "Hey, Fred, bring another pitcher over here."

While Fred brings the pitcher of beer over to the table, Charlie glances down and sees a familiar name on the golf register: Steve Johnson. He signed in at 10:12 a.m. Charlie decides to pull up a chair until Mr. Johnson comes walking through the door, as Charlie hopes he will soon do.

Charlie waits only twenty minutes until four guys come walking into the clubhouse. They all sit down at a table near Charlie, focusing their attention on the TV. One of the guys goes over to the counter and buys a pitcher of beer. Charlie casually looks over at the group while the beer is poured into four mugs.

One of the professionals on TV misses an easy putt.

One of the four men announces, "I believe I could have made that shot, and I'm just a rookie."

Another one says, "Steve, you have to get the ball on the green before you can even attempt to putt the ball into the hole." He and two of the other men then roar with laughter.

"Oh, very funny, Raymond," says Steve. "I'm not that bad."

"Oh no? How many strokes did you have on thirteen?"

There is a long pause, and then Steve finally answers, "I'd rather not say."

More laughter comes from the table of four.

Charlie remains in his seat, working up his courage to talk to the four men. They remain at the table, enjoying their view of the TV. As one of the guys reaches down to rewind the tape in the VCR, Charlie makes his approach.

"Would anyone of you like to play nine holes?" Charlie asks. All four men, including Steve, turn to look at Charlie. "The guy behind the counter says I can't ride by myself, so I was just wondering if one of you guys would like to play."

One of the men says, "Steve, you are the one who needs the practice."

Another one says, "Practice? Steve could practice for the rest of his life and still not get the ball on the green in under ten strokes. Well … maybe nine."

The three men once again roar with laughter.

Steve stands up and looks at Charlie. "Don't pay any attention to these clowns. I'm not all that bad."

One of Steve's friends says, "No, he's not that bad. He's worse."

Laughter resounds from the table.

Steve, looking humiliated, says to Charlie, "That's it! Come on. I'll play nine holes with you, but then I've got to go home."

Steve walks around to the other side of the table where Charlie is standing. "By the way, what's your name?"

"Charlie. Charlie Delaney."

"My name is Steve Johnson."

Charlie smiles like he has just hit a home run in the World Series.

Steve looks back at the table and then at Charlie. He then introduces the three other guys. "The thin dark-haired clown is David. The goofy redheaded clown with the shit-eating grin is Gary, and the one with the big mouth is Raymond Lineberry."

Charlie smiles at the three sitting at the table and says, "Glad to meet you all."

One of the guys asks, "What did you say your name was?"

"Charlie Delaney."

Raymond says, "You'd better watch Steve. He has a bad habit of knocking his ball into the woods and finding it in his back pocket."

Raymond, David, and Gary again roar with laughter at Steve's expense.

Steve looks over at Charlie and says, "Come on, Charlie, let's get out of here."

"All right, let's go."

So the two golfers walk over to Fred. Charlie pays for his nine holes, And Fred hands him the rental clubs. Charlie also buys balls, tees, and a glove. Steve only pays for the golf cart. Since he is a member, he doesn't have to pay for the greens fee.

"Okay, Charlie, let's go," says Steve.

Charlie smiles gleefully as the two depart the clubhouse and walk toward the golf carts.

Steve hops into the cart while Charlie straps his clubs in the back.

"Where are your clubs?" asks Charlie.

Steve replies, "I'll drive the cart to where I parked my car. My clubs are in the trunk."

Charlie can't believe how well everything is going.

As Steve drives, Charlie says, "I guess you have played eighteen holes already today."

"Yeah, I played eighteen holes with those three guys you just met."

"What did you hit?"

"I'm not very good yet. I shot 90."

"That's not too bad. I probably won't do much better, if I do that well."

Charlie notices the blue Chevelle as they get closer to it. Steve parks the cart, gets out, and takes his clubs out of the trunk of his car.

Charlie asks, "What kind of clubs do you have, Steve?"

"Mine are Wilson 1200s. They are a pretty good set of clubs, but the set I want costs five hundred dollars."

Charlie studies Steve as he puts his clubs in the cart and straps them in. Now that they are set, Steve and Charlie drive over to the first hole. The brisk January wind blows with a slight chill, but it is not too gusty. It gives the golf course a brisk, adventurous air. Over to the left of the first hole, though, there is a large dark cloud.

The two men get out and approach the first tee.

Steve asks, "Do you want to go first?"

Charlie replies, "No, you go ahead."

Steve takes his driver and tees up. He swings a few practice swings and then drives the ball straight ahead, about 250 yards.

"Nice drive, Steve!"

Steve smiles with pride and happiness. "Thanks Charlie. I wish those clowns in the clubhouse could have seen that."

Charlie takes his driver and walks over to the tee. He tees up his ball, takes a few practice swings, and then strikes the ball, slicing it to the right.

Steve snickers to himself and says, "Don't worry about it, Charlie. We have all sliced one before."

"Yeah. I just need to keep my eye on the ball a little better when I start to come down."

Steve and Charlie get into the cart and drive to where Charlie's ball is located.

Charlie, seeing it, points and says, "There it is."

"I see it," Steve says, driving over to the ball.

Charlie gets out of the cart. "What iron do you think I should use, Steve?"

"Try your 2-iron; you'll need all the distance you can get."

Charlie takes out his 2-iron from the bag and proceeds to address the ball. The ball doesn't go far, landing near the center of the fairway. It was a decent shot. Steve is clearly feeling good now that it's apparent he is a better golfer than Charlie. Charlie, on the other hand, feels great, because his plan is working out better than he ever thought possible.

Steve drives the cart once again to where Charlie's ball is lying.

Charlie gets out and asks Steve, "Do you think a 3-iron is too much club?"

"Oh yes, way too much club. You'd better use a 5-iron instead."

Charlie takes out his 5-iron and strikes the ball smoothly. It lands just above where Steve's ball is lying, and a little to the right.

Charlie shrugs his shoulders, like an actor on a stage, and says, "Here I am, lying three, and here you are, lying one."

The look on Steve's face plainly shows that he feels a little proud of himself.

Charlie enjoys seeing this expression on Steve's face. He enjoys seeing his ego inflated.

The two of them get back into the golf cart, and Steve drives up to his ball. Charlie studies Steve as he drives.

Steve takes out a club, and with a very proud look, he says, "I believe my 8-iron will put my ball right into the hole."

He takes a few practice swings as Charlie remains quiet. Steve addresses the ball sharply. The ball goes straight up. It bounces one time and rolls onto the green.

Charlie yells, “Great shot, Steve! That was perfect! I don’t think you could have hit it any better.”

Steve says, “Thanks, Charlie. It was a pretty good shot. Damn, I’m good. I wish that loudmouth Raymond could have seen that shot.”

Charlie watches as Steve’s face glows with pride.

Charlie grins and then says, “Since you used an 8-iron, I will too.”

Charlie takes his iron and strikes the ball. It takes off again to the right, another bad slice.

“You know what you are doing wrong, Charlie?”

“No, Steve. Please tell me.”

Steve acts like a pro as he gives advice to Charlie. “First of all, you aren’t keeping your eye on the ball. When you swing, your eyes have a tendency to move upward.”

“You’re right, Steve, they do.”

Charlie’s response inflates Steve’s ego even further.

“Second of all, you need to hold your club in more,” Steve says, and then he demonstrates to Charlie how he should hold the club.

Charlie takes the club from Steve and says, “Oh yeah! I believe you are right again, Steve.”

Continuing to talk like an expert, Steve says, “It just takes practice. Bad habits are hard to break, so try to keep your eye on the ball until the momentum of your body pulls your head upward.”

“I’ll do that, Steve. Thanks!”

They both get into the cart, and Steve drives over to Charlie’s ball.

Charlie takes out a 9-iron and hits the ball straight up in the air. They both look on with great anticipation as the ball finally bounces on the green.

Steve lets out a loud, “Great shot, Charlie!”

Charlie shows a wry smile and says, “Thanks to you, Steve. It’s amazing what the club will do if you just keep your eye on the ball and your mind on the green.”

Steve and Charlie drive up the path to where the green is. They both get out, pull out their putters, and begin to walk toward their balls.

“I believe your ball is farther away, so you go first, Steve.”

"Okay, Charlie. Just watch this."

Steve lines up his ball for a birdie putt. He strikes the ball gently, but the ball misses the hole. Steve mutters a few curses, and then pulls out a dime and marks his ball. After picking up the ball, he throws it deep into the woods.

With a puzzled look, Charlie asks, "Why did you throw your ball into the woods?"

Steve angrily replies, "Any ball that can't fall in for a birdie from that distance doesn't need to be used again."

Charlie thinks to himself, *What a jerk! He thinks the ball is supposed to just go in all by itself.* Charlie doesn't say anything negative to Steve, but he does look at him with a little disgust.

Charlie approaches his ball and putts it. The ball falls right into the cup.

Steve can't believe his eyes!

Charlie looks over at Steve and casually says, "It's amazing what you can do when you set your mind to it."

Charlie watches Steve closely. He is quiet and shows a serious look, but he doesn't say anything. He then walks over to his ball one more time, putting it in for an easy par and grinning like an opossum.

Steve and Charlie walk back to the golf cart.

As they put the putters away, Steve asks, "Did you get six, Charlie?"

"Yep, I got six."

"And I got four."

Steve records the score on the card, and then he drives the cart to the second hole.

They both get out of the cart and pull out their drivers.

Charlie looks at Steve and thinks to himself, *Maybe I should get him to talk about that little honey Mr. Bowman was telling me about.*

Steve proceeds to tee up. He takes a few practice swings and then addresses the ball right down the middle of the fairway.

Charlie says, "Wow! Nice shot, Steve. Right down the middle!"

With a proud grin on his face, Steve says, "Thanks, Charlie. I love to see the ball leave here like that."

"I hope mine will take off and leave here in the same direction—or somewhere close."

Charlie tees up his ball. He takes a few practice swings, just like Steve did. He addresses the ball, and once again, the ball takes off to the right.

Steve snickers a little bit before saying, "Maybe you need to turn the club in more, Charlie."

"I believe I need to turn the club in a whole lot more, Steve." Charlie decides to probe Steve a little.

As they drive to the golf balls, Charlie asks, "Are you married, Steve?"

"No, I'm not married. Are you, Charlie?"

"Oh no … at least, not yet."

Steve remarks, "I don't think I want to get married. I'm having too much fun being single."

Charlie grins. "I'll bet you have got girls coming out of the woodwork."

Steve opens up a little to Charlie. "Well, I do have a few following me around. You ought to see this cute little blonde I have been banging. I met her over at the tennis courts. Yum-yum! Eat 'um up."

Charlie listens with his complete and undivided attention.

Steve continues. "Yeah, she is a baby doll. She is twenty-one and lives with her parents, and her parents are rich. She has got some enormous boobs, almost as big as my main girlfriend's."

"You have a main girlfriend?"

"Yeah, I have been going with her for nearly six years. I love her to death, but she doesn't fool around any. You know, a virgin."

Charlie happily asks, "You mean that? She is really a virgin?"

"Yeah, no doubt in my mind, since I'm the only guy she has ever gone out with."

Charlie takes all this in with great enthusiasm.

"Yeah, if I ever do decide to get married, she would be the one," Steve says.

Charlie is about to say something, but at the last moment, he decides to keep it to himself.

Steve drives Charlie right next to his ball. Charlie takes out his 3-wood and drives the ball long, but to the right. Steve remains silent, except for a snicker or two.

As he and Steve drive off, Charlie says, "You know, Steve, women are a lot like golf: If you keep your eyes on them and address them properly, you will always know where they are. If you don't keep your eyes on them, or if you address them improperly, you may lose them in the thicket of the woods."

Steve looks at Charlie with a little savor. "You know something, Charlie, I believe you are right about that."

Steve drives up to his ball. He pulls out a 2-iron. Charlie watches carefully as Steve swings his club. Steve then addresses the ball. He tops it, and the ball rolls only a short distance. Steve begins to swear and curse, using very nasty language. Charlie watches with a distasteful look as Steve continues to bellow out the disgusting vocabulary. Charlie doesn't say a thing to Steve, so as not to make him even more upset. Charlie doesn't want Steve to be upset. Steve then walks to where the ball is and strikes it again. This time, the ball soars into the air and lands on the fairway, about 125 yards from the pin.

"Great shot, Steve!"

"I just wish I had done that the first time."

"Yes, Steve, there are things in life we wish we had done the first time, but for some strange reason we did not. Then, after we fail to do so, we wish we had done things differently. But no matter how hard we wish, nothing will change what we have already done. We must then accept what appears before us and try not to make the same mistake twice."

Steve gives Charlie a very curious look, and then he says, "You know something, Charlie, I believe you are right again."

They both get into the cart, and Steve begins to drive the golf cart once again.

Steve looks up and sees a very large black cloud. "I sure hope it doesn't rain."

Charlie, looking concerned, says, "It sure does look black over there."

Steve stops at Charlie's ball. Charlie gets his 4-iron and addresses the ball. The ball leaves the ground in a hurry. Charlie puts the club back in the bag and sits down in the cart as they both proceed to Steve's ball. Charlie tries to get Steve to say something nasty about Karen so he can put his plan into action, but the clouds in the background dominate the conversation. A chilly breeze blows calmly.

Charlie asks, "So how often do you see this blonde over at the tennis courts?"

"Oh, just now and then, usually on Wednesdays. Her folks work very late on Wednesday nights, for some reason. After we play a game, I follow her home. There is nobody there to bother us for several hours. She is real pretty but a little on the dumb side, if you know what I mean. She makes up for that in bed, though. Boy, does she ever!"

Charlie laughs a little, just to make Steve feel comfortable.

Steve stops the cart and gets out. He grabs his 9-iron and strikes his ball with great force. The ball goes straight up and lands just shy of the green.

Steve remarks, "Well, I'm lying near the green in four." Steve happily walks back to the cart.

As Steve drives Charlie to his ball, Charlie says, "You know, Steve, I have an idea. Why don't you and that little blonde come over to my house tomorrow night? You can meet my girlfriend."

Steve pauses for a moment and then says, "I don't know what she will be doing tomorrow night, Charlie. Maybe some other time."

"Okay. Just let me know, and we will double-date sometime."

Steve doesn't say anything; he just keeps on driving until he reaches Charlie's ball. Charlie takes out a club and strikes the ball with authority. It bounces on the green and rolls all the way off.

"We are both lying four … right, Charlie?"

"That's right, Steve. We both are lying four."

Steve drives the cart up the path, just shy of the green. They both pull out two clubs and proceed to their balls. Steve is farther away, so he chips first. The ball rolls past the hole and off the green. After Steve finishes swearing and acting like a complete idiot, Charlie walks up to his ball, and chips. Just like Steve's ball, Charlie's ball rolls past the hole and off the green.

Charlie says, "These greens sure are fast."

Charlie doesn't get mad at all; he just takes it in stride.

Steve takes his putter and putts his ball. The ball stops shy of the hole by about three feet.

Charlie looks at Steve and thinks, *He sure is taking this game real seriously. I believe he is trying hard just to impress me.*

Charlie takes his putter, and putts. Charlie's ball doesn't get close to the hole but manages to stay on the green. Charlie sees a delighted grin on Steve's face now that he is sure to win the hole. Steve seems to enjoy seeing Charlie's ball roll far away from the hole.

Steve, with a shit-eating grin on his face, says, "I guess it's still your turn, Charlie."

Charlie walks over to his ball, and putts. It stops just shy of the hole. Charlie marks his ball with a dime as Steve makes ready for his putt. He putts the ball into the hole. He acts like he has done something fabulous. Charlie just stands and watches Steve act silly. This gives Charlie time to size up Steve totally. Steve ends up with a seven as Charlie tries to putt one more time. He puts the ball down where his dime is and putts. He misses the hole by just a little.

Steve, seeing this, laughs loudly and says, "Too bad, Charlie! You should take a little more time to think about what you're doing."

Charlie gives Steve an unfriendly look, but he doesn't say anything. Instead, he just taps the ball into the hole for a nine.

Steve and Charlie walk back over to the cart.

As they are putting their clubs back, Steve says, "I can't believe you missed such an easy shot."

Charlie feels like jumping on him and pounding on his head, but he manages to control himself until the right moment.

"I guess I should have studied on the putt a little longer and waited until the right moment. I guess I acted too soon, Steve. I won't make the same mistake twice."

Steve tees up his ball for the third hole. Just as Steve swings his club and hits the ball high into the air, the bottom falls out of the sky. The rain starts to fall in a downpour.

Steve cries out, "Put your club back into the bag, Charlie, and let's head back to the clubhouse!"

Charlie does this, and the two jump into the golf cart and head back to the clubhouse as fast as the golf cart can take them.

As they reach the clubhouse Steve says to Charlie, "There is no way we can finish the game today, Charlie. We will have to finish it some other time."

Charlie grins. "Yes, Steve, we will finish this some other time."

Steve pulls the cart under a little shelter. Charlie gets out and removes his clubs. Steve does the same.

As the thunder echoes in the background and the rain comes down hard, Steve looks over at Charlie and says, "I'll catch you later, Charlie. I am going home now."

Charlie quickly replies, "I'll be here next Saturday at one o'clock sharp, and we will finish what we have started."

Steve answers, "Fine. I will call and get a tee time reserved."

Charlie says okay.

Steve, with that shit-eating grin on his face, adds, "I will understand if you don't show up."

Charlie happily replies, "I wouldn't miss it for the world. I will be here."

"Fine. We will start off on the third hole, right where we left off."

Without another word, Steve runs into the clubhouse to return the golf cart key, and then he comes back, gets his clubs, and dashes to his car.

Charlie carries the golf clubs inside the clubhouse, glad to get out of the rain. Once inside, he turns to the man who rented them to him and says, "I guess I won't need these anymore today."

"Since you didn't use them because of the rain, you can use them next time free."

"Really? Well, the next time will be next Saturday at one o'clock. You can go ahead and put down a tee time down for Steve and me."

The man walks over to a schedule book and writes down the reservation.

He looks at Charlie and asks, "What is your name, sir?"

"My name is Charlie Delaney."

Charlie smiles at the man, turns toward the door, and smoothly walks out.

Later in the evening, Karen is getting ready for her date with Steve. The rain has stopped, but it is fairly chilly outside. Karen has decided to have a heart-to-heart talk with Steve tonight. She has made up her mind exactly what she wants to say; she just hopes she has the courage to finally say it. Mrs. Thomas is in the kitchen, washing the dishes. Karen walks into the kitchen, carrying two dresses.

She gets her mother's attention and asks, "Which one do you think I should wear?"

Her mother looks at the two dresses carefully. "The red one will be fine."

"I like the yellow one."

"Then why did you ask me which one I liked?"

"I was hoping you would pick the yellow one. The red one is more seductive."

Mrs. Thomas shakes her head. "Honey, they're both seductive."

"Then I won't wear either one. I don't want to look seductive tonight."

Mrs. Thomas gives Karen a very stern look. "I guess you are going to tell Steve about that new fellow you've met."

"No! I'm going to do no such thing, and I hope you don't say anything to Steve about Charlie either."

Mrs. Thomas looks at her daughter, confused. "Then what are you going to tell Steve? Nothing?"

"I'm going to talk to Steve about seeing other guys, but I'm not going to mention any names. And I want you to promise me that you won't mention Charlie's name either."

Karen and her mother stare at each other in silence, each waiting for the other to speak.

Karen finally says, "Well? Are you going to promise me you won't say anything, or not?"

"Okay, I promise not to tell Steve about this guy Charlie, but I hope you know what you're doing, young lady."

"I know just what I'm doing. I also know what I'm going to tell Steve."

"What? What are you going to tell Steve?"

Karen pauses for a moment. "I'm going to tell him I want to start dating other guys, and I don't want to be tied down to him anymore."

"You mean, you want to break up with him?"

"No, I didn't say that. We can still date once in a while, but I'm not going to devote all my time to him anymore."

"He might get mad and stop seeing you altogether."

"If that's what he wants, fine! He can do whatever he wants to, mama. I hope Steve won't act that way, but if he does, so be it!"

Karen rushes out of the kitchen. She comes back in only a few seconds.

She looks at her mother, disturbed, and says, "He has had plenty of time to make up his mind if he wants to marry me. I'm not going to wait around forever."

Mrs. Thomas softly replies, "You need to give him a little more time."

With her voice raised, Karen says, "Time! He has had plenty of time. He is twenty-one years old now, mama. He works for his daddy, and he has a good job. You know, we haven't ever even talked about getting married."

"After tonight, he might never talk about it."

"Whatever, mama! I'm not going to wait around forever until he's ready."

Mrs. Thomas, seeing that Karen is upset, changes the subject. "What time is Steve supposed to be here?"

Karen calms down a little bit. "He is supposed to be here at seven-thirty, but he will probably get here at around eight."

"I just hope you are nice about telling him your plans. Don't be mean about it."

"Mean? When have I ever been mean about anything?"

Mrs. Thomas shakes her head in disbelief. "You know you have a hot temper, dear. When you get upset, your emotions fly off the handle, and you do and say things that you are sorry for later."

"What are you talking about, mother? You know I'm not like that … very much."

Mrs. Thomas just shakes her head again.

Karen smiles at her mother and says, "I'll try to be as nice as I can be. Just as long as he gets the message I'm trying to send."

Mrs. Thomas looks at the wall clock. "You'd better hurry up and get ready. You know, Steve might surprise you and get here early."

"Tell me which dress I should wear."

"The yellow one will be fine, dear."

"You know, mama, I believe you are right. I'm glad I asked you."

Mrs. Thomas smiles and shakes her head a third time.

Karen leaves the kitchen to finish getting ready as her mother goes back to the sink to wash a few more dishes. Before long, Mrs. Thomas finishes washing the last dish. She walks into the living room, turns on the TV, and sits down on the couch to relax.

Karen walks into the living room, wearing the yellow dress. She walks over to the couch and sits down beside her mother.

Showing a very apprehensive look, Karen says, "Mama, do you think Steve will understand about me wanting to see someone else?"

"I think Steve will probably understand, dear. Just be polite, and tell him in an understanding way."

As the time draws closer to seven-thirty, Karen looks more and more concerned.

With a worried look, Karen says, "I sure hope Steve understands. Mama. I will tell him in a straight way."

"I think everything will work out, dear."

"I will be glad when it's all over and done with. I have been putting this off too long now."

Karen and her mother watch TV, saying very little for the next half hour.

At eight o'clock, a car pulls into the driveway. The lights shine into the living room, and Mrs. Thomas gets up and goes to the window.

"Karen, Steve is here."

Karen remains in her seat until she hears a knock on the door.

Mrs. Thomas walks over to the door and opens it. She greets Steve with a smile. "Hello, Steve, come on in."

Steve kisses her on the cheek and says, "Hello, Mrs. Thomas. You sure look nice tonight."

Steve walks inside and sees Karen standing next to the TV. "Hello, Karen. Are you ready?"

Karen walks over to him and says bluntly, "I see you are late as usual."

"Oh yeah … I guess I kind of forgot what time it was getting. No harm done. I'm here."

"I guess so, Steve. I guess so," Karen says.

Karen walks over to the closet and gets her coat. She puts it on and casually says to her mother, "I'll be in early, mama."

Steve, hearing this, looks very surprised but doesn't say anything.

Mrs. Thomas, looking like a mother would look, says, "You two have fun. Drive carefully, and have a good time."

Steve and Karen walk to the door and exit the house.

As soon as Steve shuts the door, he asks Karen, "What do you mean, you will be in early?"

"Come on. Let's go."

Karen walks over to Steve's car and gets in. He does likewise.

Steve looks over at Karen and says, "Why do you need to be in early?"

With a reluctant look on her face, Karen says, "I'm pretty tired tonight, Steve. I don't want to stay out too late."

"Don't you feel well?"

"Oh, I feel fine. I just don't want to stay out late tonight, that's all."

Steve starts the car but is confused by Karen's behavior. He pulls out of the driveway and starts off down the road.

As he drives, Steve looks over at Karen and says, "Where do you want to go?"

"I'm hungry. Let's get something to eat."

"Sounds good to me. How about McDonald's?"

Karen, with her voice raised, says, "McDonald's! Are you crazy! I don't want to go to McDonald's!"

Steve gives her a mean look. "Well, where do you want to eat?"

"Someplace nice."

Steve calmly replies, "McDonald's is nice."

"I don't care. I don't want to go to McDonald's."

Steve thinks a bit and then says, "All right. How about Hardee's?"

Karen, looking even angrier, replies, "Hardee's? I don't want to go Hardee's either. I want to go to a nice place!"

Steve gives Karen an unhappy look. "Just tell me exactly where you want to eat, and we will go there."

"How about the new place next to the mall? The Napoleon Steak House."

Steve turns his nose up and says, "I don't care about going to a place like that."

"Why not?"

Steve pauses before giving her a reason. "That place is way too expensive. It would probably cost thirty or forty bucks to get out of there."

"So? Just look how nice it will be."

"Nice? I don't see paying forty bucks just to see something nice."

Karen doesn't say anything, but she gives him a very unhappy look.

A few moments pass, and then Steve breaks the silence. "That's what's wrong with you, Karen. You think money grows on trees. I'm the one who will have to pay for it, not you."

This upsets Karen greatly. "Don't you think I'm worth spending thirty dollars on once in a while?"

"Sure, once in a while but not every week. I'm trying to save up enough money to buy me a new set of golf clubs."

"Golf clubs! What's more important, me or those stupid golf clubs?"

"I don't want to argue about this anymore. Let's talk about something else."

"I don't want to talk about something else. Which is more important, me or those golf clubs?"

Steve is quiet for a moment.

Karen breaks the silence. "Answer me, Steve! Which is more important?"

Compelled to answer, Steve says, "Okay, you are more important."

"It sure did take you a long time to answer my question."

Steve pauses again and then says, "Why don't we go and get some seafood over at the Fisherman's Paradise?"

Still angry, Karen reluctantly agrees.

As Steve pulls up to the restaurant, he looks over at Karen and says, "Is this all right with you?"

Karen softly replies, "This will be fine."

The two get out of Steve's car and walk into the restaurant.

Steve notices there isn't a line. "You see, Karen, this is much better than that fancy place over near the mall."

Karen doesn't say anything, but she is agitated about Steve's remark.

"That place over near the mall probably has a one-hour wait."

"Let's just drop it, Steve. We are already here, so please just drop it. Okay?"

Steve doesn't say anything else.

After Steve and Karen are seated, Karen opens her menu and starts to look over the selections. She glances over at Steve and notices he isn't looking at his menu.

"Aren't you going to eat anything, Steve?"

"Why, of course I am, silly."

Karen becomes very agitated at being called silly but doesn't say anything about it. "Then why aren't you looking at the menu?"

"Because I know what I want: the flounder. I don't have to look at the menu; I know they have flounder."

"But that's what you always get. Why don't you look at the menu, and order something different?"

"Because I don't want anything different; I know just what I want, and that is flounder!"

"You don't have to be so hostile about it."

"I'm not being hostile about anything. I just like flounder, and I don't want to look at some stupid menu when I know it is on it."

Karen is becoming more and more agitated. She looks back over at the menu until the waitress comes over to take their order.

The waitress asks, "Are you all ready to order now?"

Karen begins to answer the waitress, but Steve interrupts. "Yes, I'll have the medium flounder plate, with french-fries and iced tea."

The waitress quickly writes down Steve's order. She turns to Karen and asks, "What would you like, dear?"

Karen continues to stare at the menu as the waitress waits.

Steve says, "Why don't you order the flounder plate like me; you know that's what you want."

Karen gives Steve a very stern look. "Because I don't want the flounder plate, Steve."

"Well, tell the waitress something."

Karen continues to look over the menu.

The waitress asks, "Would you like for me to come back later to get your order?"

Karen replies, "Maybe that's a good idea. You can bring me some iced tea, though."

"Fine. I'll be right back." She smiles politely at Karen and then walks away.

Steve gives Karen a shit-eating grin. "Just like a woman, can't seem to make up her mind."

Karen quickly replies, "I'm not like you, Steve. I don't like ordering the same thing every time I come into a restaurant. I like to look over everything and order something different each time."

Steve remarks, "I guess that's the difference between men and women: men know what they like and stay with it; women, on the other hand, always want to change things around and be different."

"What's so bad about wanting to be different?"

"Nothing, but when something is perfect, leave it alone, and don't change it around just to be different."

"Eating the same thing time after time gets to be boring. If you try something new every once in a while, you might like the difference."

"I guess so, Karen, I guess so." Giving her a look, Steve asks, "Have you made up your mind yet?"

Karen, still studying the menu, says, "I think so. I'm stuck between the fried shrimp and the fried oysters."

"Make up your mind. The waitress will be back soon. Here she comes now."

The waitress walks up to the table with their tea. She puts the two glasses down and asks, "Are you ready to order now?"

Karen, with her eyes still glued to the menu, says, "I can't seem to make up my mind. I have narrowed it down to two items: the fried shrimp and the fried oysters."

The waitress waits patiently, ready to take Karen's order.

Steve says, "Why don't you get a combination plate? That way you can have both."

Karen smiles at Steve and says, "I think that is the best idea I have heard you suggest all evening, Steve."

The waitress asks, "Is that what you want, dear?"

"Yes, I think that will be just what I want."

The waitress asks, "Would you like french-fries or a baked potato?"

"I'll be different tonight and get a baked potato."

The waitress writes down Karen's order, and leaves.

Karen decides to talk to Steve about her new plans now.

Before she starts the conversation, Steve says, "I was hoping we would go to the movies tonight."

"I'm not sure I want to go to the movies tonight, Steve." Karen gives Steve a provocative look.

Steve looks back and says, "You have been acting a little strange tonight. Is there anything wrong?"

Karen looks at Steve, turns her head away for a second, and then looks back, right into Steve's eyes. "Yes, Steve, there is something I want to talk to you about."

"What? What is it?"

Karen gives him a compassionate look as she says, "Steve, I have been thinking … you know … about us."

"What about us? What do you mean?"

"I have been thinking that our relationship is not at all what it should be."

Steve looks at Karen with great concern.

"By now, Steve, we should have a better understanding of how we feel about each other."

Steve, showing a puzzled look, replies, "I thought we did, Karen."

"That's the problem, Steve. We don't have that understanding. You think we do, but we don't."

"I don't know what you're trying to say. What are you getting at?"

"What I'm getting at, Steve, is that we have been dating each other for so long that neither one of us has had a chance to see what else is out there."

Steve, showing an angry look, says, "What are you getting at?"

Karen pauses for a moment and then gets an idea. "Steve, it's like that flounder you always order." Steve scratches his head as Karen continues. "Never trying anything different, always getting the same thing because you like that one item. You don't even know all the other things you might enjoy. That's the way our relationship has been going for the last few years."

Steve, not liking what he's hearing, replies, "What does my liking flounder have to do with how our relationship is going?"

"Let me try to explain." Steve shows great concern as Karen continues. "You see, Steve, we have known each other for so long that we take each other for granted. It's like eating flounder every day for the past five years. Not experiencing anything new. It's made our relationship dull and boring."

"Oh, so now I am boring!"

"Not you, Steve, just our relationship. It's our relationship that has become boring. It's the same old thing time after time after time after time."

Steve, looking convincing, says, "But I like the same old thing."

"That's it, Steve, you like the same old thing. But I don't."

Steve gives her a very mean look. "What exactly are you trying to say?"

Karen clears her throat and says, "What I'm trying to say is that I need a different routine. I need a change in our boring, uncaring relationship."

The waitress walks up to the table with two plates in her hands.

Steve and Karen cease talking about the matter until she leaves.

Steve takes his fork and starts to cut his fish. He then puts his fork down and says, "What are you trying to say? You have been talking like this for over a week now. Do you want to break up?"

Karen takes a sip of her tea and says, "Not exactly, Steve. I just want a change."

"What kind of a change do you want?"

"I just want to start seeing and dating other people. I want you to start seeing other people too."

"I don't want you to start seeing other people!" Steve slams his fist down on the table.

People from other tables begin to stare at them.

Karen, showing anger, speaks with determination. "Don't you make a scene! People are beginning to stare."

"I don't give a damn if people are staring."

Karen, not liking Steve's attitude, replies, "That's your biggest problem, Steve, you don't give a damn about anything or anybody but Steve Johnson."

The waitress returns to the table, carrying a small pitcher of tea.

Steve manages to get control of himself.

The waitress fills their glasses and leaves the pitcher of tea on the table. She asks, "Is there anything else I can get for either of you?"

Karen answers, "No, I think we have everything we need, thank you."

The waitress walks off.

Steve looks over at Karen with mischievous eyes. He speaks in a very fiendish tone. "Who have you been seeing?"

Karen looks at Steve with a frightful glare. "I haven't been seeing anyone in that manner, Steve. Stop looking at me like that."

"But you have been seeing someone, haven't you?"

"You quit talking to me in that manner right now, or I will walk out of here and stop dating you altogether."

He listens to Karen and doesn't press the matter any further.

"You ought to know that I wouldn't be secretly seeing someone behind your back. You ought to be ashamed of yourself, Steve."

Steve picks up his fork, cuts off a piece of fish, and puts it in his mouth. As he chews, Karen can see his mind thinking of something devious. She takes her fork and also begins to eat her meal.

After a few minutes of uninterrupted quiet, Steve looks over at Karen and says, "I know you wouldn't do anything behind my back, Karen."

Karen smiles and says, "Well, I'm glad you don't think I would."

"I'm just curious. Has anybody asked you out for a date?"

"Well … maybe someone has asked me out for a date."

Steve angrily replies, "Who! Tell me! Who!"

"I will do no such thing. I'm not going to tell you who, because it makes no difference at all."

"It makes a difference to me if someone is moving in on my girlfriend."

Karen gives Steve a long mean look. "From here on out, I am not your girlfriend."

"What do you mean, you are not my girlfriend?"

"I mean, I am not your girlfriend, in the same sense of the word.

What I need is space from you, Steve, so I can see other people. We can still date each other if you behave yourself. I won't be seeing you as your girlfriend, only as a friend. Understand?"

There is a long silence.

Steve looks at Karen with very sad eyes. He softly and tenderly says, "I don't want you seeing anybody else, Karen."

"This is best for both of us. I want you to start seeing other girls also, but—"

"But what, Karen?"

"I want you to promise me that you won't sleep around with any of them."

Steve turns his head away from Karen briefly and then turns back to her. "What about you?"

Karen opens her mouth, bewildered. "Steve Johnson! You should be ashamed of yourself! You know I am a virgin."

"Yeah, I know you are, but for how long?"

This angers Karen greatly. "How dare you ask such an awful thing like that?"

"I'm sorry, Karen. I didn't mean to say that. I guess I wasn't thinking."

"You know I wouldn't do anything like that."

"Yeah, I know."

"I want you to promise me the same thing: that you won't sleep around with anyone."

Steve looks at Karen, with shame and guilt written all over his face.

He agrees to her demands, saying, "Okay, Karen. I won't sleep around with anyone. How long is this arrangement going to last?"

"I don't know how long. We will just let nature take its course, and see."

The waitress comes back. Karen motions for her to go away, and she does.

Steve shows a very sad and unhappy face. Karen tries to eat her fish, and so does Steve.

After several minutes of quiet, Karen says, "If you do meet someone you like a whole lot, and you want to see her in a serious relationship, I want you to come and tell me before you get into a physical relationship with her. I think you owe me that much. Is that agreed?"

"Yes. Agreed."

Karen smiles at Steve. "It's not like we are breaking up. It's just like this combination plate."

"Huh?"

"It's just like when I couldn't make up my mind on what I wanted to order, and so I ordered the combination plate. I got two different items, not just one."

Steve still looks confused as Karen continues. "Instead of just one guy, I will see two. That is, if you still want to see me."

"I do. I do. I truly want to keep seeing you."

Karen, happy with herself, says, "Good. I just want to be up front with you about this, because I will be seeing someone else from now on."

Steve, brewing like a volcano, says, "I understand. I don't like it, but I understand."

"Fine. I'm glad that's over with."

Karen finishes her meal in a happy, positive frame of mind.

Steve pushes his food around with his fork, distress showing on his face. He doesn't eat any more, for he has lost his appetite. Soon the waitress brings Steve the bill. As the two rise, Steve pulls out two dollars and places the money on the table. He then goes to the front and pays the bill as Karen waits at the door. They both walk out to Steve's car and get in.

Steve, breaking his silence, says to Karen, "Please don't start seeing anyone else. I know I haven't been the best boyfriend in the world, but I will change. Please, Karen, let me show you."

"Steve, I think this is what's best for both of us. Let's just go ahead with what we have talked about and see what happens. Okay?"

"I think you are making a mistake, but I will show you that I will change. I will treat you better than I have ever treated you in the past."

"Let's not talk about it anymore tonight."

Steve stews as he starts the car and begins to drive off.

"Will you please take me home, Steve?"

Steve doesn't try to talk her out of taking her home. He begins to head in the direction to her house. He doesn't say anything else until he pulls into her driveway.

After he stops the car, he gently asks, "When can I see you again?"

"We can go out next Saturday night, if you promise me something."

"What?"

"Promise me you won't call me, or come by the house, until next Saturday night. You can pick me up at seven-thirty."

Steve reluctantly agrees to Karen's demands.

"I mean it this time, Steve. Don't call me or come by here until next Saturday night! Do you understand me!"

"Yes, ma'am! I promise!"

"Well, I hope so, because if you call me one more time, or if I see you drive by my house one time, we won't go out next Saturday night! And I mean that!"

"I said I promise. Next Saturday night, we'll go to that fancy steak place near the mall. Will that be all right with you, Karen?"

"Yes, that will be fine. I'll be looking forward to it. But you just remember what I said."

"You won't have to worry about me, Karen. I promise not to call you or come by here until next Saturday night."

"Fine. I'm glad you understand how I feel, Steve. I'm glad we got this settled."

Steve looks at Karen like he has lost his best friend. He walks her to the front doorstep, wraps his arms around her, and hugs her tightly.

After a few moments, he releases her. "Karen, I love you so much. Please keep on seeing me. I love you, Karen."

Karen looks at Steve sympathetically. "That's the first time I have ever heard you say that to me. I must go now." She leans over and kisses him on the cheek, and then she smoothly breaks Steve's grip and opens the door.

"I am glad you have understood so maturely, Steve."

He looks at Karen sadly.

"I will see you next Saturday."

Steve unhappily walks back to his car, gets in, and drives off.

As Karen walks into the living room, her mother greets her, eagerly awaiting to hear how things turned out.

"So how did it go, dear?"

Karen, with a happy smile on her face, says, "It went perfectly, mama."

"Come here and tell me how Steve took the news."

Karen walks over to the couch and sits down beside her mother. "I waited for the right moment, and then I told him that I wanted to start seeing other people."

"How did he react?"

"Oh, he reacted about the way I thought he would."

"Did he get very mad?"

"Well, mama, he did get angry, but I managed to suppress it. We were in a crowded restaurant, so that made it easier."

"Are you going to date him anytime soon?"

"Yeah, I told him if he behaves himself and does not call me or come over, we will go out next Saturday night."

"Well, dear, you seemed to know what's best. I hope this new guy is worth it."

"Oh, he is, mama. He is worth it."

As the week goes by, Charlie stops at the pizza place every day after work to see Karen. He doesn't get to talk to her for very long, but he does talk to her some on the phone in the evenings. They grow closer and closer with each passing day. Karen looks forward to seeing Charlie walk in every afternoon at around four-thirty. Her eyes light up when she spots his kind, loving face. Her happy expression brings joy to Charlie's heart, and Charlie's happy expression brings joy to her heart also.

During the week, Charlie also continues to study and work on the project of his secret little book. He is looking forward to finishing the golf game with Steve on Saturday; he has his plan all worked out.

When Saturday arrives, Charlie is ready and prepared to continue his little adventure with Steve Johnson at the South Park Country Club. He walks out of his house and gets into his truck at high noon, driving carefully until he reaches the country club.

Charlie gets out of his truck and walks to the clubhouse, and just as he gets to the door, he hears a voice call out.

"Here I am, Charlie!"

Charlie turns to see Steve sitting in the golf cart, with two sets of clubs tied to the back of the cart.

"Hello, Steve. How long have you been waiting?"

"Not too long. Hop in, Charlie. I've already got your clubs in the cart."

"How?"

"Fred told me you rented these clubs last week and he gave you a rain check for them. Hop in! I have already signed you in too."

So Charlie walks over and puts his balls and tees in the cart. He then gets in and says, "Okay, Steve, let's do it."

Steve looks over at Charlie and says, "I thought you might not come."

Charlie smiles, but his expression is a little remote as he says, "I wouldn't miss this for the world."

With a proud smirk, Steve replies, "Oh really! Would you like to make a wager on the game?"

Charlie pauses for a moment and then says with a grin, "Make it easy on yourself."

"You sound like you might beat me today."

"Yes, Steve, I believe I will."

"Why don't we put ten dollars on it?"

"Is that all?"

"Well, how about twenty dollars, then?"

With a self-assured grin, Charlie replies, "Sounds good to me."

"Then it's a bet. Twenty dollars on whoever wins eighteen holes. Agreed?"

Charlie gazes over at Steve with a look of authority and clearly says, "Agreed!"

Steve drives the cart past the first hole.

"Hey, Steve, where are you going?"

"I thought we agreed to finish the game at the point we stopped last week. Right?"

"Yeah, but you are four shots up on me."

"That's what we agreed on. We would start on the third hole, with me up by four shots. If you want to back out of the bet, I will understand. Ha, ha, ha!"

Charlie grins and says, "No, I don't want to back out. If that's what we agreed on, then that's what we will do."

Steve drives past the first and the second holes, stopping the cart when they arrive at the third hole. Pulling out the same scorecard he had last week, Steve pulls out his driver and tees up. He addresses the ball, and it goes straight down the fairway.

"Wow! Nice shot, Steve!"

"Okay, Charlie, see if you can top that," Steve says with a proud look.

Charlie walks over to his bag, pulls out his driver, and tees up. He takes a few practice swings and then addresses the ball. It goes straight but not nearly as far as Steve's. The two jump in the golf cart and drive over to Charlie's ball. Charlie jumps out, grabs a club, and hits the ball. Charlie then walks over to the cart and jumps in. Steve drives over to his ball. He takes out a club and hits the ball. The ball lands near the green.

"I can see it now, Charlie, that I'll be twenty dollars richer before the day is out."

"Before the day is out, I will be richer than I have ever been in my life, Steve."

Steve gives Charlie a very puzzled look. Obviously not sure what Charlie meant by that remark, Steve simply laughs it off.

Steve and Charlie continue their game—or *games*—playing until they arrive at the ninth hole.

Steve looks over at Charlie. "Okay, Charlie, you get to go first this time."

Charlie tees his ball up and strikes it. The two watch as Charlie's ball slices into the woods.

Charlie disappointedly says, "You know, Steve, I just can't seem to stop doing that."

"What you are doing wrong is you're not keeping your eye on the ball. Here, watch me, and I'll show you how to do it."

Charlie looks on as Steve strikes his ball hard and straight.

Steve grins. "That's all you have to do, Charlie. Just keep your eye on the ball, and strike it in the center."

Charlie, playing to Steve's ego, says, "Boy, Steve, you sure know a whole lot about playing golf!"

"Maybe someday I will give you a few lessons … for a small sum, that is." Steve laughs as Charlie listens in silence.

They drive over to where Charlie's ball went into the woods.

Steve says, "I guess you ought to just throw out another ball, Charlie. You will never find that one."

"I guess you are right, Steve. It went pretty far in there."

Charlie throws out another ball and strikes it. This time, it goes down the fairway, to about the same spot where Steve's ball landed on his first shot.

Charlie, acting inferior, says, "Here I am, in three, Steve, and here you are, in one."

Steve begins to laugh as he jumps out and grabs a club. He strikes the ball, and it lands just shy of the green.

"Damn! I knew I should have used a 3-iron instead of a 4-iron."

Charlie remains calm. He observes how Steve reacts to everything he does. Charlie sizes him up by how he talks and acts after each shot. Charlie takes out a club and carefully strikes the ball. It lands near Steve's. Charlie tries to keep his ball near Steve's. The two drive up to their balls. Steve chips first. His chip rolls all the way off the green to the other side. He swears awfully, and Charlie remains silent, trying to tolerate Steve's foul mouth. Charlie chips. It lands about three feet from the pin.

"Wow! Did you see that, Steve?"

Steve doesn't say anything as they hop back into the cart and drive to the green.

Charlie, seeing his ball on the green, remarks, "Wow! I'm about three feet from the hole. I should be able to drop it in from there."

Steve seems to show a bit of jealousy as he walks over to his ball. He brings a 7-iron and a putter with him, takes a few practice swings, and then chips the ball sternly. The ball rolls right past the hole, off the green, and to the other side again.

"Damn! Damn! Damn!" shouts Steve.

Charlie observes Steve's childish behavior but doesn't say a thing. He just stands there, showing no emotion, as Steve walks to his ball. This time, Steve takes his putter and putts the ball more smoothly and with greater caution. It stops at about the same distance as Charlie's ball: about three feet from the hole, in the other direction. Steve's ball is now facing Charlie's.

Charlie walks over to his ball and says, "Steve, I believe we are both lying five now."

"Yes, that's right. Go ahead and putt, Charlie."

So Charlie walks over and pulls the pin out. He takes his putter and gently taps the ball. It goes directly into the cup.

"Hooray! Yes! Double bogey, six!"

Steve watches in cold silence as Charlie walks over to his ball. Steve then walks over to his ball and taps it gently. It stops just shy of the hole. Steve yells, "Damn! Damn! Damn! How could I be so stupid!" He walks over and taps the ball in for a seven.

Charlie notices that Steve is really upset about his performance, and he wants to be a friend in need. "Don't worry about it, Steve. Tell you what—why don't we go into the clubhouse and let me buy you a cold beer."

Steve, hearing this, begins to feel better. "Okay, Charlie ole boy, that sounds good to me."

So the two head to the clubhouse for a beer.

Just as Steve stops the cart in front of the clubhouse, Charlie asks, "Oh, by the way, Steve, what is the score?"

Steve pulls out the scorecard and writes down the score for the ninth hole. He adds the numbers up and then announces, "You have fifty, and I have forty-five. I am winning by five strokes."

"Well, I guess I will have to improve some on the back nine."

Steve, looking a little better, quickly replies, "Yeah, it sure looks that way, Charlie."

The two get out of the card and walk into the clubhouse.

Charlie and Steve enter the establishment.

Seeing the man named Fred standing behind the counter, Charlie walks over and says, "Let me have two cold beers, please."

Fred pulls two beers out of the cooler and places them on the counter. "That will be three bucks."

Charlie pulls out his wallet and gives Fred a five. Fred goes over to the cash register, places the five in it, and pulls out two singles. He walks over and gives Charlie his change.

With a happy smile on his face, Charlie says, "Thank you. Just go ahead and keep it."

"Thank you, sir!"

"Call me Charlie."

Fred gives Charlie a wink as he picks up the two beers and walks over to the table where Steve is sitting.

"Here you go, Steve." Charlie slides one of the beers over to Steve.

"Hey, thanks, man! For someone who is losing, you sure are a good sport."

Charlie flashes a grin of authority and says, "Oh, but the game isn't over yet, Steve ole' boy. Before the day is done, I will be the winner of the game. Ha, ha, ha!"

Looking puzzled, Steve says, "Oh, you think so?"

"Yes, I believe so." He smiles delightfully at Steve.

Charlie then lifts the beer to his dry lips. He begins to drink down the cold beverage. Charlie lets the brew go down his parched throat as if it were water. When he puts the bottle down on the table, half of it has been devoured with just one guzzle.

Steve says, "Hey, you drink beer pretty good, but this is how you are supposed to do it."

Steve brings the cold bottle up to his lips. He turns the bottle up and begins to guzzle the ice-cold beverage also. Air rushes up inside the bottle at every swallow. Steve keeps the bottle tilted up more and more, until the bottle is only filled with air. Steve looks over at Charlie and grins like an opossum. He puts the bottle down on the table with authority. It makes a loud noise as the hard glass slams against the wooden table.

"That is how you drink beer, Charlie! Ha, ha, ha!"

Charlie smiles and then looks over at the man behind the counter. "Hey, we would like two more over here, please!"

Steve, hearing this, says to Charlie, "Are you paying?"

"Sure, Steve, sure. Don't worry about it; I've got it."

When the man comes over with two more beers, Charlie whips out his wallet and hands him three dollars.

"You know something, Charlie, you are a pretty nice guy."

With a somewhat devious grin, Charlie says, "I try to be … at least most of the time. Ha, ha, ha!"

As Charlie laughs, Steve gives him a very curious stare but doesn't say anything.

Steve picks up the beer and starts to drink the ice-cold beverage. He doesn't guzzle this one, but he does drink it fast.

Charlie, still drinking the first one, looks over at Steve. "Is the back nine harder or easier than the front nine?"

"Oh, the back nine is much more difficult than the front nine. There are a lot more obstacles you have to overcome just to get on the green. Then, when you get on the green, you have to watch out because they are fast and somewhat curvy!"

Steve looks at Charlie, still drinking his first beer. "You are going to let that beer get warm if you keep nursing it in your hand. Ha, ha, ha!"

"Is that right?" Charlie turns up the bottle and downs the remains. He looks at Steve. "Do you want me to get a few more brews to take with us?"

"Sounds good to me!"

Charlie gets up and walks back over to the counter. "Your name is Fred, isn't? I heard some of the other guys call you by name last week."

"That's right. I'm Fred Jackson."

"Well, Fred, do you have any spare trash bags nearby?"

"Yes, I think I have a few. What do you want with one?"

"I was wondering if you would put a six-pack in it, and also some ice."

Fred, nodding his head, replies, "I guess I could."

Fred goes in the back and comes out with a garbage bag. He walks over to the cooler, takes out six beers, and places them in the bag. He then walks over at the ice bin and puts three scoops of ice in the bag. He slowly walks back over to where Charlie is. "That will be nine bucks."

Charlie pulls out a ten and hands it to Fred. "Since you put some ice in there for me, you can just keep the change."

Fred smiles gladly and says, "Thanks, partner!"

Charlie then says to Fred, "Last week, I only paid for nine holes. Steve and I are going to play eighteen."

Fred figures out the difference. Charlie pays Fred and then walks back over to the table.

Charlie, with a look of strength, says to Steve, "Are you ready to get beaten?"

Steve gives a carefree laugh and then says, "You sound like you have a little more confidence now."

Charlie, showing a wry smile, says, "I feel like your luck is going to change now, Steve. Ha, ha, ha!"

"Well, let's go and see."

Steve gets up, and the two walk out the door.

Charlie looks over at Steve and says, "Here, put these beers in the cart, and don't hesitate to drink any of them."

"You are all right, Charlie!"

Steve takes the bag from Charlie and puts it in the back of the golf cart. He takes out a beer and then hops into the cart. Steve sucks down the brew before they pull up to the tenth tee. Charlie gets out first and looks for his driver, noticing that Steve drank another one fast. He just smiles as he pulls out his driver. Steve gets out of the cart fast and begins to retrieve his driver also. Charlie walks up to the tee and begins to take a few practice swings. As Charlie is warming up, Steve places his ball on a tee and gives the impression that he is going to go first. Charlie walks over and, without saying a word, takes his driver and hits Steve's ball off his tee.

"Hey, what are you doing?"

Charlie just looks at him casually and says, "I won the last hole, or have you forgotten?"

"Oh yeah, I almost forgot. Go ahead."

Charlie places his ball on his tee, takes three practice swings, and then addresses the ball swiftly and expeditiously. It goes high and straight down the fairway, but it doesn't go very far.

Steve remarks, "Come on, man, put your back into it. You only half swung the club."

"I may not have hit the ball very far, but I at least hit it in the middle of the fairway. I will have a good second shot."

"I guess so, Charlie. I like to knock the fire out of the ball when I drive."

Steve puts his ball on his tee and addresses the ball with fury. It goes long and fades to the right. Steve shakes his head and swears a little as Charlie casually walks back to the cart.

Steve, still disappointed with his shot, looks over at Charlie. "Do you want to drive?"

Charlie shakes his head and says, "Oh no. I like for you to drive me around."

"Okay with me. I just thought you might want to drive these last nine holes."

Charlie reaches over and picks up his beer as he sits down in the cart. Steve reaches in the back and pops open another cold beer. This time, he doesn't guzzle; he just sips. Steve drives over and locates his ball. He gets out and reaches for a club as Charlie stays in the cart, smiling and drinking his cold beer. Steve swings, and the two watch the ball sail into the air.

"Nice shot, Steve! I wish I could hit a 2-iron like that."

"Thanks, Charlie. It was a damn good shot, wasn't it?"

Steve drives the cart to Charlie's ball.

As Steve drives, Charlie says, "Man, it sure is a beautiful day. The sun is out, the sky is clear, and there is a no wind blowing. There is only a slight chill, just enough to make the air crisp."

"Yes, it sure is, Charlie. We couldn't ask for a more beautiful day, especially in January."

Steve drives until he comes upon Charlie's ball. Charlie gets out of the cart, pulls out a club, and walks over to his ball.

Steve yells over to him, "Come on, man! Put your back into it this time."

Charlie takes his time and strikes the ball with about the same swing he did on his drive. It goes straight but not very far.

"I should be on the green next time," Charlie says.

"If you had hit the ball harder on your drive and on your second shot, you would have been on the fringe now."

"All I want to do is hit good-quality shots. That is the most important thing I want to do today; quality not quantity."

Steve shakes his head as he says, "I guess so, Charlie. I guess so."

The two continue their game until they reach the seventeenth hole. Steve is still winning, and by now, he has drunk most of the six beers.

Steve drives the cart up to the hole and pulls out his driver once again. As he looks over at Charlie, he flashes an intoxicated grin and then says, “Well, Charlie ole’ boy, you are down by seven strokes, with only two holes to go.”

Charlie gives Steve an enchanting grin. “Yep, that’s right, Steve ole’ boy.”

Charlie walks over and pulls out his driver, and the two walk up to the tee.

Steve places his ball on his tee and addresses the ball aggressively.

“Nice shot, Steve!”

“Thanks, Charlie. It went a little to the right, but I will take it anyway.”

Charlie walks over and tees up his ball. He takes his time. He takes a few practice swings and then strikes the ball like he has before. It goes straight and narrow, but it doesn’t go very far.

“You are still not hitting the ball hard enough, Charlie.”

Charlie just smiles at Steve and says, “Maybe so, Steve, but at least it went straight. That’s what I want it to do—go straight.”

As Steve and Charlie begin to drive to Charlie’s ball, Steve shows that he is intoxicated by the way he drives.

“So what are you going to do tonight, Steve ole’ boy?”

“I am going out with my girlfriend tonight.”

Charlie detects a slur in Steve’s speech.

“Oh really? Where are going to take her, Steve?”

Steve pauses for a moment, and then he opens up to Charlie about his plans. “First, I am going to take her out to dinner, and then I am going to take her to the Walker Hotel and screw her.”

Steve laughs as Charlie remarks, “Oh really?”

Steve laughs even more, talking more loosely and quite freely. “Yeah, Karen and I never did it. She and I have been dating too long for me not to have had her by now.”

Charlie just listens in silence.

“She told me last week that she is going to start dating other guys now, so I think I will take what is rightfully mine. She’s not going to dump me for someone else after all these years.”

Charlie says, “Go on, Steve. You can tell me.”

Steve smiles a devious smile and says, “Tonight, I am going to give her something she has never had before. Ha, ha, ha!”

Charlie says, "So this is the virgin you have been seeing all these years."

"Yeah, Charlie, that's her. She has been seeing another guy, so I thought I would bang her tonight before he does."

"Oh really? What did you say her name was again?"

"Karen. Karen Thomas."

Charlie pauses for a moment. "I thought you were banging another girl also, Steve ole' boy."

"Yeah, I have been banging this cute little blonde who's a member here, but I'm getting tired of that stuff. She is just too stupid to develop anything with, and I mean a real loony bird. I want some of Karen."

Charlie, staying in control, just watches as Steve's intoxicated face gets more and more vile.

Steve says, "Yeah, it has been long enough now. I will be her first." Steve begins to laugh and talk nasty and disgusting. He relays his plan for tonight to Charlie, quite openly and in mostly four-letter words. Steve acts carefree as he talks about these things.

As Steve stops the cart at Charlie's ball, Charlie quickly gets out and strikes the ball. Steve proceeds to drive to his ball.

Charlie, needing a little more information, asks, "So how do you get along with this girl's mother? Karen's mother, I mean."

"Oh, I get along pretty good with the stupid old hag."

Steve laughs as Charlie intriguingly asks, "What makes you say that she is stupid?" Charlie listens intently for Steve's response.

Giving Charlie a drunken stare, Steve says, "All the years I have known her, she has got to be the dumbest female I have ever known. She doesn't drink. She don't date anyone. All she thinks about is Karen. I get along with her fine; it's just that she is stupid, and I don't like stupid people."

The two continue their golf game until Steve asks, "So how many beers have you drunk today, Charlie?"

"Only three."

Steve, with a bragging tongue, remarks, "This is my seventh one. It looks like I'm going to beat you drunk, Charlie."

Steve gets out, addresses his ball, and watches as it goes up near the fringe. Charlie watches Steve act a little silly as he walks back to the cart. Steve then drives up to Charlie's ball.

Charlie looks over at Steve and says, "You say her mother is stupid?"

"Yeah. Karen is pretty stupid too. There are times she is just like her mother: stupid."

"Then why do you still see her?"

"I don't know. I guess it's because I love her … and because I haven't been inside those silky soft panties yet—but I will. Ha, ha, ha!"

Charlie sits quietly as he takes all this in. Steve stops at Charlie's ball, and Charlie gets out and quickly hits it. He gets back into the cart, and then Steve drives them both up to the green and stops. They both get out and walk to the green.

Charlie chips his ball onto the green first. With deep concentration, Steve takes his time and then chips, also onto the green. Charlie putts in for a bogey, and Steve does likewise. They both put their clubs back into their bags, get into the cart, and proceed to the last hole.

Charlie looks over at Steve and asks, "You haven't said how you get along with this girl's father."

"Oh, he's dead. He died in Vietnam a long time ago."

"Oh really? I guess you don't know much about him, then."

"No, not a whole lot, except he was stupid too. He was shot down over there and got killed."

"What makes you say that he was stupid?"

Steve, with a carefree expression, replies, "That idiot could have stayed away from that war if he had wanted to. He signed up three times to go over there. He could have gone one time and then come home. If he had, he would be alive today. He was a stupid idiot for going back! I believe the whole family grew up on the stupid side of town."

Steve puts the score down on the scorecard.

Showing a confident look, Steve happily remarks, "Well, Charlie ole' boy, it looks like you are still down by seven strokes. I believe it's about over."

Charlie doesn't say a single word as Steve tees up his ball and addresses it. It takes a bad slice to the right. Charlie silently puts his ball on his tee and then, without making any practice swings, strikes the ball as hard as he can. The ball takes off like a bat out of hell. It goes straight down the fairway.

"Wow! Damn! I bet that ball went three hundred yards, Charlie!"

Charlie doesn't say anything.

"I told you if you put your back into it, the ball would go farther. I guess you finally learned something from me today, Charlie."

"Oh, I've learned a whole lot from you today, Steve ole' boy."

So Charlie and Steve once again hop into the cart as Steve drives to his ball.

As the two drives toward Steve's ball, Charlie looks over at him. With a frown, he says, "So tell me, Steve, what are you going to do if this girl says she doesn't want to fool around tonight?"

"I won't take no for an answer tonight," says Steve.

Steve stops the cart, grabs a club, and proceeds to walk over to where his ball is lying. He looks back and notices Charlie walking behind him.

Steve turns to Charlie and, with a big proud look on his face, says, "When I get her back to the hotel, I will tell her we are going to see a friend of mine there. Then, once I get her in the room, I am going to f—— the hell out of her. Ha, ha, ha!"

Steve then swings his 2-iron, knocking the white ball straight and high.

Charlie doesn't even look at where the ball went. He just gives Steve a mean stare.

"Wow! Did you see that?" Steve happily remarks about his shot.

All of a sudden, Charlie gets right up in Steve's face and roars out, "Listen, you low-life drunk, you ain't gonna do no such thing like you're fixing to do to Karen! You hear me?"

Charlie throws a left jab into Steve's face, then another one, and then another one. Charlie throws a right hook into Steve's gut. He then jabs two more times into Steve's terrified face. Finally, Charlie throws a hefty right cross and watches as Steve falls to the ground in a drunken stupor.

Looking up with a horrified expression, Steve asks, "What the hell are you doing?!"

Charlie plainly answers, "What does it look like, stupid! I am kicking your ass, you low-life piece of shit."

Charlie jumps on Steve's chest and begins slapping his face repeatedly. Steve is dumbfounded by Charlie's actions.

Steve cries out, "Why? What? What's wrong with you?!"

Charlie, showing a look of vengeance, replies with a loud voice, "There is nothing wrong with me, asshole. Let me explain. First of all, from this moment forward, Karen is my girlfriend! Second of all, don't you ever let me see you near her again!"

Steve lies powerless as Charlie takes his open hand and smacks Steve across the face several more times.

Charlie continues. "You see, bozo, I happen to be in love with that girl, and you happen to be getting in the way!"

An expression of terror erupts on Steve's drunken face. He shakes with fear as Charlie pins his arms back with his knees.

"You don't deserve Karen, you good-for-nothing drunk." Charlie slaps Steve hard with his open right hand.

Steve begs, "Please stop! Please stop hitting me!"

Charlie answers in a mean tone, "I will stop hitting you when you tell me you will never see her again!"

Steve, looking scared and confused, answers, "Huh?"

Charlie bellows, "Say it! Say you will never call her or see her again!"

"Get off me, Charlie!"

Charlie takes his left and right hands, and slaps Steve's face like a bongo drum.

Steve cries out, "Okay! Okay! I will never see her again!"

Charlie then gets up and looks down at Steve. "See what we can accomplish if only we talk things out. Ha, ha, ha!"

Charlie pulls Steve up, gets right into his face, and viciously says, "So remember, bozo—don't you ever let me see you near Karen again, or I will give you something like this." Charlie throws a hard right hook into Steve's gut, then another one with his left, and then he pushes him onto the ground.

Charlie grins at Steve politely and kindly says, "And to let you know there are no hard feelings, I will take your clubs and put them up against your car for you. Isn't that nice of me?"

Steve doesn't say anything.

Charlie angrily bellows, "I said, 'Isn't that nice of me?'!"

Steve answers quickly, "Yes, Charlie! That will be very nice of you!"

So Charlie walks over to the golf cart, gets in, and begins to drive off. He drives halfway up the fairway of the eighteenth hole before he remembers something. "Oh yes, I almost forgot," he says aloud. Charlie turns the cart around and starts to drive back to where Steve is. Steve has just gotten up from the ground when he sees Charlie coming back. His expression of terror intensifies as Charlie gets closer to him. He waits, shaking with fear. Charlie pulls the golf cart right up to Steve. Charlie gets out of the cart and pulls out his wallet. He pulls out a twenty-dollar bill and shoves it into Steve's front pocket.

Charlie stares into Steve's eyes as he says, "Here you go, chump! Don't ever let it be said that Charlie Delaney doesn't pay off his bets." Charlie then throws a shot to Steve's gut and pushes him back onto the ground. Charlie hops back into the cart and leaves the scene, smiling and laughing.

Charlie drives the golf cart up to the front of the clubhouse. He looks for Steve's car and drives over to it. He then does just what he told Steve he would: puts Steve's clubs up against his car. Charlie then drives the cart back to where all the other carts are. He takes out his rental clubs and carries them inside the clubhouse.

Fred is standing behind the bar when Charlie walks in.

Fred says, "So, how did you come out?"

Charlie walks over to Fred, grinning from ear to ear. "I made out very well, Fred."

Fred, acting surprised, asks, "Oh, you mean you beat Steve?!"

Charlie, with a smile on his face, says, "Yes, sir! I beat him so badly, he will never forget this day as long as he lives. Ha, ha, ha!"

Fred cracks a smile for the first time and says, "I'm glad you had such a good time. You will have to come back sometime."

"I don't know, Fred. I think I will give up golf now that I am ahead, but you never know, I might still want to swing my stuff another day. I believe I will take up bowling. You know, you don't have to chase down a bowling ball; it comes back to you automatically. Ha, ha, ha!"

Fred smiles at Charlie and says, "I guess so, Charlie, I guess so."

"You have a good day, Fred. And If I don't ever see you again, you have a good life."

Fred, with a puzzled look, replies, “I will, Charlie, I will. Would you like a cold beer to top off the day, on the house?”

Charlie shakes his head. In a soft voice he says, “No thanks, Fred. I don’t like to drink and drive. And besides, I have a lot of things to do today, a whole lot of things to do.”

Fred shakes Charlie’s hand and says, “It has been nice seeing you around here. It’s good to have fine gentlemen like you come in here, instead of all these worthless, irresponsible braggarts. You know what I mean?”

Charlie laughs a loud joyful laugh and says, “I know just what you mean, and it is fine to see such a good-natured man as you too, Fred.”

Fred just shakes his head and smiles gladly at Charlie.

Charlie then gets an idea. He pulls out two dollars and hands the money to Fred. “Oh, by the way, Fred, when Steve walks in here, bring him a beer on me, and tell him something.”

Fred takes the money and asks, “What’s that?”

“Tell him he swings a mean 2-iron.”

“I will tell him.”

Charlie tosses Fred the keys to the cart and leaves the establishment in a joyful frame of mind.

Ten minutes go by before Steve finally walks in the front door.

Just as Steve walks through the door Fred walks over to the cooler and pulls out a cold beer. Before Steve has a chance to say anything, Fred says to him, “Hey, Steve!”

Steve plops down at a table and turns to Fred.

Fred says, “Your buddy Charlie wanted me to give you this.” Fred sets the cold beer down at his table. “He also wanted me to tell you something.”

Steve is too sore to move, but he asks, “What’s that, Fred?”

Fred then says, “He wanted me to tell you that you swing a mean 2-iron.”

Steve just puts his head down on the table.

Fred, seeing this, says, “You know something, Steve? You shouldn’t take losing a game of golf so bad.”

Steve lifts his head and looks at Fred, confused.

Steve tries to tell him what happened, but Fred interrupts, “You know, Steve, that Charlie Delaney is one hell of a nice guy. We need more men like him around here."

Steve just shakes his head and puts it head back down on the table once again.

Fred, looking at Steve with a concerned look, says, "You know, Steve, I think you have drunk enough beer for one day. Why don't you let me put this one in the cooler, and you can drink it some other time?"

Steve keeps his head on the table.

Fred speaks again. "You need to go home and get some rest, Steve. You look like somebody beat you with an ugly stick."

Steve gets up, and without saying a word, limps to his car and goes home.

Charlie, on the other hand, isn't on his way home at all. He drives his truck to the mall, gets out, walks into the giant shopping center, and starts to look for a jewelry store.

When he finds the store that looks like it will have the most-expensive jewelry, he enters.

Once inside, it isn't long before a salesperson asks, "May I help you, sir?"

Charlie turns to see an older-looking woman smiling at him attentively.

Charlie replies, "Yes, ma'am. I am looking for a fairly expensive friendship ring."

"Are you buying it for your girlfriend?" the woman asks Charlie in a very nice way.

"Yes, ma'am! What do you have?"

The lady walks over to where the ruby and diamond rings are located. She reaches into the glass display and pulls out a beautiful ruby-and-diamond ring. It has three rubies on the top, three rubies on the bottom, and a quarter-carat diamond in the center. She shows it to Charlie.

Charlie reacts with excitement. "Wow! That's just the type of ring I came in here for. I will take it!"

The lady smiles at Charlie and says, "You haven't heard how much it costs yet. You might change your mind."

"I won't change my mind," Charlie says as the lady hands him the ring. He looks it over admiringly and then asks, "So how much do I owe you?"

The lady softly replies to Charlie, "One thousand two hundred fifty dollars, plus tax."

Charlie's eyes open wide and his jaw drops as he looks at the lady. He swallows hard and then tries to smile at the lady.

He casually says, "I will take it! The more I spend, the more I will enjoy it."

Charlie pulls out his wallet and hands the lady the money in hundred-dollar bills, as if he'd been prepared to spend that much all along.

The lady says, "She must be a very special girl."

"Yes, ma'am. She is someone very special."

The lady takes Charlie's money and walks over to the cash register. She soon comes back with Charlie's change.

As she hands the change to Charlie, she says in very happy way, "Would you like for me to wrap it up for you, sir?"

"Oh no! That won't be necessary, ma'am. I thank you very much!"

The lady looks at Charlie in a very curious manner and says, "Do you think it will fit her finger?"

"Yes, ma'am! It looks like it was made for her and her only, so it should fit just fine."

The lady eagerly replies, "If it doesn't fit, you come back with her, and we will size it for free. All right?"

"Yes, ma'am. I sure will. You sure are a nice lady."

The lady blushes a little at Charlie's words. "Thank you, young man. It sure has been nice waiting on you."

So Charlie walks out of the mall with the ring. He walks back to his truck and drives directly to Little Tony's Pizza, where Karen is going to get the surprise of her life.

When he gets to the pizza place, Charlie sits in his truck and mentally goes through the details of his plan. He soon starts to laugh out loud and can't seem to stop. His thoughts sure have made him feel good. He remains inside his truck until he gets control of himself. Once he stops laughing, he goes through his plan again, just like an actor at a rehearsal. He gets everything down pat in his mind, and then he gets out of his truck and walks through the parking lot.

As he gets to the front of the pizza place, he looks in the window. There are a few people inside, waiting for their orders. Karen is inside too, but she doesn't see Charlie. He waits patiently for all the customers to leave before he makes his approach. After the last customer has left, Charlie opens the door, walks in, and rushes over to Karen.

His face full of excitement, Charlie says, "Karen! Karen, I must talk to you!"

Karen looks at Charlie with amazement and concern. Her excited expression activates Charlie's game plan.

"What is it, Charlie?" she asks.

Charlie looks at Karen, his expression a mixture of nervousness and excitement.

"Karen, I must talk to you!" he says again. "Something happened a while ago that I must tell you about!"

"Calm down, Charlie! Please tell me what is the matter."

Just as Charlie begins to tell Karen, another customer walks in. Charlie glances over, sees the man, and then looks at Karen again.

"I can't tell you here, Karen. It is something very important!"

Karen is clearly growing angry at being kept in suspense. She demands, "You tell me right now, young man. What is the matter!"

Charlie looks into Karen's curious eyes and says in a very innocent way, "Karen, I believe I have just accidentally kicked your boyfriend's ass!"

"What! … What! … Huh!"

"I believe I have accidentally kicked Steve's ass."

Karen, looking dazed, says, "You have done what!"

"It's a long story. I will tell you the whole story when you get off work!"

Karen's curious look turns into a very angry, hostile stare. Pointing her finger at Charlie, she says in a very stern voice, "You stay right there, young man!"

Karen hurries to the back to talk to her manager. "Bob! I need to get off, right now! I have an emergency to take care of!"

Bob looks at Karen, then at his watch, and says, "You were supposed to stay until five. Is this really important, Karen?"

"Yes, sir. This is very important. I must get off right now!"

Bob, seeing Karen's urgent expression, says, "Okay, Karen, you can get off."

"Oh, thank you, Bob! I sure do appreciate it."

Karen walks back to where Charlie is standing.

Still looking angry, Karen says, "Okay, Charlie, you come with me!" She grabs Charlie by the hand and leads him out of the pizza parlor.

Once outside, Karen gives Charlie a mean look. "Okay, Charlie, you tell me what you have done. Right now!"

Charlie, looking innocent, says, "This is not the place. Jump into your car, and drive home. I will meet you there!"

Karen tries once again to get Charlie to talk, but Charlie just says, "For now, all I will tell you is that your honor has been protected. I love you very much, and I won't let anyone hurt you."

Charlie then quickly slides the ruby-and-diamond ring on Karen's finger, turns, and heads for his truck.

Karen doesn't even have time to respond to Charlie's sudden gift.

Charlie turns around and calls out, "I will see you at your house!"

Karen quickly gets into her car, and Charlie gets into his truck. They both drive directly to Karen's house.

As he drives up to Karen's house, Charlie snickers and talks out loud to himself. "Tee, hee, hee. Everything is going just as planned. I hope it succeeds as I planned it too."

Charlie gets out of his truck just as Karen pulls into the driveway. Karen gets out of her car and walks over to Charlie.

She quickly asks, "Okay, Charlie, tell me what you have done!"

Charlie grabs Karen by the hand and says, "Let's go inside so your mother can hear this also."

The two walk into the house.

Mrs. Thomas is in the kitchen when the two walk in.

Karen yells, "Mama! Come in here!"

Mrs. Thomas rushes out of the kitchen and sees that Karen is upset.

Karen cries, "Mama, Charlie has something he wants to tell us."

Mrs. Thomas, with a curious look on her face, sits down in a chair. Karen and Charlie sit down on the couch. Charlie looks at the two women, an innocent and humble expression on his face. His sweet and innocent look captures Karen and her mother's attention.

Charlie politely says, "Hello, Mrs. Thomas."

Karen interrupts, "Enough with the introductions! Tell us!"

Charlie then explains what happened. "Well, this guy, Steve Johnson, and I were playing a game of golf today."

Karen and Mrs. Thomas listen in silence, giving Charlie their complete and undivided attention.

Charlie continues. "As we were playing golf, he started talking about you, Karen." Charlie turns to look at Karen. "And then, he started talking about you, Mrs. Thomas." Charlie then turns toward Mrs. Thomas, giving her that same innocent, convincing look.

Karen and Mrs. Thomas look at each other, but neither says a word.

"As the game continued, he started talking nasty talk," Charlie says.

Karen interrupts. "What type of nasty talk?"

"I'm not going to say the real nasty things he said, but he did say that you were … well … he said you were stupid."

Karen's curious expression turns angry. "Is that why you beat him up?"

"Charlie, do you mean to say that you beat up Steve today?!" Mrs. Thomas interjects.

Charlie again turns toward Mrs. Thomas, giving her a look like a basset hound that has just disobeyed its master. Nodding his head, Charlie says softly, "Yes, ma'am, I did, but it wasn't because he called you and Karen stupid."

Mrs. Thomas says, "You mean, Steve called me stupid also?"

Charlie answers in a gentle tone, "Yes, ma'am. He sure did."

Mrs. Thomas, looking skeptical, replies, "I don't believe you, Charlie. Steve would never say such a thing."

"Oh, but he did, Mrs. Thomas!" Charlie says. "But, like I said, that's not the reason I beat him up."

Karen interrupts again, her tone very angry. "Well, why did you beat him up, then?!"

"Well, as I was saying, Steve Johnson and I were playing golf, and as the game came to an end, he began saying awful things about you three. I must confess, he was drinking a whole lot of beer when he was saying these terrible things."

Karen, looking puzzled, says, "Saying things about us three? What three?"

Charlie looks over at Karen. "Yes, Karen, you three: you, your mother, and your daddy."

With her voice raised, Karen says, "What did he say about my daddy?!"

Charlie answers softly, "I didn't want to tell you about what he said about your father because I knew it would upset you greatly, but since I already said one thing, I guess I should tell both of you everything he said."

Both Karen and her mother listen to Charlie attentively. They are quiet but angry.

Charlie takes a breath and then continues. "He said that when your father went to Vietnam, Karen, serving his country those three hitches … well … Steve said that your father was stupid. Then he went on and on about how all three of you were stupid. It was very upsetting to hear. It really was."

Mrs. Thomas says, "Steve actually said that word, 'stupid'?"

"Yes, ma'am. He said that specific word time after time after time. It made me very upset hearing him talk that way about a man who gave his life serving our country."

Mrs. Thomas says, "Please continue, Charlie. What else did Steve say?"

Charlie, with a sad face, continues. "This is what made me get really angry."

Though clearly still angry, Mrs. Thomas and Karen listen very patiently and very attentively.

Charlie turns to Karen and says, "Tonight, when you were supposed to go out with Steve, he had planned a scheme to get you to go to a hotel. He was going to rape you there."

Karen jumps up from her seat. With intense emotion, she cries, "What! Do what!"

Mrs. Thomas shakes her head in disbelief. With a disturbed and concerned look on her face, she says, "What exactly did Steve say, Charlie, to make you think this?"

Charlie looks first at Karen, then at Mrs. Thomas, and then at Karen again. "Karen, Steve told me he was going to tell you that he wanted you to meet a friend of his who came in from out of town. I believe the hotel was the Walker Hotel. Once you took the bait, he was going to pressure you into having sex with him. He said, 'I'm going to screw her when I get her back there.' He was going to force himself on you. He won't now. I made sure of that!"

Karen's angry expression turns fearful, And Mrs. Thomas's concerned expression becomes angry.

Charlie then says, "After I heard what he had planned for you tonight, I guess I lost my head and acted violently."

Karen softly asks, "What did you do to him, Charlie?"

Charlie says gently, "I told him wasn't going to do any such thing to you, Karen. And then, as I said earlier, I beat him up. I tore into him like a white tornado. When I was done with him, I made sure he wasn't going to do anything to the girl I love!"

Mrs. Thomas asks, "You didn't break anything, did you? I mean, you didn't put him in the hospital or anything like that, did you, Charlie?"

Charlie convincingly replies, "Oh no. I didn't break anything but his pride. He will be sore for a few days, though."

Karen asks, "How in the world did you know where Steve was playing golf?"

"Huh? … Well … I …" Charlie's voice trails off.

Mrs. Thomas says, "What difference does it make? If this story is true, then I owe you, Charlie. Karen and I both owe you a great deal of thanks."

Charlie, turning a light shade of red, replies, "It is true, Mrs. Thomas! I wouldn't make up such a story."

Without saying a word, Karen gets up and heads for the door.

Mrs. Thomas asks, "Where are you going!"

"I am going to check out this story on my own. I am going over to Steve's to see with my own two eyes and hear with my own two ears *exactly* what Steve said and did today!"

Mrs. Thomas quickly retorts, "You aren't going anywhere near Steve unless I go with you!"

So the two get ready to pay Steve a little visit.

Charlie subtly says, "I guess I should go now."

Karen bluntly replies, "No! You sit down and stay right where you are, young man! If your story doesn't check out, I don't want to spend any time tracking you down. You just stay right where you are until we get back."

"Yes, ma'am. I will stay right here."

Karen pauses for a moment, and then she says, "Just to make sure you are telling the truth, give me the keys to your truck so I will know you won't leave."

Mrs. Thomas says, "Do you think that will be necessary, dear?"

Charlie reaches into his pocket, pulls out his keys, and willingly hands them to Karen. "Here you go, Karen. I will be here waiting for you when you get back."

Karen takes the keys from Charlie and walks toward the front door. Her mother follows.

"If there is any trouble, don't hesitate to call me!" Charlie says.

With a face filled with fire and retribution, Karen says, "Oh, there is going to be trouble! I promise you that! But it will be trouble for Steve, not me."

So Mrs. Thomas and Karen climb into Mrs. Thomas's car and head for Steve's house. They leave with great furor and vengeance.

Charlie, on the other hand sits back on the couch in the Thomas's living room, puts up his feet on the coffee table, and turns on the TV with the remote control. "Yes, I think everything is going to be fine, just fine." He flips through the channels comfortably, just like he does at home.

After a while, Charlie lies down on the couch and takes a nap.

As Mrs. Thomas and Karen drive up to Steve's house, they see only one car sitting in the driveway: Steve's. They get out of the car and eagerly walk up to the front door. Karen rings the doorbell. When there's no response, she rings it again and again and again.

Eventually, Steve opens the door, surprised to see the two hostile and acrimonious women. Steve looks at Karen, noticing she is a very angry and very upset girl.

Karen doesn't wait to be asked inside. She pushes past Steve and storms into the house. Mrs. Thomas follows in right behind her.

Karen shouts, "Okay, buster, I have a few questions for you!" Steve doesn't say anything as Karen continues. "Did you or did you not call my daddy stupid for serving his country in Vietnam?"

Steve, looking puzzled, says, "Well … huh? I don't remember."

Mrs. Thomas, equally angry, demands, "What the hell you don't remember? Either you said it, or you didn't!"

Steve looks at the two women, fear filling his eyes. He can't seem to get the words out of his mouth.

Karen says, "Well? … Did you or did you not say that, Steve!"

Steve, looking scared, replies, "I don't know exactly what I said. I was drinking at the time when I might have said something about your father."

Karen asks, "Did you say that my mama was stupid also?"

Steve looks at Karen with amazement. He again tries to confuse the issue by saying he was drinking.

With fury in her eyes, Mrs. Thomas says to Steve, "Did you plan to fuck my daughter tonight?

Consternation fills Steve's eyes as he looks at the two angry women. He doesn't say anything. He just looks at them, and then he turns his head away in shame.

Karen says, "I don't hear you denying anything that we have confronted you about."

Steve finally says, "I got drunk while playing golf with this guy, and the next thing I knew, he was on top of me, beating me up!"

Karen asks, "What did you say to him to make him beat you up?"

"I don't know."

Karen counters, "I don't hear you denying those mean things you said about my family."

Mrs. Thomas angrily remarks, "You don't hear him denying them because he did say them. Didn't you, Steve?"

Mrs. Thomas points her finger at Steve. In a stern voice, she says, "Isn't that right, Steve? You did say those things about us, didn't you!"

Steve, groggy, just looks at Mrs. Thomas, and then he says, "I don't know."

Karen, with her voice raised, bellows, "You know! You just can't seem to admit it, you coward!"

Karen leaves the room and walks up the stairs into Steve's bedroom.

Steve nervously asks, "Hey, where are you going?"

Karen doesn't answer Steve's question, but Mrs. Thomas does. "Don't you worry about where she is going you … you … good-for-nothing, lying drunk! I couldn't believe my ears when Charlie told us what you said about us today. I thought you were an upstanding young man, Steve. You are nothing but a backstabbing son of a bitch."

Steve has heard all he can take. He goes upstairs to his bedroom to see what Karen is doing. Mrs. Thomas follows close behind. As Steve walks into his bedroom, he sees Karen looking around for something.

"What are you looking for, Karen?"

Karen doesn't answer his question. Instead, she asks, "Where were you going to take me tonight, Steve?"

A sudden jolt of fear explodes on Steve's face.

Steve's voice cracks as he says, "Oh, nowhere in particular. I hadn't thought much about where we would go tonight. Where would you want me to take you?"

Mrs. Thomas then walks into the bedroom. She overhears Steve's question.

She asks, "Go out with you! Karen isn't going out with you, stupid. She will never go out with you until you tell us the truth, Steve!"

Just then, Karen finds something lying on a table near Steve's bed. It is a room key from the Walker Hotel. She picks it up slowly. She doesn't say anything; she just looks at Steve. Tears well up in her eyes. The whole bedroom is silent for a few moments.

Mrs. Thomas breaks the silence, saying in a hushed tone, as if talking to herself, "He was right. Charlie was right. It's just like Charlie said."

Steve looks at Mrs. Thomas, frightened; he then looks over at Karen. "I can explain. I can explain! A friend of mine came into town on Friday, and he wants me to come over tonight to see him."

Karen says, "I thought you just said you hadn't thought much about where we were going tonight."

Steve shows a worried, blank expression on his face. He turns a shade of magenta as he tries to talk.

Mrs. Thomas walks over and takes the key out of Karen's hand. She looks at Steve sternly says, "What is the name of your friend, Steve?"

Steve pauses for a moment and then says, "John. John Deer. I think you both should leave now. My mother and father should be home soon."

Mrs. Thomas replies, "We aren't going anywhere until we get to the bottom of this."

Karen takes the key from her mother and notices a phone number on it. She walks over to the phone and dials the number.

Steve, looking more scared, says, "Hey, what are you doing! I said that I think you two should leave now."

Karen doesn't say a thing.

Mrs. Thomas shouts, "Shut up, Steve! You just shut up!"

After hearing this, Steve shuts up. His face is red with fear and anxiety.

All is quiet in the room.

Karen waits for her call to connect.

Soon a voice on the other end of the line says, "Hello. This is the Walker Hotel. May I help you?"

Karen says, "Yes, I found a key to one of the rooms to your hotel. The number on the key is 22. Could you please tell me who is staying there?"

The voice on the other end says, "Will you please hold for one moment?"

"Yes, ma'am, I will hold."

Karen gives Steve a mean look as she holds the phone close to her ear. The silence in the bedroom is deafening. The atmosphere is full of anticipation.

The woman at the hotel gets back on the line. "Thank you for holding. The person registered for that room is Steve Johnson."

Karen begins to cry. She nods her head toward her mother.

The voice on the phone says, "If you would come by and bring the key to us, we will make sure Mr. Johnson gets it."

Controlling her tears, Karen speaks into the phone in a pleasant tone. "Yes, ma'am. We will make sure you get your key returned." She then puts the phone down without saying another word.

Karen turns to Steve and softly says, "You were going to rape me tonight, weren't you?"

Steve answers, "Are you crazy? I would never do anything like that to you, Karen."

Mrs. Thomas jumps in, "How could you! How could you plan out such a mean and awful thing like that!"

Steve tries to explain to Mrs. Thomas, but as he speaks, Karen looks over and sees one of Steve's leather belts hanging in his closet. She walks over to it. Steve, facing Mrs. Thomas, doesn't see Karen grab the belt. Karen quickly walks up behind Steve. He turns around just as Karen draws back the leather belt. She then strikes the leather weapon hard up against the side of Steve's face. The belt makes a loud slap. Steve cries out in agony. Karen draws back and slaps Steve again.

Mrs. Thomas doesn't hold Karen back; she lets her enjoy herself.

Karen strikes Steve with the belt again and again.

Steve cries out, "Stop, Karen! Stop! Stop hitting me!"

Karen becomes a savage, raging maniac. She throws an upper cut with the belt, landing yet another clean blow on Steve's face. Steve falls to the floor and curls up into a ball. He lies there on the floor, and just like a dog, takes everything Karen gives him; he doesn't even put up a fight. Karen just keeps hitting him, again and again. The belt lands on Steve's back, hard. She gives him the beating of a lifetime. Steve looks up at Karen, partially protecting his face. He looks up at Mrs. Thomas, showing his extremely red face. He begs for mercy.

"Please stop hitting me, Karen. Tell her to stop, Mrs. Thomas! Please tell her to stop hitting me!"

Mrs. Thomas, showing no sympathy toward Steve, says to Karen, "That's enough, dear."

Karen looks at her mother with surprise.

Mrs. Thomas takes the belt from Karen and begins to strike Steve with even more fury! She hits him repeatedly. She hits Steve harder and with a lot more power than Karen did. Steve cries out in pain. His agony doesn't stop Mrs. Thomas's powerful blows.

She then stops to say, "You are getting everything you deserve, you weasel!"

Steve lies on the floor, curled up so Mrs. Thomas's painful blows don't strike his red face anymore. He doesn't put up a fight at all. He just lies there, screaming for Mrs. Thomas to stop beating him.

After a few minutes, Karen says to her mother, "You must be getting tired. Here, let me have that belt."

Karen takes the belt from her mother. She unleashes her rage and indignation, proceeding to beat Steve where her mother left off. Karen starts to administer those loud pops with the leather belt once again. The pops from the belt bring out yells and cries from Steve every time. She keeps hitting him time after time after time. Steve, realizing that Karen isn't going to stop, jumps up, grabs his car keys, and runs from the room. Steve runs into the hall and down the stairs. As he gets down to the last step, he stumbles and falls.

Karen and Mrs. Thomas run out of the room, right behind Steve. They both see that he has fallen. Karen runs down the stairs, with Mrs. Thomas following. Karen gets to Steve first. He looks up at Karen, and his face is as red as a stop sign. He puts his hands up to block his face. His facial expression shows fear and terror. Karen looks down at the broken-spirited man, still holding the belt in hand. She holds it behind her so that she won't alarm her victim.

Karen then orders Steve, "Put your hands down to your sides and show me your face, you coward!"

Steve follows Karen's orders, putting down his hands without question. Just as his hands clear his face, Karen swings the leather weapon and strikes Steve's face, hard. The powerful impact of the belt striking Steve's face makes a loud and profound sound.

Steve's agony is expressed immediately on impact. "Aauugghh!!! Aauugghh!!!"

His screams make Karen hit him harder and harder.

Steve finally jumps up and runs out the door. Karen follows, hitting him all the way to his car. He gets into his car and puts the key into the ignition. Karen manages to strike his face with the leather belt a few more times before he's able to shut the car door. Steve finally drives off, tires squealing until he is out of sight.

Mrs. Thomas comes out of the house, walks up to Karen, and says, "Well done, Daughter. I am proud as hell of you right now."

Karen, with a face of invincibility, proudly replies, "I am proud as hell of you too, mama. I love you so much."

The two embrace with an affectionate hug, holding each other lovingly. They laugh out loud, and tears of joy trickle from their eyes.

Mrs. Thomas says, "Let's go home now, dear."

Karen looks at her mother with spunk and says, "First, I want to get every photograph of me out of that house. I don't want Steve to have any images of me to look at ever again."

Mrs. Thomas replies, "Okay, honey, I will help you gather them."

So the two ladies walk back into Steve's house to remove all the pictures of Karen. Mrs. Thomas holds her daughter's hand as they walk back into the house.

"You take the upstairs, Karen, and I will take the downstairs."

"Okay, mama."

The two gather all of Karen's photos and put them into Mrs. Thomas's car. They shut the front door of the house behind them, get into Mrs. Thomas's car, and drive home.

As they are on their way home, Mrs. Thomas notices something. "Dear, where did you get that?" She points to the ruby-and-diamond ring on Karen's finger.

"Oh this?"

"Yes, that. I haven't noticed you having such a nice ring before. Where did you get it?"

Remembering how she got the ring, Karen says, "Would you believe Charlie gave it to me, mama?"

"He did! When did he give it to you?"

"He gave it ... well ... he didn't exactly give it to me. He just reached over and slid it on my finger without even mentioning it."

"He did?"

"Yeah, he came over today while I was at work to tell me what he did to Steve, and then he just slipped it on my finger. He was so nonchalant about it. He didn't ask me anything; he just slid it on my finger and then drove over to the house."

"It sure is pretty! If those are real rubies and a real diamond, he must have paid a whole lot for it."

Just then, Karen starts to giggle. She gets an idea.

"Mama, drive over to the shopping center where I work. There is something I want to do."

Mrs. Thomas, showing a curious look, says, "What in the world for? Charlie is waiting for us."

With a devious look, Karen says, "There is a jewelry store located in the shopping center: Paul's Precious Gems. I want Paul to look at the ring and test it to see if it is real."

Mrs. Thomas, showing a surprised look, says, "Karen Thomas! You ought to be ashamed of yourself. Do you think they are still open?"

Karen laughs as she says, "Yes, I hope so. The only way to know is to go by there and see."

So the two curious women make their way to the jewelry store. They soon arrive and waste no time hurrying to the entrance, happy to see that the store is still open.

Karen walks into the store first, and her mother follows close behind. A man stands behind the counter. He wears glasses with a magnifier adjacent to them. He is short and looks about fifty years old.

Karen approaches the man. "Hello. Are you Paul?"

The man smiles at Karen and says, "Yes, ma'am, I sure am."

"Could you help me?"

The man stops what he is doing. "Sure thing! What can I do for you, little missy?"

Karen takes off the ring and places it on the counter. She timidly asks, "Could you tell me if this ring is real?"

Without saying a word, Paul picks up the ring. He slides the magnifier down and looks through it as he holds up the ring. Studying the ring for only a few seconds, he says, "Sure looks real to me."

Karen and her mother look at each other in a surprised yet joyful way.

Paul then says, "Just to make sure, let me test it with my diamond tester." He reaches down and brings up a strange little device. It is about seven inches across and resembles the handle of a gun. The device has four lights and an on/off switch.

Karen asks, "What is that?"

"That is a diamond tester."

Paul takes off the cap. The tip has a point, about the size of the lead in a pencil. He turns on the little device. "It will take a few moments for it to warm up."

Not long after Paul turns the device on, a little light comes on next to the printed word *ready.* Paul carefully picks up the little ring in one hand and takes the diamond tester in the other hand. He places the head of the diamond tester on the diamond. The tester then makes a beeping sound.

Hearing the noise, Paul says, "It's real, for sure."

Mrs. Thomas asks, "Could you tell us how much it is worth?"

"Do you want to sell it?"

Karen replies, "Oh no! It's not for sale. I just wanted to know if it was real."

"In that case, it's probably worth anywhere from eight hundred to eighteen hundred dollars. It's hard to say. Higher quality diamonds sell for much more. This diamond is truly a high-quality stone, and the rubies are real and also of very good quality."

Karen, with her eyes gleaming, says, "Thank you so very much for your help."

Paul smiles and says, "Just glad to be of assistance to you, young lady."

Mrs. Thomas asks, "How much do we owe you, sir?"

"You don't owe me a thing. I am just glad to help out."

Mrs. Thomas opens up her handbag, pulls out three one-dollar bills, and lays the money on the counter.

"Here you go, Paul. I would feel better if you would take this anyway."

Paul just smiles as the two ladies turn and head for the door. Right before they leave the store, Paul reaches over and picks up the money.

Karen and Mrs. Thomas get in the car, and Mrs. Thomas drives home.

Charlie's truck is still parked in the driveway as they drive up. Karen opens her door first and hurries to the front door. Mrs. Thomas gets out and quickly follows Karen into the house.

There's Charlie: lying asleep on the couch, with the TV on.

Karen looks over at Charlie. With her head to one side, she says, "Wake up, you handsome, blue-eyed darling."

Charlie moves a little bit but doesn't wake up.

Karen walks over to the couch and lays a big kiss on sleepy lips. This wakes Charlie up!

Karen continues to kiss him.

"Did everything check out the way I told you?" asks Charlie.

Karen happily replies, "Yes! Yes! Yes, my love!"

Charlie's eyes open up tremendously. "What did you say?"

"I said, 'Yes, my love.' I love you, Charlie. I love you. I love you. You are my knight in shining armor. I love you so much!" She then lays another big kiss on his lips.

Thomas, with a tear in her eye, walks over and sits down on the other side of Charlie. She wraps her arms around him and starts to kiss him profoundly—not on the lips, just on both cheeks.

Charlie asks, "Mrs. Thomas, do you love me too?"

"Yes, Charlie, I love you too. And from here on out, you don't have to call me Mrs. Thomas. You can start calling me 'Ma,' if you would like to."

Charlie smiles and says, "All right, Ma. I will do that."

So Karen and her mother sit beside Charlie and flood him with their love and affection.

Charlie's struggle is over. He has won the game!

Chapter 3
TIME TO BUILD A MEANINGFUL RELATIONSHIP

Charlie and Karen begin to see a whole lot of each other. Their lives focus mainly on seeing each other. The love bug has bitten them both, with a most powerful bite. Charlie's thoughts center on his young, attractive, redheaded girlfriend. He wakes up every morning with love, joy, and a special happiness glowing in his heart. His heart has been captured by Karen's innocence and charm. Karen wakes up every morning, in a similar fashion. She thinks about Charlie, with a happy vision of love planted deep in her mind. They pick and carry on, just like a pair of silly teenagers, frolicking around without a worry or a care in the world. Karen is still the tender age of nineteen and won't turn twenty until September; this gives the relationship a more youthful splendor, along with a more playful and innocent character.

Mrs. Thomas enjoys watching the two lovebirds and takes great delight in seeing them pick and tease each other. She really loves Charlie. She begins to take up for Charlie more so than her daughter.

Charlie is so happy with Karen, and Karen is so happy with Charlie. It is so wonderful to be young and in love. That is the most wonderful thing life has to offer!

Charlie becomes a regular fixture at the Thomas's home. He and Mrs. Thomas get along better than ever. Karen thinks even more of Charlie now that her mother has taken such a liking to him. The three of them develop a very caring and loving relationship.

After Karen gets off work one day, she drives home and notices Charlie's truck in the driveway. She gets out of her car and proceeds to walk into the house. She finds Charlie lying on the couch, fast asleep. This gives her an idea: she walks over and ties Charlie's shoelaces together, without waking him up. She then walks back over to the door, and with a little devious smile on her face, opens the door and slams it shut.

Karen then calls out, "Charlie! Charlie! Come here, Charlie!"

Charlie jumps up, and when he takes his first step, he falls flat on his face.

Karen then bursts out laughing.

Charlie, seeing his shoelaces tied together, gives Karen an I'm-going-to-get-you look. He pulls off his shoes and starts to chase Karen around the house.

Charlie cries out, "You little varmint! You wait till I get my hands on you!"

Karen runs around the house, laughing as Charlie chases her. She and Charlie end up in the kitchen. Charlie tries to catch her, but she keeps running around the kitchen table so that he can't.

She sticks out her tongue and then says, "What's wrong, big boy, can't you catch me?" When Charlie doesn't respond, she imitates the high-pitched laugh he always makes. "Tee, hee, hee!"

"That was a mean thing to do!" Charlie says. "Why did you tie my shoelaces together like that?"

Karen laughs normally. "Because I just felt like it. You want to do something about it?"

"Yeah! You just wait till I get my hands on you, you little varmint!"

Charlie keeps chasing Karen around the table until she runs back out into the living room. Finally, he catches up to her and pulls her playful little body into his grasp.

Just as soon as Karen is captured by Charlie, she throws her arms around him and says, "I'm sorry, Charlie. I am so sorry. Please don't beat me up. Tee, hee, hee!"

Charlie starts to poke her in the sides to make her jump. He then starts to tickle her.

Charlie, now in control of her, says, "If you are so sorry, then what was that 'tee, hee, hee' all about?"

With an innocent look on her face, Karen says, "What are you talking about, Charlie?" Just as she says this, she pulls out of Charlie's grasp, runs toward the couch, and picks up Charlie's shoes. She runs farther away from him.

Charlie calls out, "Hey! You come back here! Hey! You come back here with my shoes! You come back here right now, young lady!"

Charlie gets up and starts to chase Karen around the house all over again.

Karen gets him to chase her upstairs. She goes into one of the bedrooms, and Charlie follows right behind her. As Charlie gets closer to her, Karen throws the shoes right out the window!

With a surprised and puzzled look, Charlie says, "What are you doing?"

Karen playfully replies, "I ain't doing nothing now. I have already done it, silly boy."

Charlie, staring at Karen's mischievous grin, says to her, "I ought to put you across my knee and give you a spanking, young lady!"

Karen, still with that feisty, playful look on her face, says, "You and who else, big boy? Tee, hee, hee!"

Charlie walks over, grabs her, and playfully throws her on the bed. He begins to tickle her.

Karen cries out, "Stop it! Stop it!"

Charlie, not letting up, says, "Say, 'Please forgive me, master, for being a little stinker today.'"

"I ain't! I ain't gonna say no such thing. Let me go."

Charlie continues to tickle her until she submits.

"Okay, okay. Please forgive me for being a little stinker."

"That isn't what I told you to say. I told you to say, 'Please forgive me, master, for being a little stinker.'"

"I ain't gonna call you 'master.' Are you out of your mind! I ain't . . .!"

Charlie pokes Karen's ribs unrelentingly until finally she surrenders to his demands.

"Okay! Okay! Please forgive me, master, for being a little stinker."

Charlie then stops tickling her. He stares into her eyes as the two tired sweethearts lie still on the bed. Charlie then reaches over and begins to kiss Karen. She wraps her arms around him as he kisses her.

Right after Charlie's lips separate from Karen's soft, tender mouth, Karen pushes Charlie off the bed and right onto the hard floor.

Charlie looks up at her, confused. "Hey! What did you do that for?"

"That's what you get for making me call you 'master,' master. Tee, hee, hee!"

Charlie gets up off the floor and proceeds to chase her again. He jumps on the bed just as she jumps off. Charlie does manage to grab her and pull her back on the bed. They begin to wrestle around a little bit until they both hear something downstairs.

Karen speaks first. "Hey, mama's home! If she finds us up here lying on the bed, she will take a belt to my ass. Come on, Charlie, let's go downstairs, right now!"

"Right, you go first, and I will follow you."

Karen jumps off the bed and hurries downstairs. Charlie follows a good distance behind her.

Karen finds her mother in the living room. "Hello, mama. How did your day go?"

Mrs. Thomas looks at her daughter with a stern look, "Fine. Is that Charlie's truck I see out in the driveway?"

"Yes, it is. He's upstairs."

Just as the words come out of Karen's mouth, Charlie comes down the stairs in his stocking feet.

When Charlie sees Mrs. Thomas, he walks over to her and kisses her on the cheek. "Hey, Ma, did you have a good day?"

"Yes, Charlie, I had a pretty good day. How did your day go?"

"Well … I guess it went okay."

"You sound like there's something wrong, Charlie."

"Well …" He looks over at Karen and then back at Mrs. Thomas. "There is, Ma. It's your daughter. Do you know what she did?"

Mrs. Thomas looks down and notices Charlie is not wearing any shoes. She then looks over at Karen, who has a shy, innocent expression on her face. Mrs. Thomas gives Karen a concerned look.

Mrs. Thomas turns back to Charlie and says, "What has she done now, Charlie?"

"What has she done? Let me tell you what she has done. First of all, she tied my shoelaces together. I was lying on the couch, resting, and she comes in and wakes me up by slamming the door and yelling, 'Charlie! Charlie!' I jump up to see what's the matter, and what happens? I fall flat on my face."

Mrs. Thomas looks over at Karen, who is trying to hide a grin. "Are you responsible for that, young lady?"

Karen, smiling innocently, says, "Well … uh-huh. I was just playing with him, mama. All I did was tie his shoelaces together. Tee, hee, hee!"

Charlie then says, "That's not all she has done today, Ma."

Mrs. Thomas listens closely to Charlie as he speaks.

"She grabbed my shoes and ran upstairs with them. As I tried to get them back, she threw them out the window. She did! She really did!"

Mrs. Thomas turns to her daughter, looking at her with disbelief, "Did you do that, young lady!"

Karen looks innocent as she speaks. "Mama, I was only picking. Can't a girl pick a little with her boyfriend?"

"You should be ashamed of yourself. You apologize to Charlie right now!"

"I will not!"

"Young lady, you apologize to Charlie."

"But, mama, I have already apologized to him."

"Did she Charlie?"

"Yeah, Ma, she sure did, right before she pushed me on the floor."

"Karen Thomas! You apologize to Charlie right now!"

Karen gives Charlie a mean look.

"Okay, Charlie, I'm sorry."

Charlie gazes over at Karen, sticking his tongue out. He then gives his high-pitched laugh: tee, hee, hee. "Goody, goody!" Charlie says, reaching over and giving Mrs. Thomas a great big hug and kisses her on her cheek several times.

Karen frowns. "I hope you are happy now, Charlie."

Charlie replies, "I am, meanness, I am."

Mrs. Thomas then says to Karen, "Now you go outside, pick up Charlie's shoes, and bring them into the house."

"I will not!"

"Young lady, don't you talk back to me."

Charlie counters, "Yeah, you should have more respect for your mother."

Karen gives Charlie another mean look.

Mrs. Thomas impatiently says, "Okay, young lady. Charlie is waiting for you to go outside and bring back his shoes, so snap to it."

Karen, without saying anything else, goes outside to get Charlie's shoes.

As she comes back inside, she says, "I hope you both are happy."

Charlie unties the shoelaces and puts his shoes back on.

With a big grin, he says sarcastically, "Poor baby! Is my little girl mad? Tee, hee, hee."

Karen gives Charlie another mean look. She quickly sticks out her tongue at him. He does likewise, but in a few minutes, she is back to hugging and kissing on him like nothing happened.

Mrs. Thomas turns to Karen and says, "Will you try to behave yourself while I go to the grocery store? I just remembered something I need. I will be gone for about twenty minutes. Do you think you can behave that long?"

Karen grins mischievously. "Of course I can. I don't know why you would ask such a thing." Karen glances over at Charlie, giving him a devious little grin. She then says, "Sure, mama, I can be good for twenty minutes … well … maybe. Ha, ha, ha!"

"Well, just try dear. I know it will be hard for you, but at least try."

"Sure, mama. Hey, wait a minute. There are a few things you can get for me."

Karen writes down a page of things she wants her mother to get for her.

Mrs. Thomas shakes her head and says sarcastically, "Is that all, dear? Are you sure you aren't leaving anything out?"

Karen thinks for a moment. "Well … maybe there are a few more things I might need."

"I was just being sarcastic, dear. I will be back shortly. So don't burn the house down."

"Okay, mama."

Mrs. Thomas turns to Charlie. "Is there anything you want me to pick up for you, Charlie?"

"No thanks, Ma. Well … there is one thing you might pick up for me, if you can find one."

"What's that?"

"Pick me up a paddle. When Karen misbehaves, I will have something to give her a spanking with."

Karen quickly replies, "Do what? Oh no, you're not. You ain't gonna spank me."

Charlie replies back, "I am just kidding, meanness."

Charlie walks over to Mrs. Thomas and openly whispers, "Make sure it is a big paddle, one with holes in it."

Karen glares at Charlie and angrily shouts, "Hey, I heard that!"

Charlie sounds off with his high-pitched laugh. "Tee, hee, hee."

Mrs. Thomas says, "I would like to stay and listen to all this, but I have places to go and things to buy. Both of you try to behave until I get home."

Charlie kisses her cheek and says, "Okay, Ma, I will try to keep Karen in line."

Mrs. Thomas leaves to go to the grocery store. Just as soon as she leaves the house, Charlie goes over to the TV and turns it on. He walks back over to the couch and sits down. Karen is in the kitchen, with her nose in the refrigerator.

Charlie calls out to her. "Cubby! Cubby, come here for a minute."

Karen walks out of the kitchen and joins Charlie on the couch.

"What do you want, Charlie?"

Charlie gazes at his beautiful damsel. Her eyes are as blue as the ocean. Her long red hair dangles down below her shoulders. Charlie doesn't say anything; he just looks deep into her eyes. She likewise looks deep into his eyes. Charlie reaches over and kisses Karen gently on her soft, sweet, innocent lips. Karen sits back, paralyzed by Charlie's kiss. Charlie puts his left hand up around her neck and kisses her again. The kiss soon becomes more passionate and arousing. Charlie begins to caress the side of her neck, as his lips continue to kiss his young scarlet-haired beauty's soft mouth. Charlie's hands begin to slowly go downward. His eager hands begin to get close to Karen's large, full breast. He slowly and tenderly begins to rub her soft right bosom with his left hand. Just as Charlie presses deep into Karen's large, soft bosom, he hears a loud pop, and then his face begins to burn like fire.

Realizing he has just been attacked, Charlie cries, "Hey! Why did you slap me!"

With a stern look, Karen says, "Why do you think!"

Charlie, rubbing his face, says, "That hurt! Damn, that hurt. What is wrong with you?!"

"What do you mean? Nothing is wrong with me. Let me tell you something, young man. You don't put your hands there!"

"Huh?"

"I said, you don't put your hands there! You don't put your hands on my breasts! That is something you just don't do! Do you understand me, young man!"

"What's with this 'young man' stuff? I am seven years older than you. If you didn't want me to touch your breasts, all you had to do was push my hand away. You didn't have to slap the hell out of me!"

Staring at Charlie with anger in her eyes, Karen says sharply, "Go home!"

Charlie pauses for a moment as he tries to comprehend what Karen has just dictated to him.

With a confused and disoriented face, Charlie softly says, "Huh? Go home? What did you mean when you said 'go home'?"

Karen gives Charlie another stern, mean look. "I think it is self-explanatory! Go home. Go home, right now, Charlie Delaney."

Charlie now realizes that he has made Karen extremely mad. He pauses again for a brief moment, still dumbfounded at what has just taken place.

With a sad and sorry expression on his face, Charlie looks at Karen. "Cubby, please don't make me go home. I didn't mean to make you angry."

Karen, still in the same state of mind, says, "If you think I am going to let you touch me there in that manner, then you can just go home. Let me make something perfectly clear to you, Charlie Delaney, I am not some two-bit whore you can take those kinds of liberties with. I have never let anybody touch me there in that manner, and I ain't gonna start now! So if—"

Charlie interrupts. "Yes, ma'am! Yes, ma'am! I understand! I fully understand. You see what we can accomplish when we just sit down and talk about it! I understand perfectly now how you feel about that. So please don't make me go home. I will behave. Please …"

Karen pauses for a moment as she stares at Charlie. "Well … I guess I could overlook it this time. Just make sure you don't forget. You can kiss me, but don't you try to make those kinds of advances again. I am a lady, and I expect you to treat me with respect. Because if you don't, I will introduce 'Mr. Right' once more across your face! Do you understand!"

"Yes, ma'am! I fully understand! You don't have to worry about that anymore."

"Good. I am glad we have a better understanding about this matter. So I guess you can stay."

Charlie smiles with relief as he sits quietly beside Karen, too afraid to even hold her hand. He dares not kiss her. They both continue to sit quietly until Mrs. Thomas arrives back home with the groceries.

Mrs. Thomas enters the house, carrying two bags in her arms.

Karen gets up from the couch and says, "Do you need any help, mama?"

"No, dear, this is all of them. You can help me put them up if you want to."

Karen gently bites her lower lip as she tries to suppress a smile.

She glances over at Charlie and says to him in a nice way, "You stay here, Charlie, I won't be long. Okay?"

Charlie, still distraught at what has just transpired, says a quick, "Yes, ma'am."

Karen gets up and goes into the kitchen to help her mother.

Karen enters the kitchen, laughing. "Hey, mama, guess what?"

"What, dear?"

Karen puts her hand over her mouth and then brings it down. She giggles and then says, "I finally broke Charlie in. Tee, hee, hee."

"Did you pop him like I told you to?"

"Yes, mama. I did just like you instructed me to. It worked like a charm. He is like a little puppy dog now."

Mrs. Thomas smiles gladly as she replies, "The harder you slap a man, the more he will respect you."

"I've got him saying yes, ma'am. Tee, hee, hee."

Karen puts her fingers over her lips as she laughs.

Mrs. Thomas cracks a devious little grin of her own. "Well … I am glad you finally broke him in, dear. I was wondering why Charlie was taking so long. Oh well … I guess some men take longer than other men do. I'm just glad you have finally broken Charlie in."

The two women giggle and laugh with a feminine glee as they put up the groceries. They soon finish, come out of the kitchen, and go into the living room, where Charlie is still sitting in the same spot, afraid to move.

As Mrs. Thomas sits down, she chuckles softly to herself. She glances over at Charlie, who still looks like a scared rabbit.

Karen walks over and sits on Charlie's lap. She kisses him on his forehead as the three sit there and watch TV.

Mrs. Thomas looks over at Charlie and notices the bright red mark across his left cheek. She doesn't say anything to Charlie about it, but she does give her daughter a girlish grin.

"So, Charlie, what did you and Karen do while I was gone?"

Charlie looks at Mrs. Thomas, a little apprehension showing on his face. "Oh … nothing … nothing too much."

Charlie then looks at his watch. "Oh my! Just look at the time. I'm sorry, but I am going to have to leave now. I have a few things I need to do at home."

Charlie gets up to leave.

Mrs. Thomas calls after him. "Okay, Charlie. You come back when you can stay longer, all right?"

"Sure thing, Mrs. Thomas … I mean, Ma. I will be seeing you two ladies later."

Karen follows Charlie to the door. Giving Charlie a friendly smile, she says, "You don't have to leave Charlie. I told you that you could stay."

"I know, but I have a few things I need to do. I will see you tomorrow. Okay?"

Charlie tries to leave, but Karen leans over and kisses him good-bye. Charlie kisses her back, for just a brief lip encounter.

"So long, Ma!" he calls to Mrs. Thomas.

"Bye, Charlie! You behave yourself. Okay?"

"Yes, ma'am. I will."

Charlie exits the house, and Mrs. Thomas and Karen sit back and have themselves another girlish laugh.

The next day, Charlie is back to his old self again. Although he has learned not to touch Karen in a provocative manner, the temptation is still there. He has learned his lesson, but it's difficult. He goes by the little pizza place after work to see his feisty little girlfriend.

Just as he walks in, she glances over at him. "Hello, Charlie. How's your face?"

Charlie blushes a little as he notices a few customers sitting there, waiting for their pizzas.

Karen giggles as she says, "I see the red is growing, Charlie. It's all over your face now. Tee, hee, hee!"

Charlie walks over to Karen and speaks to her in a whisper. "Young lady, there are people listening to you."

Karen sticks out her tongue and says, "You want a pizza?"

"Well … I don't know."

"You come into a pizza place, and you don't know if you want a pizza."

"Yes, little girl, I will have a medium pepperoni pizza with mushrooms, onions, and green peppers."

"Charlie, I was just picking. You don't have to order a pizza."

"I don't have to, but I am. So hop to it, little girlie."

She holds her right fist up and says, "I'm going to hop to it, all right. I'll hop one of these across your—"

"Okay, young lady, I would rather have a pizza. They are a lot easier to digest."

Karen laughs another girlish laugh and says, "Okay, Charlie, coming right up."

Karen writes down Charlie's order and takes it to the back.

Charlie just gazes at the sight of his redheaded love. Her beauty would make angels jealous. Her pure, sweet, innocent face, those radiant blue eyes, and her long, straight, luscious red hair all captivate Charlie's entire being. For a young girl with such a small frame and slender waist, she has unusually large breasts. Anyone in close contact with her front will surely discover an eye-popping view, one which arouses Charlie's sensual appetite.

As Charlie waits for his pizza, Karen motions for him to come to her. Charlie walks over and looks down at her virtuous face.

She then speaks in a very soft tone. "Charlie, are you mad at me?"

The words melt Charlie from within. "No, Cubby, I'm not mad at you. Are you mad at me for acting so aggressive yesterday?"

Karen looks at Charlie, her eyes warm and caring. She pauses for a second and then gently says, "Yes, I am." She immediately grins, and Charlie realizes she is picking. Karen takes Charlie's hand and says, "No, Charlie, I ain't mad at you."

Charlie replies, "There is no such word as *ain't*."

Karen sticks out her tongue quickly and then replies, "I'll say 'ain't' if I want to."

"I believe you will do anything if you want to." Charlie reaches over and gives her a quick kiss on her tender lips.

Charlie stands there in a daze as he looks at Karen's extraordinarily lovely face. He then picks up his pizza and throws her a kiss, as she waves good-bye by holding her right hand with her left.

Charlie goes home and devours the entire pizza. He goes to sleep happy and content, thinking of his beautiful red-haired girlfriend.

As the weeks go by, Charlie and Karen develop a beautiful, irreproachable relationship. They get to know each another more through their picking and playing. Each is always picking on the other as a way of getting the other's attention. Sometimes, though, they get out of control with this playing, resulting in one getting his or her feelings hurt. But the one who didn't get hurt always apologizes to the other, and everybody ends up happy. Karen does most of the apologizing, since she does most of the picking. But there are times when Charlie gets her back by deliberately making her mad.

One Saturday afternoon, Charlie is home, working on his truck. As Charlie he works on replacing the spark plugs, Karen drives up in her car. She parks her car near Charlie's truck, gets out of her car, and with a devious look on her face, walks up to Charlie's truck. Charlie sticks his head out of the engine for a moment and gives her a quick wave.

He then proceeds to finish what he was working on. Karen, not getting the attention she expected, walks over to the driver's side and opens the door. She reaches in and presses down on the horn. She laughs profusely as she holds it down, continually blaring out the loud, irritating noise. Charlie jumps back, trips, and falls to the ground. Karen finally releases the horn and stops the loud annoying racket. She walks to the front of the truck and sees Charlie lying on the ground. He gives her a very mean look.

She innocently says, "Charlie, I don't think you need to fix the horn. It works just fine. Tee, hee, hee."

Charlie gets up and begins to chase Karen around the yard. Just as he catches up to her and grabs her, she quickly wraps her arms around him and gives him a big hug.

She lovingly says, "I'm sorry. Please don't beat me up. I know I was a bad girl. Will you please forgive me?"

Charlie gazes down at her innocent face and says, "I'm not angry at you for blowing by horn, I'm mad at you for stealing my laugh."

Charlie bends his head down and kisses Karen, and she responds intensely.

Charlie then kindly says, "Why don't you go inside the house so I can finish working on my truck? It shouldn't take long, Miss Pick Pick."

"I'd rather stay out here and watch you work. I know! I could be your little helper. How does that sound, Charlie?"

Charlie shakes his head at her mischievous little face. "You little rascal! I'll just bet you want to help me. The first time I turn my head, you will be planning some other little mean trick."

"Who me? Now Charlie, why would you say such a thing?"

Charlie starts to poke her in the sides to make her laugh.

"Stop it! Stop it! You'd better stop that."

Charlie grins as he says, "I'd better stop that, or what, little girl?"

"Well … you'd better stop, or I'll not help you anymore."

"In that case …" Charlie pokes her in the side more and more.

"Now cut it out, Charlie! Enough is enough."

Just as Charlie stops, he bends his head down and steals a kiss. Karen responds by wrapping her arms around his waist. She puts her head on Charlie's chest. They both stand there, holding each other in a gentle rocking motion.

"Hey, Cubby, how would you like to do me a favor?"

"Sure, Charlie. You know I am willing to help you out. What is it?"

"Why don't you go inside my house and clean it up. There are some dishes in the sink, the floor needs to be vacuumed, and my room is full of dirty clothes."

"Are you crazy? I'm not your maid, Charlie Delaney. Are you out of your cotton-picking mind?"

"I'm like Roy Clark; I never picked cotton. Tee, hee, hee. Come on, Cubby, please."

Karen gives Charlie a good long stare.

Charlie tries to use a little reverse psychology on Karen. "You don't have to if you don't want to, Cubby. I just thought you might want to help me out, that's all. You don't have to."

"Sure, Charlie. I guess a little housework won't hurt me."

"Well, I have to finish working on my truck. I will be in shortly. Don't break anything."

"Okay, Charlie."

Just as Karen turns and begins to walk away Charlie pats her on her behind.

Karen smiles as she cries, "Hey! You'd better watch it, Charlie."

Charlie grins and says, "I did watch it. That's why I patted it. Tee, hee, hee."

Karen gives Charlie a feminine smirk as she turns to go inside and clean up the house.

Charlie finishes working on his truck in about thirty minutes. He decides to go inside the house to see what mess Karen has gotten herself into. Just as Charlie walks inside, he sees his lovely damsel vacuuming the living room. Charlie quickly walks into the kitchen without her seeing him. All the dirty dishes that were in the sink have been washed and put up. Charlie is impressed! He opens the refrigerator and takes out a bottle of soda. He remains in the kitchen until he hears the vacuum cleaner stop. He gets up and proceeds to walk into the living room.

Karen is putting the vacuum cleaner away in the closet as Charlie says, "I can't believe it! I just can't believe it! I am proud of you, Cubby.

Well done, young lady. I knew you were more valuable than just your good looks. Oh, by the way, have you started washing the clothes in my bedroom yet? I don't hear the washing machine going."

Karen gives Charlie a mean look. "Listen here, young man, I have been working hard trying to get this place in order. I have been working real hard …"

"I know, meanness, I know. I was just playing with you. Here is your reward for washing the dishes."

Charlie leans over and gives her a big kiss.

"Is that all I get?"

"What else did you have on your mind?"

Karen pauses for a moment and then says with a provocative smile, "Oh … I thought that since this is Saturday, you would take me to the New York Dinner Theater tonight. I have never been, and I thought—"

Charlie interrupts. "Hey, wait a minute. Isn't that the place where you eat dinner, and then a stage comes down from the ceiling and you watch a show?"

Karen smiles happily and says, "Yep! That's the place."

Charlie grins and shows a look of intrigue.

Charlie walks over to Karen, a bewildered expression on his face, and says, "Uh-huh! I see now. I see what you're up to. You cleaned up a little around my house just so I will take you there tonight, isn't that right?"

Karen shakes her head with her typical innocent expression. "Oh no, Charlie! I cleaned up your house out of the kindness of my heart. I had no intention of accepting anything in return—just a little bread and water so I won't starve. Tee, hee, hee."

Charlie shakes his head with a grin. "Well, for your information, you have to make reservations for a place like that. I don't know if we could get them now."

"But if we do get reservations, you will take me? Hmm?"

Charlie leans over and lightly kisses her tender lips. As they break, Karen responds by opening her mouth. For the first time in their relationship, she pulls Charlie's head closer, closer, until her open mouth bonds with his. She keeps her mouth open as Charlie slides his tongue into her wet mouth. She allows him to kiss her this way for only a few moments. She then gently breaks away from Charlie's seductive kiss.

Charlie rubs her nape tenderly. He kisses her lower neck wildly and then moves to her ears, where he whispers gently, "If we can get reservation, we will go."

Karen pulls his head to her face. She opens her mouth for the second time before a kiss. Charlie's head gets closer, as Karen turns her head sideways and places her hand on Charlie's neck. She closes her eyes as Charlie does likewise, and their mouths lock into a loving, passionate kiss. Charlie's eager tongue slides once again into Karen's mouth. She only allows him to kiss her like this for a short period of time, breaking the kiss with a simple turn of her head. She hugs Charlie with a strong grip.

Charlie stands there, bewildered at how she has allowed him to kiss her. This passionate kiss shows him that her feelings toward him have developed greatly. He continues to hold her quietly in his arms. He feels loved by her affectionate touch. His mind is in a happy state of wonder, and he marvels at her willingness to let him kiss her that way.

Karen's young heart begins to feel loved in a different way by Charlie's gentle and caring touch. She may only have allowed Charlie to kiss her that way shortly, but she wanted him to never stop. Even though Charlie's tongue went in her eager mouth, Karen's tongue remained dormant and still, while he moved his around her warm mouth. She acted like she was in a helpless, paralyzed state when Charlie's tongue was first introduced to her wet, young, tender, sensuous, mouth.

As they hold each other in this gentle, caring way, Charlie says softly, "I love you, Cubby."

She gives him a heavenly smile, with an aroused, sensual look in her eyes. She looks up at Charlie and says in a meaningful tone, "I love you too, Charlie."

Karen then buries her face in Charlie's chest as she holds him tightly.

The loving embrace continues until Charlie says, "Hey, Cubby, if we are going to the New York Dinner Theater tonight, I guess I'd better make those reservations."

Charlie releases Karen from his gentle but strong hands. He walks over to the phone and starts to thumb through the phone book.

Karen looks at him, a guilty expression on her face. She reluctantly does nothing until Charlie finds the number.

Just as Charlie begins to dial, Karen takes a deep breath, and then she says, "Hey, Charlie. You don't have to make that reservation."

Charlie moves the phone away from his ear. "What? What did you say, Cubby?"

"I said, you don't have to make that reservation. I already did. Tee, hee, hee."

"You did what? When?"

"I made it yesterday. They are all booked up now. You have to call them in advance. It's a good thing I took the initiative to make the reservation yesterday, or we wouldn't be able to go tonight. Aren't you proud of me, Charlie?"

Charlie looks at her fawn-like expression and says, "You little varmint! You had this whole episode planned out to the last detail."

Karen laughs. "Tee, hee, hee."

Charlie, hearing this, gives her an intriguing stare. "You told me you hate when I laugh like that."

"Oh, I do, Charlie, I do. But I never said I didn't like it when I laugh that way. Tee, hee, hee."

"What am I going do with you, little girl?"

"Take me to the theater place. But, Charlie, ain't you proud of me for making the reservation?"

Charlie gazes at her fawn-like expression once again. He smiles at her and says, "Yes, dear, I am proud of you."

Karen gets all excited when she hears this. "Oh boy! I was hoping you would be. I try so hard so you'll will be proud of me. Tee, hee, hee."

"If you don't quit stealing my laugh, I'll take you to McDonald's for a cheeseburger instead."

Karen's face suddenly gets sad. "You wouldn't do that, would you?" The sad look touches Charlie's heart immensely.

"I was just kidding, Cubby. I wouldn't do that, sweetheart."

"Good. Tee, hee, hee."

Charlie shakes his head as Karen flashes her captivating grin once more.

"I guess I will go upstairs and wash your clothes, now that I have accomplished my … I mean done what I … well, you know what I mean, Charlie. Tee, hee, hee."

"Yes, I know, Cubby. I know."

Karen jumps up in a happy way and disappears upstairs. Charlie stares at her sexy behind all the way up. He shakes his head in disbelief at how she devised and executed her plan so thoroughly. *She is something,* he thinks.

While Karen is upstairs, Charlie decides to go outside and wash her car for her. He loves her so much that he feels the need to do something else for her. It takes Charlie about thirty minutes to finish the task. When done, he feels pride looking at the shiny red Mustang. The chrome is polished, the tires are shiny and black, and everything sparkles as if it were new. He can't wait to see Karen's expression when he tells her what he has done.

Charlie eagerly walks back inside, with great anticipation, until he sees what Karen has done to his house.

Charlie stares at Karen, dumbstruck. "What in the heck have you done to my house?!"

Karen gives Charlie a concerned look. "What's the matter, Charlie? Have you been out in the cold too long?"

Charlie gazes at Karen, then his house. All the furniture in the living room has been rearranged. Charlie is furious.

Seeing his hostile expression, Karen quickly says, "Now, Charlie, don't look at me that way. I was only trying to make this dull house a little bit more attractive."

Charlie just stands there with his mouth open.

Karen continues. "You see, Charlie, after I threw your clothes in the washing machine, I didn't have anything else to do. I looked out the window and saw you washing my car, so I thought I would do something nice for you."

Charlie is still dazed at seeing all that furniture moved. The view of the room disturbs Charlie immensely.

"How on God's green earth can such a small, fragile girl like you move—excuse me, desecrate—my house in such a short period of time!"

Karen gives Charlie a stern look. "It's a good thing I don't know what *desecrate* means. It doesn't sound like a very nice word."

Karen continues to move a chair out of the room when Charlie cries, "Hey! Stop that! Will you stop that?"

"Now, Charlie, don't get so upset. This chair needs to go in some other room."

"What! Are you crazy! That is my favorite chair. It is my most favorite chair. How could you do this?"

Karen holds up her right arm and tries to make a muscle. With a bright smile, she says, "Sheer power. Never underestimate a girl with determination on her mind."

Charlie quickly runs into the other rooms to see if Hurricane Karen has swept through them too. Charlie is relieved to find them still intact; only the living room has been hit. Charlie goes back into the living room to find Karen dragging his chair down the hall.

Charlie runs over to her and says, "I thought I told you that was my favorite chair."

"I heard you, Charlie. You don't have to make such a big deal of it."

"Then why are you still trying to move it?"

Karen scratches her head and then happily says, "Because I don't like it. I especially don't like it in the living room. It doesn't go with the way I've arranged everything else."

"I don't understand you, Karen! This is my house, not yours."

Karen laughs as she says, "Charlie. I know that, silly boy. Just because you have a house doesn't mean you have to brag about it. What this house needs is a woman's touch. I am only doing this so you will be proud of me. Aren't you proud of me, Charlie?"

Charlie stares at her innocent, fawn-like expression and says flatly, "No! I am not proud of you, young lady. I want you to put everything back the way it was."

Karen hears this and begins to laugh. "Are you crazy? I have worked hard, real hard, just to get this room the way I want it. I'm not going to undo all the hard work I've done just because you have been out in the cold to long. Tee, hee, hee! Silly boy."

"Young lady, I am getting very upset with you. I liked my house the way it was. I was happy with it the way it was, so I want you to put everything back, right this instant. Do you understand me, young lady?"

"I'm too tired, Charlie. Why don't you think it over a little longer?

You may like what I've done after you get used to everything. Hey, I know! How would you like something to drink?"

"All I want is my house back the way it was. That is all I want in the entire world!"

Seeing Charlie angry with her gives Karen an idea, or better yet, an invitation to pick some more on him.

She gives Charlie a mischievous grin as she says, "Are you going to make me?"

Charlie, not in a good mood now, says, "Listen, Karen, what you have done has made me very upset. This house is my sanctuary away from this mean world. When I come in here, I don't want anything moved or put out of its place. This distracts me, and it also bothers me a great deal when I look around and see everything out of its usual place."

Karen takes this information and uses it to her playful advantage. "I have worked too hard just to put everything back. Let me take this old chair out to the garage, and then we will discuss—"

Charlie interrupts loudly. "You aren't taking that chair anywhere! That's *my* chair!"

Karen snickers. "I'm only doing this so you will be happy, Charlie. You shouldn't yell at me for doing something that will make you happy."

Charlie looks at her for a few seconds in complete silence. He then gently says, "I'm sorry I yelled at you, Karen. I didn't mean to talk to you like that."

Just as Karen hears this, she begins to drag the chair down the hall.

Charlie cries, "Stop that! Stop that, right now!"

Karen, acting tough, says, "You gonna stop me?"

"Yeah. I sure am gonna stop you, little girl."

"Oh yeah? You and who else, big boy?"

Charlie smiles a little bit now. "It's three of us: me, myself, and I."

Karen goes right back to dragging the chair, as if she wants to see Charlie do something.

Charlie's smile disappears as he says, "You move that chair any further, and I will—"

Karen playfully snaps back, "You will *what?*"

Charlie, not knowing what to say, finally says, "I'll … I'll … I'll lock you in a closet and feed you to the moths."

"I would like to see you try. I would just like to see you try."

So Charlie grabs her and makes her walk over to the nearest closet.

"Stop it! Stop it! You'd better not! You'd better—"

Charlie opens the closet, and on impulse, gives Karen a quick little push. He shuts the door and locks it.

Charlie then cries, "Goody, goody! You wanted to see me try; well, I not only tried, I succeeded." Charlie lets out one of his high-pitched laughs. "Tee, hee, hee."

Karen begins to pound on the door, yelling, "You let me out of this closet! You open this door and let me out of this damn closet right now, Charlie Delaney!"

"Tee, hee, hee. You said a naughty word. Little girls who say naughty words like that one have to stay locked in the closet a little longer."

"You let me out right this instant, young man!"

The angrier Karen gets, the more Charlie enjoys it. He laughs louder every time Karen demands to be let out.

Karen begins to pound on the door more and more. "Let me out of this damn closet, right now!"

"You said that naughty word again. You will have to stay in there a little longer. Tee, hee, hee."

"You stop laughing like that! You know I hate to hear that 'tee, hee, hee'! Let me out! Let me out! Let me out!"

Charlie continues to laugh, which in turn makes Karen even more furious. Charlie then gets an idea. He runs quietly to the front door then out to Karen's car. He pops the hood up and removes the distributor cap. He removes the rotor button and then pulls down the hood. He takes the small device back into the house.

He listens for about five more minutes as Karen screams for him to let her out. He lies down on the couch and laughs as she yells.

Karen, hearing his laughter, grows angrier and yells louder. After about ten minutes locked in the closet, Karen gets very quiet.

Charlie, not hearing anything, walks over to the closet and says, "Hey, are you still in there?" He gets no response. "Hello in there! You ain't no fun if you don't make any noise." Charlie once again hears no sound. He decides to open the door and let his angry young girlfriend out. Charlie gently opens the door and peeps inside. Karen is sitting on the floor. Her angry face looks up at Charlie as he opens the door all the way. She is silent.

"Okay, meanness, I guess I will let you out now. You seem to be tamed now. Come on out."

Karen, hearing this, decides not to follow his orders. She persists in pouting, and remains sitting on the floor in the closet, but with the door open.

Charlie, not knowing how she would react, simply walks over to the couch and sits down.

He doesn't say anything for a few moments, but then says, "You can come on out now, Cubby. Your punishment is over for today."

Karen, hearing this, decides to stay just where she is. The house becomes quiet and still, each waiting for the other to make the first move.

After about five minutes of sitting in the closet with the door open, Karen finally sticks her head out.

Charlie, seeing this, erupts with laughter.

Karen jumps up and runs over to the couch.

"You … you … you are the meanest man I have ever known. I can't believe you did that."

Charlie hears that and bursts out laughing again. He lies down on the couch in an uncontrollable fit of laughter.

He gets enough control of himself to say, "Don't beat me up. Don't beat me up." Charlie then laughs a little more before saying, "You sat locked in that closet for ten minutes because you were a bad girl, and then you realized that the punishment wasn't adequate enough, so you decided on your own to remain another five minutes. Now you're telling me you don't believe it. I sure do."

Charlie goes back to his laughing fit as Karen gets red with anger.

Karen listens to the laughter for a few seconds and then loudly says, "You are horrible! You are mean! You are terrible!"

Charlie, with tears in his eyes from laughing, replies back, "No. I'm Charlie. Tee, hee, hee. You know what you are?"

Karen pauses for a moment. "What?"

Charlie smiles and says, "You're peeved. Ha, ha, ha!"

"I am not! I am not peeved!

"You're peeved."

"I'm not peeved!"

"You're peeved, you're peeved."

"I am not peeved, so quit saying that!"

"You're peeved. You're peeved. You're peeved."

"I ain't peeved, Charlie Delaney!"

"Yes, you are. You're peeved. Tee, hee, hee!"

"I ain't peeved, and stop making that laugh."

Charlie stares at Karen and says, "There is no such word as *ain't,* Miss Peeved."

Karen looks at Charlie, peeved, and says in a loud voice, "I am not peeved, and you'd better not say that word anymore."

Charlie, realizing she has reached her highest tolerance point, decides not to push her anymore. He just looks at her, and snickers. And then, without warning, he makes that high-pitched laugh of his once more: "Tee, hee, hee!"

Karen puts her hands on her hips and gives Charlie a mean stare. "Oh! You know I hate that laugh."

"If you hate it, why do you use it so much?"

Karen sputters, "You locked me in that closet like a … a … caged animal. What do you have to say for yourself?"

Charlie, still laughing, stops momentary to say, "When a little girl misbehaves, her place is in the closet." Charlie roars with laughter once again.

Karen thinks about this quietly while she studies Charlie, fury burning in her eyes.

She waits until she has Charlie's attention and then says, "You don't sound like you're sorry one bit. You aren't repentant of your sin at all, are you Charlie?"

Charlie, gazing at Karen's tender eyes, says in a clear voice, "No." Charlie then begins hitting the floor while he continues to laugh.

Karen, having heard enough, says, "You either apologize to me right now, or I'm leaving! And if I leave, I ain't—that's right, *ain't*—going to the dinner theater place with you tonight. How do you like those potatoes, Mr. Happy?"

Charlie stops laughing only to say, "I usually like my potatoes fried, but sometimes I like them mashed, with just a little bit of gravy. How do you like your closets, large or small?" Charlie roars with laughter.

Karen turns and walks toward the door. She turns quickly so Charlie won't see her laugh also.

Just as she gets close to the door, Charlie calls out, "Hey, Cubby, come here. Come on, Cubby, will you please come back over here?"

Karen slowly walks back over to the couch, and Charlie says, "You ain't leaving, are you?"

"I thought you said there is no such word as *ain't.*"

"There isn't, I just thought since you have stolen my laugh so many times I could steal your ain't."

Karen stands there impatiently as Charlie refuses to apologize.

"Well?"

"Well, what?"

"Well, are you going to apologize?"

Charlie plainly says, "No."

"Then what did you call me over here for?"

"Since you were leaving, I was just wondering if you would do something for me."

Karen, looking very irritated, says, "What?"

"I was just wondering if you would get me a bottle of soda out of the refrigerator. I sure have developed a powerful thirst with all this laughing, and since you are closer to the kitchen than I am, I thought you wouldn't mind getting that for me."

Karen blows her stack. "You … you … you have a lot of nerve asking me that! Sure! Sure, if that's what you want, then let me get you one right now!"

Karen runs into the kitchen and comes out with a bottle of soda. She throws the bottle at Charlie, who just so happens to catch it.

Charlie gives Karen a stern look. "Hey! You ought to be ashamed of yourself! You could have made a mess."

Charlie looks around the living room and says, "I mean, you could have made another mess."

He goes back to laughing as Karen heads for the door. This time, Charlie lets her leave. Just as soon as Charlie hears the door slam, he jumps up and goes next to the window. He watches Karen storm to her car and get in. He puts his hand over his mouth as he snickers. He watches as Karen gets in and puts her key in the ignition. She turns it, but her car won't start. She tries again and again. It turns over, but it just doesn't seem to start. She keeps trying and then looks up at the house. Charlie stands near the window, his face full of laughter. When he sees that she is looking at him, he quickly moves away from the window.

Karen, realizing what he has done, says out loud, "That shit ass! That shit ass! He sabotaged my car; that's why he never apologized to me. I am going to kill him. Ooh! That man! Ooh!"

Karen quickly gets out of her car and walks right back up to the house. She opens the door and walks inside. She finds Charlie lying on the couch nonchalantly, pretending to be reading a newspaper. She walks over to him, but he pretends that he doesn't know she is there. She then takes the newspaper away and stares at him with a mean look. Charlie doesn't say a word.

Karen calmly and softly asks, "Okay, Charlie, what did you do to my car?"

Charlie erupts into another laughing fit! It looks like he is having a convulsion. He tries to get control of himself as he cries out, "I just knew you were going to ask that." He starts hitting the floor hard, laughing uncontrollably.

Karen listens to only a few seconds of his uncontrollable fit, and then she hits the roof. Her voice filled with fury, she says, "You are awful! How could you be so mean? You are the meanest man I have ever met. You are impossible!"

Charlie stops laughing as he says, "The only thing impossible is your car—impossible to start, that is. Tee, hee, hee."

With that, Karen begins to cry. "You have locked me in a closet, you have torn up my car, and now you're making fun of me. The only thing you haven't done is beat me up, and I wish you had done that instead of laughing at me."

Not knowing where to turn or what to do, Karen decides to run upstairs. She runs into Charlie's bedroom and collapses on the bed, crying away.

Charlie hears the sad sounds of her crying sounds and realizes that his happy time of fun and games has come to an end. He thinks about running up there that instant but decides not to. Hearing her cry is bad enough; he doesn't want to see her sad, teary eyes.

Instead, he decides to put back the furniture. As Charlie puts back the last piece of furniture in its original place, he feels content that his house is finally back in order. It takes him thirty minutes to finish the task. He gets a drink from the kitchen, and then he runs out to Karen's car and easily puts the rotor button back on. He eagerly walks back into the house but slowly walks up the steps to his bedroom.

Karen lies on Charlie's bed, growing very impatient at how long it is taking Charlie to come up and apologize. She continues to lie there, sad but not too hurt. Her pride has been stepped on, so the only thing that will make her feel better is Charlie's apology. She lies there, still and quiet, and soon hears Charlie's footsteps in the hallway.

Charlie enters the room.

Karen rolls over to make sure it's Charlie, and she then rolls back to face the opposite direction.

Charlie softly says, "Hey, there. Is my little Cubby still angry with me?"

Karen doesn't respond.

Charlie lies down next to her and begins to rub her back gently.

"I guess I have been a bad boy today, haven't I?"

Karen remains silent.

"You still mad at me, Cubby?"

Finally, Karen softly says, "Yes." After a pause, she adds, "Now that you have torn up my car, I guess I am just a prisoner here."

"Yeah, I guess you are. My prisoner of love."

Charlie continues to rub Karen's back gently, feeling a sense of tenderness and warmth toward her. By allowing him to rub her back, Karen gives Charlie the feeling of being wanted and needed.

After a few moments, Charlie says, "You have every right to be mad at me, Cubby. Locking you in that closet was the meanest thing I have ever done. I feel bad about it now. I'm sorry."

Karen rolls over, her face still wet with tears, and says, "That's all I wanted to hear you say, Charlie."

Karen kisses Charlie tenderly, and her wet nose rubs up against his cheek. They kiss tenderly and lovingly, but not passionately; just a lot of pecking on each other's lips and faces. Kissing multiple times, but only for short periods, they lightly touch each other's faces.

"Aren't you forgetting something, Charlie?"

"What?"

"Aren't you going to apologize for tearing up my car?"

"I didn't tear up your car; I only temporarily dismembered it. It works now."

"Aren't you sorry for tearing it up, though?"

"I didn't tear it up, and no, I am not sorry."

"Then stop kissing me."

"Why? If I had not torn up your car, you wouldn't be here, kissing me. You would be driving down the road somewhere in an angry fit. So aren't you glad I tore it up?"

Karen thinks about this for a moment and then says, "Go out there and tear it up again."

Charlie gazes at Karen's radiant eyes.

They delicately kiss each other for several more minutes, and then it starts to get passionate.

After staring into her soft blue eyes for a while longer, Charlie tells Karen, "Cubby, I hate to run you off, but I have to get ready for tonight. I have to take a shower and put on my suit."

Karen gives Charlie a heavenly smile; her face has a magical glow.

"Go ahead, Charlie," she says "I'll wait here."

Charlie grins as he says, "Oh no! You don't think I am going take a shower while you are loose in my house, do you?"

"What's the matter, Charlie? You don't think I would try to peep at you while you were naked in the shower, do you? Tee, hee, hee!"

"I'm not worried about that. I'm worried you might try to destroy my living room again."

"What do you mean, 'again,' Charlie?"

"Oh … didn't I tell you? I went ahead and put everything back as it was."

Hearing this, Karen becomes agitated. "What? You did what!"

Giving her a surprised look, Charlie says, "I put all that furniture back in its original place. It finally looks like home again."

"All that hard work I did was for nothing. Damn! … Ain't life a bitch?"

Karen gets up and exits the bedroom in silence. She goes downstairs, gets in her car, and drives home, without even kissing Charlie good-bye.

Charlie just scratches his head in wonderment at her reaction. "I can't believe that girl sometimes," he says aloud. "She actually thought she was doing me a favor. Women try so hard to please a man, but when their intentions were really more to please themselves, they only wind up feeling confused and disappointed."

Charlie showers, puts on his suit, and drives over to Karen's house to pick her up for their date. He pulls into the driveway, gets out of his truck, walks to the front door, and rings the bell.

Mrs. Thomas answers the door and invites Charlie in. He kisses her on the cheek and says hello.

Karen, standing nearby, says, "Hey, buster, why is it you always kiss mama first when you first get here?"

"Because she answers the door, I guess."

Charlie gazes at his beautiful damsel. Karen is wearing a fancy silky pink dress. She has her hair looking really glamorous and diamond earrings dangle from her ears, highlighting her entire face. She smiles at Charlie now that she has got his attention.

"Wow! Wow!" Charlie says, and then he kisses Mrs. Thomas on the cheek once more.

Karen gives Charlie a very curious look. "Hey, why did you kiss her? I'm your date."

"I kissed her because she is the woman who brought you into this world; if it wasn't for her I wouldn't have ever met the most beautiful girl in the world." Charlie reaches over and gently kisses Mrs. Thomas again on the cheek for the third time. His face is full of awe. His intoxication with Karen's beauty fills the room with a spectacular splendor of excitement and wonder.

After they say good night to Mrs. Thomas, Charlie takes Karen's hand as they walk to his truck.

When he opens the door for her, she says, "Charlie, Why don't we take my car? Your truck doesn't seem to fit the occasion."

"Anything you say, my love. Anything you say. I can't disagree with you on anything tonight. You are so beautiful in that dress that you have captivated me completely."

Karen turns her head sideways, and then she says, "Well … in that case, after we get back from the dinner theater tonight, what do you say we go over to your house and move the furniture back! Tee, hee, hee."

Charlie gives Karen a blank look, and she says, "I'm only kidding, Charlie. I am only kidding."

Charlie and Karen get into Karen's shiny red Mustang, and he drives to the New York Dinner Theater. They have a wonderful dinner and then watch a very funny comedy.

When Charlie drives Karen home, she tells him that this has been the most wonderful day and night of her entire life. Her face glows with happiness. Charlie walks her up to the front door and gives her a respectable good-night kiss. Charlie waves good-bye, and Karen does likewise.

Karen walks into her house, filled with the most wonderful feeling she has ever had in her life. She thinks about Charlie all night, experiencing the glorious feeling of being young, innocent, and in love for the first time.

As the weeks go by, Charlie and Karen's most fun date is playing putt-putt. Charlie always wins. Karen gets more enjoyment from trying to get Charlie to mess up while he is putting; she doesn't really care about the score. She is always picking and teasing him right before he putts the ball. Charlie usually does fairly well, but Karen plays lousy. She is too busy picking on Charlie to concentrate on her game. Sometimes she gets frustrated when she misses an easy putt. A few times, she has picked up the ball in anger and thrown it away. Charlie always runs after it and brings it back. He kindly cheers up his aggravated little sweetheart. Karen loves the attention Charlie gives her. This is one of the main elements of their happy relationship: the kindness and support he gives her when certain circumstances arise, always there to say a kind word. In almost every game Charlie and Karen play, she gets upset because of some simple mistake she makes, but Charlie is always there to make her smile once again. This type of caring is the magnetic field that brings Charlie and Karen ever closer together. They always end the game of putt-putt with a trip to McDonald's, where they each have a vanilla milk shake. Always.

McDonald's also becomes a routine place to go when Karen is upset. The atmosphere there gives Charlie a pleasant mood to be in when he talks to her in that special way. He tells her those things a girl likes to hear when she is down. He always compliments how pretty she is and makes a point of telling her how glad he is that she is his girlfriend. He makes her feel important and loved. She really enjoys these moments. She really loves the special attention he gives her when she has acted quite childish. They never really fight with each other, but they do tend to get mad once in a while because of what one may have said or done. Neither one of them can stay mad at the other for very long, though. The tender love they have for each other adds to their harmony, and it develops into a very strong and meaningful part of their relationship. Their simple dates and innocent, pure conversations give the foundation of their loving relationship a splendor of a rare quality.

One Friday afternoon, Charlie and Karen happen to be walking around the local shopping mall. Karen sees the pet store on the top floor, so she pulls Charlie by the hand, and off they go. Karen's innocent face is full of anticipation and excitement. She is a very happy girl. Charlie sees this happiness rub off on him. He doesn't know when he has ever been so happy, and neither does Karen. As Karen pulls Charlie along, in her fun-filled way, they finally arrive at the pet store. Charlie and Karen hold hands while they look over all the different animals there. They watch the tropical fish swimming in the aquarium, they listen to the talking parrots, they laugh at the hamsters running in their cages, and they delight in all the adorable creatures. Karen is soon compelled to walk over to where the cute little puppies are.

Karen spots a cocker spaniel looking at her.

She points at it and then, her voice filled with tenderness and emotion, she says, "Charlie, just look at that poor innocent little dog in that terrible cage."

Just then, someone from the store walks up and says, "Would you like for me to take her out of that cage so you can hold her?"

Karen looks at the store clerk, turns to Charlie, looks back at the clerk, and says, "Yes, would you, please?"

The clerk takes the keys out, goes around to unlock the cage, and retrieves the little puppy dog, handing the pup to Karen.

Karen displays great joy and happiness while she plays with the little pup.

Charlie gets the feeling that if he doesn't get that puppy off her mind, they will be taking it home with them.

Karen impulsively says, "Charlie, will you buy this cute little dog for me? Please!"

Charlie shakes his head as he smiles. "Karen, there is a lot of responsibility in taking care of this little mutt. I mean, puppy."

Karen, surprised to hear him say this, says, "That was a terrible thing to say to this sweet little dog. You ought to be ashamed of yourself, Charlie Delaney."

"Karen, you can't keep it in the house all the time. You'd need to get a doghouse, plus it will need to go to the vet for its shots—"

The store clerk, listening in, interrupts. "She has already had all of her shots."

Charlie looks surprised, and Karen halfheartedly sticks out her tongue at him.

"Well, what about your mother? You need to ask her if it will be all right."

This strikes home with Karen. She would never do anything unless she asked her mother first.

Charlie takes the dog from Karen and hands it back to the clerk.

Karen gives Charlie a very disappointed look.

Charlie kisses her forehead and then says, "I promise you, Karen, before your birthday comes in September, I will buy you a puppy. I promise."

"I want *that* puppy. That one is the one I want."

Charlie kindly says, "That's the first one you saw, Karen. You didn't give the other puppies a chance. You shouldn't be so impulsive. Take your time, look things over, think about it for a while. You may find one you like even better."

This doesn't influence Karen's decision in the least. Charlie takes her by the hand as they leave the pet store. Karen looks back one last time, a sad expression on her face. She looks as if she is leaving her best friend.

When they get home, Karen doesn't waste any time asking her mother if it would be all right if she got a puppy.

Mrs. Thomas says she doesn't mind, as long as Karen takes care of it and it doesn't shed hair all over the furniture.

Hearing this, Karen says, "Come on, Charlie! Let's go back to the mall and buy Gypsy."

Confused, Charlie asks, "Gypsy? Who is Gypsy?"

Karen turns her head sideways and gives Charlie an intriguing look. "Gypsy is the name of that cocker spaniel at the pet store. You know, my little dog."

Charlie has made himself comfortable on the couch. "*Your* little dog? She isn't yours, Karen."

"Mama said it would be all right, and you promised me that you would buy me a puppy before my next birthday. Didn't you say that, Charlie?"

Charlie turns his stunned face toward Mrs. Thomas, who glares at him as if to say, "If you promised her, then you'd better fulfill that promise." So Charlie says, "I'll tell you what, Cubby, tomorrow is Saturday, so if you still want that dog tomorrow, we will go down there, and I will buy it for you."

Karen jumps up and down. "Yippee! Yippee! I love you, Charlie Delaney! I love you! I love you! I love you!"

Karen throws her arms around Charlie's neck, as if he had just proposed to her. With great enthusiasm, she kisses him all over his face.

Mrs. Thomas doesn't know what to think. She hasn't seen Karen this happy in a long time.

Charlie just sits there, enjoying Karen's love and affection.

For the rest of the evening, Karen sits on Charlie's lap, hugging and kissing her knight in shining armor.

The next day, Charlie arrives at Karen's house at just about noon.

Karen, waiting eagerly at the window and hoping to see his truck pull up, turns to her mother as soon as she sees it. "Bye, mama. Charlie's here." She doesn't wait for an answer; she just runs out the door to Charlie's truck.

Charlie has just gotten out when Karen rushes up to him, saying, "Where are you going?"

"I thought I would come in, kiss Ma on the cheek, and say hello to her, just like I always do."

Karen steps closer to Charlie and sticks out her cheek. "Go ahead and kiss me instead."

Charlie grins as he kisses her cheek.

Karen excitedly says, "Hurry up! Let's go!"

She runs over to the passenger side of his truck, opens the door, and gets in.

Charlie continues to grin, amused by her excitement. He gets in, starts the truck, pulls out of the driveway, and heads toward the mall. Charlie parks the truck in one of the spaces.

Karen gets out, runs around the front of the truck, and grabs Charlie's hand as he gets out. Her face is excited as she smiles gloriously at him. "Come on, Charlie! Let's go!"

Karen, still holding Charlie's hand, heads directly to the pet shop. She releases his hand as she walks over to where the puppies are. Karen looks with great expectation for her little friend, but … her little dog isn't in any of the cages. A few tears begin to trickle out of Karen's eyes.

Charlie, seeing this, asks one of the store clerks, "Excuse me, where is the little yellow cocker spaniel you had here yesterday?"

"Just a minute, sir, and I will go see," the store clerk says, walking back behind the counter and looking at a chart.

Charlie tries to comfort Karen while they wait.

Charlie says softly, "Hey, Cubby, don't worry; they probably just took her in the back to give her a bath."

Karen doesn't say anything.

Charlie points to another cocker spaniel. "Hey, look at that one: she has red hair like yours! If the yellow one is gone, I'll buy you the red one."

"I don't want a red one or a blue one or a purple one. I only want Gypsy."

Charlie puts his arm around Karen as the store clerk approaches them

With a look of disappointment, he says, "I'm sorry, but that pup was sold just last night."

Charlie says, "But we were only here yesterday afternoon!"

"The time of sale was nine o'clock, sir. The lady who bought the pup took her right home. I am truly sorry. We do have another cocker spaniel, a red one, would you like for me to—"

Karen interrupts. "We won't be interested in any other dog."

Seeing that Karen is disappointed, Charlie says, "Come on, Karen, pick out another puppy. Look at the one with all those wrinkles, and look at that one over there …"

Charlie's voice trails off as Karen grabs his hand and leads him out of the store.

She looks up at Charlie and sternly says, "I don't want any other dog. Will you please just take me home?"

Charlie doesn't argue. He walks her out to the truck and takes her home.

As they drive along, Karen begins to cry. Soon she is sobbing uncontrollably.

Charlie decides to take her to McDonald's for a vanilla milk shake. Seeing the Golden Arches, he says, "Boy! I sure could go for a vanilla milk shake." He looks over at Karen, who doesn't respond to Charlie's remark.

Charlie pulls his truck to the drive-through.

As they wait, Charlie kindly asks, "Would you like to have one, Cubby?"

Karen doesn't speak; she just shakes her head. Her crying has calmed down a little since Charlie stopped at the drive-through.

Charlie rolls down his window to place the order. "I will take two vanilla milk shakes, please; and also, a yellow cocker spaniel named Gypsy."

Karen looks at Charlie as if he's crazy. Her face is smiling, though; just what Charlie wanted to see.

The voice on the drive-through says, "What! What did you order, sir?"

"I'll just have two vanilla milk shakes, please."

Charlie doesn't wait to hear a response. He drives up, pays for the milk shakes, takes the order, and pulls into one of the parking spots. Charlie then sits back, sucking away on one of the milk shakes; the other one he keeps between his legs.

Karen looks at him, wondering why he hasn't offered her one of the milk shakes. She begins to smile a little bit as Charlie deliberately makes that sucking sound to stir her appetite for the milk shake.

With a robust voice, Charlie says, "Man! That sure is good. Yum-yum!"

Charlie peeps over at Karen, who softly asks, "Aren't you going to offer me that other milk shake, Charlie?"

"Oh, I thought you didn't want one."

Karen, not getting the milk shake, sternly replies, "Well … if that's the way you want to be, you can just keep it."

"Okay. Tee, hee, hee."

Karen, wanting that milk shake more than ever, now boldly cries, "Give me that damn milk shake, right now!"

Charlie picks it up and hands it over to her, moving it away when she tries to grasp it. After a moment, he lets her take it.

Karen sweetly and softly says, "Thank you, Charlie.

She face smiles lovingly as Charlie reaches over and gently kisses her soft, innocent lips.

Taking Karen's hand, Charlie says tenderly, "Cubby, there is something I want to say to you."

Placing the straw to her lips, Karen listens as Charlie looks at her.

"Cubby, there are a lot of things in this world you are going to want. You are going to want them an awful lot; but, Cubby, you aren't going to get everything you want in this world. Life isn't always going to be nice. You are young and haven't experienced things like I have. You will be faced with a lot of adversity as life goes on, and when something happens that you don't like, you can't just run in a corner somewhere and cry about it. Feeling sorry for yourself will only make matters worse."

Karen gazes at Charlie while he talks. Her complete attention is focused on Charlie as she slowly sucks on her milk shake.

Charlie tenderly looks into her eyes and then continues. "I know you wanted that specific puppy dog. She had her own unique personality. You looked at her not just as another dog, but as an individual. Another dog would not have been the same dog. You didn't want just a dog, you wanted the one you fell in love with."

Karen smiles, moves her mouth from the straw, and bites her lower lip. Her tender eyes well with tears, as her emotions are completely controlled by Charlie's words.

Charlie gently smiles when he sees the delicate reaction on her face. "I just want to remind you, sweetheart, that life isn't always going to be nice and pleasant. You have to learn how to deal with the not-so-nice things too. You need to learn to accept things a little better. Once you accept things as they are, then you can deal with them; that way, you'll be ready to cope better the next time. There are going to be other things you will want in your life, more so than just a little puppy. There will be things your heart will ache to have—and I mean ache badly—but you won't get them. You must learn to be able to handle disappointment, because life is full of disappointment."

Charlie sees Karen's face get sad again, so he decides to tell her a joke to bring her spirits up a little bit.

"Cubby, have I ever told you the joke about the little girl who went to a pet store?"

Karen smiles briefly and then says, "No, Charlie."

"Well, let me tell it to you. This little girl walks into a pet shop, and she sees big green parrot in a cage. The little girl walks up to the parrot, and the parrot says, 'Aarrgghh, Polly wants a cracker. Then you can take me home.' The little girl gets real excited when she hears the parrot talk. She runs over to the pet-store owner and says, 'Mister, how much is that talking parrot? I want to buy him.' The man looks down at the little girl and says, "That parrot can't talk, little girl. I could let you have him for ten dollars if you still want to buy him.'"

With great amusement, Karen listens to Charlie as she sucks on her milk shake.

Charlie continues. "Well, the little girl runs home and tells her mama. 'Mama! Mama! Come with me to the pet store. I found this talking parrot, and the man running the store said I could buy him for only ten dollars!' So the little girl and her mother hurry down to the pet store. The little girl runs up to the parrot and says, 'Talk for me, Mr. Parrot, like the way you did a while ago.' Well, the parrot just sits there and doesn't say anything. The little girl, her mother, and the pet-store owner listen carefully, but the parrot just looks at them and says nothing. The pet-store owner walks away and disappears into the back of the store. The little girl's mother says, 'That parrot isn't going talk. Come on, let's go home.' The little girl's mother walks out of the store. The little girl looks up at the parrot and says, 'Thanks a whole lot, Mr. Parrot. I don't understand why you didn't talk!' The parrot looks down at the little girl and says, 'Aarrgghh, no cracker, no take me home! Aarrgghh.'"

Karen pulls the straw out of her mouth, and laughs.

Charlie gazes at her, smiling at the sound of her heavenly laugh, and says, "Now that's what I have been waiting for: to see and hear my beautiful girlfriend smiling and laughing again. Oh my, what a beautiful sight that is!"

Karen's eyes glow with joy, twinkling at Charlie. She leans over and kisses him sweetly. This ignites a spark in Charlie, who throws his milk shake out the window and then hugs his happy redhead. Charlie covers her mouth with his as they share a sensational loving moment.

Karen's disappointment has been altered into a happy event. She loves Charlie more now than she has ever in the past. He gazes into her eyes as she looks at him with love and admiration.

Charlie's soft words reach Karen's sensitive ears. "Cubby, every time life deals you a bad hand, I want to be there to dry your tears and bring a smile to your lips. I want to make you happy as much as I possibly can."

Karen turns her head sideways and smiles at Charlie, a special aura glowing from her sweet, innocent face. She looks him in the eye and says, "Oh, Charlie! I love you. I love you so much."

"I love you too, Cubby. I really do. I love you more than I have ever loved anyone."

Charlie kisses Karen passionately. He presses her lips apart and slides his tongue into her mouth. Charlie flicks his tongue all around Karen's mouth as she slowly moves her hands around his neck. The kiss becomes more and more passionate. The passion grows stronger as Charlie presses Karen's head closer to his. And for the first time, Karen begins to move her tongue around Charlie's mouth. Her heart begins to feel the powerful emotion of lust. She feels her blood boil as the burning desire fills her teenage body. Charlie breaks the passionate kiss, and gently rubs her arms and shoulders. Karen puts her head on Charlie's chest. She begins to caress Charlie's chest and stomach. They both sit quietly for a few minutes until Charlie breaks the silence.

"You know something, Cubby?"

"What?"

"I never told anyone this, but …" Charlie's voice trails off.

In a state of total tranquility, Karen listens to Charlie, and this encourages him to continue.

"When I was a little boy, I found a little dog near my house. I played with him all day long. I fell in love with that little dog."

Karen looks up at Charlie, continuing to listen wordlessly.

"I wanted that dog more than anything in the world. I asked my parents if I could keep him. They took one look at him, and decided no. He wasn't a beautiful dog. He was just a mutt. He was short and hairy, but that dog loved me. I guess that's why I wanted him so much. He played with me as if he understood what I was saying to him."

"Why didn't your mama and daddy let you keep him?"

"I don't know. I guess they just didn't understand how I felt about him. I really don't know. They just said that I couldn't keep him. The next day, when I got off the school bus, he was gone. I was so upset. I was mad at both of my parents for weeks. I sure did miss that little dog. I got really depressed after that."

Karen reaches over and picks up her milk shake. She sucks on it for a few seconds and then raises the straw to Charlie.

He takes a good slurp. "Man! That sure is good. It's even better coming from your cup."

Karen sticks out her lips, and Charlie gives her a quick peck.

"I know it may sound silly, but I have been depressed ever since then. I don't know why. I loved that innocent little dog, and he loved me, just as I was. But then, my parents took him away from me. That was the first little disaster I had to go through in life. A little dog will capture your heart more than anything … Well, except maybe a red-haired, blue-eyed virgin."

Karen's eyes light up with youthful glee. She finishes her milk shake, looks at Charlie, and says, "Do you want the rest?"

Charlie takes the empty cup and says, "Hey, this cup is empty."

Karen wraps her arms around Charlie and giggles. She then looks into his loving eyes and says, "Oh well … another one of life's little disappointments."

Charlie hugs her in a warm loving hold. Karen takes the empty cup from Charlie and tosses it out the window effortlessly.

She whispers to Charlie, "Charlie, I am so glad you're my boyfriend. I am so glad you're here with me right now."

Charlie cuddles Karen in his masculine arms and says, "I am so glad you are my girlfriend, Cubby. I am glad you are here too."

After a few more minutes of some tender cuddling, Charlie starts up his truck and drives back to Karen's house. As he drives, Karen snuggles up to him as close as she can. The two enjoy the drive home tremendously.

Karen still thinks about the little dog she wanted, but she accepts that she will never get that particular pup. She is content just to have Charlie beside her. As they drive along, Karen begins to think about making love to Charlie. Her mind goes wild as she fantasizes about Charlie. In the mood she is in now, Charlie could easily take her virginity away, but when Charlie pulls his truck into Karen's driveway, the erotic dream diminishes.

Charlie walks his love up the front steps, through the door, and into the house.

Mrs. Thomas is in the living room, eagerly awaiting the new arrival.

When Charlie and Karen walk in, empty-handed, Mrs. Thomas curiously asks, "So where's the cocker spaniel? Didn't you get it?"

Karen's face becomes sad again as she says, "No, mama. She was sold last night to someone else."

Mrs. Thomas, hearing this, becomes deeply disappointed. She looks at Karen with great concern, knowing her daughter doesn't handle things like this very well.

Mrs. Thomas looks over at Charlie. "Didn't they have any other dog that she liked?"

Charlie just shrugs and says, "There was a cute red cocker spaniel there. I offered to buy it for her, but she had her heart set on the yellow one. I told her I would buy her any dog she wanted, but she didn't want any of the others. Her mind was made up; she didn't want a substitute."

Karen, trying to change the subject, says, "There is no need to go on about this anymore. What's done is done. I'm hungry. Anybody want a sandwich?"

Charlie quickly says, "Yeah, I do."

Mrs. Thomas, bewildered by Karen's controlled behavior, says, "I'll help you, dear."

Just as Mrs. Thomas gets up, Karen says, "No, mama. You stay in here and entertain Charlie. I will fix them."

Karen leaves the room to go fix the sandwiches.

Mrs. Thomas walks over and sits down next to Charlie. She softly says, "Charlie, I don't know what you said to Karen, but I just want to thank you." She leans over and kisses Charlie on his cheek.

Charlie blushes a little as he says, "Thank you! That's almost as good as a vanilla milk shake."

Mrs. Thomas gazes at Charlie with fascination and says, "Charlie, I just want you to know something. Karen has never handled disappointment very well. I thought she would be crying hysterically by now. She thinks life is always going to be wonderful and pleasant. When she doesn't get her way, she gets extremely upset, and I mean *extremely upset*."

Charlie takes Mrs. Thomas's hand as she continues. "One time, when she was just a child, we were in a store. Karen was probably around five years old, and there was something she wanted. I told her she couldn't have it. Well, let me tell you something Charlie, she threw a fit you wouldn't believe! She started to cry like the end of the world was coming. She rolled around on the floor, hollering and screaming, 'Mama! Mama! Buy it for me! Buy it for me!' I could not get control of her, even if my life depended on it. I didn't have a husband to give me any moral support in raising her. So after about ten minutes of trying to stand my ground, I finally gave in. I said, 'All right, Karen, I will buy it for you.'"

Charlie laughs a little, and Mrs. Thomas continues. "And do you know what she said after I gave in to her?"

"What?"

"Mind you, we are talking about a five-year-old girl. She looked up at me and said, 'It's about time! Why didn't you decide that before I started crying?' Charlie, I could have slapped her, but I didn't."

Charlie laughs even louder, holding Mrs. Thomas's hand in both of his.

Listening to Charlie's laughter makes Mrs. Thomas laugh also. Looking at Charlie with great admiration, she says, "Since Karen is my only child, I gave into her almost all the time—I still do. I admit it: I have spoiled her rotten. She has always gotten her way. Now that she is growing up, she is going to find out that life isn't always going to let her get her way."

"That's about what I told her, Ma."

Mrs. Thomas looks at Charlie, a twinkle of gratitude shining in her eyes, and she says, "Charlie, I am glad Karen has found you. I believe you will be good for her. She is a very sensitive girl. She is a very delicate girl. But she has got an atrocious temper."

"Ma, you don't have to tell me that. I have seen Karen's temper get riled up, so I know what you mean."

"Tell me, Charlie, what do you do when she gets like that?"

Charlie smiles gladly as he says, "Ma, the best way to handle her when she gets like that is to laugh at her. This burns up her. The angrier she gets, the more I laugh. I do this until she starts to pout. She doesn't like it when I laugh at her, and it may be mean, but it does make her pout. She is cute when she pouts. When she starts to pout, then I know I have won. Tee, hee, hee."

"I'll have to try that sometime, Charlie."

"Ma, if you do, try to make this laugh: tee, hee, hee."

"I don't know if I can, Charlie, but I will try. Tee, hee, hee."

Charlie says, "That was good, Ma. Anytime Karen throws a fit and you don't know what to do, laugh at her in just that way. It drives her crazy. It really does."

Just as Charlie finishes his statement, Karen comes walking into the room, carrying a platter of sandwiches. She notices that Charlie is holding her mother's hand.

After she hears her mother try to laugh like Charlie, Karen says, "Okay. What are you two talking about?"

Mrs. Thomas answers, "We are talking about you, dear."

Charlie adds, "I was just teaching Ma to make that laugh you like so well."

Karen puts her hands on her waist and glares down at Charlie. "Now, Charlie, you know I don't like that laugh."

"She really does, Ma. She likes it so much that she even tries to make it."

"Is that all you two were talking about?"

Mrs. Thomas smiles a motherly smile at her daughter as she replies, "We were just talking about what you were like when you were a little girl."

Charlie says, "That could mean from the day you were born until this very moment."

Karen, giving Charlie a mean look, says, "That wasn't very nice, Charlie."

"I know. I'm sorry, Karen."

Charlie glances over at Mrs. Thomas, and then he says, "Do you want to tell her, or do you want me to tell her?"

"Tell me what?"

Charlie, with a playful expression on his face, says, "We were just trying to find the words to tell you."

Karen looks curiously at Charlie as she says, "Find the words? What words, Charlie?"

Charlie, still holding Mrs. Thomas's hand, whispers in her ear.

He then turns toward Karen, showing her a serious look. "Karen, I hope you are mature enough to hear this … Ma and I are running off together. Our plane leaves in about an hour. I hope you can overcome the loss of both of us. I hope—I mean, we hope—you can bear the sadness and loneliness of our leaving. Tee, hee, hee."

Karen, showing a wry smile, says, "Very funny, Charlie, very funny. If you are trying to make me jealous, you are wasting your time. It's kinda hard to make me jealous of my own mama."

Karen returns to the kitchen and quickly comes back out with three soft drinks.

With a stern look at both of them, Karen says, "Here, put your hands on one of these."

"Hey, Ma, look! She is jealous! See, I told you! She is jealous."

Mrs. Thomas laughs merrily, amused by Charlie's words.

Karen says in a determined voice, "I ain't jealous. Don't be ridiculous, Charlie."

Karen looks over at her mother and says, "Mama, will you go into the kitchen and get the napkins?"

"Sure, dear, sure."

Mrs. Thomas gets up and walks into the kitchen. Just as she does, Karen runs over and sits down beside Charlie, right where Mrs. Thomas was sitting.

When Mrs. Thomas comes out of the kitchen, she says, "Hey, young lady, that's my seat."

"I'm sorry, mama, but this seat is taken by Charlie's girlfriend. You'll just have to find another one."

Charlie and Mrs. Thomas laugh as Karen takes a bite of her sandwich. Karen looks at both of them, a nonchalant expression on her face.

Charlie and Karen sit on the couch as they watch Mrs. Thomas walk away. She disappears to her bedroom in a very quiet way.

Sensing something a little off about Mrs. Thomas, Charlie says, "Karen, why doesn't your mother date? She doesn't really even go places or do other things. She kinda stays in her room a whole lot. How come?"

Karen softly says, "Charlie, I'm not supposed to tell anyone about this, but … Promise me you won't tell mama. You have to promise me."

"Sure, Cubby, I promise."

"Well … you see, Charlie, ever since my daddy died in Vietnam, mama has had a problem with her heart."

Charlie gives Karen a very serious look.

"It's nothing too bad, Charlie. The doctor just keeps telling her to take it easy and not to do anything stressful. That's why she only works at the florist a few days a week."

Charlie feels sadness in his heart when he hears this.

"You say she has had this problem since your father died in Vietnam?" he says.

"Yes, Charlie, that's how long she has been taking the medicine."

"You mean, Ma has to take pills for it?"

"Yes, Charlie, but don't you ever say anything about it to her. She doesn't want anybody to know, so please don't ever bring it up. Okay?"

"Okay, Karen. I will never say anything about it. Thank you for telling me, though. I care a great deal about your mother, and I would always want to know if there's anything wrong."

"Thank you, Charlie. I know you care about mama, and I am glad you and she are so close. That means a whole lot to me."

Charlie and Karen remain sitting on the couch, talking, cuddling, and petting each other for another hour or so.

Karen then gets up and goes upstairs to check on her mother. She comes back downstairs and goes into the kitchen, returning with two more bottles of soda: one for herself and one for Charlie.

As Karen walks back into the living room, Charlie says, "Karen, will you do something for me?"

"What?"

Charlie takes his shoes off and lies down on the couch. "Will you rub my back?"

Karen gives him an are-you-crazy look. After thinking about it, though, she walks toward the couch and starts to rub Charlie's back, without saying a word.

Karen enjoys doing things for Charlie, not because she has to, but because she wants to. These things she does for him give her a very special sense of joy that fills her heart.

Charlie and Karen's relationship has developed into something wonderful which most people never get a chance to experience. They have established a true, loving relationship built on respect, kindness, and love. They care for each other, not because of some pleasurable, lusty, sexual act, but because of caring about what the other feels and needs. They have done this in a very unselfish way. Their relationship is like a rosebush: It takes time for the plant to establish itself. It needs time to adapt to its new environment, and it does so by remaining in the ground for several weeks before any type of fertilizer is added. If fertilizer is added before the establishment of the plant takes place, the roots of the rosebush will burn up and die. So it is with Charlie and Karen. If the sexual aspect of the relationship began before its right time, it would surely have burned up the true feelings of love, caring, respect, and admiration they have for each other. It would have prevented the proper development of the relationship, which grows from the small things—the tender moments, the delicate conversations, the playful moments, and the heartfelt love—to properly establish a sturdy foundation to build on.

Now the foundation of Charlie's and Karen's relationship has been established, and established in the purest and most loving way, by becoming friends and confidantes first. By doing so, the mental and emotional stage of the relationship has also been created. The physical nature of this pure relationship has begun to take hold. More and more, with each passing day, Karen thinks about Charlie in a sexual way. Charlie, on the other hand, has always thought of Karen as a sexy, young delicacy, but his controlled behavior—along with Karen's right hook—has kept their relationship from burning up and dying at this early stage. But now that the first stage of love has been developed, the physical part becomes more and more of an obstacle to overcome.

For the first time, Karen has kissed Charlie with passion and desire in her heart. Her tender years of being a virgin are becoming harder to maintain. Her sensual thoughts and Charlie's affection and playful attention are beginning to blossom into a sexual fantasy—a fantasy ready to become a reality. Her sweet, innocent eyes have never seen the naked body of a man. She has never even seen pictures of any nude man in magazines or any other form of media. But her aroused curiosity begins to stimulate her more and more.

Her mother has talked to her many times about men. Some of these conversations were very provocative and stimulating. But Karen's eyes have never been exposed to a man's physical nature, not even one time. Her curiosity is as big as a mountain. And now that Charlie has come into her life, she feels the need to ask questions about sexual matters. Her mother is the only person she can trust on this subject. She asks many questions, but her mother, who hasn't been with a man since Karen's father died, isn't very helpful answering many of those questions.

Charlie and Karen have constructed their foundation, and now is the time for the relationship to go to the next level. Their time spent holding hands and kissing tenderly and cuddling is quickly giving way to a yearning to know each other in a more physical way. The lust growing in their bodies may be more than they both can handle.

Chapter 4
JUST WHEN EVERYTHING WAS GOING SO WELL

Charlie and Karen date each other for two wonderful months, without any problems. Everything is going so well for the happy couple. They develop a genuine, true, loving relationship. Their relationship is full of respect and admiration for each other. Lust doesn't enter the relationship at this developing stage. And by not doing so, it prevents the love they have for each other from being spoiled.

This is a time to nurture the true unselfish feeling that a long-lasting relationship needs to have. The developing stage for Charlie and Karen is now complete. It is time for the relationship to take root and grow more abundantly.

The sexual desires in Charlie's and Karen's hearts soon begin to overcome their own physical structures. Like a drug addict needing more and more heroin to achieve the same high, Charlie and Karen begin to need more and more of each other's affection. Just being around each other and kissing and cuddling doesn't seem to be enough to express their true feelings anymore.

They each begin to think and fantasize about making love to the other. These thoughts are strong and demanding, and they are about to surface.

Neither one has ever engaged an intimate act with anyone else. Because of their strong religious beliefs, and their respect for each other, they have developed a pure, true, dedicated, and virtuous loving relationship for each other. But the lust in their bodies begins to take its toll.

Charlie and Karen begin to talk about marriage, but not always in a serious way. Charlie remembers the promise he made to his mother. Although she is no longer around, Karen is. The thought of being close to Karen's extremely sexy and beautiful flesh begins to seep into Charlie's heart. He feels compelled to bring this to Karen's attention.

One day, Karen and Charlie are having a wonderful time playing putt-putt at one of their favorite courses. Charlie is winning, as he usually does. They have just finished playing the first nine holes. They are sitting down, resting and having a soda. As Karen looks over the scorecard, Charlie looks over Karen.

"Karen, I love you."

Karen stops looking at the scorecard and looks over at Charlie. "I love you too, Charlie."

Karen's radiant gaze grabs Charlie's attention; he can't take his eyes off her.

"Charlie, why don't we make love to each other? I have been thinking about it for a long time now. I just can't seem to think about anything else. Why don't we make love?"

Charlie continues to stare at Karen, but now his expression is dumbfounded. Her blunt remark activates Charlie's impulse mechanism.

"Sure!" he says. "Yeah! All right! When do you want to?"

"Everybody else is doing it," Karen says. "I know I love you, Charlie, so why not?"

"You mean it? Really?"

"Yeah, Charlie, I mean it."

"How about right now!"

Karen, with her head turned sideways, says, "Not so fast, Charlie. We must think this over carefully. We should plan it out. This will be our first time, so let's plan it out together."

"Okay. How about tomorrow?"

"Charlie! If you aren't going to discuss it any better than that, then—"

Charlie interrupts. "Okay, Karen, let's just sit here and plan out when. When would you want to, Cubby?"

"Well … how about Saturday night?"

"That will be great! Now that we got that settled, where do you want to go?"

"I don't know, Charlie."

"We could get a hotel room somewhere out of town, or we could just go to my house."

Karen thinks for a moment. "Yeah, that would be better, Charlie. Over at your house will be better."

Charlie gets very excited when he hears Karen say this and sees her face light up.

"Can you stay the whole night?" he asks.

"I don't know, Charlie. My mama will suspect something if I don't come home."

"Could you tell her you're staying the night with one of your girlfriends?"

"I probably could, but mama might call to check up on me or something. You know mamas."

So Charlie and Karen sit quietly, thinking on the subject awhile.

"Come on, let's finish our game. Maybe we can think better if we are moving around." Karen shows a seductive grin as she gets up.

They proceed to the next nine holes of their game of putt-putt.

After they've played a few holes, Karen says, "I think I can arrange it so we can spend the whole night together, Charlie.

"Okay, Cubby. So it is set for Saturday night, right?"

"Yes, Charlie. It is set."

Charlie and Karen kiss each other, and then they stroll around the putt-putt course, holding hands. Soon they finish playing. Charlie wins, as usual, beating Karen by ten strokes.

Charlie and Karen go by McDonald's for a milk shake, their typical routine to finish off a date. Charlie then takes Karen home. He walks her to her front door.

"I will talk to you tomorrow, Cubby."

Charlie leans over and kisses her tenderly. Karen looks at Charlie, her eyes shining.

"I can't wait till Saturday night, Charlie."

"I can't wait either."

Charlie kisses Karen one more time, and then he goes home.

Charlie pulls into his driveway, happy as a fat rat in a cheese factory. He has something spectacular to look forward to now. The time he has been waiting for has almost arrived.

After entering his house, he goes up to his room, takes off his clothes, and takes a shower. Shortly after his shower, he goes to bed. Charlie falls asleep fairly fast. He then begins to have a very strange and quite unusual dream.

Charlie is at his childhood townhouse. He sees his mother sitting on the couch in the living room. She gives him a very angry look. Charlie watches as his mother points her finger at him. She motions for him to come over to the couch. Charlie walks over and sits down next to her.

His mother gives Charlie a sad look. She then begins to cry.

"Mama! Mama! Why are you crying?"

"Why are you lying to me, Charlie? Why are you lying to me?"

Charlie becomes frightened by his mother's words.

"Why are you talking to me that way, mama?"

"You promised me that you would not fornicate until you were married. Why are you lying to me?"

Charlie becomes to get very upset.

"But, mama, I wouldn't lie to you."

Charlie hears his mother's voice get louder and meaner.

"Why are you lying to me? Why are you lying to me?"

"Mama! Quit talking to me like that. Quit talking to me like that, mama."

The front door opens. There, standing in the doorway, is Charlie's father. Charlie gets a fright when he sees his father's face. He looks right at Charlie, giving him a very mean and angry look.

"Why are you lying to your mother?" Charlie's father asks. "Why are you lying to your mother, Son?"

Charlie gets up and tries to walk over to his father. As he approaches his father, Charlie hears his mother crying again.

"Mama! Why are you crying? Why are you crying?"

"I am crying because you are lying to me. Why are you lying to your poor old mother?"

Charlie walks away from her and then runs into the kitchen. As he turns, he sees his father standing in the kitchen. His father is crying too.

"Why have you lied to your mother, Son?"

"Why do you keep saying this? I haven't lied to her."

Charlie runs back into the living room. When he gets there, he looks around but doesn't see anybody. He cries out, "Mama! Mama! Where are you?" Charlie still doesn't see anyone. He runs back into the kitchen. He can't find his father either. He looks around, but he can't find either one of them. "Where are you? Mama! Daddy! Where are you?"

And then Charlie wakes up.

Charlie realizes he has had a bad nightmare. He is sweating profusely. He jumps up out of bed, runs into the bathroom, and washes his face. He is still shaking from the bad dream. Charlie looks over at the bedside clock; it reads 3:00 a.m. He can't believe how real the dream actually felt. He washes his face some more, until he gets control of himself, and then goes back to sleep and doesn't wake until morning.

When morning does come, Charlie doesn't forget about the nightmare like he usually does with his dreams. He thinks hard about it, and he feels a strange sense of guilt.

After work, he goes by the Little Tony's Pizza to see Karen. He walks into the little restaurant and spots Karen standing behind the counter. Her bright eyes open wide when she sees him.

She throws up her hand in a wave and says, "Hello, Charlie. Am I glad to see you!"

Charlie walks over and says hello to Karen.

"I have everything worked out, Charlie," Karen continues. "I told mama that I'm going to stay with you Saturday night. She understood. She didn't get angry or anything. I guess she knows how I feel about you, so she said it would be all right with her."

"You mean, you just told her that you were going to spend the whole night with me, and she said it would be all right?"

"Yep. That's what I did. I didn't want to make up a lie to her. I have never lied to my mama, and I don't want to start."

Charlie then has a flashback of the dream he had last night. He sees his mother crying. In his head he hears his mother saying, "Why are you lying to me, Charlie?" He sees a vision of her crying face. The voice is coming from inside Charlie's head. He understands every syllable she speaks. He even recognizes the voice as his mother's. He stands there, in somewhat of a trance, as Karen tries to get his attention.

"Charlie! Charlie, are you all right? Charlie! Hey, Charlie!"

Charlie then snaps out of it. He begins to sweat profusely. He looks over at Karen and says, "Yeah, I'm fine, Karen. Would you happen to have a towel? I need to wipe my face off."

Karen notices the sweat running down his face. She runs to the back and returns with a towel.

"Here you go, Charlie." She hands Charlie the towel, looking at him with concern. "Are you all right, Charlie? You are white as a sheet. You look like you have just seen a ghost."

Charlie notices the concerned look on Karen's face. He tries to calm her down.

"It's nothing, Karen. I'm all right." Charlie smiles a big grin at her. He leans over and kisses her.

Karen smiles. "I guess you are all right. You kiss like you are all right, but you scared me for a moment there."

"I guess I just had a rough day at work. Some days down there can really get to me."

"I know just what you mean, Charlie. Working here isn't exactly all fun and games; sometimes it can be a real headache."

Customers begin to come in.

Karen says playfully, "Okay, Charlie, you get out of here. I have got to go back to work."

"Okay, meanness, I will see you on Saturday night."

"Okay, Charlie."

"What time do you want me to pick you up?"

"Oh … about seven will be fine."

"Good! There is a party I have been invited to Saturday night. We can go there for a little while until we—"

Karen interrupts. "Okay, Charlie. We can talk about it later."

Karen's arousing, alluring, luminous eyes entice Charlie to stay a few moments longer.

Karen speaks in a playful tone again. "I thought I told you to get out of here."

"That was before you started to look at me that way. Now that you have my attention, I think I will just stay here forever."

Karen shakes her head. "You will stay here for how long?"

"Oh … maybe just until I get a pizza. I will take my usual. You do still sell pizzas here, don't you?"

"I think we still do."

Karen fills out his order and takes it to the back. One medium pepperoni pizza with mushrooms, onions, and green peppers—Charlie's favorite pizza!

Charlie hands her the money and waits.

As Charlie waits for Karen to serve the other customers, he has another flashback. He sees a vision of his mother. This vision isn't the one he had in his dream. This vision is the one he had when she was still alive—the one when she asked him to make her those three promises, right before he graduated from high school. He sees her clearly: she is sitting on the couch, just like when it happened, her true, sincere face looking right at him.

Charlie sees his mother's face as if she were really there. He watches her take his hand and place it on the Bible. He then hears her say in a soft way, "Charlie, promise me that you won't practice the act of fornication until you marry."

As if someone else were speaking, Charlie hears himself say, "Yes, mama. I promise."

Charlie then jumps up from his seat.

People around him look at him in a disturbed manner.

Karen looks at Charlie in surprise. "Charlie, are you all right?"

Charlie looks over at Karen. "Oh … I guess so, Karen. I think I will go home."

Charlie begins to walk to the door.

"Hey, Charlie, aren't you forgetting something?"

Charlie pauses.

"Your pizza, Charlie, your pizza."

"Oh yeah, my pizza."

Just then, someone in the back rings a bell and places Charlie's pizza on the bay where the other pizzas are. Karen picks up the pizza and hands it over to Charlie.

Charlie takes the pizza from her. He looks at her a little strangely. "Thanks, Karen. I will see you later. Okay?"

"Okay, Charlie. I hope you get to feel better." Karen gives Charlie a very concerned look.

"Cubby, I will be all right. After I get something on my stomach, I will be fine. Love ya."

"I love you too, Charlie. Call me tomorrow so I'll know you are all right. Okay?"

Charlie nods his head and gently says, "Okay, Karen. I will talk with you tomorrow."

Charlie departs the little pizza place.

As Charlie drives home, he begins to feel very guilty. He remembers the promise he made to his mother very well now. He remembers the day like it was yesterday. He feels the atmosphere of that that long-ago day. Charlie tries to put it out of his mind, but he can't seem to forget about it. He drives up to his house and sits outside in his truck for several minutes before getting out.

He thinks to himself, *Dear God in heaven, what should I do? If I break the promise I made to my mother, I will never be the same. What should I do, Lord?*

Suddenly, an idea floods Charlie's mind. *I know! I will go down to the mall and see if I can buy Karen a wedding ring. Then I will propose to her on Friday night. We could get married right then! That way, we will be married on Saturday. Why didn't I think of that sooner?*

So Charlie starts his truck back up and begins to drive to the mall. He decides to go to the same jewelry store where he bought Karen the friendship ring.

Charlie arrives at the mall shortly. He looks down at the pizza and pulls out a slice. He eats it as he plans out what he wants to do.

Let's see. I will go to the store and buy … damn! That store doesn't take checks, and all the banks are closed. How am I supposed to buy the ring if the banks are all closed? Hmm … maybe the nice lady in the store will let me take the ring on credit. Yeah, that's it! She might just let me have it on credit.

So Charlie thinks about what type of ring he wants to buy before he even gets there. He eats only one slice of pizza by the time he arrives at the mall. Finding a spot, he parks the truck, gets out, and makes his way to the store.

When Charlie enters the store, he finds the same lady who waited on him the time before.

"Hello there. Can I help you?"

"Yes, ma'am! I am looking for a diamond engagement ring. I am thinking about asking this girl I've been dating to be my wife."

The lady notices the excitement on Charlie's face.

"Well, I am glad to see you came here to buy that all-important ring. Let's see what we have."

The lady walks around and shows Charlie a display full of diamond solitaire rings.

"Here we go. How much do you want to spend?"

"Money is no object. Just show me one of your finest quality rings."

"Well! This must be someone very special. I don't think I have ever had a customer say that. Let's see if I can find you one over there."

The lady shows Charlie to a seat by a table, and then she brings him a small array of rings. They are in a small golden chest. She places it on the table.

"Here we go. This is the nicest one we have. It's a little more than a carat; 105 points, to be exact. It is the cream of the crop, as far as quality goes. The clarity is IF. That means it is flawless. The color is D; that's extremely good, the best. The cut is a round brilliant cut. The ring is mounted on an eighteen-karat gold setting."

Charlie holds the ring in his hand. "Wow! Just look at it sparkle! Wow! That's got to be the most beautiful diamond I have ever seen. Wow! Would you just look at that!" Charlie is dazzled as all the colors of the diamond radiate before him. The stone sparkles attractively, as if it had some mysterious power over him. He becomes enraptured by its beauty.

Charlie notices the ring doesn't have a price on it, just a number on a tag tied to the ring with the string. He looks at the ring for a few more moments.

"This is the one I want," he tells the lady. "I don't want to look at any more rings. This is it! I want Karen to have the very best."

"It is the very best. There is not another of this quality anywhere around here; you'd have go to New York or overseas. It is simply the best diamond that can be found."

Charlie confidently replies, "I will take it. How much is it?"

"Let me see. With tax, it comes to $31,498.95, and we will size it for free."

Charlie's mouth falls open. He then falls out of his seat and lands on the floor, with his mouth still wide open.

"Are you all right, young man? Would you like for me to call an ambulance?"

"Huh? How much did you say it was again?"

The lady helps Charlie off the floor and back into his seat.

"The ring by itself is $29,999.00 When I add 5 percent sales tax, it comes to $31.498.95."

"That's what I was afraid you said. Oh boy … oh my …"

The lady then realizes that the ring is just a little bit too expensive for Charlie.

"We have a lot of other ones that are not as expensive," she says.

"No. I don't want any other one. That is the one I want. It's just that I don't quite have that much to spend for it right now."

Charlie picks up the little jewel and holds it in his hand. He is mystified by it once more. His eyes become glassy as the ring's dazzle continues to entrance him. His mind goes blank. He stares at the ring as though it has control of his mind.

"I know it is beautiful. We have some that are almost as beautiful, but a little less expensive."

"I can't believe how beautiful it really is," Charlie replies, enraptured. "I have never thought much about diamonds, but this one, well … this one is something." Charlie slowly hands it back to the lady.

The lady puts the ring back into the gold chest, which she takes and puts away. She walks back to where Charlie sits, a very depressed look on his face.

The lady tries to cheer Charlie up. "Now let's see—here is one that is almost a carat."

The lady hands the ring to Charlie, who is still unnerved. Charlie looks at the ring, but he doesn't take it. After a long pause, he looks at the lady, as sad as if he'd just lost his best friend.

"No thanks, ma'am," he says to the lady. "I really had my hopes set on that particular one. Maybe I will come back some other time. Right now I am not in the mood to look at any others."

The lady looks disappointed. She puts the ring back into the display and says, "I know you had your hopes set on that one. Maybe I shouldn't have shown you one that was so expensive."

"No, you did right. I wanted to see the very best. You showed me what I wanted to see. I will just have to think it over. Maybe I will come back and look at the others you have some other time. Thank you for your time."

"Sure thing. I am sorry I couldn't be of any help to you. Please come back."

Charlie gives her a sad nod as he leaves the store, a very distraught and depressed look on his face.

Charlie walks over and sits down on one a bench he finds near the wishing well. As he sits, he thinks about how badly he wanted that ring. The sudden disappointment triggers a very bad, depressive mood in his mind. He is in a very confused state and doesn't know what he wants to do. He just sits there, confused, as he thinks about what to do next. The more he thinks, the more confused he gets. He thinks back to when he was a little boy, to the time when he found that little puppy dog he described to Karen. He wanted to keep that little puppy dog, but his mother and father wouldn't let him keep it. He remembers how sad he was. He feels just like he did then.

Charlie sits there for hours, in this confused and depressed state, until he hears a familiar voice.

"Hello, Charlie."

Charlie looks up, and guess who he sees? Dee!

Charlie's sad expression disappears as he says, "Hey, Dee, how have you been?"

"Oh, pretty good, how about yourself?"

Standing right next to Dee is a little boy.

"Oh, I have been doing pretty good." Charlie smiles at the little boy beside Dee. "Who is this?" he asks.

"This is my little boy, Daniel."

"He sure is a handsome little guy. So where is your other half?"

Dee shyly replies, "Oh, you mean Danny. We got divorced several years ago. We only stayed married for about five years."

Charlie listens intently as Dee and Daniel sit down beside him on the bench.

"So you got divorced? What went wrong?"

"Oh, I guess you could say we just couldn't get along. We were always fighting over money. We never had time for each other. We never talked. There was always something else more important coming between us. After fighting over those stupid things for so long, it became time to explore greener pastures."

"I am sorry to hear about that. I hoped you would have stayed happily married forever, but I guess things don't always work out the way we want them to."

"You are absolutely right, Charlie. Things just don't work out the way we hope they would."

"So what brings you down here to the mall?"

"Oh, I thought I would come down here and buy Daniel a toy. Have you ever been in the Toys "R" Us store?"

"No, I don't think I ever have."

"I have never seen so many toys in all my life. Daniel has the best time when he walks in there. You ought to see him. His whole face just lights up."

Charlie, smiling at the youngster, says, "I'll bet he does."

The little boy grins at Charlie and then looks away.

"So tell me, Charlie, have you ever gotten married?"

Charlie pauses for a moment and then says, "Funny you should ask that, Dee. I came down here to buy an engagement ring for the girl I have been seeing."

Dee shows a very disappointed look. She tries to smile, though.

"Well, did you find one?"

"Yeah … I found one, all right. Boy, did I find one. I was ready to take it home with me until the lady told me how much it cost."

Dee shyly asks, "If hope you don't think I am prying, but how much was it?"

Charlie laughs. "I believe she said $31,400 or something like that."

Dee's eyes get as big as marbles.

"What! How much did you say!"

"Thirty one thousand four hundred, plus …"

They both begin to laugh wholeheartedly.

"Yeah, I know, Dee. It sounds crazy, but you know what is even crazier?"

"What, Charlie?"

"I wanted to buy it anyway."

They both roar with laughter.

Charlie continues. "That's why I am sitting here. I just don't know what to do."

Dee stops laughing. "You aren't serious about buying it are you, Charlie?"

Charlie pauses. "I doubt it, Dee. I sure do want to, though."

"She must be some girl."

"Oh, she is, Dee, she is."

Charlie stops talking as he stares at Dee. She stares back at him in total quiet.

Charlie says softly, "You know, Dee, ever since I have known you, I have always wanted to be yours and you to be mine. It seems like there was always something trying to prevent us from ever getting together. Have you ever felt that way?"

"You know something, Charlie, I believe you are right once again. It seems that there was always something in the way."

"I have never told you this, Dee, but I was in love with you while we were in school."

Dee's eyes light up when she hears this. "Why didn't you ever tell me, Charlie?"

"I don't know. I guess I was just too stupid. I was really shy back then. I wonder how it would have turned out if we had gotten married."

Dee looks surprised at Charlie after hearing these words.

"I guess we will never know, will we, Charlie?"

Dee and Charlie look at each other, curiosity showing in their eyes, and continue their conversation.

"So, tell me Dee, where do you work?"

"Have you ever heard of the Dodge City Saloon?"

"Yeah, I have heard of it."

"Well, that's where I work. I am a cocktail waitress there."

"Really? Come on!"

"That's right, Charlie. I dress up in a dress like the old saloon girls used to wear. When I am in my costume, I look like one of the girls on the old *Gunsmoke* TV show."

"Really?"

"Yeah. It pays the bills. I make pretty good money there, at least in tips."

"Well, how about that! I would like to see you in one of those costumes."

"Drop by sometime, Charlie, and bring your girlfriend. I would like to meet her. I really would."

"Maybe I will, Dee, maybe I will."

"Yeah. Do that, Charlie. I would like to meet the girl you want to spend thirty one thousand dollars on. Ha, ha, ha!"

"What nights do you work?"

"Every night except Sunday, Monday, and Tuesday, most of the time. So come on by and see me in my outfit. I know you will like it."

"I will be looking forward to it."

"Well, Charlie, I guess I'd better be going now. It's past Daniel's bedtime."

"It sure has been good seeing you, Dee. You take care of yourself. All right?"

"Sure thing, Charlie. Oh, by the way, don't buy that ring. No girl in the world is worth a diamond like that."

Dee smiles enticingly at Charlie as she says this. Charlie is moved by this look.

"Okay, Dee. Maybe …"

Luckily, Dee and her son leave.

Charlie watches Dee disappear from sight. He gets up and looks at his watch. "Jesus Christ! It's nine o'clock! I have got to get home. I will have to come back some other time to buy Karen a ring."

Charlie hurries to his truck and drives home.

The week goes by, and Saturday night arrives without a hitch. Charlie forgets about the idea of proposing to Karen. He is in a very happy mood. He can't wait until he brings Karen home. His hopes are at the highest they've ever been in his life. He has forgotten all about the scene he made at the pizza place. He has also forgotten about the strange dreams he had earlier this week. All he has on his mind is making love to Karen.

Charlie makes sure all his clothes have been washed, dried, and hung up. All the dishes have been washed and put away. He cleans up his house like he hasn't done in a long time. Everything is set, and Charlie refines all the last details of his game plan. He has an album of soft music ready on his turntable. The room smells fresh and clean. Everything is in place. All he has to do now is go and pick up Karen.

The first item on his agenda is to take Karen to a party one of his friends is having. After the party, he will bring her home. His hopes are high. He is very excited about the evening.

When Charlie leaves his house to go pick up Karen, he is full of confidence. It is late spring, and there is a warm breeze blowing. Charlie wears a red short-sleeved shirt and white slacks. He gets into his truck at around six-thirty and drives quickly down the road, feeling very anxious and excited about what is to come. He feels like he could climb Mount Everest. He is filled with nervous energy that is ready to be released.

Charlie holds his breath as he drives up to Karen's house. He pulls into the driveway, gets out of his truck, and eagerly walks up to the front door. He knocks on the door three times. Karen opens the door. She is wearing a beautiful red dress. Her hair looks beautiful, just like the hairstyles on models in magazines. She takes Charlie's breath away. Her diamond earrings sparkle against her face, and she looks more beautiful to Charlie than ever. He stares at his scrumptious delicacy as if in a trance.

Charlie, with his eyes wide open, says, "Wow! Pardon me, miss, but I must have the wrong address. I am looking for Miss Karen Thomas."

"Well … who are you, may I ask?"

Charlie, still stunned, says, "It is I, my love. It is your knight in shining armor who has come to take you away to paradise."

Karen looks at him a little apprehensively. "Well, Mr. Shining Armor, while you were out fighting dragons and wizards, didn't you think to call me like you were supposed to have done!"

Charlie, in a silent stupor, continues to gazes at Karen. Finally, he says, "Huh? Oh … that's right, I was supposed to have called you, wasn't I? Ha, ha, ha! Since I didn't, why didn't you call me instead?"

"Oh! I didn't think I was supposed to call you. You were supposed to call me. Didn't you know I was worried about you?"

"You must not have been *too* worried. If you had been, you would have called me to find out if I was all right."

Karen looks at Charlie sternly.

Charlie, seeing this look, suddenly wraps his arms around her and gives her a big hug. He then kisses her before she has a chance to say anything else.

Charlie says tenderly, "I love you, Karen. Tell me you love me."

Karen looks up at Charlie. "I love you, Charlie."

Charlie bends his head down, not noticing the gleam in Karen's eye as he kisses her once more. Karen then pinches him on his side, hard.

"Ouch! Hey! What was that for?"

"That was for not calling me this week. You had Wednesday, Thursday, Friday, and today to call me." Karen gives Charlie a mean look.

Charlie gives Karen a melancholy look, and then he gazes deeply into her eyes. Holding her gaze for a moment, he then turns his head and whispers in her ear. "I'm sorry, Cubby. I am really sorry. Please don't be angry with me, my love."

Charlie then gently kisses Karen's soft red lips and gives her a loving hug. He looks into her radiant blue eyes and says, "Will you forgive me? Hmm … will you forgive me, Cubby?"

Karen looks up at Charlie, with those beautiful baby blues, and says softly, "Well … yes, Charlie. I forgive you." She reaches up and lightly kisses him.

"So where is Ma?"

"She is over at a friend's house. I asked her not to be home when you got here tonight."

"How come?"

"I just didn't want her to say anything to you about me staying … you know."

"Oh. Has she said anything to you about staying over with me tonight, sweetheart?"

Karen steps back as Charlie walks into the house.

"Well, Charlie, everything was going just fine until last night. Just before I went to bed, she came up to my room, and we had a little talk about it."

"How did it go?"

"At first, it went fine, but as we kept talking about it, she gave me the impression that she didn't exactly approve of me staying over with you."

Charlie sits down on the couch, listening in silence as Karen continues.

"You see, Charlie, I told her that I was old enough to start making my own decisions about things like this. I simply told her that I wanted to stay with you because I love you. To make a long story short, Charlie, I told her that I am the one who should decide when I want to love someone."

"How did she react?"

"Well … she gave me a very concerned look. I think it hurt her feelings somewhat. After I told her that I wasn't going to change my mind, she just got up and left my room. She didn't say anything after that."

Charlie again sits quietly as he looks at Karen, showing concern.

"So you say we are going to a party first?" Karen says.

"Yeah, over at Wayne Scott's house. He told me he was going to rent some videos and have a few people over tonight."

"Oh really? What kind of videos did he say he was going to rent?"

"I believe he said he was going to rent some old Super Bowl tapes."

"Super Bowl tapes! We're going to sit around and watch football tapes!"

"Uh-huh."

"Ugh! … I hate football, Charlie. I don't know anything about that silly game."

"Look at it like this, Karen, it's not what we watch, but who we watch it with. Are you ready to go?"

Karen shakes her head in disbelief and says, "I guess so, Charlie."

"We will only stay for an hour or so. Trust me. You will have a good time."

"Okay, Charlie, let's go."

So Charlie and Karen turn out all the lights in the house, lock the door behind them, and drive to the party.

As Charlie drives his truck, Karen snuggles up to him very affectionately. She rubs his hand softly; she even changes the gears as Charlie pushes in the clutch. She rubs his leg, and she then takes her hand and begins to rub his chest. Charlie doesn't say anything while Karen is caressing him.

"Charlie."

"Yes, Cubby."

"Tell me you love me."

Charlie takes Karen's hand. "I love you, Cubby. I love you more than I love anybody else in the whole world. I love you more than I love myself."

"I love you too, Charlie."

Karen puts her head on Charlie's shoulder as he continues to drive to the party at Wayne Scott's house.

Charlie and Karen arrive, and Charlie gets out of his truck, runs over to the other side, and opens Karen's door. She giggles as she gets out. Charlie then gently kisses Karen on the lips. She wraps her arms around Charlie's waist, and he gives her a strong, loving hug. They then walk up to the front door of the house, arm in arm.

Charlie rings the doorbell.

Wayne Scott opens the door, greeting Charlie and Karen with a jolly welcome.

"Well, hello, Charlie. How the hell are you, buddy?"

Charlie smiles gladly at his friend. "Hello, Wayne. You know Karen."

Wayne smiles at Karen. "Hello, Karen. How have you been?"

"Fine, Wayne. How have you been?"

"Can't complain too much. You all come on in and join the party."

So Charlie and Karen follow Wayne into the living room, where the party is under way. All the other guests sit comfortably, watching the TV.

Wayne says, "Hey, Karen. I want you to meet my Uncle Henry."

Just then, an elderly man stands up. He is wearing overalls; it looks like he has been wearing them for quite some time. His right cheek is full of tobacco. He has an open pouch of chewing tobacco in his hand, and he stuffs his face with more of the chew. A shit-eating grin spreads across his face as he looks at Karen.

Karen timidly says, “Glad to meet you, Uncle Henry.”

Uncle Henry puts away his pouch. He steps closer to Karen and then spits into his spittoon.

“Honey, you are purtier than a bucket full of hog livers!” Uncle Henry says.

Karen gasps for breath as everyone in the room laughs out loud. Her face turns as red as her hair.

“Well, thank you, I guess …” she manages to say.

Charlie, snickering, says, “Hello, Uncle Henry.”

Uncle Henry gives Charlie a shot in the arm. “Hello there, boy. You mean this purty little thang is yours?”

“That’s right, Uncle Henry, she is mine.”

“It’s a good thing I ain’t twenty-five years old again.”

“How come you say that, Uncle Henry?”

“’Cause, boy, if I were twenty-five years old again, I would kick your ass and take this purty little thang home with me. Tee, hee, hee.”

Everyone in the room laughs as Charlie’s face begins to turn red.

“Well, I guess I am glad you aren’t twenty-five years old anymore, Uncle Henry.”

Grinning like an opossum, Uncle Henry says, “I am just playing with you, boy. Golly Jesus. She sure is real purty. She sure is.”

Charlie and Karen move farther into the room, find a seat, and sit down.

Karen begins to kiss and love Charlie, but he gently pushes her away.

Charlie whispers, “Not in front of everyone, Karen. People are looking at us.”

Karen gives Charlie a stern look.

Everyone focuses their attention on the TV.

Karen holds Charlie’s hand, but when a football player on the TV makes a touchdown, Charlie pulls his hand out of Karen’s grasp, raising both his arms in a cheer.

“Hey, Charlie. Do you want a beer?”

“Sure thing, Wayne.”

Charlie then looks over at Karen, who has a disturbed expression on her face.

Charlie whispers, "Karen, I will only have a few beers. Come on, Karen. Let me see a smile on your face."

Karen continues to look at Charlie, and then she gives him a quick smile.

"Would like one?"

"I ain't gonna drink no beer."

"Come on, Karen. You can drink *one.* Come on."

"Well … maybe just one."

Wayne brings Charlie a beer, grinning as he says, "Here you go, buddy."

Charlie takes the beer from Wayne. "Thanks, buddy. Hey, would you bring Karen a beer?"

"Sure thing, man."

Wayne goes back into the kitchen and comes out with another beer. He hands it to Karen and says, "Here you go, Karen."

Karen thanks Wayne, opens the beer, and takes a sip. Making a sour face, she says, "Yuck! This stuff tastes awful! It tastes like cold cabbage soup."

Charlie laughs and then guzzles down some of the brew. He sticks out his tongue as Karen shows him a playful smile.

Everyone else continues to watch the football game.

After a few minutes goes by, Karen reaches over and begins to love Charlie some more. Once again, Charlie gently pushes her away. He then gets up and sits down on the floor where the other football fanatics are sitting.

"Hey, Wayne!" Charlie says. "This is where he throws the long bomb and gets on the four-yard line."

Wayne watches, excitement showing plainly on his face.

All the others watch in silence as the quarterback throws the pass just as Charlie predicted.

Karen feels lonely and neglected.

As the party continues, the doorbell rings. Wayne gets up, opens the door, and greets the pizza man. After paying the man for the pizza, Wayne walks back into the living room, carrying two large pies.

"Hey, everyone! The pizza is here!"

Everyone gets excited as the girls pass out plates.

Karen brings a plate to Charlie. He is too occupied with his male acquaintances and the game to pay her much attention. She feels more and more lonely, neglected, and left out.

They all eat pizza, drink cold beer, and watch the football game.

Charlie drinks another beer. Karen attempts to drink hers but finds the taste revolting. She tries to be one of the boys, but she hates the taste of the golden beverage.

Charlie gets up from the floor and sits down on the couch. Karen casually gets up from where she is sitting and walks over to Charlie. She sits down on his lap. She wraps her arms around his neck and kisses him on his lips.

Charlie, showing a dislike for her affections, says, "Not now, Karen. Can't you see I am watching the game now? There are people watching us. Why don't you go into the kitchen where the other girls are? We guys would like to watch the game. Okay?"

Contemptuously, Karen remarks, "Whatever you say, Charlie. I wouldn't want to interrupt your football game!" Karen angrily stands up and walks into the kitchen.

One of the girls sitting at the table in the kitchen says, "Football! Football! Football! That's all Bobby thinks about!"

Another girl says, "Don't feel like you are the only one who has to put up with it. I just don't see what they see in a bunch of men killing each other over a stupid football."

Karen says, "I don't care for it either, but since it is something they like, I guess it's all right with me."

"Wait till you get married, dear, and football season comes around. Nothing you say will register. Every Sunday afternoon, it's football, football, football! That's all you will see the men do: watch football. They will plop down in front of the TV and do nothing but watch football!"

As the other girls continue to talk, Karen hears Charlie's voice say, "Karen! Karen! Come here." Karen happily smiles, hearing Charlie call out her name. She eagerly gets up and walks back into the living room to see what Charlie wants of her. She walks over to Charlie and sits down beside him.

"Yes, Charlie?" she asks.

"Would you go out to my truck and bring in the briefcase I have in the bed?"

Karen looks at Charlie, as if to say, "Why don't you go get it yourself?"

Charlie turns his head sideways and says, "Please … I don't want to miss any of the game; it's just about over, only two minutes left to go, and—"

Karen interrupts. "You don't have to explain, Charlie. I will be glad to get it."

Karen gets up, walks out to Charlie's truck, and retrieves the briefcase. As she walks back into the house, everyone's eyes are fixed on the TV.

Karen walks over and sits down beside Charlie. "Here you go, Charlie."

"Just lay it down for now, Karen."

So Karen lays the briefcase down, without hearing Charlie thank her for going out and getting it for him.

Karen then tries to hold Charlie's hand, but he once again pushes her hand away.

She sits there quietly and, like everyone else, watches the final moment of the game.

The coach sends someone in with the play. The ball is hiked. The quarterback throws the ball, long. The receiver catches the ball. He runs and then turns toward the goalpost.

Just as he crosses over into the end zone, Karen yells, "It's a home run!"

Everyone stares directly at Karen. And then, without warning, everyone bursts out laughing. The room is filled with people laughing directly at Karen. Even Charlie laughs at her remark. He doesn't laugh as hard as everyone else does, but he does chuckle some.

Karen is very embarrassed. She feels completely humiliated. She looks at Charlie, her face red with embarrassment. The laughter continues for a long while. Karen sees the laughter on Charlie's face also. She glares at him like she wants to kill him.

Before long, everyone settles down, and the room is once again quiet and still.

Karen remains completely silent for the duration of the party.

Charlie detects that Karen is upset by the way she looks at him. He then takes something out of his briefcase and shows it to Wayne. It's a book of Super Bowl records. The two of them look at it for a while.

After about twenty minutes or so, Charlie leans over and whispers to Karen. "Are you ready to go?"

"Yes, I am."

Charlie goes over to Wayne and says, "Hey, buddy. I believe Karen and I will leave now. I sure have enjoyed the party."

"Hey, buddy, what's your hurry? The party is just starting."

"I know, but I think we will go anyway."

Wayne looks over at Karen. He sees she is still upset over the remark she made earlier.

Wayne says softly, "Hey, Karen, I am glad you came to the party. I hope you aren't upset over the remark you made. Nobody meant any harm by laughing, so don't let it bother you. Okay?"

Karen tries to puts on happy face. She looks at Wayne shyly. "Thank you, Wayne."

"See you later, buddy," Charlie says to Wayne.

"Right. You drive safely now."

"We will. Later, man."

Charlie and Karen say their good-byes to the others, leave the party, and walk to Charlie's truck.

Just as soon as Charlie starts his truck, he looks over at Karen. She is mad. She is *really* mad. Charlie tries to cheer her up.

"Hey, Cubby, did you hear about the gay communist terrorist? He went to blow up a car, and he came back with third-degree lip burns."

Charlie laughs, but Karen just sits there, in total silence.

Charlie begins to drive away.

Karen is still silent.

"Do you want to change the gears?" Charlie asks her.

"No!" Karen says quickly, her voice sharp.

Charlie reaches over and tries to hold Karen's hand. She doesn't let him.

"Hey, Cubby. Don't be that way. Don't be mad at me."

Karen toward Charlie, giving him a mean look.

"What do you mean? You have some nerve to say, 'Don't be that way, Cubby'! All evening, you have pushed me away. All evening, you have ignored me. Now you tell me not to be that way."

"Cubby … hey … I just don't feel comfortable kissing and hugging in front of other people. I love you."

Karen just sits there.

"Didn't you hear me, Cubby?"

Karen doesn't say anything.

"I said, 'I love you.'"

"If you love me so much, then why are you ashamed to let me love you in front of others?"

"Hey, I am not ashamed of you. It's just that guys don't like to act that way in front of other people, that's all."

"Well, if you don't feel comfortable with me in front of others, then why don't you just take me home?"

Charlie gets very upset when he hears these words. "Take you home! I don't want to take you home! Don't you remember? This night is supposed to be our time together."

"Some time together, huh! You didn't call me earlier this week. You ignored me at that party, and worst of all, you laughed at me. I have never been so humiliated in all my life!"

"Hey, that wasn't my fault. I didn't laugh at you."

Karen gets furious when she hears his denial. "What do you mean, you didn't laugh at me? I sat there and watched you laugh at me like all the others. The only one who didn't laugh at me was Wayne!"

Charlie now gets angry too. "Hey! I said I didn't laugh at you. If you had not made that silly remark, nobody would have laughed at all."

"Silly remark! That's it! Take me home! Take me home, right now, Charlie Delaney!"

Charlie's anger diminishes as he drives.

"Hey, Cubby, please don't make me take you home, sweetheart.

Hey-y-y …" Charlie looks over at Karen with soft compassionate eyes. His voice becomes very soft. "Hey, Cubby. Can I tell you something?"

Karen, unmoved by Charlie's sweet tone, asks sharply, "What!"

"First of all, I just want to say that if I laughed at you at the party, I want you to know that … well, I'm sorry. I really am. Okay?"

"*If?* There is no if; you did laugh at me."

"Okay. Okay, Cubby. I am sorry I laughed at you."

"You don't mean it. I can tell by the way you said it."

"Huh? I am sorry I laughed at you at the party. Isn't that good enough?"

Karen waits a moment before saying, "No, it's not. Take me home! Take me home, right now!"

Confused, Charlie looks over at Karen, not knowing what to say to her next. He is dumbfounded by the way she is behaving. He begins to feel depressed, but decides not to get angry like he did a while ago. Instead, he decides to use a little reverse psychology this time, acting happy so as not to set Karen off again.

Charlie glances at Karen. Seeing the angry look in her eyes, he says, "You know something, Cubby? You are cute as hell when you are angry."

"I ain't."

"Yes, you are too. Tee, hee, hee."

"Are you laughing at me again?"

"No. Not quite. It's just that you look adorable with that mean look in your eyes." Charlie smiles.

"Well?"

"Well, what, Cubby?"

"Well, are you going to take me home?"

Charlie just looks back over at her, the smile still on his face, and says, "No. Tee, hee, hee."

Karen gets furious. "You take me home, right now, young man!"

"Who are you calling 'young man'? I am seven years older than you are, young lady. Tee, hee, hee."

"Stop this car right now!"

Charlie laughs a little more as he replies, "We aren't in a car, silly. We are in a truck."

This makes Karen even more distraught. "Fine, then. Stop this truck!"

"Uh-uh. I will not stop until you say, '*Please* stop this truck.'"

"I ain't playing, Charlie. You take me home right now! Or, you stop this truck, and I will walk home!"

Hearing this, Charlie laughs out loud. And then he says, "You mean you will walk all the way home?"

"That's right. If I have to, I will."

"Come on, Cubby. Let's not fight. We have never had a fight before. Hey, guess what?!"

Karen looks surprised at Charlie's question. "What!"

"We are having our first fight. Right now! Wow! I was wondering if we would ever have one, and we are having one right now. Isn't that great, Cubby?"

"Huh? What's so great about having a fight?"

"Not just *a* fight, but our *first* fight. This is something we can tell our kids about someday."

"Are you crazy? I think you had too many beers."

"Nah, it's not that. I only drank three, Cubby."

"Well, getting back to the subject at hand, I want you to take me home. I am only going to ask you one more time, Charlie. Are you going to take me home, or aren't you?"

Charlie is a little puzzled by the way she put it. He replies, "Nope. I am having too much fun to take you home."

"I hate to spoil your fun, young man, but I am getting off the boat."

As Charlie is driving down the road, he comes up to a traffic light. It is red. Just as he stops his truck, Karen opens the door and gets out. She starts walking down the road, turning right at the light.

Charlie rolls down the window and says, "Hey, come back here! Come on back here, Cubby!"

Just as Charlie bellows out these words, the stoplight turns green. The driver in the car behind Charlie begins to honk the horn, and Charlie is forced to pull off, leaving Karen walking down the dark street.

"What is wrong with that girl?" he mumbles. "Sometimes I just can't figure her out. I'll just drive around the block. That will give her time to think about how silly she has acted. Then, when I drive up, she will be glad I came back for her."

So Charlie drives around the block slowly. It is very dark now. He turns at the same traffic light and begins to drive down the road Karen had started to walk down. He soon comes across Karen, walking along. He pulls up to her, continuing to drive slowly alongside her as she walks.

"Hello there, marathon girl. Are you getting tired of walking?"

Karen turns and peers into the truck, glaring at Charlie. She still has a mad look on her face. She doesn't say anything; she just keeps on walking.

"Hey, baby, you looking for a ride?"

Karen just keeps on walking, without saying one word.

"There's one thing I will give you credit for: you walk a mean mile. Ha, ha, ha!"

Karen tries to hide her smile, but Charlie catches it.

"Hey, don't you hide that grin. I saw you! Did you ever hear the one about the girl who wanted to walk around the world? She walked halfway around, got tired, and then decided to walk back home. Ha, ha, ha!"

This time, Karen laughs.

"Hey, Cubby, come on. Please get back in. I am responsible for you. Somebody might try to harm you walking around in the dark like this. Please get back in."

"Will you take me straight home?"

With a grin, Charlie says, "I will take you anywhere you want me to, sweetheart."

Karen gives him a stern look. "Promise me that you will take me straight home."

"I promise to take you straight home. Okay?"

Karen stops walking. She opens the door, and with a pouting expression, gets back into the truck.

As she gets back in, Charlie says in a soft tone, "When you say you're going to do something, you really mean it."

Karen doesn't say anything. She just gives Charlie a peeved look.

As Charlie continues to drive down the road, he passes a little store.

"Hey, just look at my gas gauge. I am going to need some gas."

Karen looks over and sees there is still half a tank. With her head turned sideways a little, she looks at Charlie. Her face shows that she is still peeved.

"It won't take me long to fill up my tank."

Karen does not question his decision.

He whips his truck around to the gas pumps, fills his tank, and walks into the little store to pay. He comes out, carrying two cans of Dr Pepper.

As Charlie gets back into his truck he hands one can of Dr Pepper to Karen. "After walking so much tonight, I thought you might be thirsty."

Karen takes the beverage from Charlie and says in a soft tone, "Thank you, Charlie."

Hearing Karen speak is like music to Charlie's ears.

"Well, you can talk too." Charlie smiles as he starts his truck. He drives it over near the store, and parks.

Karen takes one sip of her Dr Pepper and then begins to look sternly at Charlie. "Where are you going? I told you I want to go home!"

Charlie takes a big swig of his soda and says, "I know you said you want me to take you home. I just want to talk to you for five minutes. That's all: five minutes." Karen turns her head sideways again. The look she gives makes him say, "Okay. Let me have just three minutes. Okay, Cubby? Hmm … Please …"

Karen takes another sip from her beverage and says, "Well, all right, Charlie. You have three minutes. No more."

"That's why I love you so much. You are so nice to me."

"You are wasting time; I am timing you." Karen looks at her watch.

Charlie reaches over and takes Karen by the hand. This time she lets him.

Charlie looks at Karen with complete sincerity. His voice is soft and kind. "Cubby, I know I haven't been the most considerate person tonight." Charlie pauses for a moment as Karen looks deep into his eyes. "I know I haven't paid you the attention I should have, either. And I know I haven't acted in the sweet way that I usually do. But I just want you to know that if I have said something wrong tonight, or if I haven't said something I should have, I just want you to know that … well … I'm sorry." Charlie's eyes are full of love as he says these words.

Karen looks at Charlie and then turns away from him.

She is quiet for a moment, and then she says, "Are you finished?"

Charlie sees that she is still upset.

"No, I ain't finished," he says. "I just want you to know that I truly love you. I really do. I love you more than I have ever loved anyone else. Now I am finished."

"Okay. Take me home."

Charlie is astounded. He can't believe Karen didn't crack.

"Okay, Charlie. Your time is up! Are you going to take me home now?"

Charlie just shakes his head in amazement. "Come on, Cubby. Don't make me take you home. I have been looking forward to this night all my life."

"So that's it. You are just being nice to me so you can take me home with you. You just want to have sex with me."

With his eyes as big as marbles, Charlie says, "Huh! What! Do what? I can't believe you said that! For your information, young lady, it was your idea all along."

"My idea! What makes you think it was my idea?"

"Don't you remember? We were playing putt-putt, and then you said to me, 'Charlie, why don't we make love to each other?' Remember?"

Karen, mad as a hornet, says, "All I want to know is, are you going to take me home!"

"Not until you admit this was your idea."

Karen opens the door, gets out of the truck, and walks over to the phone booth next to the store.

Charlie gets out slowly and follows close behind her.

Karen opens her purse, takes out a quarter, and drops it into the slot in the pay phone.

"Who are you calling?!"

"I am calling mama to come pick me up."

Charlie gets very angry.

"Oh no, you're not!" Charlie presses down the switch that makes the quarter drop.

This infuriates Karen. She points her finger at Charlie and starts to say something, but Charlie stops her.

"Don't bring Ma into this," he says.

"You listen here! …"

"Okay, Karen, okay. You win. I will take you home right now. Okay?"

Karen looks at Charlie, fire burning in her blue eyes. "This will be your last chance. If you don't take me home this time, I promise you I will call mama. Do you understand?"

"Yes, ma'am. I understand. I understand completely."

So Charlie walks Karen back to his truck. She gets in, and does likewise. Charlie starts his truck and drives off. He doesn't say a word for a long time; neither does Karen.

Several minutes go by before Charlie breaks the silence.

"You know, Karen, you are acting very childish about this whole thing."

"I ain't acting childish. You are the one who is acting childish."

"What! What makes you think that?"

"I would rather not discuss this matter anymore."

Karen pouts as Charlie says, "I just can't understand why you want me to take you home so early. Cubby, I just don't understand."

Karen just sits there in silence.

Charlie begins to get very upset. "You know something, there are a lot of other girls who would love to have me as a boyfriend."

Karen looks over at him, her face filled with rage. "What exactly is that supposed to mean, Mr. Delaney?"

"Mr. Delaney? Mr. Delaney? So now I am Mr. Delaney. What happened to Charlie?"

"Don't change the subject. What exactly do you mean when you say that there are a lot of other girls who would like to have you as a boyfriend?"

"Me, change the subject? That's a good one."

"Well?"

Charlie sees Karen is getting impatient for an answer.

"Well … it just means that you aren't the only girl in the world."

Charlie looks over at Karen and sees a very angry face looking back at him.

"Okay! Then why don't you just go find someone else, Mr. Delaney! You aren't the only guy in the world either, you know."

Charlie gets very angry when he hears her say this.

"Well, maybe I will, Miss Thomas!"

Karen looks at Charlie sternly and says, "What exactly do you mean by that remark!"

"I think it is self-explanatory, Miss Thomas!"

"Are you saying that you are breaking up with me?"

Charlie is surprised by Karen's question. He is angry and surprised at the same time. Hearing Karen ask this string of questions has really agitated him completely.

"Yeah! I think that will be just fine with me, Miss Thomas."

"Is that official? Do you mean it?"

Charlie gives Karen a very angry look. "Yes! It is official. As of right now, you are no longer my girlfriend, and I ain't your boyfriend anymore, either."

Karen begins to cry. "If that's the way you want it, Mr. Delaney, then that will be just fine with me!"

Just as soon as these words come out of Karen's mouth, she pulls off her friendship ring, the one Charlie gave her, and throws it out the window.

Charlie, seeing this, bellows, "Why in hell did you do that!"

"I didn't have use for it anymore."

As Karen continues to cry, Charlie starts to drive faster. He passes a little store as he drives. He marks it in his mind as the store where Karen threw the ring away. Karen does likewise. Charlie is fit to be tied now. That act really got his goat. He is furious, and his spirit is broken.

Charlie says softly, "I don't know why you did that. You didn't have to throw it out the window." Charlie looks up toward the sky and says, "Jesus Christ in heaven, did you see her throw my ring out the window! Did you see her do that, Lord?"

Karen begins to feel awful about doing that. Her soul is flooded with guilt. Most of the tears she is crying now are for throwing the ring out the window.

Charlie is devastated. He is more upset than he has ever been in his life. He just can't believe Karen threw his ring out the window. He drives her straight home, without saying another word.

When Charlie gets to Karen's house, she jumps out of his truck and runs inside. Charlie, still stunned by Karen's actions, just sits there, confused. He doesn't understand why everything happened the way it did. His fury has been replaced by disappointment and distress. He feels lonely and sad. He waits in his truck, hoping that Karen will come back outside.

As Karen runs into the house, she slams the door behind her. Her mother is sitting peacefully in the living room, watching TV, when Karen runs in.

Mrs. Thomas quickly jumps up from her restful spot.

"Dear, what is the matter?!"

"It's Charlie, mama. He broke up with me!"

"Come here, dear, and tell me what happened!"

Mrs. Thomas looks out the window and notices that Charlie's truck is still on the driveway; Charlie is still sitting in the truck, and the parking lights are on.

"Mama, Charlie broke up with me." Karen begins to cry profoundly.

"Dear, calm down. Calm down. Tell me exactly why Charlie broke up with you."

"He didn't pay any attention to me, then he laughed at me, then he broke up with me, then I threw his ring out the window, then I—"

Mrs. Thomas interrupts. "Slow down, dear, slow down. You threw the ring Charlie gave you out the window. Why in hell did you do that!"

Karen stops crying when she hears her mother speak this way. "Mama, I don't really know why I did it. Charlie and I had this stupid fight, and the next thing I know, I threw the ring right out the window. I don't know why I did that."

"Well, if you don't know, that's makes two of us." Mrs. Thomas begins to shake her head at Karen. "Dear, just because you and Charlie had a fight doesn't give you the right to throw away the ring he gave you. To be honest with you, that was plumb stupid!"

"That's right! Take up for Charlie. You always take up for Charlie. You never take up for me!" Karen continues to cry even more.

"It's not that, dear. It's just …" Mrs. Thomas lets her voice trail off as she walks over to the window. She notices that Charlie is still sitting out there in his truck. "Hey, Karen. Why don't you go out there and apologize to Charlie for throwing away his ring!"

"I thought you taught me not to run after boys."

"Dear, Charlie isn't a boy, he's a man, and you are a woman now. Women have always given in to the men they love; it is just an unwritten law. We are the ones who keep everything together. We do this by giving in to them from time to time."

"But, mama, you don't even know what we were fighting about."

"What were you fighting about?"

Karen is silent for a moment, and then she says, "I don't know! I mean … well … I don't know what we were fighting about. He broke up with me, and then I got angry and threw the ring out the window."

"Do you mean to tell me that you don't even know what you were fighting about?"

Karen just shakes her head, sitting there and looking as innocent as a fawn.

"Young lady, don't you think you should go out there and apologize to Charlie? You don't really want to break up with him, do you?"

"I guess not, but I can't go out there."

"Why not?"

"Because I am ashamed of myself. I feel just awful for what I did. And at the same time, I am angry with him for breaking up with me. Part of me says I should go out there, and the other part of me says I shouldn't. What should I do, mama?"

"Don't ask me! All I know is Charlie isn't going to sit out there all night. So you'd better decide, and decide fast, on what you want to do."

Karen just sits there, confused.

"Mama, I just can't go out there right now. I just can't make a fool of myself."

"You can't make a fool of yourself? Young lady, when you threw that ring out the window, you made yourself the fool."

Karen just gives her mother a worried look.

"How many times have I warned you about that temper of yours? Charlie probably paid several hundred dollars for that ring."

"That's right, mama, make me feel worse than I already do! You always take up for Charlie. You always take his side."

"Honey, I am not taking up for anybody. I just want you to understand what that temper of yours has caused tonight. Why don't you tell me about the fight you two just had?"

So Karen begins to tell her mother about the confrontation she just had with Charlie.

Meanwhile, Charlie, still sitting in his truck with the parking lights on, thinks to himself, *I wonder if she will come back out. I will forgive her for throwing away my ring. I know she didn't mean to. She only did that because she was angry. I don't know why she got so angry, though.* Charlie hits himself on the head. *Yeah, I do know why she got so angry: because I broke up with her. How could I be so stupid? How could I be so ignorant? Why on God's green earth did I break up with the girl I love? Hmm … maybe I should go inside and apologize to her. I think I will wait a few more minutes first. Maybe she will have second thoughts about that stupid fight we had.*

Charlie continues to wait, hoping that Karen will come back outside.

Back inside the house, Karen has just finished telling her mother about the fight she just had with Charlie. She has calmed down somewhat.

Mrs. Thomas keeps looking out the window from time to time, to see if Charlie is still out there.

"Dear, why don't you go out there and ask Charlie to come inside?"

"Mama, I just can't go out there. How can I explain throwing away that ring?" Karen begins to cry once more.

"Honey, why don't I go out there and ask Charlie to come inside? I know you two don't want to break up for good, but I also know he isn't going to sit out there all night, so you'd better do something."

"How long has he been sitting out there, mama?"

"I guess it has been about twenty minutes. Would it be okay with you if I go out there and have a talk with him?"

"No, mama! I don't want you going out there. I don't want you to get involved; besides, you are on his side anyway."

"I told you, Karen, I am not on anybody's side. I just don't want you to make a terrible mistake that you will regret for rest of your life. Why don't you let me go out there and talk with Charlie?"

"I said no, mama! If anybody is going out there, it is going to be me. I just can't seem to work up enough courage to face him. He probably hates me now. I know he does. I just know it!"

Mrs. Thomas walks over and sits down next to her daughter. "Dear, if Charlie hated you, do you think he would be still out there? Hmm …?"

"I guess not, mama. I just don't know what to do. I just don't know what to do."

While Karen debates whether she wants to go outside to talk with Charlie, Charlie is thinking seriously about the situation too.

Charlie says to himself, *She probably threw away my ring because she hates me. Why else would she throw it away like that? Why did she do that?* Charlie then begins to think about the situation further, with a false perception of what Karen did. *What am I saying? I paid a whole lot for that ring. That ring represented my love for her. When she threw it out the window, she didn't just throw away a ring, she threw away the love I have for her. Who the hell does she think she is anyway? I shouldn't be the one to apologize. She is the one who should apologize! Why should I crawl back to her, huh?! She told me to go ahead and find another girl. Maybe I ought to do just that! That will pay her back for making me feel so … Hey, I know! I will talk to Dee! I think I will go and see if Dee is still at work!"*

So, as Charlie is planning his revenge, Karen is still in the house talking to her mother.

"Mama. Do you think Charlie will forgive me if I go out there and apologize to him?"

"I don't know, honey. But I will tell you one thing, Charlie hasn't been sitting out there for nothing."

Karen walks over to the window and peeps out. "Maybe I should at least go out there and try. I don't really want Charlie to think I don't love him."

"You better hurry up and make up your mind, Karen. He has been waiting out there for thirty minutes now."

"I think I will, mama. I think I will go out there and apologize to him. Maybe he will forgive me for being so mean to him."

Mrs. Thomas and Karen suddenly see Charlie's headlights come on. They hurry to the window, only to see Charlie backing out of the driveway.

Karen hurries out the door, but it is too late. Charlie begins to drive away into the darkness of the night. Karen is left standing outside as she sees Charlie's truck disappear from sight. Mrs. Thomas goes outside to join her daughter.

Karen yells, "Charlie! Charlie! Come back, Charlie!"

"It's too late, dear. Charlie has gone."

Karen sobs as she says, "Oh no! He has left me."

Karen begins to really cry. Her eyes pour out tears of loneliness and sadness.

"Charlie! Please come back! Please, Charlie. Please come back. I am sorry. I am sorry."

Looking sadly at Karen, Mrs. Thomas says, "Come on back inside, dear. He has left. Let's just go back inside."

As her mother puts her arm around her, Karen cries like a child.

"Calm down, dear. He will be back. He loves you too much just to break up with you this way. He will be back. Mark my words, Karen, he will be back."

"Do you really think so, mama?"

"Yes, dear, I really do. He will be back."

Mrs. Thomas and Karen walk back into the house and shut the door.

As Charlie drives away, he mutters aloud to himself, "So she wants me to find another girl. Well, I know just the girl! I will show *her*."

Charlie heads to the Dodge City Saloon, driving with a vengeance. Before long, he arrives, drying his eyes as he gets out of his truck. He proceeds to walk up to the front entrance and goes up to the man standing behind the window.

In a loud and clear voice the man says, "That will be five bucks, buddy."

Charlie pulls out his wallet and takes out a five-dollar bill. He hands it to the man, who takes the money and then stamps Charlie's hand.

"Okay, buddy, you can go in now," the man says.

Charlie walks around the strange, crowded saloon, feeling like a visitor from another time. He thinks to himself, *Dee sure was right. It looks just like the saloon in* Gunsmoke. Charlie keeps walking around until he spots what he came there for.

"Hey, Dee. Guess who?"

Dee looks surprised to see him. "Hey, Charlie! Good to see you."

Dee wears the saloon girl outfit she described to Charlie, complete with feathers and a garter belt. The dress is very short in the front.

Charlie gets to see Dee's nicely shaped legs for the first time.

"So where is this lucky girl I am so eager to meet?" asks Dee.

With disappointment in his eyes, Charlie looks at Dee. "Well, Dee, she and I … you see … we kinda broke up tonight. We had a terrible fight, and the next thing I knew, well … we aren't going together anymore."

Charlie's eyes are sad when he tells Dee the news, but she goes on to smile after hearing the story.

"Well, I am sorry to hear that, Charlie," says Dee.

Charlie sees a smile on Dee's face. He also notices a twinkle in her eyes. They seem to gleam with excitement.

"Come with me, Charlie. I will find you a table." Dee smiles sweetly at Charlie as she takes him by the hand.

They walk through the horde of people at the crowded bar, and finally Dee finds a seat for Charlie.

"Here you go, Charlie. Can I get you a drink?"

Charlie hesitates for a second and then says, "No. I think I will just sit here for now. Thanks anyway, Dee."

Dee smiles, a sparkle of seduction glowing in her eyes.

She pleasantly says, "I'll be back later. Okay?"

"Okay, Dee. I will be looking for you."

Dee comes back shortly after that, holding a glass in her hand.

"Here you go, Charlie." She puts a mixed drink on his table.

Charlie looks puzzled as Dee says, "This drink is on me. I thought it might cheer you up some. I hope you like gin and tonic."

Charlie smiles with a glimmer of excitement and gratitude. "Thank you, Dee. I'll try it." He doesn't waste any time drinking the drink.

Dee sits down at Charlie's table.

"So tell me, Charlie, what did you and your girlfriend fight about tonight?"

Charlie takes another taste of his drink.

"I really don't know, Dee. I really don't know. We just started arguing, and the next thing I knew, I broke up with her."

"Oh, so you broke up with her."

"Yeah, that's right."

Dee smiles gladly when she hears these words.

"Charlie, I would love to sit here and talk with you, but I have to go back to work now. If my boss sees me sitting around, he might get mad."

"I understand, Dee. You go ahead, but from time to time, just stop by. Okay?"

"Sure, Charlie. Gotta go now. I will talk with you later."

"Okay, Dee. I will be waiting for you."

Dee gets up and goes back to serving the other customers as Charlie sips his drink.

As the night goes by, Charlie orders several more drinks. Dee comes by and talks with him periodically. Charlie gets more and more depressed as the night goes on. He blames Karen for the way he feels. Charlie just sits in the same seat all night. He only gets up to go to the bathroom or to get another drink.

Eventually, it's time for the saloon to close. Charlie remains in his seat until one of the bouncers comes by.

"Hey, fella, it's time to hit the ole' dusty trail. All drinks have to be off the table by one o'clock. State law!"

Charlie raises his glass and downs the rest of his gin and tonic.

"Here you go, fella," says Charlie. "My drink is off the table."

The bouncer takes the glass as Charlie just sits back, intoxicated.

Dee comes by Charlie's table, looking at him with seductive eyes. She says softly, "Hey, Charlie, are you going to be all right?"

Charlie is now under the influence, big time. He gives Dee a cockeyed look. "What are you going to do now, Dee Bee?"

"Dee Bee? Charlie, I think you have had enough to drink."

"Yep. Yeehaw! It's a good thing too: all drinks have to be off the table before the cuckoo clock hits one o'clock. Tee, hee, hee."

"Charlie, I have never seen you like this."

"That makes two of us, baby. I have never seen you like this either, Dee Bee. Tee, hee, hee."

Dee knows now that Charlie is drunk.

Looking concerned, Dee says, "Charlie, I can't let you drive home in the condition you are in. Would you like for me to take you home?"

Charlie doesn't waste any time giving Dee an answer. "Yeehaw! I thought you would never ask that, Miss Kitty. Tee, hee, hee."

With that, Dee helps Charlie up from his seat, out the door, through the parking lot and into her car.

After Charlie gets into Dee's car, he calms down a little bit.

"I want to thank you so much for taking me home, Dee. You are a good girl."

"You have to tell me how to get to your house, Charlie."

"Oh, that's no problem; I know where it is."

Dee laughs at Charlie's remark.

As Dee exits the parking lot Charlie waves good-bye to his truck.

"So long, pick-'em-up truck. Don't you go nowhere until we meet again."

Charlie looks over at Dee. His expression is humble and innocent. "I was just saying good-bye to my truck. You know, it's the best friend I have in the whole wide world."

Dee laughs again, amused by the way Charlie is carrying on.

"You know something, Dee Bee, you have a beautiful laugh. Where did you get it?"

"I don't know, Charlie. I guess I was just born with it. So, tell me, Charlie, which way do I go?"

Charlie tells Dee how to get to his house, and they soon arrive there.

"Here we are," says Charlie. "We have arrived at my castle."

Dee pulls her car right up to the front of his house. They both get out of Dee's car and proceed to enter Charlie's house.

Dee holds on to Charlie as they walk inside.

"My, my, Charlie! You have a really nice house."

"Thank you, Dee. I kinda like it too."

They walk into the living room, where they both sit down on the couch.

"I want to thank you again for bringing me home, Dee. I don't know how I would have gotten home without you."

Charlie reaches over and takes Dee's hand. Dee looks at Charlie; her eyes are very seductive eyes. He leans over and kisses her on the lips very passionately.

Charlie looks deep into Dee's eyes. "I have wanted to kiss you like that for a very long time."

Dee softly replies, "I have been wanting you to kiss me like that for a very long time also."

Charlie is still a little intoxicated but is slowly sobering up.

Dee, rubbing Charlie's hand, says, "You know something, Charlie?"

"What?"

"All our lives, there has always been something to prevent us from being together. Always. There was always something pulling us apart … until tonight."

He listens, lust filling his eyes.

"But tonight is different. It's like something is pushing us together, something with a powerful force. Do you feel it too, Charlie?"

"Yes, Dee, I do."

Dee's eyes are like Charlie's now: filled with lust and seduction.

"Charlie, I sure am thirsty. Would you mind if I go into your kitchen to get a glass of water?"

"Let me."

"No, Charlie. You just sit there. I will go get it."

"Sure, Dee, whatever you say."

"Would you like me to get you something to drink?"

"Yeah. I believe I will have a soda."

"Fine. I believe I will have a soda, too."

Dee gets up and walks into the kitchen. She goes over to the refrigerator. As she does, she notices a telephone hanging on the wall. With a devious little grin on her face, she walks over to the phone, takes down the receiver, and lays it on the table nearby. She then goes back to the refrigerator and grabs two sodas. Cutting the lights, she exits the kitchen and walks back into the living room.

"Here you go, Charlie."

Charlie takes the soda, and Dee sits down beside him.

"Thank you, Dee."

Charlie drinks down most if his in one guzzle.

Dee only takes a small sip of hers, as if she weren't really thirsty at all.

Soon after, they both put their beverages on the coffee table.

Charlie looks over at Dee, and love and admiration glow in his eyes. She looks at him the same way. He leans over, kissing Dee very passionately once again. She responds warmly and very affectionately to Charlie's seductive kiss.

Charlie then caresses Dee's neck and ears. He slowly moves his hand down to caress Dee's small but plump breasts. She responds by rubbing Charlie's chest. She unbuttons the top buttons of Charlie's shirt. Their kisses become more and more intense. Charlie starts to kiss Dee's neck. Her feminine moans show Charlie that she enjoys this. Charlie begins to blow lightly in her ear. This makes Dee's moans grow louder. As Charlie continues to rub Dee's soft breast, she turns to Charlie and looks deep into his eyes. Her eyes are full of lust and desire.

"Charlie! Oh, Charlie! I love you, Charlie. Ahh … ooh … Charlie."

The effect of the alcohol swimming around Charlie's brain has taken control of his entire body. He thinks of nothing but the feeling of Dee's soft body. Her warm, soft, eager flesh close to his fills his heart with unruly and uncontrollable desire. Giving in to his lusty urges, he kisses Dee madly.

Dee continues to unbutton Charlie's shirt. As she unbuttons the last one, she reaches in and begins to caress his bare chest. His hand then begins to go downward, all the way to her knee. He then quickly begins to move his hand upward.

Just as Charlie's hand disappears up Dee's dress and into her warmth, she takes Charlie's hand and says to him sweetly, "Oh, Charlie! Take me to your bedroom and make love to me."

Charlie looks at Dee, desire and want filling his eyes. "Oh-tay, Dee."

Charlie takes Dee by the hand, and they both rise from the couch and begin to walk upstairs to the bedroom.

The two smile at each other as Charlie escorts her to the top floor. Dee giggles a little as she walks along with Charlie. Charlie enters the bedroom first. Dee, still holding Charlie's hand, follows right behind him. She releases Charlie's hand so she can shut the door, and then she seductively walks over to Charlie. She rubs his chest while kissing him. He just stands there as she takes his shirt off.

Turning around, Dee says, "Would you like to unzip me, Charlie?"

Charlie, stunned by her words, only says, "Uh-huh."

Charlie then lowers the zipper in the back of Dee's dress. The dress falls to the floor. She removes her undergarments very quickly and climbs into Charlie's bed, quickly pulling the covers over her naked young body. She behaves like a shy fawn in a forest.

Charlie is left standing there as Dee watches he from underneath the covers. He eagerly pulls off his shoes and socks, quickly unbuckles and removes his belt, and pops the catch on his white slacks. As he pulls down his zipper, Dee waits impatiently to see Charlie's full length. He pulls off his white slacks, focusing his attention on the look in Dee's eyes. He throws his slacks aside. He pulls down his underwear without taking his eyes off Dee. Dee's eyes suddenly go down to view Charlie's stiff masculine feature. Charlie walks over, turns off the lights, walks back to the bed, and pulls back the covers. As his eyes adjust to the dimness of the room, Charlie can see just how beautiful Dee's naked young body is.

Charlie climbs into his bed and begins to kiss Dee madly once again. His passion is like a raging animal. Without any foreplay, he climbs on top of Dee. He penetrates Dee, and begins to move fast and quick. He kisses her neck wildly, and she responds to him passionately, with loud erotic moans and groans of sheer pleasure. Charlie soon reaches his climax. It was the most pleasurable thirty seconds of his life.

Back at the Thomas's house, Karen is on the phone, trying to reach Charlie.

Karen, with a discouraged look on her face, says, "Mama, the line is busy now."

Mrs. Thomas, sleepy at this late hour, says to her daughter, "He probably got tired of hearing it ring. You have been calling for hours now."

"I know, mama, but now it is busy. Do you think there is something wrong?"

"No, dear. I don't think there is anything wrong. Charlie probably just doesn't want to talk to you tonight, and he probably just took the phone off the hook so he wouldn't have to. I think you should just go to bed."

"Maybe I should go over there to see if everything is all right."

"At this hour! No, young lady! Charlie took the phone off the hook for a reason. You can go over there tomorrow, but for now, I think you should go to bed."

"Maybe you are right, mama. Maybe I should."

"I *am* right, dear. Tomorrow is another day. You two can work it out then. Let's go to bed. I am bushed."

"Me too, mama. Thank you for waiting up with me. I am glad you did."

"You're welcome, dear. That is what mamas are supposed to do."

Mrs. Thomas and Karen go to their bedrooms and retire for the night.

Just as soon as the sun rises, Karen is ready to go see Charlie. She has her clothes on before Mrs. Thomas is even out of bed. Karen walks into her mother's bedroom to say good-bye.

"Mama, I think I will leave now."

Mrs. Thomas rolls over and looks at the bedside clock. "Jesus Christ, Karen! It is only seven o'clock in the morning. You can't go over there now."

"Why not, mama?"

"Because, it is just too early. You don't want to give the impression of being too eager."

"But, mama, I *am* eager."

"Yes, I know, dear, but you don't want to look like you are. What about the ring? Are you going to go look for it any?"

"Oh yeah. I almost forgot about that. Will you help me look for it? Maybe if we both look for it, we might just find it. Will you help me look for it, mama?"

"I guess so, dear. I guess so."

Mrs. Thomas slowly gets out of bed, hurrying to get dressed so she can go help Karen look for the ring.

Neither one of them fixes any breakfast. They both are eager to locate the ring. Mrs. Thomas and Karen lock up the house and walk outside.

"Let's see. I tell you what, Karen. You take your car, and I will take my car. I will follow you to the store you said you remember passing. Okay?"

"Okay, mama. We will do that. You just follow me."

So Karen drives her car, and Mrs. Thomas follows her in hers.

Karen drives until she comes across the store. She pulls in and parks. Her mother follows, parking also. Mrs. Thomas then gets into Karen's car, and Karen drives down the road where she thinks the ring might be.

"This is it! This is where I threw it out, mama."

Karen pulls her car off the road, and parks. They both get out of the car and begin to look for the ring.

"This is like looking for a needle in a haystack."

"Just keep looking, mama, just keep looking."

The two women continue their search for about thirty minutes.

As Mrs. Thomas looks closely at the ground, she hears Karen shout out, "Yippee! Yippee! I found it! I found it! I can't believe it! I found it!" Karen begins to jump up and down.

Her mother runs over to her to share the excitement.

"Let me see it!"

Karen hands the ring over to her mother.

"I can't believe it! I can't believe you found it! I really can't believe it!"

"I did, mama, I did! I did! I did! Oh boy! Will Charlie ever be happy now!"

The two women jump up and down, celebrating the victory of finding the ring!

Only a few cars drive by at this early morning hour, and the drivers look at the two women like they are crazy.

"Mama, I have got to go and show Charlie that I have found his ring. I am so happy!"

Karen looks up to the sky and says, "Thank you, Lord, for guiding me to find this ring! Thank you, God! Thank you."

Mrs. Thomas, knowing that Karen is very fortunate to have found the little ruby-and-diamond ring, is happy for her daughter.

Mother and daughter continue to rejoice with great happiness and jubilation.

"Take me back to my car, honey. I know you are eager to go and see Charlie."

Karen quickly drives her mother back to her car.

When they get back to the store where Mrs. Thomas's car is parked,

Mrs. Thomas says to Karen, "I will see you back home, dear. I am so glad we found the ring."

She sees a glow in Karen's expression that she has never seen before.

"Okay, mama. I will see you at home … later."

Karen hugs her mother, thanking her for her help.

"I love you, mama!"

"I know, dear. I love you too."

After Mrs. Thomas gets into her own car and starts it up, Karen pulls away from the store and drives over to Charlie's house.

Karen is full of anticipation and joy as she drives down the road. She can't wait to apologize to Charlie for being so childish last night. The joy disintegrates as soon as Karen pulls into Charlie's driveway. She sees a strange car sitting there and begins to worry when she doesn't see Charlie's truck. Her heart begins to beat faster than the pistons in a Corvette going a hundred miles an hour. A thought of horror surges through her soul as she gets out of her car.

She walks up to the front door, feeling great apprehension, and knocks on the door gently.

"Charlie … Charlie …" Karen says as she turns the knob on the door. The door opens, and Karen puts her head into the doorway.

Stepping inside, Karen speaks in a curious and somewhat louder tone. "Charlie! Are you home, Charlie?"

Upstairs, Charlie is awakened by Karen's voice. Dee doesn't hear anything. She remains asleep, her arms wrapped snugly around Charlie.

At the sound of Karen's voice, Charlie wakes up in a horrible fright.

"Oh shit! Oh shit! No! No! It can't be! Please Lord, it can't be!" Charlie says aloud, hearing Karen's voice once more.

"Charlie? Are you up there, Charlie?"

He jumps to his feet and hurries to put on his underwear. Dee is startled by Charlie's sudden movements. He grabs his bathrobe and quickly puts it on. He then runs out of the room and down the stairs, finding Karen standing in the living room.

Karen looks at Charlie with great curiosity. "Charlie, where's your truck?"

"Well … it's … well …" "Whose car is outside, Charlie?"

Charlie again acts confused.

Karen sees guilt written all over his face.

Karen looks upstairs as she goes on to say, "What's going on, Charlie? Charlie! Tell me what is going on!"

Just then, Dee comes walking down the stairs. She is wearing only her panties and one of Charlie's shirts.

"No! No! No, Charlie! How could you!" Karen cries. "Charlie! How could you!"

"Let me try to explain, Karen."

Karen erupts like a volcano. She screams at the top of her lungs, "No!! No!! It can't be true!! Charlie!!" Her innocent face turns into a demon from hell! Her face turns as red as a pepper. "Don't you dare try to explain it to me, Charlie! Aauugghh!! Aauugghh!! I can't believe you could do such a thing!"

"Please let me explain it to you, Karen."

"You animal! You heathen! How could you do such a thing!"

Dee gets into the battle. "Hey. Don't you talk to Charlie like that!"

"Come on, Charlie. Let's go upstairs and make love some more."

"Oh boy. Did you have to go and say that?" says Charlie.

Karen runs out of the room and into the kitchen. Her face is red and full of tears. She sees the phone receiver lying on the table. She quickly grabs a towel to wipe her tears, and then she proceeds to run back into the living room.

"So that's why I couldn't reach you on the phone. You had it off the hook so you wouldn't be disturbed while you were with *her*. Ugh! How could you do such a thing, Charlie?"

Charlie gives Karen a look of utter shock and amazement. "Hey! I didn't take that phone off the hook," he says.

Karen tries to get control of herself. She takes out the ring and shows it to Charlie. "Here, Charlie! Look here! Mama and I went out early this morning to look for this ring. I finally found it."

Charlie puts on a half-assed smile and says, "Hey, that's great!"

Karen throws the ring at Charlie as hard as she can. "I threw it away once, now I will throw it away again! You turd, you!"

Karen then turns and runs out of the house.

Charlie just stands there, dumbfounded.

Dee then casually says, "I wonder if it was something I said."

Charlie gives Dee an angry look. "Did you take the phone off the hook?"

Dee gives Charlie a look of surprise. "Yes, Charlie. I didn't want anything to interrupt us this time. This time, nothing did."

Charlie shakes his head in regret. His heart is full of guilt and shame. He looks up to the ceiling and cries out, "What have I done, Lord? Dear God in heaven, what have I done?"

Charlie tries to get control of himself, but he goes berserk. He falls to the floor and sees a vision of his mother crying, not because he disobeyed her wishes, but because she feels his suffering.

"Mama! Mama! Please don't cry anymore, mama."

Suddenly, the vision diminishes.

Charlie looks around and then slowly gets up from the floor.

Dee is devastated by Charlie's actions. She doesn't know what to think.

Charlie looks up and sees Dee still standing there, in nothing but her panties and his shirt.

"Go get dressed, quickly! I need for you to drive me to my truck. Move it!"

Dee quickly goes upstairs. Charlie hurries up the stairs to dress also. They get dressed without saying one word to the other. Dee then drives Charlie back to the Dodge City Saloon, where his truck is still parked.

Charlie hops into his truck. He doesn't even say good-bye to Dee. He races as fast as he can to Karen's house. Charlie gets out of his truck and runs up to the front door. He doesn't even knock on the door before he enters.

Mrs. Thomas is sitting at the kitchen table as Charlie enters the house. She is crying; Karen has already told her what happened.

"Ma! I need to talk to Karen!"

"Ma? Don't you call me 'Ma' ever again! How could you, Charlie? How could you? Tell me! I must hear it from your own lips. Did you have sex with another girl last night?"

Charlie is now in a state of panic. Tears are running down his face.

"Please don't hate me, Ma. I don't know why I did it …"

"I told you to never call me 'Ma' again!"

Mrs. Thomas's voice echoes throughout the house. Her face is full of anger and hate.

"Tell me, Charlie! Tell me, right now! Did you have sex with another girl last night?"

Charlie is forced to admit it. "Yes, ma'am. I sure did."

When Mrs. Thomas hears this, she explodes into a hysterical fit. "Get out! Get out of this house, you low-life insect! Get out!"

Hearing this Charlie rushes out of the house, leaving even more upset than he was when he first arrived.

Mrs. Thomas chases after him, cursing him until he gets back into his truck. Her words are extremely vulgar, especially for a Sunday morning. "Karen told me that you and she were going to spend the night together last night, Charlie Delaney. I didn't want to say this, but I am very disappointed in you. My daughter isn't some whore for you to relieve yourself on. If you wanted to have sex with Karen, why didn't you ask her to marry you? Maybe you don't think she is worth marrying! Why didn't you think to make a respectable girl out of her, instead of treating her like a whore? I am very disappointed in you, Mr. Delaney, very disappointed!"

Charlie doesn't say anything. He just drives away, and a feeling of deep, dark sadness and depression fills his heart and soul.

Charlie goes straight home. He doesn't leave his house for anything. He cries like a child as he realizes what a terrible mess he has made. He waits at the phone, hoping that Karen will call. She doesn't. He sits there alone, crying. He prays hard and long for God to help him. He is plagued with an undeniable feeling of guilt.

"Dear God in heaven," he whispers feverishly. "What have I done!"

Chapter 5
TRYING TO WIN BACK HER LOVE

The next day, Charlie calls in sick. His illness is mental, not physical, but he knows he will be unable to get through the day at work.

Charlie stays in the house all day. The only thing he does throughout the day is work out in his gym. He hasn't used his gym in a very long time, but he works out until he almost reaches exhaustion: lifting weights, jogging on the treadmill, and riding the exercise bike until he almost passes out. He works out very hard, trying to relieve some of the mental pain and agony he is experiencing.

Soon Charlie begins to have thoughts of committing suicide.

So Charlie picks up the Bible and starts to read it as if he had never read it before. It does give him some comfort and help in this most difficult time. He finds a little relief from the awful depression that has set in. Reading the Bible doesn't remove the terrible guilt he feels, though. He thinks about how badly he has hurt Karen, and he knows that what he did was a very stupid thing to do. Also, he feels really bad knowing that Mrs. Thomas doesn't love him anymore. He really loves Mrs. Thomas, and he feels guilty as much for hurting her as for hurting Karen. He remembers the awful look Mrs. Thomas gave him yesterday, and the stern, angry way she talked to him. The more Charlie thinks about the subject, the worse he feels.

The next day, Tuesday, Charlie again calls in sick. He tells his boss that he just can't make it in. His boss tells him that he will find someone to cover for him.

Once again, Charlie doesn't leave his house for anything. He doesn't even go outside to take the mail out of the mailbox or to retrieve the newspaper. When the depression gets so bad that he can't stand it, he jumps on his exercise bike and pedals until he almost passes out. He uses the other equipment, too. Exercise is the only thing he can turn to.

Charlie thinks about calling Karen, but after the scene she made the other day, combined with the way Mrs. Thomas acted, he decides to give them a little while longer before contacting them. He tells himself that maybe they will have calmed down by the next time he tries to talk to them. He wants so badly to talk to Karen. His heart is heavy with a ponderous burden of guilt he can't seem to shake off.

He collapses in the living room after working out. He turns on the TV in attempt to distract himself, but after watching only a few minutes of any particular show, he loses interest. The only thing on TV that Charlie can watch all the way through is the news. He does feel somewhat better when seeing others who are worse off than he is. The saying "misery loves company" has becomes true and real for Charlie.

The next day, Wednesday, Charlie's life quickly gets worse than the two previous days combined. Charlie once again calls in sick, but his boss gets very angry this time. Telling Charlie he can't tolerate much more of this, he instructs him that if he doesn't make it in tomorrow, he will need to get a doctor's excuse to be out any longer. He tells Charlie this in a very harsh way.

Charlie puts the phone down and goes back to bed, even more depressed than he was before he made the call.

While asleep in his depressive state, Charlie has another bizarre dream. He sees a stream of flowing water and begins to walk toward it. The sound of the stream has a hypnotic effect on Charlie, drawing him like a magnet. As Charlie gets closer, the stream begins to flow more slowly. The blue water puts Charlie in a very tranquil state.

Charlie walks right up to the bank of the stream, and he sees something on the other side. It looks like a person.

Charlie calls out, "Hey! Who goes there?"

With that, Charlie sees the figure begin to walk toward him. As the person gets closer, Charlie begins to feel very strange.

The figure moves closer to Charlie, wading through the water very slowly. Charlie realizes that it is a man. He look at the man's face, but he can't tell who it is. When the man gets close enough for Charlie to be able to distinguish his facial features, he is jolted by the realization of who it is. Charlie looks for a second time, just to make sure. It is Jesus! Charlie sees his face and simultaneously feels a wonderful feeling rush through his entire soul. The face is so true and real. But then, the full awareness of whose presence he is in begins to dawn on Charlie, and he gets scared and frightened.

Charlie hears him speak. "Charlie, my friend, do not be frightened." The sound of the voice makes Charlie know for sure who he is. His voice is clear and pleasant. It is as if Charlie has known that voice all his life.

"Jesus. It is you! It really is you … isn't it?"

Jesus looks at Charlie, giving him a joyous and peaceful smile. "Yes, Charlie. It is I. Listen to me earnestly. I have come to tell you three things."

Charlie, with joy and excitement in his eyes, says, "Tell me, Lord. Please tell me, Lord!"

Charlie listens patiently and quietly as Jesus speaks.

"Verily, verily, I say unto you: first, the sin of fornication that you have committed has been forgiven. Let it bother you no more. Soon everyone who has suffered because of this sin will forgive you also. Your mother doesn't want you to hurt from this act anymore. Verily, I say unto you, don't let it trouble you any longer."

Charlie gets excited when he hears of his mother.

"Tell me, Lord, is my mother all right? Is she doing fine? Can I see her? When can I see her? May I talk with her?"

None of Charlie's questions are answered. Jesus just kindly looks at Charlie, his expression filled with love and compassion.

"Verily, verily, I say unto you this second thing: search for the third element. This element will make you feel better. It will relieve you of the evil spirit which has plagued you for such a long time. It is the substance that will rid you of this demon."

Charlie looks at Jesus, confused. "But Lord, what do you mean? What is this third element? Tell me, Lord. Please, Lord, tell me what this third element is!"

Once again, Charlie's questions are not answered.

This time, Jesus just gives Charlie a blank, expressionless stare.

"Verily, verily, I say unto you this third and last thing: You are being tested by the evil one. He is trying to get you to rebel against me. He will try again and again. Put your faith in me. Love me with all your heart, mind, and soul. If you do this, Charlie, he will not succeed. Do not be deceived to rebel against me. I have prepared a place for you. But remember my words: you should not ever rebel against me or hate me for anything that happens in your life. Verily, verily, I say unto you: You will be tested again. You have a place in my kingdom waiting for you. If you don't enter my kingdom, it will be because you choose not to. Take heed of my words; you must not rebel against me."

Charlie listens intently to Jesus, dropping down to his knees and saying, "I will never rebel against you, Lord. I promise I will never do that. No matter what happens in my life, I promise I will never rebel or hate you."

Jesus smiles at Charlie, his eyes filled with joy.

"I must leave you now, my friend. Hold true to my words which I have just spoken unto you."

Jesus then turns and begins to walk back to the other side of the fast-flowing stream. This time, Jesus walks on top of the water.

Charlie cries out, "Please don't leave, Lord! Take me with you. Please, Lord, take me with you!"

Just then, he sees Jesus pass over to the other side of the stream. The water begins to flow even faster. Charlie hesitates to walk across the stream now because the water is flowing too powerfully. As he looks across the water, he sees Jesus disappear.

The sound of the ringing telephone rouses Charlie from his dream, jolting him awake.

He jumps up in a hurry to answer the phone. "Hello? Karen! Hello. Is that you, Karen? I was hoping you would call …"

The voice on the other end of the line interrupts him. "Charlie, this isn't Karen. It's me … Dee. How have you been, Charlie?"

Charlie is very disappointed.

"Oh … I … um …well, I don't really know," he stammers.

Dee seductively says, "Sounds like you need some loving. I haven't seen you in three days. Would you like for me to come over and—"

Charlie cuts her off. "No! I don't want you to ever come over. I don't want to sound mean, Dee, but I don't want you to come over again. I am trying to get back with Karen, if she will ever have me back."

"Don't you love me, Charlie?"

"Dee, please don't make this any rougher than it already is."

"Don't you care for me?"

The way Dee says this cuts through Charlie like a knife through bread.

"Part of me will always love you, Dee. I fell in love with you a long time ago, when I was a lot younger. This is a different world we live in now, Dee. I love another girl now."

Charlie hears Dee begin to cry on the other end. The sound makes Charlie feel blue.

"I care for you, Dee. I always will, but ..." Charlie's voice trails off.

"But what?"

"But I am in love with someone else. I really love Karen. I want to marry Karen. I want Karen to be the mother of my children. I don't want to hurt you, Dee, but I have got to put Karen first in my life. I am trying to get her back. If she came over here and saw you here again, I would never get her back. Please don't come over here."

"Well, Charlie, if that's the way you want it."

"It is, Dee, it is. And another thing: please don't call me again. You only make it more difficult when you do."

Dee's crying gets louder, and then she says, "Well, Charlie, then I don't know what I'll do. I love you. I love you so much. It's hard not to call someone you love."

With that, she begins to sob uncontrollably.

Dee's crying begins to tear at Charlie's emotions.

"Dee, I have got to go now. Please don't be angry with me, but I have got to go."

"Well, I ain't through with you yet, Charlie! What if she doesn't want to take you back?"

"Dee, I don't want to think about that. Karen loves me. She will always love me. She is just angry with me right now. She will come around; I know she will. Please don't make matters any worse."

"But, Charlie, I love you!" Dee starts to cry again.

Charlie realizes that he must end this conversation, and fast.

"Dee, I am going to hang the phone up now. Okay?"

He hears no reply, just some sobbing.

"Say 'good-bye, Charlie', Dee."

"Good-bye, Charlie."

"I am glad you said that, Dee. Bye, Dee."

Charlie attempts to put the phone down, but he Dee continue to talk. Charlie pauses for a moment, but then he hangs up the phone while she is talking.

Charlie looks at the clock. It is 3:30 p.m.

"Holy cow! Karen will be getting off work soon. I think it's time I paid her a visit."

So Charlie gets dressed and prepares to go see Karen. He gets into his truck, drives to a nearby florist, buys a dozen red roses, and heads off again.

As he drives he thinks to himself. *Hmm … I don't think it would be a wise idea to go over to her house. After what Ma said to me the other day, I don't think that would be a very smart thing to do. I think I will just wait for Karen to get off work. That's it: I will be waiting for her out in the parking lot. Maybe she will talk to me. I sure hope so. Jesus told me that everyone will soon forgive me for my sinful act. Maybe not today, but she will, sooner or later.*

So Charlie happily drives over to the little pizza place to wait for Karen.

Charlie lets down the tailgate on his truck and sits down. He has the dozen red roses in his hand, ready and waiting. A little after five o'clock, Charlie finally sees Karen coming out of the restaurant. He deliberately parked his truck right beside Karen's car.

As Karen walks toward her car, Charlie notices that she sees him. She then walks up to Charlie.

"Hello there. Don't I know you?" Charlie says.

Karen doesn't say anything.

"Hey. I bought these roses for you. I sure would be grateful if you'd take them."

Again, Karen doesn't say anything.

"Hey, Cubby, I know you are still angry with me. You have every right to be mad at me. I don't blame you one bit for feeling the way you do. I just want you to know that I feel like the lowest form of life on this planet."

Karen turns away, opening her car door as if Charlie were not even there. She starts her car and begins to drive off.

"Hey. It sure was good to see you again. You sure are pretty in that cute little outfit."

Karen looks at Charlie's sad expression as she drives off. She leaves him there, still holding the roses in his hand.

Charlie watches in sadness as Karen disappears from sight. He just shakes his head in sorrow.

"Well, Charlie ole' boy, tomorrow is another day," he mumbles. "Maybe she will say something then."

Charlie gets back into his truck and drives home.

When Karen gets home, she goes straight to her bedroom and has herself a good cry.

Her mother comes home soon afterward. When she walks into the house, she calls out for Karen but gets no response. She walks upstairs and knocks on Karen's bedroom door.

"Karen? Are you all right, dear?"

Mrs. Thomas opens the door and sees her daughter lying on her bed.

Karen rolls over toward her mother. Her eyes are red and sad.

"What's the matter, dear?" Mrs. Thomas walks over and sits down on the bed.

Karen sits up, and her mother gives her a hug.

"What's the matter, Karen? Did Charlie do something?"

Karen speaks in a very soft and gentle tone. "When I got off work today, Charlie was waiting in the parking lot for me."

"What happened then, honey?"

"Oh, nothing much, mama. He had a dozen roses in his hand. He tried to give them to me, but I wouldn't accept them."

"Did he say anything that bothered you?"

"No, mama. He just talked the same sweet way he always does. Mama?"

"Yes, dear?"

"I didn't say a single word to him, not even one."

Mrs. Thomas just sits there, holding her daughter lovingly.

After a few tender moments, Mrs. Thomas breaks the tranquil silence. "You know something, Karen?"

"What, mama?"

"I kinda miss Charlie. I mean, I … well … it was just nice to have a real man around the house. He was a perfect gentleman until …"

Karen gets up from her bed. "Yeah, mama, he was a real gentleman until he went to bed with that … that whore."

"Now, dear, don't start talking like that. That's not going to make you feel any better."

"It might not make me feel any better, but it does make me stop crying."

Mrs. Thomas sits quietly, watching Karen.

Karen picks up a brush and starts to brush her hair.

"Would you like for me to brush it for you, dear?"

"No, mama. I would rather do it myself."

Karen continues to brush her hair, but her strokes become harsh. She moves the brush wildly and uncontrollably, more and more. Her hand moves across her head with fast, quick strokes, and then she bursts into a crying fit.

"Mama!" she cries as she runs over to her mother.

Mother and daughter embrace each other with love and compassion.

"Mama, you know something?"

"What, dear?"

"I miss Charlie too."

"I know, dear. I know."

Karen keeps crying, and the two sit there and hold each other until Karen gets control of herself. Mrs. Thomas cries a little too. Her tears are for the sadness that her daughter is going through, and also for the emptiness resulting from Charlie's absence.

Meanwhile, back at his house, Charlie still feels the awful pain and agony of depression. He tries to figure out what Jesus meant when he referred to the third element. As Charlie thinks about what it might be, he realizes that he's going to need some help for his depression. He calls the Heath Care Center he belongs to at work and makes an appointment to see a doctor for his depression. The receptionist tells him to come in tomorrow and fill out a questionnaire. It will take about an hour to fill out the form, and he can come in anytime he wants to. After he fills out the questionnaire, they will schedule him to see a doctor. Charlie is happy and relieved to know that he is finally on the path to get some help for his depression.

The next day, Charlie gets up and goes to work. His boss is glad to see him. Charlie tries to catch up on all the work that wasn't done while he was out. His mind is busy for most of the day as he tries to get his workload under control. When Charlie gets off work, he decides to go home first. He wants to pick up those red roses he bought for Karen yesterday; he's kept them in the refrigerator so they'll stay fresh. He decides to pay Karen another visit at the pizza place.

Charlie drives over and parks his truck right next to Karen's car, just like he did yesterday. He waits on the tailgate, with the roses in his hand, and watches as Karen walks out the door. As she draws nearer, she sees Charlie sitting there and pretends not to notice him.

"Hello there, young lady. Let me introduce myself. My name is Charlie Delaney. I am a very lonely and stupid man. I acted like a complete jerk earlier this week. I was wondering if you would like to adopt me."

Karen looks over at Charlie, smirking slightly, but doesn't say a word. She unlocks her car door and proceeds to get in. Once again, she acts as though Charlie isn't even there.

"You sure do look pretty, young lady. You are so pretty, you could win a prize." Charlie offers the roses to Karen, sticking the blossoms through her open window.

Karen just turns her head and begins to drive off.

Stepping back, Charlie says, "Well, it sure has been nice talking to you. You drive carefully now."

Karen gives Charlie a stern look as she drives off. Charlie looks back at her, his face filled with a very sad, unhappy expression. Karen doesn't show any emotion whatsoever to Charlie. As she drives off, she glances over at his sad expression while he holds the roses in his hand.

Charlie stays there for thirty minutes, hoping Karen will come back. When she doesn't, he gets back into his truck and drives to the Health Care Center.

Charlie takes the elevator to the second floor, walks into the psychiatry department, and approaches the lady at the desk.

"May I help you?"

"Yes, ma'am. My name is Charlie Delaney. I was told to come here to fill out some type of questionnaire."

The lady flips through a file. "Yes. I will be right back. They are in another room."

Charlie waits at the desk as the lady leaves. He looks around, noticing how modern and nice everything is.

The lady comes back shortly, bringing the questionnaire. As she hands the questionnaire to Charlie, she says, "Here you go, Mr. Delaney. Just fill out your name, address, and the other simple data requested on this sheet. Then, try to answer all the questions on this sheet. Mark the answers with this pencil. If you make a mistake, erase the area completely and then mark the correct answer accordingly. If you can't make up your mind, simply put no as your answer, but answer all the questions. If you have any questions, feel free to ask me."

"Thank you very much."

Taking the pencil and the two documents from the lady, Charlie begins to complete the paperwork. It takes him a little longer than an hour to fill out both forms.

When he finishes, he takes the forms to the same lady and hands them to her. "Here you go, ma'am."

The lady takes the forms and flips through them. "Okay, Mr. Delaney. We will be calling you sometime next week."

"I work during the daytime hours, but I'd prefer if you don't call me there."

"Sure thing, Mr. Delaney. I will make sure we call you at home."

"I get home at around four-thirty."

The lady writes this down on a little yellow piece of paper and sticks it on one of the forms.

"Okay, Mr. Delaney, someone will call you at your home number on Monday or Tuesday, after four-thirty."

"That will be fine. Thank you for your help."

Relieved, Charlie walks out of the Health Care Center, gets back into his truck, and drives home.

The next day, right after work, Charlie rushes home to get the red roses out of the vase of water he has them in.

He looks at the flowers with dismay, murmuring, "If she doesn't take these flowers home today, I guess I will have to throw them away. The roses are beginning to droop a little. They sure don't look like they did when I first bought them."

Charlie hurries to get to the pizza place before Karen leaves for the day. He carries the roses to his truck, drives to the parking lot, and parks right beside Karen's car.

This time, Charlie parks his truck so close to Karen's care that she won't be able to open the door on the driver's side. He does this so that maybe she will say something to him. He doesn't care if it is something harsh, just as long as she speaks to him.

Charlie pulls down the tailgate, just like he has for the past two days, and calmly waits for Karen. Karen comes out of the restaurant and heads for her car. Charlie sees her coming and prepares to win her over one more time.

"Well, hello there! Funny bumping into you here. It sure is a beautiful day. The sun is shining. The birds are singing. Wow! What a beautiful day for a walk."

Karen approaches her car and sees that she can't get in. She looks Charlie straight in the eye, with a very mean glare.

"Oh? Is my truck blocking you from getting into your car?"

Charlie waits for Karen to say something. She just keeps staring at him with that same mean look.

"I'll tell you what, young lady. If you will give these poor roses a nice home, I will be glad to move my truck. Is that a deal?"

Karen still doesn't say anything. She does take the roses from Charlie, though. Karen waits for Charlie to move his truck.

"Now that I have your attention I just want you to know how sorry I am for behaving the way I did. Please say something, Karen. Please talk to me."

Karen's expression shows that she is getting very impatient with Charlie's stalling tactic.

"I know I have done wrong. I will spend the rest of my life trying to make it right with you. Please, Cubby, say something to me. Please talk to me, sweetheart."

Karen sees the sad expression in his face. She sticks to her guns hard, though. She doesn't say anything, not one word. She just walks over to the passenger side and unlocks the door.

"Hey, wait a minute. Okay! Okay! I will move my truck, just like I promised I would."

Charlie gets into his truck and starts it up. He moves up just far enough for Karen to open her car door, and then he quickly jumps out of his truck and runs back over to where Karen is standing.

"You see, Karen, I can be trusted. Cubby, I miss you so much. I will not let that girl come over to my house anymore. I promise on a stack of Bibles that I won't. I know you are mad at me, and I don't blame you one bit. I just feel so bad about this whole mess. All I want in the whole world is for you to speak to me. Yell at me. Scream at me. Cuss me out. Call me a name. Anything. Just say something to me."

Karen looks at Charlie like she's fixing to break down and cry, but then, just as Charlie stops talking, Karen walks over to her car and gets in. She does take the roses with her. She starts her car and gives Charlie a mean look before she drives off. He continues to keep his eyes on her. Just as soon Karen pulls out of the parking lot, she throws the roses right out the window. Charlie shakes his head in disgust as he watches the red beauties topple to the ground.

Charlie waits there again for thirty minutes, hoping that Karen will feel bad about throwing the roses away and come back. She doesn't. Charlie goes home, with his depression in a very ugly state. Charlie goes to his room and straight to bed.

When Saturday comes, Charlie is relieved he doesn't have go to work. Remembering the dream he had earlier in the week, Charlie tries to figure out if it was really something to take seriously.

I wonder if I am going crazy. Did I really see Jesus? Was it real, or was it just another dream? What is this third element? What could it be?

Charlie just lies in his bed, in a confused state, pondering the subject.

The depression takes away his will to do anything. It burns his mind with an awful pain of sadness, despair, and emptiness. After thinking about it, Charlie decides to go to the library to see if he can solve this mystery. It takes all his strength and willpower to get out of bed. He struggles to the bathroom to take a shower. After the shower, Charlie feels a little bit better. He puts on his clothes and forces himself drive to the library. When he gets there, he almost decides to turn around and go back home, but his recollection of the dream gives him the faith to go inside.

Once inside the library, Charlie walks up to the librarian and says, "Pardon me, Miss, could you help me for a moment?"

The librarian says, "Yes, sir. What can I do for you?"

"I was just wondering if you would know what the third element is."

"The third element of what, sir?" The librarian asks this with confusion on her face.

"Well … I don't really know. That's why I am asking you."

"Are you talking about the third natural element?"

"Well … yes … I guess so. What is it?"

"I don't know what the third one is. The first one is hydrogen. The second one is helium. After that, I don't really know."

Charlie scratches his head.

The librarian says, "I could help you find a book that might have the answer."

"Yes, ma'am. That would be great!"

So the librarian helps Charlie find a book on the natural elements.

Charlie takes the book from the librarian, finds a seat, and begins to look through the book. He flips through the pages casually until he gets to the very back. He then looks up the third element of matter.

Hmm … here it is. Lith … lithium. Lithium? What on God's green earth is lithium? It sounds like something you would put in a nuclear bomb! This can't be what I am looking for. It must be something else, but I don't know what.

So Charlie goes through several more books, trying to find out what this third element is. He remains at the library all day long.

After coming to the conclusion that he won't find what he came there to find, Charlie leaves the library. He is deeply disappointed, and he doesn't even check out any of the books he read over. He just walks back out to his truck and drives home. His depression doesn't get any better. He thinks how wonderful it would be if Karen would simply call him up and tell him that she isn't angry with him anymore, but he feels in his heart that won't happen.

Charlie goes to his bedroom, lies down, and falls asleep. He wakes up several times during the night, in a very bad, depressed state. He walks into his bathroom and opens up the medicine cabinet. He takes out a bottle of antihistamine cough suppressant, drinking two small cups of it, just so he can go back to sleep.

Charlie sleeps all day Sunday. He doesn't even get out of bed. When he wakes up late Sunday night, he still feels very sleepy. He manages to activate his alarm clock so he won't oversleep and be late for work on Monday. He sleeps until he hears his alarm clock go off, and then he forces himself out of bed and into the shower. He gets dressed and manages to get to work on time.

After work, Charlie goes straight home. He hopes to hear from the Health Care Center. He waits for the phone to ring, but it doesn't. After waiting for several hours, Charlie goes straight to bed. He pulls out the alarm button on his alarm clock and then collapses on his bed. His depression takes away all of his will. He doesn't want to do anything, not even things he really enjoys doing. He would rather just lie on his bed and try to sleep.

The next day comes before Charlie is ready. His depressive state gets the best of him. He just can't seem to face work today. He walks over to the phone and calls in sick. His boss begins to wonder what Charlie's problem is. Charlie tells him he just can't make it in today. His boss OK's his request but makes Charlie feel terrible and very guilty for not coming to work.

Charlie falls back into his bed. He is relieved to know he doesn't have to go to work today. Charlie lies still in his safe haven. He lies there, just staring up at the ceiling.

Dear God in heaven, what is wrong with me? Will somebody please help me? How long do I have to go on like this?

A tear begins to run down Charlie's face. He wishes his life would end. He thinks about committing suicide but hasn't got the nerve to carry it out. He continues to sincerely wish that his life would end. His manic-depressive state hits an all-time low.

Charlie lies back and falls asleep. The dreams he has are full of evil and false things. He sees visions of people at work giving him a hard time. He sees events of tragic circumstances happening all around him; nothing makes any sense. The dreams are full of stupid things, bizarre images of weird and strange things. Charlie tosses and turns in his bed until …

Until the telephone rings, bringing Charlie out of this unpleasant and grievous state of depression.

Charlie rushes over to the phone. "Hello."

The voice on the other end says, "Hello. Mr. Delaney?"

"Speaking."

"This is Carol Jennings. I am with the Health Care Center. How are you doing today, sir?"

"About the same."

"I am calling to set up an appointment for you to see Dr. Dixon about your depression."

"That sounds fine! When!"

"Would next Monday morning at ten o'clock be all right with you?"

"Don't you have anything sooner?"

"I am sorry, Mr. Delaney, but Monday at ten o'clock is the soonest I can get you in."

"Then that will be fine."

"Fine. I will put you down to see Dr. Dixon at ten o'clock, next Monday. Just come to where you filled out the questionnaire."

"Okay. I will be there."

"Okay. You have a good day. Good-bye."

Charlie puts the phone down as soon as the lady hangs up. He then starts to jump up and down.

"Thank you, Lord!" he says aloud. "I just know you are listening to me. I know you are helping me. I just want to thank you for answering my prayers."

Charlie goes into the kitchen and fixes himself something to eat. He sits back in his living room and watches a little TV until he retires to bed.

Meanwhile, at the Thomas's house, Karen is going through a

depressive state of her own. She is in her room, crying. She has been crying every day since the breakup and the fight.

Mrs. Thomas hears Karen sobbing in her room. She decides to try to cheer up her daughter.

Mrs. Thomas taps on the door and then opens it. "Karen, are you all right?"

"Yeah, mama. Can't you see I am all smiles?"

"Dear, you have been crying every day now. Did you see Charlie today?"

"No. The big dummy didn't come by work today."

"Did you want him to?"

"Me? Want him to come by? No way … well … I was hoping he would come by anyway."

"How many times has he come by now?"

"Three times, mama."

"Have you spoken to him any of those times?"

"No, mama. I haven't spoken to him since the fight."

"Why not? You look like you want to."

"I don't know what's wrong with me, mama. I kinda want to, but just as soon as I see him, I get angry all over again."

"I think I know what you are going though, honey. You want to talk to him, but your self-pride just won't let you."

Karen stops crying and then looks at her mother, intrigued. "You think that is what's the matter?"

"Yes, dear. That's what I think is the matter.

"But, mama, after Charlie cheated on me like he did, I just can't seem to forgive him."

Mrs. Thomas sits down beside her daughter, reaches over, and holds her hand.

"Dear, the first thing is Charlie never really cheated on you."

"What!"

"Now let me explain something to you. When you and Charlie broke up that night, he was no longer obligated to you."

"Huh?"

"You see, Karen, now I don't agree at all that what Charlie did was right, but he did not go to bed with that girl while you two were going together; therefore, he didn't exactly cheat on you, now did he?"

"Well ... since we did break up, I guess he didn't cheat on me, but—"

"But nothing. He was not your boyfriend at that moment, so don't try to make it sound like he was."

Karen's looks down at the floor as her mother brings her chin up.

"Now don't hate Charlie for cheating on you, because he didn't. Do you think you would cry so much if you didn't feel guilty about that fight?"

"Well, mama, I don't know. I just keep seeing those visions of Charlie having sex with that girl. It just makes me feel so ..."

"Don't think about those things, dear. Nothing on earth will ever undo that. You are going to have to accept it. Can I ask you something, Karen?"

Karen looks at her mother with sad, innocent eyes. "Yes, mama. What?"

"Do you still love Charlie?"

Karen thinks a moment and then begins to nod her head. "Yeah, mama, I still love the big dummy."

The two women laugh, and then Mrs. Thomas says, "You know something?"

"What?"

"I love the big dummy too."

The next day Charlie gets up and goes to work. He tells his boss that he has got to have Monday off so he can go see a doctor at the Health Care Center. His boss seems more understanding now that he knows Charlie is seeing a doctor. Charlie doesn't tell him the doctor is a psychiatrist. Charlie's boss likes him a whole lot; as a result, he doesn't press Charlie for more information.

After work, Charlie goes home and takes a shower. He jumps back in his truck, deciding to drive over to see Karen again. This time, Charlie doesn't bring any flowers with him. Instead, he brings an old football. Charlie pulls into the parking lot, parks his truck, pulls down the tailgate, and waits patiently for Karen to come out of the restaurant.

Just after five o'clock, Karen comes out of the little pizza place and begins to walk toward her car. When she sees Charlie, she begins to feel the anger once more.

Charlie has the football in his hands when Karen walks up to him. "Hello there, pizza girl. It sure is good to see you again."

Karen doesn't say anything.

"I thought I would bring you something," Charlie says as he tosses the football to Karen.

She instinctively catches the football, giving Charlie a strange, curious look.

"You're probably wondering why I just gave you that football."

Charlie waits for a response but doesn't get one.

"Cat still got your tongue? I brought you this football because you have such a strong arm. You throw things so well that I thought it would be a waste to let such a talented arm not have anything to throw anymore. So now, when you don't have anything to throw, you can pick up this football and throw it. Tee, hee, hee."

Karen still doesn't say anything, but she does manage to snicker softly.

"I was just wondering, Cubby, if you would let me explain what happened the other week. You will probably understand things better if you'd let me explain. I sure would like to tell you about it."

Karen's snickering smile disappears, quickly replaced by the angry look.

Undeterred, Charlie continues. "That girl wasn't just some girl I picked up. She was a girl I went to school with a long time ago."

Karen stops listening and turns to unlock her car door.

"I know that one's a boring story, so why don't I tell you the one about the man who is lonely and doesn't know how to get his girlfriend to forgive him for acting like a stupid idiot."

Karen tosses the football in her car as she gets in. She still doesn't say anything.

"I hope you enjoy the football. As much as you like to throw things, I thought it would be an appropriate gift and something you would enjoy."

When Karen hears these words, she bursts out laughing. She looks at Charlie, and her laughing face glows. She starts her car and drives.

She still hasn't said a word to Charlie, but he saw her laughing, so he feels encouraged.

Charlie tells himself, *It's just a matter of time now, Charlie ole' boy. Soon she will break. I know she still loves me. It is just a matter of time now.*

Once again, Charlie sits in the parking lot for thirty minutes, hoping Karen will come back. She doesn't. So Charlie puts up his tailgate, gets in his truck, and drives home. He feels a little bit better about things than he did earlier.

On Thursday, Charlie has a hard day at work. He is busy all day long. He is eager for the four o'clock whistle to sound. When it does, Charlie runs out to his truck and hurries home. He takes a quick shower and then heads back out to see Karen.

This time, he takes along with him a sign he made up last night. It reads, "Idiot," in big letters, and it has a string around it. Charlie puts it on the seat next to him and then drives to the pizza place.

Charlie pulls his truck right next to Karen's car, just like he has done before. He picks up the sign, walks around to the back of his truck, pulls down the tailgate, and sits down on it. He puts the sign around his neck and waits for Karen to come out of the restaurant.

Karen comes out right after five, just like always. She walks toward her car and sees Charlie sitting on his tailgate. He doesn't say anything this time. He just sits there in silence. When Karen approaches him, he gives her a sad look. Karen looks at him and then quickly turns her head away. But then she looks back and sees the sign hanging around Charlie's neck. After she reads it, she bursts out laughing. When Charlie sees Karen laugh, he laughs also.

"Hey! What are you laughing at, little girlie?"

Karen looks like she is going to say something, but then she changes her mind. She pauses before putting her key in her car door.

As she opens the door, Charlie says, "Do you think the sign is big enough?"

No response.

"I could get one as big as my truck, but it might be hard to wear. Even if I could wear it, I believe it would still be too small."

Karen listens to Charlie until he finishes, and then she starts up her car. With a smiling snicker on her face, Karen slowly looks right back over at Charlie and again explodes into laughter. She puts her car in drive and pulls away, leaving Charlie sitting on his tailgate, with the sign still hanging around his neck.

Charlie looks humble as Karen drives off. He sadly takes the sign off, once again sitting there for about thirty minutes. He patiently waits, hoping she will come back to him. She doesn't. So Charlie shrugs his shoulders and then drives home. He leaves with an empty and lonely heart.

The next day is Friday. Charlie is so glad that Friday has finally come. He goes to work and puts in another hard day at the office. When the four o'clock whistle blows, Charlie runs out to his truck and drives home. He takes a quick shower and prepares himself to pay Karen another little visit.

This time, Charlie brings with him a box of candy: chocolate-covered cherries, Karen's favorite. He hurries to his truck. As Charlie drives to the shopping center parking lot, he starts to eat the candy. By the time he gets there, he has eaten most of the chocolate. He gets out, pulls down his tailgate, and sits down. He continues to eat the candy.

Karen comes out of the restaurant, right on time. She sees Charlie sitting there as she walks toward her car.

"Hey, Karen. I bought you this box of chocolate-covered cherries because I know they are your favorite. But it looks like I have eaten them all. Look." Charlie shows Karen the empty box.

Karen gives Charlie a puzzled expression, and he smiles at her.

"I know you are watching your figure, so I didn't want to give you something that might make you fat. So I thought I would do you a favor and eat them for you. Wasn't that nice of me, thinking of you like that?"

Karen shakes her head in disbelief, but she laughs.

"You can have the box."

Karen gives Charlie a curious look.

"You're probably wondering why I would want to give you an empty box."

Charlie waits for Karen to say something, but she doesn't.

"You are so good at throwing things away that I thought you would like to throw this box away. Tee, hee, hee!"

Karen snickers, and the she starts to laugh out loud, a full, outrageous laugh.

"When are you going to speak to me? Say something, Cubby. Please say something to me, Cubby. I haven't heard you say anything to me for so long that I think I have forgotten what your voice sounds like."

Karen gets control of herself, and then she looks at Charlie with that same pissed-off expression. She gets into her car and drives away, without saying a single word.

Charlie just shakes his head as she disappears into the traffic on the road.

"Stubborn!" he says, frustrated. "That woman has got to be the most stubborn female who has ever lived. Tomorrow will be two weeks since she and I had that fight. I just can't understand why she won't speak to me. I have got to get her to say something to me if I'm ever going to get her back."

So Charlie sits there and tries to figure out what his next move is. After thirty minutes, he gets back into his truck and goes home. Once again, as he leaves the parking lot, he feels sad and disappointed.

Just as Charlie begins to drive off, Karen sits in her car and watches at a distance. She drove around the block and came back into the shopping center opposite of where Charlie could see her. She is crying like a child whose candy has been taken away. She sits there, bawling, until she gets control of herself. After a few minutes go by, she drives home.

When she arrives home, she goes straight to her bedroom, where she collapses on her bed. There, she really starts to cry. She knows her mother isn't home yet, so she bellows out those awful moans and heartbreaking groans. These sounds would make an angel cry. She cries out loud for Charlie. She yearns for him so much. She gazes up at the ceiling and cries out, "Dear God, please let me forgive Charlie. God, please let me forgive him. I love him so. Please let us be as we were." Karen cries until she has no more tears in her eyes. She looks at the clock and notices that her mother will be home soon, so she takes off all of her clothes and walks into the bathroom to take a shower.

After her shower, she puts on her clothes and walks downstairs. Her mother has already arrived home. She is putting up some groceries as Karen walks into the kitchen.

"Hey, mama."

"Hello, dear. How did your day go?"

Karen doesn't respond. She just starts helping her mother put the groceries up.

Mrs. Thomas notices that Karen's eyes are red again. Knowing what the problem is, she doesn't press. After all the groceries are put up, Karen grabs a bag of potato chips, walks into the living room, and plops down in front of the TV.

Her mother comes in soon afterward and sits down next to her.

"You never told me how your day went, dear."

"It went all right, I guess."

"Have you seen the big dummy this week?"

Karen smiles a little and says, "Yeah, mama. I've seen the big dummy three times this week."

"Oh really? What did he have to say?"

"Let me show you something."

Karen gets up and runs out to her car. She grabs the football and rushes back inside the house with it. When Karen walks back inside, she tosses the football to her mother.

Mrs. Thomas catches it as Karen eagerly asks, "Guess where I got that football?"

"How should I know?"

"You know that big dummy I used to go steady with?"

"Charlie!"

"Do you have to say his name, mama? His new name is 'the big dummy.'"

"Okay, dear. Why did the big dummy give you a football?" Still holding the football, Mrs. Thomas gives Karen a puzzled look.

Karen begins to laugh as she starts to think about it. "Mama, the big dummy said that since I have such a strong arm and like to throw things, he didn't want my arm to go to waste. He said this football will give me something to throw when I don't have anything else, or something like that."

Mrs. Thomas begins to laugh heartily.

Seeing her mother laughing, Karen begins to laugh hard also.

The more the one laughs, the more the other laughs. After a few minutes, the two women get control of themselves. Mrs. Thomas looks back over at Karen, who has a snickering smile on her face. The two women begin to laugh once more.

"When did you see him again?"

"I saw him Thursday." Karen's normal expression turns into a humorous one. She begins to laugh again.

"What are you laughing at now, Karen?" asks Mrs. Thomas. "Come on, tell me."

"Well, when I got off work Thursday, The big dummy was sitting on the back of his truck. He gave me this sad look, and then he was …" Karen's voice trails off as she starts to laugh again. She can't finish what she was going to say because of the laughter.

Mrs. Thomas, full of curiosity, tries to find out what is making Karen laugh so much. "Tell me. Tell me. What did he do?"

"He had a big sign around his neck that said 'idiot' in big letters."

"No! You don't say."

"Mama, you should have seen him sitting there. He was a sight to behold. That sad, innocent look, along with that sign around his neck. I burst out laughing the moment I saw him."

"Did you say anything to him, dear?"

"No, mama. I haven't spoken to him since I caught him with that girl over at his house."

"You said you have seen him three times. When, and what else did he do?"

So Karen describes the events to her mother. "I saw him again today, mama." She grins as she says this. "Guess what he did today!"

"Dear, I haven't got the slightest idea. Tell me!"

"Well, when I got off work today, he was out in the parking lot as usual, right next to my car. He was eating a box of chocolate-covered cherries."

Mrs. Thomas listens, intrigued.

"When I walked up, he said something about how he bought me this box of chocolate, but he ate the entire box. He said he didn't want it to make me fat, and so he thought he would do me a favor by eating it. And that's just what he did. He ate the whole box."

Mrs. Thomas roars with laughter after hearing what Karen just told her.

"That's not the funniest part, mama. Listen to this!"

Mrs. Thomas listens to her daughter with great interest.

"He then handed me the empty box."

"Why did he do that?"

"He said I enjoy throwing things away so much that he thought I might enjoy throwing the box away too."

Mrs. Thomas and Karen roar with laugher wholeheartedly at this. Mrs. Thomas laughs so hard that tears begin to come out of her eyes. They both laugh joyfully for several minutes.

Karen's laughter stops suddenly. She then begins to cry.

Her tears touch her mother's inner soul. Mrs. Thomas reaches over to hug her daughter.

"What's the matter, dear? You were laughing so happily."

"That's it, mama. I remember how much Charlie made me laugh. Now he isn't my boyfriend anymore."

"Now, dear, don't start crying again. Please don't start crying. We were both laughing and having ourselves so much fun, and then you start to act like this. Come on, honey, cheer up. You'll see: everything will work itself out okay."

"You think so, mama?"

Mrs. Thomas looks down at Karen's sad, innocent eyes. "If Charlie still means that much to you, why haven't you spoken to him?"

"I don't know, mama. I don't know. When I am away from him, I want so badly for him to be near me. But when he is close to me, as he has been this week … well … I just want to scratch his eyes out! I just keep remembering going to his house that day and seeing that woman there. She was standing there on the last step of the staircase, wearing nothing but her panties and one of Charlie's shirts. Ooh! I just get furious at him for what he did to me."

Mrs. Thomas sits there, reluctant to speak. She just listens to her daughter pour her heart out to her.

"If you would have seen that, mama, you would understand it a little better."

With that, Mrs. Thomas breaks her silence. "I disagree with you."

"You what, mama?"

"I disagree with you. Remember what we talked about earlier?"

Karen remains silent. She just looks up at her mother, her blue eyes filled with youthful innocence.

"Remember?" Mrs. Thomas persists. "Charlie didn't pick her up, did he?"

"Well, I guess not. His truck wasn't there."

"You weren't still going with him at that time, were you?"

"Well … no … but—"

"But nothing. We've already talked about this, dear, and I know it is hard to accept. But it seems to me that you're so enraged at what Charlie did that you can't understand what he must have been going through that night that would have made him do such a thing."

"What do you mean, mama?"

"He must have been hurt an awful lot to go to bed with that girl. I know he shouldn't have done it, dear, but he did. You must accept that so you can go on with your life."

Karen listens attentively to her mother.

"You see, Karen, men act differently than we do. They have something that gets erect, if you know what I mean."

Karen smiles at her mother shyly, a shade of deep magenta showing on her face. "Yes, mama, I know what you mean. Go on."

"Well, dear, when men feel this excitement in their bodies, they don't have the restraint to contain those sexual impulses the way we women do. When any sweet young thing comes walking by, men think there is nothing wrong with relieving themselves on that appealing young flesh—and this is all because of this strong erect impulse in men."

Karen's face marvels at her mother's knowledge as she speaks these words of wisdom to her. She continues to listen, fascinated.

"You see, dear, before that night, Charlie had something to restrain his erect behavior."

"What, mama?"

"You, honey, you. You see, dear, as long as you were going with

Charlie, he knew he couldn't tap into any other female's body, because of the love he had for you. As long as he had you, he could control himself. When you two broke up that night, Charlie didn't think you loved him anymore."

"How could he think that, mama? He knows I love him."

Mrs. Thomas reaches over and picks up the football off the floor.

"You see this, Karen?" Mrs. Thomas hands the football to her daughter.

Karen's face begins to turn red.

"Charlie gave this to you because you like to throw things. Do you remember throwing something else?"

Karen just nods her head slowly. She looks down at the floor. Mrs. Thomas lifts up Karen's chin gently, until her daughter's sad face is looking her straight in the eye. Mrs. Thomas smiles lovingly at her innocent-looking daughter. Karen slowly smiles back.

"You know, sweetheart, when you threw that ring out the window, you threw away more than just a ring. You threw away the token of Charlie's love for you. I can imagine what Charlie must have been thinking when you did that."

Karen looks at her mother attentively, and a tear runs down her cheek. Her mother pushes the tear away.

"After that moment, Charlie didn't have anything to restrain him anymore. When he went to find that girl—at a bar, or wherever—he didn't think you still loved him. In the state of mind he was in, he probably thought that vengeance was what he was looking for. He probably was so hurt that he wanted to do something that would hurt you back. Men sometimes do have some of the craziest thoughts floating around inside their minds, and drinking alcohol numbs the truth."

Karen blows her nose and then says, "It sure does, mama."

"Anyway, dear, Charlie is sorry now for what he has done. After hearing about the things he did this week, I am sure he realizes he was wrong."

Both mother and daughter are silent for a moment

"Did he really put a sign around his neck that said 'idiot'?"

"Yes, mama, he sure did. You should have seen him."

"I would have paid a hundred dollars to have seen that. I really would have."

Karen give her mother a look of intense admiration. "Mama, what do you think I ought to do?"

"Dear, I can't tell you that. You have got to make up your own mind about what you want to do. Charlie loves you. You love Charlie. Before you do anything, you have got to get these negative images out of your mind. Don't let the hate you have in your heart control your life. Be honest with yourself, and then you will come up with a solution to this problem."

"Mama, I love you!"

"I know, dear. I love you too."

Back at Charlie's house, lonely ole' Charlie lies on the couch. The TV is on, but the sound is turned down to where he can't hear it. He just watches the images as they appear on the screen. Charlie's face looks like that of a basset hound puppy that has lost his mother. He lies on the couch in a very depressed state. His mind burns with a depressive fire. His heart aches with loneliness. He doesn't know what to do. He hasn't the will to even get up and turn the sound on the TV back up. Charlie rolls over and tries to go to sleep.

At around three o'clock Saturday morning, Charlie gets up and turns off the TV. He walks upstairs and climbs into his bed. He doesn't get out of bed—except to go to the bathroom—until Monday morning.

Charlie lies awake early Monday morning. He looks over at his alarm clock and waits for it to start ringing. He keeps his eyes glued to the clock until the six o'clock bell begins to ring. Charlie doesn't move when the alarm sounds. He just keeps staring at the noisy clock for several minutes. After the racket begins to get on his nerves, he gets up from his warm haven and shuts it off. He walks to the bathroom, where he takes a shower. Charlie remains in there for over an hour.

After Charlie gets out of the shower, he walks over to the dresser, takes out a pair of underwear, and puts it on. With only his underwear on, he walks downstairs to the kitchen. He is famished; he hasn't eaten anything since Friday night. He pours what's left of a box of cereal into a giant bowl, pours some milk on it, and wolfs it all down, right to the last flake. After his ravenous hunger has devoured the bowl's contents, Charlie goes back upstairs to get dressed.

Charlie takes his time getting ready for his visit with the doctor at the Health Care Center. He thinks to himself, *I wonder if he can help me. I hope he doesn't try to admit me into some stupid hospital. I hope he gives me something—anything—to get this demon off my back.*

Charlie looks up and says out loud, "Dear God in heaven, please let this doctor be able to help me. Please, Lord, give me some help."

Charlie then sits back in the living room until nine o'clock. He then slowly walks out to his truck and drives to the Health Care Center for his ten o'clock appointment.

Charlie arrives a half hour early, so he takes his time walking into the building. He gets on the elevator, which takes him up to the second floor. Charlie walks out of the elevator and heads toward the psychiatry department, where he filled out the questionnaire the week before. The same lady is at the desk.

"Hello, ma'am. My name is Charlie Delaney. I have an appointment to meet with a doctor at ten o'clock."

The lady flips through some papers and then says to Charlie, "Yes, Mr. Delaney. Please have a seat, and we will call you."

So Charlie walks over and sits down in the waiting room.

Before long, Charlie's name is called.

Charlie gets up, and he sees a man standing near the lady. Charlie walks over to them.

The man puts out his hand and says, "Hello. Are you Mr. Delaney?"

"Yes, sir." Charlie shakes the man's hand enthusiastically.

"My name is Dr. Dixon. Come on back here with me to my office."

So Charlie follows the doctor back to his office.

The doctor ushers Charlie into the office, following closely, and then he shuts the door behind them.

"Please sit down, Mr. Delaney."

Charlie sits down in a chair in the quaint little room.

As the doctor sits down at his desk, he flips through some papers.

"I have read your questionnaire, Mr. Delaney. That's the form you filled out last week. Tell me, what brings you here?"

Charlie is a little reluctant at first, but he soon opens up.

"I have been depressed all my life. When my mother died some years ago, it amplified into a horrendous state. Since then, I have tried to push it aside, but now, I have broken up with my girlfriend. And the depression is like a roaring forest fire in my mind. It has taken control of my entire life. The burning, fiery pain in my brain has made me realize that I have got to do something about it."

The doctor listens to Charlie, giving him his complete attention.

When Charlie is finished, Dr. Dixon says, "You say this depression has been with you all of your life."

"Yes, sir."

"Can you remember the first time you felt it?"

Charlie thinks for a moment. "Well … I guess the first time I felt this pain was when I was little. I found an abandoned dog."

The doctor looks at Charlie intently. "Go on."

"I fell in love with this little dog the moment I saw it. The pup followed me home, and I played with it all that day. Well, to make a long story short, I wanted to keep it, so I asked my mother and my father if I could."

"What did they say about it?"

"They didn't want me to have it. Neither one of them did. They told me I couldn't keep it. They took the dog away from me. When I got home from school the next day, they had taken the dog away. I remember feeling the depression very strong that day. Even now, it feels like it happened only yesterday. I remember wanting that dog so badly that I cried. I cried and I cried. When my mama and daddy took it away, I was mad at them for a very long time."

The doctor looks at Charlie a bit apprehensively. He studies Charlie with close scrutiny, and then he finally speaks. "Did you hate your mother and father for doing this?"

"Yes, I guess I did."

"You said your mother died some years ago."

"That's right."

"Did you hate your mother right before she died?"

"Oh no! My mother and I were the best of friends. She was my sweetheart. I loved my mama more than I loved myself. She was the one person I truly adored."

"Tell me about your father. Was he good to you when you were growing up?"

"Well … yes, I guess so."

"Your response sounded a little reluctant."

Charlie tries to explain. "He was good to me, but he wasn't the kind of father I could talk to about anything."

"Tell me about your relationship with your father."

"Well … he was a good man, but when it came to talking, he was always right and I was always wrong. He didn't have the patience to understand anything I told him. I was always afraid to talk to him."

Dr. Dixon says in a soft tone, "Like what, for instance?"

"Well … like when I came home from school. I wanted to talk to him about things."

"Such as?"

"Well … girls for one thing. If I talked to him for any length of time, he would eventually say something that would hurt my feelings terribly. He was good at doing that. He would say things that would make me feel like a stupid idiot. He didn't think when he talked. He would just open his mouth and say something that would make me feel like crawling under a rock. I came to accept not talking to him about anything important in my life, knowing I would regret doing so."

Dr. Dixon listens to Charlie's story, curious and intrigued.

"Did you hate your father for talking to you this way?"

"Well … I don't think I hated him for doing it, but there were times he hurt me so much that I didn't want to be around him. He did make the depression worse."

"Is your father still alive?"

Charlie gives the doctor a silent stare, and then he says, "No, he's not."

"How long has he been gone?"

"He died before my mother died."

The doctor gives Charlie a look of compassion. "Well, I am sorry to hear that. Losing both parents is difficult to deal with under any circumstances. So tell me, did you hate your father before he died?"

"No! I didn't hate him."

There is a long silence in the room.

"So tell me, Mr. Delaney, do you think you are depressed now just because you have lost your parents?"

"No. I was depressed when they were both alive. When they died, it just amplified the pain of the depression, but it has always been there."

Dr. Dixon writes down something in his little notebook.

"All right. Tell me about breaking up with your girlfriend."

"Well … that's a long story. To tell you the truth, I don't know why we broke up. We just had this silly little fight, and the next thing I knew, we broke up."

"How long have you been seeing this girl?"

"About three months."

"Did you break up with her, or did she break up with you?"

"I broke up with her."

"Do you think your depression was the cause of the fight?"

"Well … I don't … it's kinda hard to put my finger on. It may have had something to do with it, but I'm not sure."

"Did you love this girl?"

"Yes, I did! I still do. I am trying hard to get back with her now."

"Well, if you broke up with her, why do you want to get back with her?"

Charlie scratches his head. "I have not the slightest idea why I wanted to break up with her in the first place. I love this girl more than I have ever loved anyone before. We just had a stupid fight, that's all."

"It sounds like your depression has caused you some grief in this relationship."

"Maybe you're right, Doctor."

Dr. Dixon pauses for a moment and then writes a little more in his notebook.

"Let's get back to your childhood."

Charlie listens with complete attention as the doctor continues.

"Would you say you had a normal childhood, Mr. Delaney?"

Charlie thinks for a moment and then says, "Yes, I had a pretty normal childhood."

"You said earlier that when your parents took away this dog, you got very angry with them."

"Yes, that is correct."

"Do you think this anger you had at that time stayed in you as you grew up?"

"I don't think so. I do know that after my parents took the dog away, felt the depression very strongly. I remember I didn't want to be around many people. I kinda stayed to myself. But I don't think I hated either one for any long period of time."

The doctor listens to Charlie thoroughly every time he answers a question.

Dr. Dixon looks at Charlie, scrutinizing him intensely. He then picks up Charlie's questionnaire and reviews his history.

"It says here that you were institutionalized in 1979. Would you care to tell me about that?"

Charlie pauses for a second. "That was when my mama died. It was the night of my high school graduation. I had just received my diploma ..."

As Charlie's voice trails off, Dr. Dixon urges him to continue. "Yes, Mr. Delaney. Please go on."

"Well, I had just received my diploma when a police officer came into my classroom."

Dr. Dixon looks at Charlie very attentively.

"The police officer told me my mother had just been in an automobile accident. She drove onto a bridge that had flooded. She drowned before the ambulance got there. When the police officer told me this I ... I ... I flipped out. I couldn't accept it. So they put me in this institution for a few months."

"I see. I see." Dr. Dixon's expression shows great sadness and sympathy for Charlie. "When you were put in this institution, did they give you any medications?"

"Yeah. They gave me some pills that made me sleep a whole lot."

"Hmm ... was that all they gave you? Just tranquilizers?"

"Yeah. That's all they gave me. I would swallow one, and the next thing I knew, I was in dreamland. Those pills made me sleep for a very long time. They just wanted me sedated so I wouldn't act wild, I guess."

"I see. They never diagnosed you as being manic-depressive?"

"No. They thought the only thing making me act the way I did was losing my mother. It was a real shock how she died."

Dr. Dixon takes a small pad of paper and begins to write something on it. "Mr. Delaney, I am going to prescribe something for you that I think will help you greatly."

"That will be fine," Charlie says, filled with hope and excitement. He waits for Dr. Dixon to speak again before saying anything else.

"But, first, I want you to go downstairs to have some blood work done," says Dr. Dixon.

"Okay."

"And then I want you to have an EKG."

"Fine."

"I also want you to make an appointment to see your regular doctor so that you can tell him you will be using lithium now and—"

At this, Charlie makes an excited gesture and interrupts the doctor. "What did you say, Doctor!"

The doctor gives Charlie a surprised look. "I said that I want you to tell your regular doctor—"

Charlie interrupts again. "I know that part. What did you say you were going to prescribe for me?"

Dr. Dixon speaks in a clear voice. "Lithium. I want you to take it three times a day."

"Yippee! That's what I thought you said! You are going to prescribe lithium for me!"

"That's right. Is that all right with you?"

Charlie's face lights up like a Christmas tree. "Yes, sir! That will be fine!"

"That's why I need you to have this blood work done. I also want you to come back Wednesday and have some more blood taken. I need to know if the lithium level will be where it needs to be."

So Charlie sits there, as happy as a fat rat in a cheese factory, while the doctor writes out the prescriptions for the lithium, the blood work, and the EKG.

Dr. Dixon hands Charlie three slips of paper. "Okay. This one is for the blood work and the EKG to be done today. The lab is downstairs, to the right. The lady downstairs will show you."

"Okay. I will do that right after I leave here."

"This second slip is for the blood work to be done on Wednesday.

Don't eat anything or take your lithium for twelve hours before you give the blood. You can drink a little water, but don't eat anything."

"Fine. I won't eat anything. No problem with that. And I'll take the lithium twelve hours before I come for the test."

Dr. Dixon hands Charlie the last slip. "This is your prescription for the lithium."

Charlie looks at the slip, marveling at seeing the word *lithium*.

"I want you to take one pill, three times a day," Dr. Dixon tells Charlie.

Charlie gives the doctor a look of joy and delight. "Yes, sir, thank you. Thank you so very much!"

"I hope this will make you feel better."

"It has already started to, Doctor. I believe this stuff will make me feel much better! Yes! I really do think it will."

"When you leave today, you'll need to ask my secretary to schedule you another appointment for next week."

"Fine. That will be fine."

"When I get the Wednesday blood results, I might call you at home to tell you to increase or decrease your medication. I will know more after I get the results."

"Okay. You can call me anytime, Doctor."

Charlie takes a slip of paper out of his pocket, writes down his phone numbers at home and at work, and gives the slip to the doctor.

Dr. Dixon looks at the slip and then at Charlie. "You work in the daytime, don't you?"

"Yes. Eight in the morning till four in the afternoon."

"I don't like calling people at work. It's just something I would rather not do. I get off at five, so why don't I call you around five o'clock Friday afternoon."

"That sounds great!"

Charlie and the doctor shake hands and walk out to the front.

Dr. Dixon's secretary schedules Charlie for another appointment, the following Monday. He shakes Charlie's hand and wishes him a good day.

Charlie gets on the elevator and goes down one floor. He finds the lab, takes a seat in the waiting room, and waits for someone to call his name. A lot of other people are waiting also; the room is filled with people. As Charlie looks around, he notices some very old people with sad, tired expressions. He sympathizes with them, touched by the misery in their expressions. Soon a lady in a white uniform comes into the waiting room and calls out Charlie's name. He gets up and follows her to another room.

Just as Charlie sits down, he realizes what is about to take place. Seeing the long needle in the lady's hand, he says, "I … I think I need to tell you something."

The lady smiles and says, "Yes. What would you like to say?"

"You see that needle?"

"Yes."

"I just so happen to be allergic to them. Every time I've had to give blood, I get sick. I just want you to know that before you stick it in me."

The nurse tries to distract Charlie by getting him to focus on something else. As she pushes the needle into Charlie's arm, she says, "So tell me, where do you work?"

"Steven's Knitting over on Broad Street."

The nurse continues to talk with Charlie until she is finished. And then she pulls out the needle. "That didn't take very long, did it?"

Just as the needle comes out of his arm, Charlie begins to feel a wave nausea coming on.

"Oh no! Lady! I believe I am going to get sick. Is there some place I can lie down?"

Charlie's head begins to spin profoundly. He sees stars and feels as though he is going to pass out. The nurse runs over to the bed in the corner and pulls out the leg extension. As she tends to the bed, she tells Charlie to put his head between his legs. Charlie is on the brink of passing out; his face is as white as a sheet. The nurse walks over to Charlie and helps him up from the chair. She manages to get him to lie on the bed before he passes out. Charlie lies there on the bed, and his blood pressure slowly begins to return to normal.

As he comes to, the nurse says, "Would you like some orange juice?"

Charlie says in a very soft tone, "Yes. Yes, that would be fine."

The nurse then pours Charlie a cup of orange juice and hands it to him.

The nurse tells Charlie, "Just lie still, and drink your juice. I will be right back." She then runs to find someone to help her.

Charlie lies there for a few minutes. The first nurse then comes back into the room, and another nurse is with her. The two nurses stand over Charlie, looking at him worriedly.

The second nurse says, "What happened to you?"

Charlie finishes his orange juice. He points his finger at the first nurse. "She stuck me with a needle."

"Did she do that? I think I will take your blood pressure, if that's all right with you."

"That will be fine with me."

"Would you like some more orange juice?"

"Yes, I sure would."

The first nurse pours Charlie some more orange juice, while the second nurse takes his blood pressure.

Charlie rests on the bed for about twenty minutes altogether. The nurse takes Charlie's blood pressure three times. Charlie drinks several cups of orange juice before he gets up from the comfortable position.

The first nurse tells the second nurse, "He has to have an EKG. I can't leave here. Would you help him upstairs so he won't have to go by himself?"

So Charlie and the nurse walk out of the room and go upstairs for his EKG. The nurse takes Charlie to the room where the EKGs are performed. She guides Charlie to the waiting room.

"Do you think you will be all right now?"

"Oh yeah. I will be fine now. Really. I am all right now."

"Okay. I will leave now. You have a good day."

"Yes, ma'am, I will. Thank you for helping me."

The nurse disappears from sight as Charlie sits down. Soon another nurse calls out his name.

"Charlie Delaney, would you please come with me?"

Charlie gets up, and the nurse takes him into another room.

"Will you take off your shirt and pants?"

Without hesitating, Charlie does as he's told, taking off first his shirt and then his pants. He is still a little queasy from giving the blood a while ago.

"Okay," says the nurse. "You can lie down on the table now."

Charlie lies down on the table, and the nurse puts electrodes on his chest, stomach, and legs. The procedure only takes a few minutes.

"Okay, Mr. Delaney, you are ready to go. You can get dressed now."

At this, Charlie quickly puts on his clothes. As Charlie puts his shirt on, he gets a fright.

"Oh no! Where is it! Where is my prescription?" he wonders aloud.

He finishes dressing and then quickly runs out of the room to find the nurse. Spotting her, Charlie rushes over.

"Miss! I have lost something!"

The nurse, seeing the panic in Charlie's eyes, says, "What did you lose, Mr. Delaney?"

"I lost my prescription! I had two slips from my doctor; one was my prescription!"

"Have you checked everything in the EKG room?"

"Yes! Yes! It isn't there!"

The nurse walks into the room and looks for the prescription herself.

Charlie's face is full of worry as he watches the nurse search the room.

"Where were you before you came up here, Mr. Delaney?"

"I had some blood work done."

"You were in the lab."

"Right! That's where I was, in the lab!"

"Come with me."

Charlie follows the nurse. They both get on the elevator and go down. Just as soon as the door opens, the nurse rushes out. She doesn't look back, not even for Charlie. She walks with authority right past the desk and straight to where the blood is drawn. Charlie follows right behind her.

"Has anyone found a prescription for Mr. Delaney?"

"Yes. I did."

Charlie looks over and sees the nurse who took his blood earlier. She is holding the prescription in her hand. Charlie walks over to the nurse and takes the prescription from her.

"Oh boy! Thank you! Oh, thank you so very much!" Charlie says, wrapping his arms around the nurse and kissing her right on the forehead."

"Well, thank you," says the nurse.

Charlie then walks over to the other nurse and wraps his arms around her also. He kisses her on the forehead three times.

"I want to thank you so much for coming down here."

"You're welcome, Mr. Delaney."

"Are you married?"

The nurse blushes a little and then says, "Well, yes, I am."

"Damn shame. Oh well. I guess I missed out again."

The nurse laughs sweetly at Charlie's remark. She gives him an intriguing feminine look, her face glowing.

He gives her another hug and smiles at her with affection. And then, without saying anything else, he slowly turns and walks away. He happily leaves the building with his prescription in his hand.

Charlie walks right across the street to the pharmacy. He happily looks at his prescription one more time before he hands it over to the lady behind the window.

"Here you go."

The lady takes the prescription and politely says, "It will take a few minutes. Please be seated. We will call you when it's ready."

"Yes, ma'am, I will." He finds a seat and sits down.

As Charlie sits there, waiting for his prescription to be filled, he feels robust joy and excitement in his soul. His mind is flooded with anticipation of what is to follow. He is so excited about everything that he can't sit still. He gets up, walks around, and then shortly returns to his seat.

When Charlie sits back down, he begins to think about the dream he had. The dream where he saw Jesus. He thinks to himself, *Oh, how true that dream was. Hmm … the third element … it was so real!*

As Charlie sits there in his seat, thinking about the prodigal dream, he finally hears his name called: "Mr. Charlie Delaney! Pick up at window 3."

Charlie jumps up and walks over in a hurry to the window which has a large numeral 3 above it.

Standing there is another lady in white. She smiles at Charlie as he walks up. "You take one capsule three times a day. You may eat something before you take the capsules, or you may take them with some milk."

Charlie smiles at the lady as he takes the bottle from her hand. "Thank you! Thank you so very much!"

Charlie signs his name on the line of the paper the lady holds toward him, and then he happily walks back to his truck. He is full of excitement and jubilation.

When Charlie gets inside his truck, he takes the top off the little bottle and very carefully pours out some of the capsules in his hand. They are the most beautiful little things he has ever seen. Charlie stares at the tiny pills for a few minutes, marveling at their rosy white color.

Charlie pours the little pills back into the bottle and drives straight to the nearest grocery store for a carton of milk. Charlie carefully opens the bottle of pills once again. He takes out one of the capsules and puts it in his mouth. He swallows the pill and then drinks down the entire carton of milk. Charlie then sits back and relaxes for a moment before driving back home.

Charlie walks into his house and goes into the living room. He turns on the TV and sits down on the couch. About three hours later, he begins to feel something.

"Hey … hey … hmm …" Charlie mumbles and then begins to smile. As he watches the TV he starts to think out loud. "Hey … oh my, my, my. Yes, I can feel it working! It feels like a cool breeze is blowing on the outer part of my brain. I thought it would take several days before I would feel anything. Oh my! This is wonderful! I can't believe this. I am feeling better! Yes! I am feeling much better." Charlie looks up to the ceiling and says, "Dear God in heaven, thank you! Thank you, Lord! I can't believe it. It's like a cool breeze blowing on my brain."

Charlie jumps up and starts to walk around his house, filled with a happy, glorious feeling.

Charlie suddenly gets an idea. He goes upstairs, puts on some different clothes, rushes out to his truck, and jumps in. He then drives down to the mall. When Charlie gets out, he smiles contentedly, thinking about what he has planned. He hurries into the mall and goes directly to the pet shop, walking over to the window where all the little puppies are. He looks them all over until he finds one that fits his personality.

Just as soon as Charlie has picked out a pup, he hears a voice say, "May I help you, sir?"

Charlie turns and sees a beautiful girl standing behind him. A smile lights up her young face.

"Yes, miss. I would like to hold that basset hound, if it would be all right."

"Yes, sir. Let me go get the key."

Charlie waits there as the sales clerk leaves to fetch the key. He stares lovingly at the little basset hound puppy.

The sales clerk comes back and opens the little cage that the dog is in. She picks up the little guy and takes it to Charlie.

Charlie takes the puppy from the girl and says, "I can tell you right now, miss, you won't have to put him back in that cage. Is it a he or a she?"

"It's a boy."

Charlie holds the dog in his arms, cradling him with love and affection.

"Wow! Would you just look at those ears!"

"He sure is a pretty little dog," the sales clerk adds.

Charlie stares at the pup's sad expression and says, "I know just how you feel, little dog. Oh boy! He has captured my heart!"

"He has had all his shots."

"I will take him."

"Fine, sir. Let me go get his papers. I will be right back."

The sales clerk leaves, and Charlie stands there, holding the puppy.

The sales clerk comes back in a few minutes. "He sure is a cute little guy. I love basset hounds. I have one myself."

"Could you tell me something?"

The sales clerk gives Charlie a curious look, and then she says, "Yes, sir. What would you like to know?"

"Could you deliver this puppy to my girlfriend's house?"

"I guess we could. It will cost a little extra for delivery."

"That will be fine. I will be glad to pay extra if you will deliver him to her."

The sales clerk thinks for a moment and then says, "Wouldn't you like to give the puppy to her in person?"

Charlie pauses for a moment. "Well … I kinda want it to be a surprise. When you deliver it, she will be surprised. Boy, will she ever be surprised!"

"That will be fine."

So Charlie pays for the basset hound puppy. He writes down Karen's address and then hands it to the sales clerk.

"Make sure you don't deliver the puppy until after five-thirty. Do you think you can deliver him tomorrow?"

"Well … I don't know about tomorrow."

Charlie thinks to himself and then gets an idea. "I will pay you fifty bucks if you will deliver the puppy exactly when I want."

"Heck, for fifty dollars, I will deliver him personally."

"Okay, here's how I want it to go. First, I want the puppy delivered at exactly five-thirty on Wednesday afternoon."

"Okay."

"Second, I want the puppy to have a red bow wrapped around him. Do you think you can handle that?"

"No problem at all."

"Good. The third thing is I want you to give my girlfriend a note."

"Sure. What kind of note?"

Charlie goes over to the counter, writes the note, and gives it to the sales clerk.

"Here you go. Make sure you give this note to Karen Thomas. Don't give it to anyone else. Okay?"

"Sure thing, Mr. Delaney. The puppy will be delivered at exactly five-thirty on Wednesday afternoon. The puppy will be wrapped in a red bow, and I will give Miss Karen Thomas this note."

"That is perfect! I want to thank you so very much for your help."

"Thank you, and please come back."

With that, Charlie leaves the pet store, in a joyous frame of mind.

After Charlie gets home, he sits around the house, plotting out his plan for what to do and say to Karen this week. He takes the second lithium pill eight hours after the first one, and then he devises his plan thoroughly before going to sleep.

The next day is Tuesday, and Charlie faces the day in a happier state of mind. The lithium seems to be working well for him. After work, Charlie goes straight home. He thinks about going over to see Karen but decides not to; he doesn't want to go by the pizza place too often. Instead, he spends an enjoyable evening at home. He takes his lithium just as Dr. Dixon instructed him to do: three times a day. Charlie sits back, full of confidence. The lithium also gives Charlie an erotic stimulation, starting at his crotch and then spreading throughout his body. For the first time in Charlie's life, the depression has been removed from his mind.

After work on Wednesday afternoon, Charlie quickly runs to his truck. He drives home, takes a quick shower, and puts on some shorts and a T-shirt. Running to his truck like a secret agent working on an important case, he drives to Little Tony's Pizza, pulls into the shopping center parking lot, and parks his truck right near Karen's car. He waits patiently until he sees Karen come out of the restaurant.

Karen walks slowly to her car, and there is Charlie, sitting on the tailgate of his truck.

She gets closer, and then Charlie says, "Hello, stranger. Long time no see."

Karen doesn't pay any attention to him. She pulls out her keys and starts to unlock her car door.

Charlie is disappointed when Karen doesn't say anything, yet again.

"You know something, Cubby, I haven't let that girl come over to my house again. Matter of fact, I told her I didn't want her calling my house either. I knew you'd want to know that, but I guess you can't find the words to ask me. Tee, hee, hee."

At the sound of Charlie's high-pitched laugh, Karen opens her car door and gets into the car.

"Hey, Cubby! Don't leave so soon. I want to talk to you. You don't have to talk me if you don't want to; I just have a few more things I want to say to you."

Karen sits in her car, glaring at Charlie with that stern, pissed-off look. She doesn't start the engine; she just sits there and looks at him.

Charlie is happy to see that Karen isn't leaving.

"Guess what, Cubby? I bought you a present. I was afraid you wouldn't accept it if I gave it to you personally, so I am having it delivered to your house. I just want you to know that I am not trying to buy your love. It is just something I thought you might enjoy."

Karen listens to Charlie with complete attention. As the stern expression disappears from her face, she turns her head away from him so that she doesn't have to look at him while he speaks.

"What I bought you is something you can't throw away. After you see it, you'll understand what I mean. It's like the love I have for you: something you can't throw away."

Karen turns her head toward Charlie and gives him a curious look.

Charlie looks at Karen with a sweet, kind, humble expression. "It is only a token of the love and appreciation I have for you. It will remind you of me when you are feeling down. I want to try hard to make up for the wrong I have done to you, sweetheart."

A tear runs down Karen's cheek.

"I love you, Cubby."

A few more tears run down Karen's cheeks. She turns the key and starts the engine, once again driving off without saying a word to Charlie.

Charlie saw Karen begin to cry before she drove off. He tells himself, *She will crack soon. Tee, hee, hee. Before too long, she will be my girlfriend again. She still loves me. It is only a matter of time now. Tee, hee, hee.*

Charlie remains in the parking lot for thirty minutes, but Karen doesn't come back.

When Karen gets home she walks slowly up to her doorstep, still crying. She manages to wipe away her tears before going inside the house.

Mrs. Thomas is sitting in the kitchen as Karen walks in. "What's the matter, dear? Did you see Charlie today?"

Karen shrugs her shoulders and sits down next to her mother. "Yes, mama, I saw him."

"Did you two talk any?"

"Well … kinda."

Mrs. Thomas shows concern at her daughter's response. "What exactly do you mean by 'kinda'? Either you did, or you didn't."

"Well, mama, he talked but I didn't. I just listened to him."

"Why didn't you speak to him, dear?"

"I don't know, mama. I just don't know."

Karen begins to cry again. Her mother puts her arms around her daughter to offer support.

"Well, what did Charlie have to say?"

"Huh? Oh … he said he bought me a present."

"What was it?"

"I don't know. He didn't give it to me. I guess he thought I would throw it away. He said he was going to have it delivered."

"Did he tell you what it is?"

"No, mama, he didn't. I guess he wanted me to ask him what it is, but I didn't."

Mrs. Thomas looks at her daughter with sadness and curiosity. "Honey, don't you think you should talk to Charlie, maybe just a little?"

"I want to, mama, I really do! But as soon as I see him, I just can't make myself forgive him enough to say anything to him."

Karen begins to cry harder. Her tears make her mother start to cry too.

"Karen, why don't you call Charlie up? Or better yet, why don't you and I go over to his house so that you and he can talk. I think it would—"

"No, mama! No! I will not go crawling back to him. I just won't do it!"

"Honey, you won't be crawling back. You'll be walking back. Ha, ha, ha!"

"Mama! That wasn't funny. I am in the worst predicament I have ever been in—in my whole life—and you're making jokes."

"I know, dear. I was just trying to cheer you up some. Don't be angry with me."

As Karen and her mother are talking, the doorbell rings. Karen gets up and walks toward the door. When she opens it, she sees a young woman standing on the doorstep, holding a little basset hound puppy wrapped in a red bow.

"Is this where a Miss Karen Thomas lives?" asks the woman.

"Yes, it is. I am Karen."

The young lady smiles gladly at Karen and says, "I have a little present for you."

Intrigued and curious, Karen looks at the lady and the little pup. After a moment, she says to the lady, "Please come in."

Just as the lady steps into the house, Karen calls out, "Mama! Mama! Come here! Come here quick!"

Mrs. Thomas comes out of the kitchen in a hurry. She sees the young woman holding the puppy, and her eyes light up like a Christmas tree.

"What have we here!" asks Mrs. Thomas.

The young woman holding the puppy looks at it and says, "Say, 'I am a basset hound.'"

Smiling, Mrs. Thomas says, "Come on in the living room."

The three women walk into the living room.

Karen's face is full of happiness and joy as she picks up the little puppy and holds it in her arms.

"Wow! What a pretty little puppy. What type did you say she is?"

"*He* … is a basset hound. He is a present to you from a Mr. Charlie Delaney."

Silence fills the room when Charlie's name is mentioned.

"Mama, isn't this the prettiest little puppy dog you have ever seen!"

"Yes, dear, he sure is."

The young lady hands Karen Charlie's note.

"What's this?"

"Mr. Delaney wanted me to give you this when I delivered the puppy."

Giving her mother a strange look, Karen says, "Mama, would you read it?"

"Oh no, young lady. Charlie wanted you to have it, not me. You read it."

Before Karen has a chance to read the note, the lady who brought the pup says, "I hope you enjoy this little basset hound. He has had all his shots for now, but it would be a good idea to take him to a vet. He can tell you how to take care of him, and he'll let you know when he will need his other vaccines. It is just a good idea for him to have his own doctor, because he is a basset hound. Basset hounds should be cared for more particularly because they are special. I'm not just saying that because I own one. I say that because they are the most adorable dogs in the whole world. I don't know why anyone would want any other type of dog."

Karen and her mother listen with joy as the young woman speaks.

"I guess people have their own tastes. My basset hound is my best friend."

Mrs. Thomas and Karen smile with admiration at the young lady.

The three women sit there, admiring the innocent and humble expressions of the basset hound puppy. The sound the little pup makes when he barks makes everyone's heart and mind feel happy and filled with love.

As the ladies sit and look at the puppy, the young woman who brought him to Karen says, "There is one thing I should tell you about basset hounds."

Karen gives her a curious look. "What's that?"

"Even though these little pups are cute and adorable, they aren't the smartest dogs in the world. Matter of fact, they are kinda on the dumb side. So be patient with him. Don't expect him to learn many tricks. These dogs are very sensitive. So please don't yell at him or hit him. Okay?"

"We will take good care of him. You don't have to worry about him," Mrs. Thomas says reassuringly.

"Oh boy!" Karen exclaims. "I have already fallen in love with him."

"Well, I must be leaving now," the young woman says. "I hope you all will have a good day."

Mrs. Thomas walks the young lady to the door as Karen continues to hug and love the little basset hound puppy. Mrs. Thomas comes back into the living room and sits down beside Karen. They both play with the little pup, happily getting acquainted.

"Have you read the note yet, dear?"

"Isn't he a nice little puppy, mama?"

"Didn't you hear me, Karen?"

Karen stares at her mother for a few seconds and then turns her head away.

"What name do you think I should give my little friend, mama?"

"I don't know, dear. What did you do with Charlie's note?"

"I threw it on the coffee table." Karen quickly points at the table while she continues to play with her little puppy. "I'll read it later … maybe."

Mrs. Thomas looks at her daughter with surprise. "Aren't you at all curious about what's in the note?"

Karen keeps her attention on the puppy. She doesn't answer at first, but then she says in a callous tone, "No, not really. I think I will call my puppy Charlie."

"Why would you want to call him that?"

Karen playfully flips the puppy on his back and laughs at him.

"Well, mama, he did give me the puppy; besides, I don't need him anymore now that I have this Charlie."

"I don't understand you, Karen. Charlie buys you this adorable little puppy which has brightened up your day, and you won't even read the note he had delivered to you."

Karen answers sharply, "I don't want to read it because it will make me cry! I know it will. I don't want to cry, so I don't want to read that stupid note! Now don't bother me about it anymore!"

Looking hurt when she hears Karen's harsh words, Mrs. Thomas gets up and leaves the room quietly.

Karen begins to feel a little guilty about what she just said. She gets up, walks over to the coffee table, and picks up the note. She walks back to the puppy and sits down. The little puppy gives his frail, innocent bark one more time as she opens the note. She pauses nervously as her hand shakes, and then she reads the note.

> Hello, Cubby.
>
> I wanted to give you something that would express to you how I am feeling. The personality of this little basset hound puppy describes it perfectly. This little dog's sad eyes show how my heart is feeling right now. The look on his face shows you how lonely I am. The long floppy ears show how long I have waited to hear your voice. The frail, innocent bark the pup makes is the same

sound my soul makes every time I think of you. I hope you like this little basset hound. His personality is the image of my own. I hope that by giving you this little puppy, I will get you to at least read this note. All I want to do is explain things to you. I know I did wrong. I will spend the rest of my life trying to make it up to you. I will see you tomorrow in the parking lot by the pizza place. I hope you will find it in your heart to forgive me. I hope you will at least talk to me. I am running out of paper, so I must end this note. I just want you to know that I love you, Cubby.

Love,

Charlie

After Karen reads the note, she begins to cry quietly.

Mrs. Thomas peeps through the doorway at Karen. She then walks back into the living room and sits down beside her. The little puppy begins to scratch and chew at Karen's foot. He is still barking that frail, innocent bark. Karen reaches down and picks up the adorable little puppy dog.

"Did you read Charlie's note, dear?"

"Yes, mama, I read it."

"Would you mind if I read it?"

"No, I don't mind."

Karen hands the note to her mother.

Mrs. Thomas reads the note, and then she looks at her daughter. "There is one thing you have to say about Charlie, dear."

"What's that, mama?"

"Charm. That man has charm. He knows just what to say and just how to say it."

"I guess so, mama."

As another tear runs down Karen's face, her mother asks, "Why are you crying, dear? It was a sweet note. Don't you think so?"

"That's just it, mama. It is *too* sweet. It makes me feel bad. It makes me feel real bad."

Mrs. Thomas looks at her daughter with concern, and then she says, "Does it make you feel bad, or does it make you feel guilty?"

"Guilty? What have I done to feel guilty about?"

Mrs. Thomas doesn't reply.

Karen pauses a moment before saying, "Well … maybe I do feel a little guilty about everything."

"Are you going to talk to Charlie tomorrow?"

"I don't know, mama. I just don't know what I am going to do."

"After reading this note, honey, don't you think Charlie is sorry for what he did?"

"Yes, mama. I know he is sorry. I have known that for quite some time now. I just can't seem to forget about him being with that girl."

"Dear, we have talked about that a few times now. I thought we got it all sorted out the other day."

"I know, mama. I know we talked about it, and I remember everything you said. I don't care, though! He went to bed with another girl. Nothing will erase that from my mind! Nothing! He had no right to do such a thing."

"It sounds to me like you can't forgive Charlie because you can't forgive yourself."

Karen looks at her mother with a shocked expression. "What? What are you talking about, mama?"

Mrs. Thomas gives her daughter a stern look as she tries to explain. "You have to remember something, young lady, Charlie would never had gone to bed with that girl if you hadn't thrown his ring out the window. You are partly responsible for his doing what he did, and until you admit that, you will never be able to forgive yourself."

"But, mama—"

"Don't 'but mama' me, young lady! The problem isn't with Charlie and what he has done. The problem is with you and what you have done."

Karen quietly listens to her mother with complete attention.

Mrs. Thomas continues. "I don't agree that what Charlie did was right, but after hearing all of the factors involved, I have come to the understanding that Charlie was hurt that night you and he broke up, very hurt. And because he was hurt, he did something stupid. Now he is feeling very ashamed about what he did. In other words, he feels a greater hurt because he knows he hurt you. Now if that isn't love, then I don't know what is."

Karen looks at her mother in silence, with her sad blue eyes watering.

"Until you admit that you are at fault somewhat in this whole episode, Karen, you will never be able to look at this matter honestly or genuinely."

Even after hearing these words, Karen still doesn't budge one bit on how she feels about Charlie.

"I think I will go to the store and buy my little dog some food."

Mrs. Thomas just shakes her head in disgust as Karen gets up and leaves the house.

Karen comes back in about an hour, with two bags in her arms. She bought the little puppy some puppy food, as well as numerous toys for him to play with. She also bought him a collar and chain. Karen takes up with the little pup very affectionately. She loves her new companion.

Mrs. Thomas just looks at Karen sternly as she plays with the dog so cheerfully.

Before it gets too late, Karen puts the collar on the puppy and takes him outside. She chains him to one of the trees in the backyard. Giving the little puppy a good-night kiss, Karen turns and walks back into the house.

"Karen, I am going to bed now," Mrs. Thomas says. "I just want you to know that Charlie isn't going to keep after you forever. Soon he will grow tired of chasing after you."

"Mama, will you lay off me about Charlie? He is getting just what he deserves."

"Young lady, one of these days you will get just what you deserve too."

Mrs. Thomas leaves the room to go to her bedroom.

Karen remains sitting downstairs in the living room, thinking about everything her mother has said.

The next day, Thursday, Charlie goes to work as usual. He feels better than he has ever felt in his life. The lithium has relieved him of all the sad depression that has plagued him for most of his life. Charlie works with a great sense of enthusiasm, showing eagerness and fervor on the job. The day goes by quickly for him. Before long, Charlie hears the four o'clock whistle blow. He runs out to his truck and drives home.

When he arrives, he races inside, changes his clothes, and grabs a bag from the closet. He rushes back out to his truck and drives to the shopping center parking lot. Pulling up to the pizza place, he spots Karen's car and parks his truck right next to it. He waits nervously, sitting on the tailgate of his truck until he sees Karen come out of the restaurant. She walks toward her car.

As Karen walks out to her car, Charlie opens the bag he brought with him and takes out a rolled-up newspaper. When Karen approaches her car, Charlie holds out the rolled-up newspaper.

"The girl at the pet store told me the best way to discipline a puppy is to spank him with a rolled-up newspaper. So here you go. It's not for the basset hound puppy; it's for me. So if you want to whack me a few times with it, I will understand."

Karen looks at Charlie's sad expression, and then she gets in her car and starts to turn the ignition.

"Hey! Don't leave! You haven't told me if you like my present."

Karen gets out of her car and walks over to Charlie. She throws an envelope at him, and then she turns and walks back to her car.

Before Charlie has time to open the envelope, Karen starts her car and begins to drive away.

Charlie calls out, "Come on, Cubby, can't you just say something to me? Please say something—anything!"

Karen puts her car in gear and drives away, leaving Charlie standing there, with nothing but the envelope.

Charlie opens the envelope after she has left his sight. He pulls out the piece of paper inside the envelope, reading it quickly:

> Thank you for the basset hound. I am still angry with you!
>
> Karen

Charlie sits back down on the tailgate, shaking his head in disappointment. *I thought for sure she would at least say something to me. I just can't see why she is acting so stubbornly. I just can't understand why she won't talk to me. Oh well … tomorrow is another day.*

Charlie doesn't wait thirty minutes this time. He just goes straight home, disappointed once again.

The next day is Friday, And Charlie is glad to see it come. He works very hard all day, trying to complete his work. Also, he works with a sense of extreme confidence. He thinks hard about how he is going to approach Karen today. He studies the matter until … *Pow!* Charlie gets a marvelous idea. He thinks about his plan extensively and devises it thoroughly. When the four o'clock whistle blows, Charlie eagerly runs out to his truck and drives straight home.

He changes out of his work clothes and into shorts and a T-shirt. He takes another capsule of lithium, with a glass of milk, and then hurries back out to his truck. He hops in and begins to drive happily to the shopping center parking lot. Charlie smiles joyfully as he drives down the road. He is eager to see Karen today.

And then, Charlie realizes something. *Oh shit! Oh no! Dr. Dixon told me he was going to call me today. Oh shit! He said he was going to call to tell me about my lithium level.*

So Charlie turns the truck around and heads back home. He rushes into the house and looks at the answering machine. No one has called, so Charlie sits down and waits for the call from the doctor.

"Ring, phone, ring! I don't have all day!" Charlie says aloud.

He looks at the clock on the wall. It is exactly 4:32 p.m.

Charlie thinks to himself, *It will take me about twelve minutes to get to Little Tony's Pizza. Karen will be walking out the door right at five. Come on, phone, ring! I have about sixteen minutes!*

Charlie waits and waits for the phone to ring. He keeps staring right at it, until it finally rings.

Charlie picks up the phone before it rings one complete time. "Hello, this is Charlie."

"Hello, Charlie. This is Dr. Dixon."

"Hello, Dr. Dixon."

"How are you feeling?"

"Oh, I am feeling much better, much better. The lithium seems to be working very well."

"Good, very good. I am glad to hear that. Are you feeling any side effects?"

"No. I'm not feeling anything unusual. I can't believe how good I am feeling now."

"Excellent! I was a little bit worried that you might feel some side effects; I am happy you aren't experiencing any." Dr. Dixon pauses and then says, "I have got the lab report back. Your lithium level seems to be low, so I want you to take four capsules a day, instead of three."

"That will be fine."

"Just take two capsules in the morning, one when you get home from work, and one more before bed. On your days off, take the third capsule at approximately the same time as you do when you get home from work."

"Okay, that sounds like a winner. I will do just that."

"Fine. I am glad you are feeling better. I have to go now. I will see you Monday at ten o'clock."

"Okay, Dr. Dixon, I will be there. Thanks a lot for your help."

"I am just glad to be of some assistance. You have a good weekend."

"I will. You have the same. Good-bye."

Charlie puts down the phone and hurries out to his truck. He drives straight to the shopping center parking lot, but when he pulls in, he sees Karen's car driving away. Charlie sits there, angry and disappointed. He sits there and thinks about another plan. He doesn't let his discouragement affect his desire to make up with Karen. Instead, it just makes him more determined than ever to get Karen to talk to him. He sits there for about thirty minutes, until he comes up with a very daring and adventurous plan. He grins a determined grin and then drives home.

When Charlie gets home, he quickly runs to the garage. He gets an empty bucket, a sponge, a few towels, and a bottle of glass cleaner. He smiles gladly as he puts these items in the back of his truck.

He thinks to himself, *I believe that is all I will need. I guess it is time to pay Miss Karen Thomas a little visit.*

Feeling determined, Charlie gets into his truck. He laughs heartily, and his ambitious expression shows that he is up to something.

Charlie drives until he reaches Karen's house. He hasn't been there in almost three weeks. When he arrives, he takes the items out of his truck and walks over to Karen's car. Charlie takes the Thomas's garden hose and begins to wash Karen's car. As he sprays the car with the water, he begins to whistle.

Mrs. Thomas is sitting in the living room. She sees a reflection, so she goes to the window. She casually looks out the window. Her eyes get as big as marbles, and her mouth falls open.

"Karen! Karen! Come here!" Mrs. Thomas runs from the living room into the kitchen. "Karen! Where are you!"

Karen comes down the stairs. "What is it, mama? What's the matter?"

"Did you see Charlie today?"

Karen gives her excited mother a curious look. "No, mama, I didn't. He didn't come by after work."

"Would you like to know where he is now?"

Karen curious look becomes a very concerned one. "Where is Charlie, mama?"

Mrs. Thomas smiles at Karen as she says with conviction, "Would you believe that dumb dumb is outside, washing your car?"

"Huh? What? He is doing what!"

Karen runs to the window and looks out. She sees Charlie washing her car. Seeing this, Karen gets mad. Anger flashes in her eyes.

Mrs. Thomas sees Karen's rage building. She tries to defuse it somewhat.

"Young lady, why are you getting so upset? I think it is quite funny."

"Funny! What is so funny about Charlie coming over here?"

"Now don't blow your top! Remember it was your bad temper that got you into this mess in the first place."

"Who does he think he is? He has got a lot of nerve coming over here. I guess I will have to go out there and give him a piece of my mind."

"Now don't be mean to him, Karen. I mean that! You have been wanting him to come over here and try to make up with you for quite some time now; therefore, don't ruin the opportunity you have."

Karen's face is indignant as she listens to her mother. She opens the door and walks outside, approaching Charlie from behind.

Karen yells, "What the hell are you doing!"

Charlie turns around and smiles gladly. With jubilance and happiness he says, "She spoke to me! Dear God in heaven, she actually spoke to me! I can't believe it! I really can't believe it! You spoke to me, Cubby."

Charlie begins to dance around with great jubilation. He says enthusiastically, "Please say those beautiful words one more time."

Karen, with anger in her eyes, bellows once again, "What the hell are you doing!"

Charlie smiles at Karen gladly as he replies, "We have been broken up almost three weeks now, and you have forgotten what it looks like to see somebody wash a car! It just goes to show how much we need each other."

Karen doesn't think what Charlie said was very funny. "I can see that you are washing my car. Why are you doing it?"

"Because it is dirty. Tee, hee, hee."

Karen gets even more furious when she hears this.

"Have I ever told you that you are cute as hell when you're mad?"

"Don't try to use that charm on me, young man, because it's not going to work."

"The only thing I want to work is us. I sure have missed you, Cubby. Have you missed me?"

Charlie waits for a reply, but Karen only looks away.

"I want to know why the hell you are washing my car!"

"You sure do cuss a whole lot now. That is just another reason why we should get back together. A good Christian girl isn't supposed to talk like that."

"So now you are telling me that I ain't a good Christian girl?"

"There is no such word as *ain't.* I think the words you are looking for are *am not.*"

This makes Karen extremely upset. Charlie sees this anger in her eyes.

"I think you are the most beautiful Christian girl in the whole world. I mean it! If Jesus were here, I believe he would agree with me. That's why it is so very important that we get back together. So you will remain a good Christian girl."

Karen, with her head to one side, says, "I *ain't* gonna ask you but one more time! Why are you here washing my car? And don't tell me it's because it's dirty!"

"Okay, young lady. Don't you remember washing my truck right before we had that silly fight?"

Karen thinks, and then she remembers that she washed Charlie's truck two weeks before they had the fight. Charlie promised her that he would wash her car for her someday. She turns her head away as Charlie continues.

"When you washed my truck, I promised you that I would wash your car someday. Well, that someday is now. Don't you remember that, Cubby?"

Charlie smiles gladly as Karen nods her head.

"I am obligated to wash your car, Cubby. Don't ever let it be said that Charlie Delaney doesn't fulfill his promises."

Karen gives Charlie a stern look as Charlie continues to smile at her.

"Okay, young man. You go ahead and wash my car if it will make you feel better; however, just as soon as you are finished, I want you to leave. Do you understand me, young man!"

"It sure is good to finally hear you talk to me. You do have a lovely voice. I guess that is the best thing about you; your sweet-sounding voice."

Charlie smiles happily as Karen cracks a grin also. She turns her head away so Charlie won't see her grin, but Charlie sees it anyway.

"Hey, Cubby, now that you are speaking to me, tell me, how do you like the little basset hound puppy dog?"

Karen doesn't say anything. She just looks at him harshly.

"Have you picked a name for him yet?"

Karen softly says, "Yes."

"So what is it? You can tell me."

"I'm not going to tell you anything I don't want to. I came out here to see what you were up to. After you finish washing my car, I want you to leave. Do you understand me?"

"You sure are cute when you are mad."

Karen bellows, "Charlie Delaney!"

"Okay. Okay, Cubby. I will do just what you said. I will leave right after I wash your car. I promise. Okay?"

"Just make sure you do." Karen turns around real quick, and then she storms back into the house.

Charlie just stands there, shaking his head, as he watches Karen angrily walk away.

Charlie thinks to himself, *I will leave, little girl. Tee, hee, hee. Yeah, I will leave all right.*

Charlie then goes back to washing Karen's car. He gazes up at the window and sees Karen and Mrs. Thomas looking out at him. Charlie throws up his hand, and waves. The two women then disappear from the window.

Charlie washes the car, scrubs the tires, and cleans the windows. Just as he finishes the job, he jumps into the car and starts it up. He grins to himself and then blows the horn.

Mrs. Thomas rushes over to the window. She looks out and sees Charlie waving at her while sitting in the driver's seat. Charlie then puts the car in gear and begins to drive off.

Mrs. Thomas calls out to her daughter, "Karen! Karen! Come here!"

Karen is in the living room, playing with her little puppy. She jumps up and runs to her mother.

"What is the matter, mama?"

"Charlie has just driven off in your car!"

"He has done what?"

Karen runs to the window and sees her car is missing.

"Ooh! That just burns me up! He sure has got a lot of nerve doing that. Mama, call the police!"

"Now, dear, you don't really want to do that, do you?"

"I certainly do!"

"That's just what Charlie wants you to do."

"Huh? What makes you think that, mama?"

"You see, dear, if you call the police and have Charlie arrested, then he will use being arrested as a way to get your sympathy. You know Charlie; he won't be gone long. He probably just wants to get your attention."

"I guess you're right, mama."

Just then, the little basset hound puppy comes waddling toward Karen, barking his little bark. She picks up the innocent-looking little creature.

"When Charlie gets back, I am going to—"

Mrs. Thomas interrupts. "I have had enough of your mean temper, young lady!"

"Huh?"

"I said, 'I have had enough of your mean temper.' You yell at Charlie with that temper of yours one more time, and he might never, ever come see you again! Ask yourself something: do you want Charlie to never talk to you again!"

Karen pauses for a long moment.

Shaking her head no, she says, "I guess not, mama. I don't know what I want."

"It is about time you finally admitted that. When Charlie comes back—and, he will be back—think about what you will say before you say something you will be sorry for. Okay?"

"All right, mama, all right. I promise I will think before I scratch Charlie's eyes out."

Mrs. Thomas shakes her head as Karen smiles at her.

Charlie is gone for over an hour. He pulls into the driveway slowly. Karen comes out of the house just as Charlie turns off the engine. She walks down the walkway and toward her car. Charlie is just getting out as Karen walks up to him.

Karen doesn't waste any time yelling at him. "Where the hell have you been in my car?!"

Charlie doesn't say anything at first; he just laughs a little.

"What's so damn funny?"

"You sure do cuss a whole lot. You see how important it is that we get back together! Like I told you before: another three weeks apart, and there is no telling what you might be saying."

Karen just stands there waiting for an answer, with her arms crossed over her chest. Her face is red and full of anger.

Charlie tries to wipe the grin off his face.

"But I have got to hand it to you, Cubby, you sure are cute as hell when you're angry."

Karen's mean look fades away as her face shifts into a cheerful grin. She puts her hand over her mouth so Charlie won't see her smile.

"Hey, Cubby. Don't cover up that smile. I see you smiling."

Karen stops smiling. "Well!"

"Well, what?"

"Well, are you going to tell me where you went in my car?"

"Say please."

"I ain't gonna say no such thing. You tell me where you went in my car, or I ain't never gonna talk to you ever again."

"Well, since you put it that way, I guess I should tell you."

So Charlie explains where he has been. "When I was washing your car I noticed that one of the tires looked a little low. I didn't want you to have a blowout, so I thought I would take it to a filling station and put some air in it."

Karen listens to Charlie attentively.

"Then, when I got there, I noticed you didn't have but a half tank of gas, and since I used some of your gas to drive to the filling station, I thought I would fill your tank up for you. Wasn't that nice of me?"

Karen continues to listen to Charlie, without saying anything in response.

"Well, then I checked your oil. You know that oil looked so black, I just couldn't let it remain in your crank case, so I got the filling station to change it, plus the filter. Then, I couldn't just let it go with just an oil change, so I told them to lube the chassis also."

Karen gives Charlie a slightly grateful look.

"Then, I took a look at your windshield wipers. They looked like they have seen better days, so I told the mechanic to replace them too. I couldn't let you drive around with worn-out wipers."

Karen just stands there in silence, with a guilty look on her face.

"I know I shouldn't have driven off in your car without telling you first, Cubby. I am sorry. I don't blame you for being angry with me.

You have every right to be mad. I just wanted to do something nice for you; that's all."

Karen gives Charlie a sad look.

"Cubby, I want to tell you about why I did what I did that night. I know that what I did that night hurt you. That's the worst thing about this whole mess, Cubby: I did something that ended up hurting you."

Karen looks at Charlie, her eyes filled with tears.

Charlie smiles a subtle grin, and then he says, "I know! How would you like to go for a vanilla milk shake? I could tell you everything. Would you like to go for a milk shake, Cubby?"

Karen stands there for a few moments and then says, "Okay, Charlie, but only for a milk shake. After that, you bring me straight home. Do you understand?"

Charlie gets very excited.

"Yes, ma'am! Yes, ma'am! That sounds like a winner."

"Just for a milk shake, and then you bring me back home."

"Okay, Cubby. I promise!"

"Let me tell mama that I am going."

"Oh-tay … We can take your car. I about forgot how much fun it is to drive this little red Mustang."

Karen turns and walks back into the house.

"Mama, I am going out for a milk shake with the big dummy."

Mrs. Thomas gives Karen a look of great surprise. Turning her head sideways a little, she says, "Are you my daughter? You look like my daughter."

"Mama, we are only going out for a vanilla milk shake; that's all. And then we will come right back home."

"I do declare, there's one thing Charlie sure has got, and that's charm. Make sure you pay for yours, dear. I know you don't want to be obligated to him. Tee, hee, hee."

Karen doesn't say anything in reply. She runs and gets her purse, gives her mother and her little puppy each a kiss good-bye, and then hurries out the door.

Karen walks to her car slowly, so as not to give Charlie the impression she is eager. Charlie is waiting, standing on the passenger side of the car and holding the door open. Karen walks over and gets in. Charlie shuts the door and then happily runs over to the other side and gets in. Charlie looks over at Karen and sees a pouting expression on her face. She looks at him and then turns her head away. Charlie starts the car and drives off.

Just as soon as Charlie pulls out of the driveway, he looks over at Karen again.

"It sure feels good to be driving this car again. Like I said, I about forgot how much fun it is driving it."

Karen doesn't say anything, but she does glance at Charlie.

"This is wonderful! You are sitting beside me, and I am driving your car. I couldn't be happier."

Charlie pauses for a moment, hoping Karen might say something. She doesn't.

"You sure are beautiful, Cubby. I mean it. You are the most beautiful girl I have ever seen. I sure have missed you these last three weeks. I never thought I could feel so lonely. My heart ached every minute that I was away from you."

Karen still doesn't say anything.

Charlie softly says, "Have you missed me any?"

Karen pauses a moment, and then she softly says, "Yeah, I guess I have missed you a little bit."

Charlie smiles gladly as he continues to drive.

"There is one thing I have learned from this ordeal, Cubby."

"What?"

"I have learned how much I truly love you. I mean … I just can't seem to cope with life without you, Cubby. I love you more now than I ever did in the past." Karen's face turns a light shade of red as she hears Charlie's words. "You mean the world to me, Cubby. I learned that you don't fully appreciate something until you don't have it anymore. I have learned these last three weeks that you are the most important thing in my life. I know you are still angry with me. You have every right to be angry with me. What I did was stupid, thoughtless, ignorant, and very dumb. I will spend the rest of my life trying to undo the hurt that I have caused. I truly mean it when I say that I am sorry."

Charlie looks over at Karen and sees her pouting expression has turned into a sympathetic look.

"Do you know what the worst part of this ordeal is?" he asks.

"What?"

"The worst thing is all the pain I have caused you."

Karen sits quietly and listens attentively.

"I know that what I did hurt you. I guess that's why I feel so miserable. Hurting you was the last thing on earth I wanted to do … the last thing I'd ever want to do. Let me try to explain how I felt that night, and maybe you will understand why I did what I did."

So Charlie tries to explain things to Karen.

"You see, Cubby, after I brought you back home that night, I didn't want to leave. I sat out in my truck for about an hour, hoping you would come back out."

Karen quickly says, "Forty-five minutes."

Karen looks over at Charlie, and they smile simultaneously.

"Okay, forty-five minutes. I was just hoping you would come back out and—"

Karen interrupts. "Why didn't you come into the house?"

"Well … You see, Cubby, after you threw the ring away, I was kinda angry with you."

"I was kinda angry with you for breaking up with me!"

"You had every right to be angry with me, Cubby. That was the stupidest thing I ever did in my entire life. To this day, I don't know why I did that. But I do know that because I broke up with you, I provoked you into throwing my ring out the window. I blame myself for that."

Karen doesn't say anything, but she does show a look of guilt.

Charlie continues. "While I was sitting out in my truck, I was hoping you would come back out. I guess my pride got out of control. I kept thinking about negative things, and those negative things were distorting the truth. I was angry, and so I wasn't thinking about things in an intelligent frame of mind. I conjured up a deceptive thought that you didn't love me anymore."

Charlie looks over at Karen and sees a tear run down her milky white cheek.

The atmosphere grows quiet as Charlie drives the car into the McDonald's parking lot. Charlie maneuvers the car to the drive-through and orders two vanilla milk shakes. He pays for them, hands one to Karen, and proceeds to park the car.

After the car is parked, Charlie and Karen sit there, sucking on their milk shakes for a few moments. The mood is quiet and tranquil.

"Would you like a cheeseburger, Cubby, or something else?"

"No, Charlie, this milk shake is all I want."

"I'll be glad to get you something else if you want."

"No, I'm fine. Thank you, though."

"You know something, Cubby?"

"What?"

"The simplest things in life are the best things life has to offer. Like this milk shake. It is so cold, sweet, good, and simple. It is as sweet as one of your smiles."

Karen blushes a little as she sucks on her milk shake.

"That night, when I was sitting out in my truck, I wasn't thinking in the right frame of mind. When I left, I was feeling sad, depressed, hurt, and … angry."

Charlie looks over at Karen with big sad eyes.

Karen gives Charlie a sad look, and then she says, "So? Go on. Tell me where you went after you left my house."

Charlie takes another suck on his milk shake as he tries to put the words together. "You see, Cubby, you are only the second girl I ever have been in love with."

Karen looks at Charlie with complete attention.

Charlie continues. "A long time ago, when I was about fourteen years old, I fell in love with a girl. Her name is … well, her name isn't important. Anyway, I was in love with her, but I never had a chance to tell her how I felt."

"Are you telling me that the girl I saw at your house was this girl?"

"Yes, that's right."

"How did you know where she would be?"

"Okay. Let me tell you. I was walking around the mall about a week or so before you and I had that silly fight. I was sitting down near the wishing well, and she walked up. She had her little boy with her. Anyway, she and I talked a little while. She told me where she worked, and I told her about you. It was a completely innocent conversation."

"Where does she work?"

"She works at a bar. The Dodge City Saloon is the name of it."

"Oh, I see."

"Yeah. I didn't just pick up some floozy. She was someone I had known a long time ago, when I was fourteen years old.

"Where was your truck?"

"You see, Cubby, when I left your house that night, I didn't really know where to go, but somehow I ended up at that saloon. When I got there, I saw Dee."

"Is that her name, Dee?"

"Uh … yeah. Well, when I got there I was feeling real bad. I never felt so bad in my life. I didn't know really what to do."

"What did you do then?" Karen says this with a stern look.

Charlie notices this. His voice is kind when he answers. "Well, I saw Dee there, and she got me a table. She then bought me a drink."

"Did you drink it?"

"Uh-huh. Like I said, I was in a very bad state of mind. Well, after I drank the drink, it kinda made me feel better, so I ordered another."

"How many drinks did you drink there?" Karen's stern look shows more sharply than ever.

"Well … I guess I drank nine or ten."

"Nine or ten! Charlie! How could you drink nine or ten drinks?"

"One at a time."

Karen's expression is furious now.

"You see, Cubby, I never would have drunk any if Dee hadn't brought me the first one. The alcohol swimming around my brain did make me feel better, so I just kept ordering them."

"Did you get drunk?"

"Uh-huh. I sure did. I got really drunk. I got so drunk, I couldn't drive home."

"So that explains it. That's why your truck wasn't there. Right?"

"You're right again. She took me home because I wasn't fit to drive. So she really did me a favor."

"Favor! She got you drunk and then took you home, some favor."

While Charlie sips more of his milk shake, Karen calms down a little bit.

"After that part, I have no worthwhile excuses. I was so intoxicated that I didn't think about the potential consequences of my actions. I didn't think about what would happen because of my thoughtless behavior. But there is one thing I should tell you."

"What's that?"

"I never took the phone off the hook. I never did that."

"I guess this girl Dee did that. What did you say her last name was?"

"Uh … well, I don't think I gave you her last name."

Karen gets a little angry. "Well, give me her last name now!

"It's not really important. So why don't—"

"You tell me her name right now, Charlie Delaney, or you can take me home!"

"Dee Swanson. Her name is Dee Swanson. Would you like me to tell you some more?"

Karen smiles at Charlie and says, "No, Charlie, I think that will be enough."

"Good! So you see, Cubby, I didn't just go out somewhere and find someone to bring home with me. It was just a combination of things that made me act the way I did. I know what I did wasn't right. I know what I did was stupid. I just want you to know that I am very sorry about this whole mess that I have caused."

Karen sits still and motionless as Charlie reaches over and takes her hand.

Charlie's voice becomes very soft and gentle. "You remember when we first drove up? I said I had a thought that you didn't love me anymore."

Karen's sad eyes look directly into Charlie's.

"Well, Cubby, do you still love me?" Charlie says this with an expression of tenderness, warmth, and compassion.

Karen sheds another tear and says softly, "Yes, Charlie, I still love you."

Charlie whips out the ring. He looks over at Karen, and love and compassion fill his eyes.

He turns his head sideways a little as he tenderly asks, "Will you be my girlfriend again? Hmm?"

Karen's sad look explodes into a happy, joyous smile.

"Yes, Charlie, I will be your girlfriend again."

Charlie slides the ring back on Karen's finger, and then he leans over and kisses her passionately. Charlie kisses Karen all over her face, over and over and over again.

They both cry tears of happiness and joy.

"I love you. I love you. I love you, Charlie."

"I love you so much, Cubby. Oh, how I love you! How could I live in this world without you?"

"Charlie."

"Yes, my love?"

"I want to apologize for throwing your ring out the window. I acted like a child that night. It was all my fault, Charlie. You would have never done what you did if it hadn't been for my childish behavior. Will you please forgive me for being such a hot-tempered bad girl?"

"You don't have to apologize to me, Cubby. I love you so much."

"But please say you forgive me. I will feel much better if you do."

"Okay, Cubby, I forgive you. I forgive you. I forgive you a million times."

Karen looks at Charlie with that special twinkle in her eyes.

"Oh, thank you, Charlie! I love you so much."

Charlie leans over again, and the two lovebirds engage in another loving kiss.

After several minutes of kissing and caressing each other, Charlie breaks away and opens the door in a hurry. He jumps out of the car.

"Where are you going, Charlie?"

"I have got to call Ma now. Now that I won you back, I have got to win Ma back too."

Charlie rushes over to the telephone as Karen shakes her head in amazement. Charlie puts a quarter in the telephone and dials Mrs. Thomas's phone number. After Charlie dials the number, he motions for Karen to come over to him.

The phone rings three times before Mrs. Thomas answers it.

"Hello," Charlie excitedly says, "Hello, Ma! This is Charlie. You know, Karen's boyfriend."

"Charlie? Is that you, Charlie?"

"Yeah, Ma! I can start calling you Ma again. Everything is fine now. Karen says she loves me again, so now you can start loving me again too."

"Is Karen there?" Karen walks up just as Mrs. Thomas asks this.

Charlie looks at Karen and excitedly says, "It's Ma! She wants to talk to you! Here she comes, Ma!"

Charlie hands the phone to Karen.

"Hello, mama. Yeah, it's true … Charlie and I are going together again."

"Are you sure that's what you want, dear?"

"Yes, mama, that is exactly what I want. I love Charlie."

"Well, dear, if you're happy, I'm happy too."

"Mama. Charlie even forgave me for acting the way I did. Wasn't that nice of him?"

"Charlie forgave you? I thought it would be the other way around."

"Well, mama, I forgave Charlie first. So all is forgiven. Mama, I am so happy now."

A tear trickles down Karen's happy face as she smiles at Charlie.

"Well, dear, I am glad to hear you are happy."

"Yes, mama, I am happier now than I have ever been in my life."

Charlie takes the phone from Karen. "Hello, Ma, it's me again. It's all right to call you Ma again, isn't it?"

"Yes, Charlie. You can call me Ma again if you like."

"Oh boy! That's great! Can I ask you something, Ma?"

"Sure, Charlie, ask me anything you want."

"Karen says she loves me again, do you love me again too?"

Charlie hears a laugh in the background, and then he hears Mrs. Thomas say, "Yes, Charlie. I love you again too."

"Yippee! You just made my day! I love you too, Ma! I do! I really do! We will be home shortly."

"Okay, Charlie."

"Tell me one more time, Ma, you know, that you love me."

"I love you, Charlie."

"Oh boy! That sounded even better than the first time!"

Charlie hears Mrs. Thomas laughing in the background again.

"We will be home shortly, Ma. Okay?"

"Okay, Charlie. I will be here waiting for you two."

Charlie grins as he hangs up the phone. He then gives Karen a huge, loving hug, lifting her up in his arms. He kisses her time after time and then carries her over to the car.

Setting Karen down gently, Charlie holds the door open for her. Karen gets in, with a happy glow showing on her face. Charlie dances over to the other side and gets in too. He starts the car and begins to drive off. Karen snuggles up close to Charlie, and he drives back to her house.

Chapter 6
SHE'S GOT TO STOP BEING JEALOUS

Charlie and Karen begin to start over again. They love each other more now than they did before the fight.

Mrs. Thomas enjoys having Charlie around the house once again. She loves Charlie a great deal more now too.

Karen and Charlie's relationship develops into a kinder, caring, and more open one. Their lives revolve around each other. They become so close that one can't function without the other. They become possessive of each other on a grand scale. Everything Charlie is interested in doing, Karen thinks she must also involve herself in; and Charlie wants to be involved in all of Karen's interests also. But Karen's demands of Charlie are extreme. She doesn't want him to do anything she can't be a part of. Her possessiveness becomes bigger than both of them.

Soon, whenever a girl looks at Charlie, something bizarre happens in Karen's mind. She gets very disturbed and sometimes becomes uncontrollable. The green demon of jealousy has set up shop in Karen's heart.

Charlie detects the way Karen is feeling by the look in her eye. He tries hard not to say or do anything to upset her, but the green demon has a powerful force over Karen's emotions. He puts false thoughts in her head. He dances the dance of rebellion and hate. Karen loves Charlie, but she believes that she is the only one permitted to love Charlie; everyone else had better back off.

Dee hasn't disappeared from the scene totally. She has waited long and patiently for Charlie to call her. She gave him her home phone number, and her work number, but is very disappointed that Charlie hasn't called her yet. She loves Charlie more now than ever. The night they spent together has given her more initiative to pursue Charlie. She has more determination now. She wants him back, but she wants him to come to her. Since Charlie has gotten back with Karen, Dee is setting herself up for a big heartbreaking disappointment. And with Karen's jealousy growing bigger every day, it is just a matter of time before the two girls have a catastrophic confrontation with each other.

Charlie doesn't tell anyone that he is going to a psychiatrist. He keeps this little secret to himself. He doesn't want anyone to know he is taking medication for depression. He keeps his pills locked away where no one can find them, just in case someone starts to look around inside his house. He takes his lithium every day, just like his doctor told him to. The substance has been a godsend for Charlie. He is happier now than he has ever been in his life. The relief from the depression has made his life more robust.

One night at the Thomas's house, about three weeks after Charlie and Karen have gotten back together, Karen is getting ready for a date with Charlie. She is very excited as she gets ready. Charlie hasn't arrived yet. Karen puts on a new dress that she just bought today. She has fixed her beautiful red hair just so; it looks like the hair of a model in a magazine. The silky red dress gives a suggestive view of her milky white cleavage and large, full breasts. The red dress has a slit up one side, and with Karen's shapely waist, it makes all of her other alluring features stand out in an even more attractive manner.

But her eyes! Her luscious blue eyes! They radiate majestic tranquility. They are true blue entities that give a hypnotic effect with each and every bat of her eyelashes.

As Karen finishes dressing, she walks down the stairs and into the kitchen.

Mrs. Thomas turns around and gazes at her beautiful daughter.

"Well, well, well! Just look at you, Karen! You have got to be the most beautiful girl in the whole world right now."

"Oh, mama, stop."

"I mean it, Karen. And just think: you are my daughter. Charlie is going to take one look at you and fall flat on the floor."

Karen smiles gladly as she rocks from side to side.

"Oh, mama, cut it out."

Mrs. Thomas just stands there, marveling at her beautiful young daughter with total and complete admiration.

"When is Charlie supposed to pick you up, dear?"

"He is supposed to be here at seven o'clock, but you know Charlie. He will probably get here at six-thirty."

"Well, I can't blame him. After he takes one look at you, it will take him thirty minutes to be able to start thinking again."

"Oh, mama, cut that out," Karen says again, but she smiles.

Karen and her mother continue to talk until six-thirty.

Mrs. Thomas hears something. She gets up and walks to the window. "Charlie's here! Be ready to catch him just as soon as he takes one look at you. Be ready."

"Oh, mama, stop teasing." Karen laughs.

Charlie knocks on the door. Karen walks over and opens it. He takes one look at Karen, and his mouth falls open.

Karen smiles at Charlie, and then she turns around and says, "Do you like it? I just bought it today."

Charlie doesn't say anything at first. He just stands there, with his mouth hanging open. He stares dumbfounded at this most beautiful spectacle that is before his eyes.

"Wow! Excuse me. I must be at the wrong house. I was supposed to meet my girlfriend here, but I must have the wrong address."

"Oh, come on in, Charlie."

"It is you! It really is you! I thought I was at the wrong house for a second. You look stunning, Karen!"

"Thank you, Charlie."

Karen escorts Charlie into the house, leading him into the living room.

When Charlie walks into the living room, he sees Mrs. Thomas. He walks over to her and gives her a big kiss on the cheek.

"What was that for, Charlie?" asks Mrs. Thomas, surprised.

Karen also gives Charlie a surprised look.

"That was for bringing into the world the most beautiful girl who has ever been born."

Mrs. Thomas smiles gladly at Charlie.

"Just look at her, Ma! Just look at Karen. Isn't she the most gorgeous creature in the entire world?"

Mrs. Thomas glances over at Karen, winks at her, and smiles.

"Yes, Charlie, I believe you are right."

Karen doesn't say anything. She just shows a sweet, girlish grin as she blushes with an innocent glow of magenta.

"So where are you two going tonight?"

"After seeing Karen, I don't want to go anywhere. I would rather just sit here and look at her."

"Huh? Are you kidding? I am starving."

Charlie laughs and then says, "Yes, I am just kidding. I guess we could go out for dinner."

"Where?"

"Oh … how does Bojangles' sound?"

"Bojangles! Are you out of your cotton-picking mind!"

"I'm like Roy Clark," Charlie says, and then he begins to sing. "I never picked cotton. Tee, hee, hee."

Karen looks peeved, but only in a playful way.

"I didn't get all dressed up just to go to Bojangles', Charlie."

"I know you didn't, Karen. We will have to go to a nicer place."

"Now that's more like it. Where?"

"Oh … I think McDonald's is much nicer. It is clean and neat. Tee, hee, hee."

Karen puts her hands on her waist and gives Charlie another peeved look.

"Charlie, before you get me too mad, you'd better—"

"Okay, okay! How about a big steak at the Ranch House?"

"Well … if that's where you want to go, that will be fine with me. You know me; I ain't hard to please."

Mrs. Thomas laughs out loud, and Charlie does the same.

"Why are you two laughing?"

Charlie and Mrs. Thomas continue to laugh as Karen begins to get upset.

"Well, if you both think something is so funny, why don't you let me in on it?"

Charlie walks over to Karen and kisses her forehead.

“There is nothing funny, Cubby. Tee, hee, hee.”

“Well, if you think it is so funny, maybe we should just stay home.”

“Hey, that’s a great idea! Ma could set out the grill, and you could cook! …”

“Be damn! I ain’t cooking nothing.”

“Young lady, you know better than to talk like that.”

Karen gives her mother a sad look.

Charlie, seeing how everything is going, suddenly grabs Karen by the hand and says to Mrs. Thomas, “We will be in late, Ma. We are going to a movie after we eat. Bye now.”

“You two have fun. Drive careful.”

“Okay, mama, we will.”

Charlie pulls Karen out the door before she has a chance to say anything else.

Charlie walks over to Karen’s car, opens the door for Karen, and she gets in. He runs over to the other side, happily gets in, starts the engine, and drives off.

“Where are we going, Charlie?”

Charlie detects the softness in Karen’s voice.

“I want to show off my girlfriend to the entire world, so we are going to the nicest place in town: the Ranch House. Is that all right with you, Cubby?”

“Yes, Charlie, that is just fine with me.”

Karen snuggles up to Charlie as he drives to the steak house.

When they arrive at the steak house, there is a long line of people waiting outside. Charlie does manage to find a parking spot. He pulls into it and parks the car.

Charlie looks at the long line and says, “Cubby, I know I promised to take you here for dinner, but—”

“I know, Charlie, I know. You don’t want to wait in line. Right?”

“Yeah. You know I don’t have the patience to stand in line. Would you like to go somewhere else?”

“Well … that line does look awful long. I guess we could go somewhere else if you want to.”

“Hey! I have an idea!” Charlie looks excitedly at Karen. “What do you say we go to the mall and walk around for a while?”

"That sounds all right to me."

"Yeah, there are dozens of places to eat at the mall. And then we could go to the movie over there. The movie begins at nine o'clock."

"Well, what are we waiting for? Let's go."

Charlie leans over, kisses Karen sweetly on her delicate lips, and then drives away.

Charlie drives to the mall, parks the car, gets out, and runs over to open Karen's door.

"I don't know how long you plan to keep doing this, so I am going to enjoy it while it lasts."

"I like to pamper you. I enjoy it because I love you so much."

"I love you too, Charlie."

Charlie and Karen embrace with a big hug and a long kiss. They walk toward the mall, hand in hand.

"I'm glad I thought about coming here. Where in the world can I show off my beautiful girlfriend more than here at the mall?"

Karen laughs a little girlish laugh as her shining eyes look happily at Charlie. Her innocent, sweet smile fills Charlie's heart with love and affection. As the two sweethearts walk, Charlie releases Karen's hand to put his arm around her. She puts one of her arms around his waist. Just before they get to the front of the mall, Charlie releases Karen completely so he can open the door for her. She walks in, giving another girlish laugh. She then eagerly wraps her arm around Charlie's waist once again. The happy couple walks around the mall, looking at all the nice things together.

As they walk, Charlie notices a lot of other pretty girls too. He glances at them innocently, but Karen sees Charlie's face light up when a very attractive girl catches his eye. Karen holds her tongue, though. As they continue to walk around the mall, Karen's green demon wakes up from his slumber. He begins to stir around, aroused by Charlie's roaming eyes.

"I am getting hungry. What do you say we get something to eat?"

"I thought you would never ask. I am starved."

"What would you like?"

"Anything that's not moving."

"How about a steak sandwich, Cubby?"

"Yeah, that sounds good."

Charlie and Karen find the place that sells steak sandwiches. Charlie orders both of them steak sandwiches, some fries, and two sodas. They sit down at one of the tables and begin to eat their meal.

As they are eating, Karen notices Charlie's eyes as the girls walk by. Just as Charlie takes another bite of his sandwich, he hears a female voice call his name.

"Charlie! Charlie Delaney! Is that you?"

Charlie turns around and sees a woman whom he works with.

"Janette! Janette Tillman! Is that you?"

"Why, hello there, Charlie."

"Please, pull yourself up a chair and sit down with us. Karen, this is Janette Tillman. Janette, this is my girlfriend, Karen Thomas."

Janette pulls up a chair and sits down beside Karen.

"Karen, this is one of the best friends I have at work. She helps me out on about everything I have to do."

Karen looks at Charlie sharply.

Glancing at Janette, Karen politely says, "Hello. Glad to meet you."

"Nice to meet you too. Charlie, you were right, she is every bit as beautiful as you said she was."

Karen blushes a little before saying, "Thank you."

"So what are you up to?" Charlie eagerly asks.

"Oh, nothing much, I thought I would come down here and see all that they have done to the mall. They sure have added a lot more stores since the last time I was here."

"Yes, they sure have added on to it. When was the last time you were here?"

"Oh … it's probably been over a year. I don't get down here very often. I thought I'd try to find something for my grandson. He is three and a half years old now, and into everything."

Karen sits as quiet as a mouse, afraid to say anything.

Charlie and Janette talk about work for a few minutes before Janette says to Karen, "I know you two have other things to do, so I believe I will be moseying along now. It sure has been nice to meet you, Karen. Try to keep Charlie out of trouble."

Karen smiles and says, "I will try."

Charlie gets up as Janette stands. "It sure was good seeing you."

"It sure was good seeing you too, Charlie. I will see you later. Bye now."

"Bye-bye, Janette. See you bright and early Monday morning."

As Janette walks away, Charlie remains standing. He focuses his eyes on Janette's buttocks and exposed legs, staring after her until she has disappeared into the crowd. He only sits down after she is out of his sight.

Karen stares at Charlie while his eyes are focused on the alluring sight.

"Isn't she a nice woman?"

Karen gives Charlie a mean look. "Maybe you would rather go to the movies with her instead of me."

Charlie looks at Karen with surprise and wonder. "Why would you say a thing like that, Karen?"

"Well, the way you were looking at her gives me the impression you would rather be with her." Karen's face is full of the green monster, jealousy.

Charlie is dumbfounded by Karen's attitude. "Huh? You must be out of your mind. That is the silliest thing I have ever heard."

"Oh! So now I am silly! Is that what I am to you, silly!

"Do you think I would rather be with her than you? How could you think such a thing?"

Charlie takes a good look at Karen. He sees she is upset. He reaches over and takes her hand.

"Come on, Cubby. Come on."

"Don't you tell me to 'come on'! I saw the way you were looking at her ass. Not to mention all the other women you have been looking at like that."

"Huh? Are you out of your cotton-picking mind?"

Karen sternly replies, "I'm like Roy Clark; I never picked cotton either!"

Karen then gets up and begins to walk away in a very angry mood. Charlie gets up and follows her.

He catches up to her and says, "Hey, Cubby. Hey!"

Karen stops walking. She stands still, looking directly at Charlie.

"I went out and spent a hundred dollars on a new dress, and all you would rather look at is another woman."

"Another woman?! That woman is a grandma. I can't believe you are … jealous! You're jealous!"

"I am not jealous!"

"You are too. You're jealous of a woman who happens to be a grandma."

"I don't think this is the proper place to discuss this matter. I think you should take me home."

Karen's anger gets more intense.

"Don't you think you are overreacting somewhat?"

"No, I don't! Every girl that walks by, your eyes drop right down to her ass."

"Huh?"

"Are you denying it?"

"Well … no, I am not denying it, but—"

"But nothing! Take me home, right now, Charlie."

Karen begins to walk away.

"Karen, please don't be mad at me."

"I said this is no place to discuss this matter."

Karen continues to walk at a fast pace, and Charlie follows right along behind her. Karen doesn't stop until she reaches the car. Charlie unlocks the door and holds it open while Karen gets in. Charlie sadly walks over to the other side and gets in. The car is filled with a deafening quiet.

Charlie thinks for a second and then says in a soft tone, "Hey, little girl, I didn't mean anything by looking at those other women. Hey-y-y-y … if I have done anything wrong tonight, I want you to know that I am sorry. Okay?"

Karen turns and sharply says, "Uh-huh! There you go! You wouldn't be apologizing if you hadn't done anything wrong!"

"You are overreacting to this. Those women don't mean anything to me."

"What about that remark Miss Janette made about how she will see you later?"

"Of course she will see me later. I work with her."

"Yeah, right! It's the way she said it that makes me wonder."

"I can't believe you. That woman is forty-two years old. Why on God's green earth would I want to see a forty-two-year-old woman when I am with the most beautiful nineteen-year-old girl in the entire world?"

"Well, I don't know why."

"Don't you know that I love you, sweetheart? Just because my eyes look at other women doesn't mean I want to be with them. Looking at other women is only natural. I think I have seen your eyes wander around too."

"Well, that's different."

"Oh really now! How is it different?"

"It's just different."

"Tell me why it is so different."

"It's different because … because I'm a girl, that's why."

"Oh, I'm glad you cleared that up for me. A girl can look, but a guy can't. Tee, hee, hee!"

Charlie keeps laughing that high-pitched laugh. His laughter makes Karen even more upset.

"Well, young man, if you think it is so funny, then you can laugh yourself all the way to my house."

Charlie stops laughing. He pauses for a second and says, "Yeah! Then, when we get home, I'll tell Ma that you got jealous over a forty-two-year-old woman."

"Oh no, you won't! You will do no such thing, Charlie Delaney!"

Charlie starts the car and begins to drive off. Once again, he makes that high-pitched laugh.

"Tee, hee, hee. Ma is going to get a big laugh out of this."

"Oh no, she's not, either. You'd better not tell her, Charlie Delaney! You'd better not tell her about anything, young man."

As Karen's face gets as red as a pepper, Charlie pulls over and parks the car at the mall Cinema.

"Where do you think you are going"?

"I, my dear, am going to the movies. The movie is going to start in ten minutes."

"I told you I wanted to go home!"

"You did, but I came down here to see a movie, and that's just what I am going to do. Tee, hee, hee!"

"Now you listen here—"

"You know something, Karen?"

"What?"

"When you are angry, you sure are cute as hell. Tee, hee, hee."

Charlie gets out of the car.

Karen gets out and calls out to Charlie, "Hey, you! I said I want to go home!"

Charlie tosses the keys to Karen. "Here you go. You can drive yourself home."

"Oh no, you don't! You don't expect me to come back and pick you up after your movie, do you?"

"I don't expect anything. Now, if you will please excuse me, I have a movie to go see." Charlie turns and begins to walk away.

"You come back here, young man! I haven't finished talking to you!"

Charlie turns and walks back toward Karen. "Yes, my love, do you want to apologize to me?"

Karen gives Charlie another mean look. "I expect you to take me home right now!"

"How can I take you home? You are the one with the keys." Charlie laughs a little as Karen holds out the car keys to him.

"Here! Take these keys, and drive me home."

"Nope. Not until you apologize to me for the way you have acted."

"Are you crazy?! Me apologize to you? You are the one who should apologize to me."

"If my memory serves me right, I did apologize to you. Then you manufactured a ridiculous argument. It just goes to show, when a woman gets her emotions riled up, she doesn't think about things in a logical manner."

"Ooh! That burns me up, Charlie Delaney!"

"Well, I finally agree with you, young lady. Your emotions are so hot right now, they are burning up your intellect! You do look cute as hell, though. Tee, hee, hee."

"Ooh! Will you quit laughing like that? It is the most irritating sound I have ever heard in my life."

Charlie leans over and kisses Karen quickly.

"I would like to stand out here and look at you all night, but the movie is about to start."

"I don't want to hear any more about that damn movie!"

Charlie gives Karen a very stern look. "You ought to be ashamed of yourself, young lady, talking to me like that. I am very disappointed in your behavior tonight."

"You listen here—"

"No! *You* listen here! You have been acting jealous ever since we got back together. You have manufactured some silly notion that I want to be with someone else. I love you! You, and nobody else! And every time your temper gets out of control, you make up something false in your head just to justify this untrue and unnecessary way of thinking. Can't you understand that I love you? I wouldn't ever want to be with anyone but you."

Karen stands there in silence, with her lip stuck out as she listens to Charlie.

"Now I am going to see a movie; the third one playing. If you want to join me, come on."

Charlie turns around and begins to walk away. He walks a short distance and then turns back around. He sees Karen just standing there next to her car. Charlie motions with his hand for her to come on.

"You'd better come back here and take me home, Charlie Delaney! I mean it! You'd better come back here!"

Charlie makes that same laugh again. "Tee, hee, hee." His face is full of laughter as he turns around playfully and continues to walk to the box office. He doesn't turn around again.

Karen is left with only her little green demon to keep her company. She gets into her car, and the two begin to wrestle about what to do. The green demon summons two of his friends to help him out. One is self-pity, and the other is his brother, self-pride. The three demons begin to attack Karen's mind.

"Ooh! That man!" she mutters aloud. "He knows better than to walk off like that. I have a notion to just drive off and let him get home on his own. That will teach him a lesson. I believe that's what I will do.

Serves him right for looking at all those other girls and for talking to me that way."

Karen begins to cry. She starts up the car and pulls off. The three demons join hands and begin to dance a little jig for their victory and Karen's defeat.

The farther Karen drives, the stronger her love for Charlie grows. Karen's love is more powerful than any negative force in her mind. Karen's love chases away all three of the demons. She turns the car around and drives back to the movie theater. She hurries to get out of her car, and then she runs all the way to the box office.

"Excuse me. I would like one ticket for the third movie."

"That will be four dollars."

Karen nervously hands the man a five dollar bill. She gets her ticket and her change.

The man gives her a pleasant smile, and then he says, "The movie has already begun, missy."

"Thank you," Karen replies.

Karen rushes to the theater and gives the usher her ticket. She enters the dark theater and slowly walks down the aisle, looking at the people in the seats. About halfway down, she spots Charlie sitting right on the aisle.

Karen taps him on his shoulder and says, "Could I sit down with you, Charlie?"

"Sure, Cubby. Is it really you? I thought I was going to have to eat all this popcorn all by myself. Come on and sit down."

Karen gives Charlie a timid smile and sits down beside him.

As Karen snuggles up to Charlie, a tear runs down her face, and she whispers, "I'm sorry, Charlie. I have been acting like a child. Will you forgive me for acting so immaturely?"

Charlie listens to Karen with love and compassion. Looking into her blue eyes tenderly, he whispers, "Yes, my love, I forgive you."

Charlie pulls out a candy bar from his shirt pocket. "Here you go. I thought you would come back, so I bought you this." It's a Milky Way, Karen's favorite candy bar. He hands it to her, with a loving smile showing on his face.

Karen takes the candy bar, whispering, "I love you, Charlie Delaney. I love you more than I love anybody else in the whole world."

Charlie smiles gladly as he whispers back, "I love you too, Cubby, more than I love anybody else in the whole world."

Charlie and Karen sit back and watch the movie, with love and happiness filling their hearts.

After the movie, Charlie takes Karen by the hand, and the two walk back to Karen's car. Karen hands Charlie the keys and then gives him a big hug. Charlie leans down and kisses Karen sweetly on her tender, soft lips. The moment is magical. They get into the car, and Charlie drives back to Karen's house. As they move along the road, Karen snuggles up to Charlie affectionately. She helps him shift gears.

When Charlie gets to Karen's house, he pulls into the driveway, opens her door for her, and walks her up to the front doorstep.

"Well, Cubby, I guess it's time for me to go home now."

"Why don't you come in for a few minutes?"

"I think I'd better go home now. It's late, and I don't think your mother would want me to be here at this hour."

"Well, okay, Charlie. I had a very nice time tonight. You aren't mad at me anymore, are you?"

Charlie smiles at Karen, his face a picture of pure love and admiration. "No, Cubby, I am not mad at you. I can't ever stay mad at you for very long. I love you too much."

"I love you too, Charlie. I know I have a very bad temper. I am trying to control it now. It will take a little while before I finally get control of it, but I am trying real hard not to let my temper get like it did tonight."

"Hearing you say those words makes me so happy. Just being close to you makes me feel like I am the luckiest man in the world."

"Well, Charlie, I am the luckiest girl in the world. I am glad you're mine."

"I will be yours forever and ever."

Charlie leans down and kisses Karen firmly and passionately.

"Are you going to church tomorrow?"

"I guess so. What time do you want me to come pick you up?"

"Oh, about ten-thirty will be fine."

Charlie gives Karen another loving kiss.

"I will see you tomorrow morning."

"Okay, Charlie. I will be waiting for you."

Charlie kisses Karen one last time, and then he walks to his truck and drives home.

Just as soon as Charlie walks into his house, the telephone begins to ring. He glances over at the wall clock: 11:50 p.m.

"I wonder who would be calling me at this hour," Charlie mumbles aloud.

He gets a feeling of anxiety as he walks over to the phone. A bad feeling rushes through him. He nervously picks up the phone. "Hello?"

A familiar voice on the other end of the line says, "Hello, Charlie. I haven't heard from you all week. I have got to see you."

"Dee! I thought I asked you not to call me anymore. I am back with my girlfriend now."

"But, Charlie, I need you. You don't know the loneliness I am going through. It is so hard to work a full-time job and take care of an eight-year-old boy at the same time. I need you, Charlie! I desperately need to be close to you, right now. Let me come over so we came make love to each other. I won't tell your girlfriend."

Charlie has to sit down when he hears this.

"Dee, you will do no such thing! Promise me you won't come over here!"

"But, Charlie I—"

"Don't you 'but Charlie' me. Promise me you won't come over here, or I will hang up on you, right now!"

"Okay, Charlie. I promise not to come over."

Charlie hears Dee crying in the background as he listens. His hand starts to shake as he hears these pitiful sounds.

"Now stop crying, Dee. I just don't want you to come over here. I happen to be in love with someone else."

"I guess things have not changed."

"What do you mean, Dee?"

"All our lives, Charlie, there has always been something to keep us apart. I thought the night we had together was a sign that those days were over. Charlie! I love you! Can't you understand that?"

"Dee, calm down. Part of me will always love you. But I am deeply in love with another girl. I am thinking about asking her to marry me."

"No, Charlie! No! Don't do that! You haven't given me a chance. I haven't been calling you lately, because I have wanted you to call me. I'll start calling you more so that you will know I care for you. I want us to feel the same way as we once did for each other."

Charlie gets very upset when he hears this.

"No, Dee! You are not supposed to call me anymore! I don't want you to keep doing this. Please understand. I am in love with Karen. Before long, I am going to ask her to marry me."

"No! No! No, Charlie! I can't stand to hear you say that! If you marry her, I will kill myself. I will, Charlie. I will kill myself! I can't live without you, Charlie."

Charlie hears Dee's crying in a tone that is even more heartbreaking than the one before.

"You will do no such thing! You will not kill yourself! Can't you understand, Dee? I love someone else."

"You loved me the night I came over to your house."

A long silence fills the phone line.

Charlie's heart begins to pound fast.

Dee breaks the silence. "Did you hear me, Charlie?"

"Yes, Dee, I heard you."

"When you made love to me, time after time after time, I knew you cared deeply for me."

"Dee, I can't keep talking about this, I just can't. I am in a very wonderful relationship with a girl—the girl I love—and I am not going to let anything interfere with it."

Dee's voice gets louder. Her tone becomes demanding and indignant as she says heatedly, "Then tell me something, Charlie ..."

"What?"

"Tell me you don't love me anymore."

There is another long pause on the phone line.

Again, Dee breaks the silence. "Are you still there, Charlie?"

"Yes, I am still here. Well, I have got to go, Dee."

"You ain't going nowhere until you answer my question!"

"Question? Did you ask a question?"

"Well, kinda. I don't know. Before I will stop calling you, you're going to have to tell me that you don't love me anymore."

"That's not a question."

"I don't care if it's a question or not, Charlie! I'm not going to stop until I hear you say that."

"Dee, I am not going to tell you any such thing. I have always cared for you, and I always will but …" Charlie's voice trails off.

"But what, Charlie?"

"But I am involved with someone else now."

"You are also involved with me. I love you, Charlie. I love you so much. You can't tell me you don't love me, because you still do."

"I can't keep going on about this matter, Dee. Please stop calling me. Please. If Karen ever finds out you are calling me, it could cause a lot of trouble."

"Oh really! I'm glad you told me that, Charlie."

"No, Dee. Don't you start any trouble between Karen and me."

"Who me? Now, Charlie! Would I do that?"

"The way you sound, you might."

Charlie scratches his head as he thinks about how to handle this situation.

While Charlie is thinking, Dee says, "You don't make love to someone the way you made love to me and then expect that person to just jump up and go away. I yearn to be close to you, sweetheart. Oh, how I want you to be close to me."

"Okay, Dee, that is enough! I can't get involved with you. I love Karen."

"But you are involved with me, Charlie. You made love to me three times that night. Don't you think that means we are involved?"

"Dee, listen here! That was some time ago when we did that. I was in a very depressed state then. I had just broken up with Karen; besides, I was also drunk that night. Try to understand that, Dee. The time when you and I had true feelings for each other was a long time ago—a very long time ago."

"But, Charlie, I can't seem to think about anything but you. These last six weeks have been hell for me. I have only talked to you over the phone. I need to feel you close to me! I need to reach out and feel your warm, naked, loving body on top of me. I yearn to touch your naked body. Oh, Charlie! Let me come over! I promise not to tell anyone. I will leave early enough so nobody will know. Please, Charlie, let me come over! Please!"

Charlie feels the lusty desire erupt throughout his nervous body.

"No, Dee! No! I am going steady with someone. As long as I am, I am going to be faithful to her. You just don't know how much I love her. You just don't know."

"You don't know how much I love you, Charlie. I have felt this way for a long time. You remember what you said a while ago?"

"About what, Dee?"

"About being in a very depressed state."

"Yeah. I remember."

"Well, Charlie, that's how I feel right now. I am so depressed, I don't know what to do."

"I can't help you, Dee. Hey, it's getting late, and I have to get some sleep now. Please don't interfere with Karen and me. Let everything get back to normal. Okay?"

"I don't know why you are treating me this way! Can't you understand that I need you, Charlie!"

Charlie scratches his head, wondering what to do. He tries not to say anything that might hurt Dee any further.

"Can I ask you something, Dee?"

"Yes, Charlie. You can ask me anything you want to."

"Have you been drinking tonight?"

"Well … kinda."

"What exactly do you mean by 'kinda'?"

"Well, I have been drinking for a few hours."

"A few hours! That explains why you are in such a depressive state. I want you to stop drinking. Do you understand me, young lady?"

"I love it when you talk so forceful to me, Charlie. If you let me come over, I will let you give me a spanking for being such a bad girl."

"Do what!"

Dee enticingly replies, "I want you to spank my horny ass until it's red! You can say you're sorry, and then you can make love to me as many times as you want to."

"Dee! I have heard enough! I want you to go to sleep now, and I do not want you to call me anymore. Do you understand?"

"But, Charlie—"

"Do you want me to hang up on you?"

"No, Charlie, don't do that."

"Then I want you to go to bed."

"That's what I've been wanting to do ever since I called you. Go to bed with you. Ha, ha, ha!"

"Well, you aren't going to. I am going to put the phone down now, Dee, and please don't keep calling me. Don't call me anymore."

"But wait, Charlie, I—"

Not knowing what else to do, Charlie simply hangs up the phone gently. He picks it back up after twenty seconds goes by. Hearing a dial tone, he leaves it off the hook.

Filled with anxiety, Charlie stands up, goes upstairs, and goes to bed.

The next day, Charlie gets up and takes a shower. He takes his medication and then fixes himself some breakfast.

As he sits at the kitchen table, he thinks about Dee. *I hope I didn't upset her too much last night. She was really in a bad frame of mind. I hope she doesn't interfere with Karen and me. I know she will try. Oh God! I was so tempted last night! I could have easily opened my mouth and said, "Okay, Dee, come on over." That would have done it! Karen and I would be through if I'd done that. I came so close to giving in to Dee, though.*

Charlie looks up to the ceiling and says out loud, "Dear God in heaven, lead me away from the temptation that I have brought upon myself. Give me the strength to say no. Don't let anything tear Karen and me apart. Please, Lord, help me!"

Charlie puts his head down on the table, feeling drained and exhausted.

Finally, Charlie manages to get ready. As he looks in the mirror, he sees that his restless sleep the night before now shows on his face. He hurries to his truck and drives over to Karen's house. He parks his truck, gets out, and walks to the front door. He doesn't knock; he simply opens the door with his own key and walks in.

Charlie looks around and then calls out, "Hello! Anybody home?"

Mrs. Thomas comes down the stairs and says, "Go ahead and sit down, Charlie. Karen and I will be down shortly."

So Charlie plops down on the couch, waiting patiently.

Soon Karen come downstairs. She walks over and sits down beside Charlie. "So, what's happening, big boy? Did you make it home all right last night?"

"Yeah, I made it home all right."

Karen gives Charlie a curious look. "What's the matter, Charlie? You look tired."

"I guess I didn't sleep too good last night. I am all right, though."

Karen doesn't say anything, but she continues to look at Charlie with curiosity.

Mrs. Thomas, wearing a lovely pink dress, comes downstairs and walks into the living room.

"Is everybody ready to go?" she asks.

Charlie looks at Mrs. Thomas, smiling with excitement.

"Wow! That sure is a pretty dress, Ma. You will get more attention than the preacher."

"You think so, Charlie? I thought I would wear a new dress for a change. Karen isn't the only one who wears new clothes around here."

Mrs. Thomas is in a wonderful mood today, full of happiness and jubilation.

She looks at the two lovebirds on the couch and joyfully says, "Well, let's go! Why don't we all pile into my car? I want to drive, if that's all right with you two."

"That's fine with me. Let's go." Karen slowly stands up, still looking curiously at Charlie.

They all pile into Mrs. Thomas's car, and she happily drives to church.

They all get out and walk inside the church. Mrs. Thomas leads the way, and Charlie and Karen follow. They sit up in the balcony. Charlie sits between Karen and Mrs. Thomas. The three sit patiently, waiting for the morning worship services to begin.

After the morning announcements and a few songs, the reverend walks up to the podium. The church becomes very silent as the reverend takes his time getting his sermon ready. The reverend looks sternly at the congregation, as if he has something important on his mind. The church is very crowded. Almost every seat is taken. He stares at the congregation, his face filled with mystery and intrigue.

The congregation gives the reverend complete and undivided attention. They all look up at him, eager to listen to his sermon. The church is filled with a deafening quiet as the reverend begins his sermon.

"Good morning to all of you this morning. I hope you all had a good week. There is something that's been going on in this country this year that has recently been bothering me. I want to talk about it to you this morning."

All eyes are focused on the reverend.

"It seems to me that this country has a big problem with corruption, in our government and in the business world. People are being lured to do all kinds of things that are wrong, that are done only for the almighty dollar. I think this needs to be talked about."

Karen reaches over and takes Charlie's hand. They hold hands as they listen attentively.

The entire church remains quiet as Reverend Heath continues.

"I saw on the news this week that a drug dealer was extradited to the United States to stand trial. Before he was arrested, he gave out millions of dollars to poor people. These people then began to riot at our embassy. They burned down buildings and a lot of other things. People were shot and killed. These common, everyday people destroyed human beings and property. After being giving money—money that was raised through selling illegal drugs—they committed these heinous acts. The temptation of this money has lured honest people into crime, making them become monsters."

Charlie pays very close attention to what the reverend has to say.

Reverend Heath continues. "Some of our political representatives take money as contributions for their election campaigns, knowing that, in time, they will have to do things that are completely wrong and immoral. They will gladly do these things because they have received this money. The power of money is one of the main things the devil has to offer, and he will use it to trick and deceive you so that he can get his evil actions done. I want to warn you!" The reverend points his finger at the congregation. His voice becomes loud and powerful. "I want to warn all of you out there that the power of temptation is strong and mighty. And every one of you will be tempted at some point in your life. You will be tempted to do something you know is wrong. You must be strong to overcome this temptation! You must be strong!"

Karen looks at Charlie and sees that his sleepy eyes have come alive.

"And money isn't the only way the devil will tempt you!" says the reverend. "Oh no! There are other things that are just as tempting. There are substances out there that will make you feel like you are the king of the world. Drugs and alcohol will make you feel wonderful, until you slam your car into a tree, or destroy everything you spent your life building. They will lead you down a path of self-destruction! And while you are traveling down that road, you will think that everything is wonderful. The pleasure these substances will give you will also give you a false sense of reality. You won't think there is anything wrong, until you feel the physical and mental anguish these substances cause."

Mrs. Thomas glances over at Charlie and notices his attentive and serious expression.

"But there is one more temptation I want to talk about," says Reverend Heath.

Charlie glances over and sees Mrs. Thomas looking at him. He reaches over and takes her hand.

The reverend continues. "Being a man, I am tempted by members of the opposite sex."

A little laughter issues forth from the congregation.

The reverend's voice grows more serious. "This world is full of lust and seduction. The people who are living together outside of marriage—the ones who have their mistresses tucked away at some cozy out-of-the-way place, and the ones who are cheating on their spouses, and I am not referring to only men—those people will one day have to answer for these actions! And when these people answer, they will then see the true reality of what they have done: used other human beings just to satisfy their own selfish desires. And on the Judgment Day, when they do see the truth of the actions, the shame will burn like fire."

Many in the congregation applaud.

The reverend continues. "The people who do these things think they won't have to answer for their actions, but they will. And when they do, they will turn and rebel against God."

The reverend begins to walk around the platform. "That's why they don't want to go to church or pray or read the Bible or worship or do anything else God commands. They don't want to believe in God because, if they do, they won't feel comfortable living their carefree, sinful lifestyles."

There is another robust round of applause from the congregation.

Reverend Heath's voice grows louder. "These people who practice fornication don't think they are doing anything are wrong. They don't! They think it is a completely natural and normal thing to do."

The reverend walks around some more, until the church is very quiet. "Using other people just to satisfy your own selfish, pleasurable desires is wrong. This is why it is wrong: women engage in this lifestyle, get pregnant, and then trot down to these death factories and pay money to a sinister monster to have their own children destroyed! That's right! More than four thousand women make that trip every day of the year! Imagine. Paying money to have their unborn children destroyed!"

There are a few angry faces in the congregation looking at the reverend now.

Reverend Heath sees this expression of discontent in a few of his assembly. He looks at these few and says to them, "I know this is a very controversial topic. I know this is something people have different views on, but as a follower of Jesus Christ, I must tell you the Christian way of thinking. Tonight's sermon will be on this topic. I don't want to branch off to it until tonight. The name of the sermon is 'John 3:3.' That's it. 'John 3:3' is the entire name. And after you hear this sermon, you will be jolted right out of your seat! It is not a pleasant sermon to listen to, but it will tell you of the most horrifying thing mankind has ever been deceived into doing. For now, I want to finish this sermon on temptation."

Mrs. Thomas releases Charlie's hand, and Karen does likewise. The reverend announces a passage in the Bible that he wants the congregation to read. Mrs. Thomas and Karen both turn to the passage. They read the passage and then shut their Bibles.

Charlie doesn't read a thing. He fixes his eyes on the reverend with intense emotion. Karen reaches over and takes Charlie's hand again, holding it tight. Charlie doesn't take his eyes off the reverend; he listens with total concentration.

The reverend walks back to the podium and opens his Bible. He flips through the pages as the church again becomes quiet and still.

In a very clear voice the reverend says, "Turn to Matthew, chapter 4, verse 1. Read silently as I read out loud:

> *'Then was Jesus led up of the spirit into the wilderness to be tempted of the Devil. And when he had fasted forty days and forty nights, he was afterward hungered. And when the Tempter came to him, he said, 'If thou be the Son of God, command that these stones be made of bread'. But he answered and said, IT IS WRITTEN, MAN SHALL NOT LIVE BY BREAD ALONE, BUT BY EVERY WORD THAT PROCEEDED OUT OF THE MOUTH OF GOD.'*

Reverend Heath pauses for a moment and then says, "This is a good example of being tempted. Jesus has been fasting for forty days and forty nights. I don't know about you, but if I miss one meal, you don't want to be around me."

There is laughter throughout the congregation.

The reverend continues. "It is hard to imagine what Jesus was going through, but remember this ... as hungry as had to have been, Jesus did not yield to the devil's temptation. He didn't give in to Satan's lure."

The congregation is silent.

Reverend Heath says, "Now I want you to read silently the second temptation the devil puts to Jesus."

Everyone looks in their Bibles as the reverend reads aloud:

> *"'Then the Devil taketh him up into the holy city, and sat him on a pinnacle of the temple. And he saith unto him, If thou be the Son of God, cast thyself down: for it is written, He shall give his angels charge concerning thee: and in their hands they shall bear thee up, lest at any time thou dash thy foot against a stone. Jesus then said unto him, IT IS*

> *WRITTEN AGAIN, THOU SHALT NOT TEMPT THE LORD THY GOD.'"*

The reverend takes a handkerchief and wipes his forehead. He pauses for a moment and then says, "Here, Jesus was tempted again by the devil. The devil wanted him to jump off a pinnacle, hoping he would kill himself. This was not a temptation of something pleasurable, but a test to see if God would run to the situation and pull Jesus out of harm's way. How many of us have tried to strike a deal with God? We might say, 'God, if you send me a million dollars, I will always be faithful to you,' or something like that. You don't test God! God will test us, but we should never test him."

The reverend begins to walk around the stage. "You see, there are temptations for physical things, like the first test the devil tempted Jesus with. But there are other temptations too, like when we try to tempt God to come running to our rescue. Now there is one more temptation the devil has for Jesus."

> The reverend walks back to the podium. He looks into his Bible and begins to read the next verse: *"Again, the Devil taketh him up into an exceeding high mountain, and showed him all the kingdoms of the world, and the glory of them. And saith unto him, all these things I will give thee, if thou wilt fall down and worship me. Then saith Jesus unto him, 'GET THEE HENCE, SATAN: FOR IT IS WRITTEN, THOU SHALT WORSHIP THE LORD THY GOD, AND HIM ONLY SHALT THOU SERVE. Then the Devil leaveth him, and behold, angels came and ministered unto him.'"*

The reverend closes his Bible, and he stands still. "This time, the devil tempted Jesus not for physical things, and not to tempt God into doing something. No! He tempted Jesus for something called power, something politicians and people in high places lust for in this mean world of ours. This temptation is something most of us never have been exposed to. But when power gets into the blood, this temptation—I have been told—is the strongest and most powerful desire of them all. Just look at all the dictators in this world. They are dictators because they have killed people to get where they are. No one votes under a dictatorship. There is no democracy in these vile governments! You do basically whatever you are told to do. And when you are told to do something wrong, the next thing you know, you start to think, 'Hey, I'm not doing anything wrong.' And these individuals who are dictators think, 'Hey, I'm not doing anything wrong either. I am above the law.' They're so blinded by power and corruption that they don't know what is right or wrong. And some of these dictators begin to use their religion to make them feel holy and righteous. These dictators live in a world where they think they are God. This temptation of power makes it easy for them to murder, destroy, corrupt, and do a host of other sinister things."

The reverend points his finger directly into the center of his congregation, fire and fury raging in his eyes. "But when you choose to start practicing these wrong acts, then the devil has won his battle!"

The congregation listens intently.

The reverend continues. "I say this because the devil knows he can't take your soul! He can only tempt you into practicing something that is wrong so that one day, you will surrender your soul to him because of what you have become."

There is a low hum of voices from the congregation.

The reverend waits until the entire church is silent once again. "I hope you all see what temptation leads to."

Everyone focuses again on the reverend.

He clears his throat and then says with conviction, "When you are being tempted—and you will be tempted in this life—make sure you fight it. You won't be tempted with something that isn't pleasurable. And don't forget, you will be tempted the most when you are the most vulnerable. Your mind and your body will feel the compelling desire to yield to the temptation, but you must make the decision to be strong; you be determined not to yield."

The reverend looks deep into his congregation. His stern expression looks out at everyone as he walks around the stage. "Just remember what Jesus said when he was tempted. He said, 'THOU SHALT NOT TEMPT THE LORD THY GOD.' In other words, when someone tempts you, just tell them, 'Hey, don't tempt me!' And if they continue to tempt you with things you desire, order them to get away from you! Don't take no for an answer. Tell them, 'Get thee hence away,' and make sure they do!"

The congregation gives the reverend another short round of applause.

Reverend Heath continues. "There are so many things in this world; so many nice things to have and enjoy. It's not the things you have that will make you happy. It's how you obtain them that counts. And once you give in to the devil's temptation, you will eventually be at his mercy. And then, he will be able to trick you into doing all kinds of hideous things, just to cover up the things you have already done … all those things that are shameful."

The reverend pauses briefly and then says, "You must always be on the alert for temptation. When confronted with temptation, just ask yourself some questions: What will happen as a result of this temptation? What awful shame will I have to endure? How many people who love me will also be hurt because of my weakness? And, finally, the most important question of all: is it really worth it!"

With that, Reverend Heath concludes his sermon.

The look up at the reverend, their faces filled with admiration and respect.

As the morning worship service continues, Charlie reaches over and takes Mrs. Thomas's hand once again. He squeezes Karen's hand, which is still clasped in his, and then he smiles happily at both of them.

Charlie whispers to Mrs. Thomas, "That sure was a good sermon. Don't you think so?"

She smiles gladly at Charlie and says, "Yes, Charlie, it sure was."

Charlie gazes at Karen, smiling at her with love and joy. He leans over and whispers in her ear, "I love you, Cubby."

Karen turns her head sideways and smiles, her face glowing with love.

She turns her head and whispers in Charlie's ear, "I'm hungry, Charlie." She laughs as Charlie shakes his head. "I love you too, Charlie."

Karen kisses Charlie lightly on the lips.

Mrs. Thomas gently slaps Charlie's knee. He rubs it like it is killing him.

"I didn't hit you that hard, but I will if you don't behave yourself."

Charlie smiles a playful smile and then leans over and kisses Mrs. Thomas quickly on her lips!

Mrs. Thomas is taken quite surprised by Charlie's sudden act of affection. "Young man, we are in church! You had better behave yourself."

Charlie smiles that mischievous little smile of his. "I am behaving myself, Ma," he whispers. "I guess that lovely dress of yours has made you so beautiful today that I was tempted to kiss you. Tee, hee, hee."

Mrs. Thomas shows a pleasant grin as she shakes her head. She pats Charlie lightly on the arm, as the choir sings the last song.

Once the worship services are over, they file out of their seats. Charlie takes Karen's and Mrs. Thomas's hands. All three happily walk, hand in hand, to the car. Charlie opens Mrs. Thomas's car door and then hurries over to the other side. He opens the door, and then he sticks out his tongue at Karen as he slides in next to Mrs. Thomas. Karen sticks out her tongue in response.

All three sit comfortably in the front seat as Mrs. Thomas drives off.

As they drive along, Karen says to Charlie, "Did you kiss my mama in church?"

Charlie glances at Karen and then says with a happy grin, "I sure did, right on the lips! Tee, hee, hee."

Karen gives Charlie a scornful look as her mother silently smiles.

"Why did you kiss my mama on the lips?!"

"I was tempted. She looks so pretty wearing that dress, I just couldn't resist. Besides, I wanted to make you jealous."

"Are you kidding? I'm not jealous, silly boy."

"You were last night. Hey, Ma, guess what happened last night at the mall!"

Karen puts her hand over Charlie's mouth. "You shut up, Charlie Delaney! You keep quiet."

Charlie's question has aroused Mrs. Thomas's curiosity. "Tell me, Charlie, what did Karen do?"

"I didn't do anything, mama. Now let's talk about something else. I'm hungry. Where are we going to eat?"

Charlie grabs Karen's hand and removes it from his mouth. "Ma, would you believe your daughter got jealous over a forty-two-year-old grandmother. Tee, hee, hee."

Karen gives Charlie a scornful look. "I want to know where we are going to eat."

Charlie playfully says, "Hey, Ma, she is only trying to change the subject. She got insanely jealous last night over this woman I work with. Tee hee, hee!"

"Oh, she did …?"

Karen reaches over and pinches Charlie's leg, hard.

"Ouch! Hey, that hurt!"

"Good! That's what you get for starting trouble. But since you brought the subject up, you owe me four dollars."

Charlie tilts his head sideways, giving Karen a curious look. "What makes you think that?"

"Because that's how much I had to pay for the movie ticket."

Charlie grins at Karen and then turns his head toward Mrs. Thomas.

"Hey, Ma, Karen got so mad last night that she sat out in the car while I went inside the movie theater. I told her to come on, but she had to pout a little longer. She had to buy her own movie ticket because I had already gone in. You should have seen her pout, Ma."

Mrs. Thomas smiles gladly as Charlie finishes telling her the story. Charlie's face is all smiles. Karen, on the other hand, is not smiling at all. Her face is red and full of disenchantment.

"Well, after fifteen minutes or so, your daughter finally decided to join me in the theater. I told her I was going to the third movie, so she wouldn't get hysterical looking for me. Wasn't that thoughtful of me, Ma?"

"Yes, Charlie. That was very thoughtful of you."

Charlie looks at Karen and laughs that high-pitched laugh again. "Tee, hee, hee."

Karen gives Charlie another pinch on the leg.

"Ouch! That hurt! Quit doing that, Karen! Ma, tell Karen to quit pinching me."

"Karen, quit pinching Charlie."

"That's right! Take up for Charlie again. You always take up for Charlie."

"I don't always take up for Charlie, dear. It's just that you shouldn't pinch anybody like that. How would you like it if Charlie pinched you that way?"

Karen turns her head away. Looking out the window, she says, "I have nothing more to say."

"Look, Ma! She is pouting again. Isn't she adorable when she pouts?"

Mrs. Thomas laughs as she continues to drive.

Charlie takes Karen's hand, even though she tries to prevent him from doing so.

"Oh no, buster, don't try to love up to me now, not after all you have said."

Charlie does manage to hold her hand. He leans over and kisses her. She looks at him peevishly.

"I think you are the prettiest when you are peeved."

Charlie then kisses Karen quickly. Karen's peeved look fades away. She looks at Charlie with a passionate, loving expression. Charlie gently tilts his head sideways as he kisses Karen passionately on her sweet, innocent lips.

Mrs. Thomas doesn't say anything as Charlie and Karen sit there kissing each other.

The story Charlie was telling before has faded away and completely disappeared from the consciousness of everyone present.

Mrs. Thomas drives until she pulls into the parking lot of a steak house. All three of the hungry individuals jump out of the car and walk to the front of the restaurant, where they wait in line.

Eventually, they are seated in the busy eating establishment. Their steaks are brought to them after a long wait.

Karen smiles gladly when they do finally arrive. Even though she said she was starved earlier, she only eats half of her meal. Mrs. Thomas, on the other hand eats everything on her plate, and so does Charlie.

"I thought you said you were starved!"

Karen puts her napkin down on her plate and says, "I was starved, Charlie."

"Then why didn't you eat all of your steak?"

Karen gives Charlie a stern look. She turns her head sideways and says, "I ate all I wanted."

"Ma, why do girls say they are starving, order something big, and then barely eat half of what they order?"

"I don't know why, Charlie. I ate everything on my plate."

Charlie turns toward Karen, looking at her with a playful expression. "Why aren't you like your mother? Look, she ate everything on her plate."

Karen gives Charlie a mean look. Charlie sees this and begins to grin.

"Why are you grinning?"

"Because of the way you are looking at me. I like to get you peeved. You get that feisty look in your eyes."

Karen gives Charlie a little kick under the table.

"Ouch! Hey, cut it out. Ma, do you know what your daughter just did?"

"What did she do now?"

"She kicked me. She did. She kicked me."

Karen gives Charlie another mean look as Mrs. Thomas gives Karen a mean look of her own.

"Young lady, you know better than that. You apologize to Charlie for kicking him."

"I will not," Karen replies sternly.

"You apologize right now, young lady!"

Karen pauses for a moment. Her punished expression gazes back to her mother. She turns toward Charlie, and with a sad, soft voice says, "I'm sorry, Charlie."

Charlie begins to make that high-pitched laugh again. "Tee, hee, hee."

He grins at Karen. Karen's sad expression disappears, turning into a stern look.

Charlie leans over and kisses Mrs. Thomas on her cheek. "Thank you, Ma. I guess that is why I like to have you around so much, so you can help me keep Karen straight. Tee, hee, hee." Charlie kisses Mrs. Thomas on the cheek again.

Mrs. Thomas looks happy about all the affection she is getting from Charlie.

"Ma, just look at that face. Isn't Karen the cutest when she's peeved like that?"

Mrs. Thomas and Charlie watch as Karen's peeved expression explodes into a happy grin.

Charlie leans over and kisses Karen lightly on her soft, sweet lips. "Do you love me?"

Karen looks at Charlie with shining eyes. "Yes, I do, Charlie."

Charlie gazes into her eyes and whispers in her ear, "Next time, eat all of your steak."

Charlie laughs as he picks up the check.

The three get up to leave. Charlie leaves three one-dollar bills as a tip.

As Charlie walks over to pay the bill, Mrs. Thomas says, "I will be glad to pay for mine, Charlie."

"I will not hear of it, Ma! I will take care of it."

"Now, Charlie, I insist you take this." Mrs. Thomas hands Charlie a ten-dollar bill.

"No, Ma, I will not take it. Please let me get it, Ma. I want to. I really do. I enjoy doing this for you and Karen. Please don't give me that money."

"Well, Charlie, if it means that much to you, then okay."

Charlie's eyes light up when he hears Mrs. Thomas's words. Charlie pays the bill, and then all three walk back to Mrs. Thomas's car. Charlie holds hands with Karen and with Mrs. Thomas.

"You sure are feeling pretty good today, Charlie."

"Yeah, for someone who wasn't feeling too good this morning, you sure are happy now," Karen remarks.

"How could I not feel good? I am with two of the most beautiful women in the entire world."

The two ladies smile gladly as Mrs. Thomas unlocks the car. Charlie gets a fast kiss from Karen as Mrs. Thomas gets into the car. She reaches over and unlocks the door. Just as Charlie bends to get in, Karen pinches him on his buttocks.

"Ouch!"

When Karen gets into the car, she gives Charlie an I'm-proud-I-did-it look. She tries to make that high-pitched laugh of Charlie's: "Tee, hee, hee."

"Oh, you think you are something, don't you, little girl?"

Karen turns her head, smiling proudly. She sticks out her tongue at Charlie.

He gives her a feisty look.

Charlie looks over at Mrs. Thomas as she starts up the car. "Ma, guess what your daughter just did?"

Karen leans over and kisses Charlie profusely.

"What, Charlie?"

"Oh, nothing, Ma. Karen has made me forget."

Karen tries to laugh that high-pitched laugh again as they drive away.

When they get back to the Thomas's house, Charlie escorts the two ladies inside. As Charlie walks inside, Karen grabs his arm and leads him into the living room. The two sit down on the couch and neck for a few seconds before Mrs. Thomas enters the room.

Charlie, sensing her presence, stops necking with Karen.

Mrs. Thomas sits down on the sofa and says, "I believe I ate too much."

"Me too, Ma." Charlie looks over at Karen and then back at Mrs. Thomas. "We all know Karen didn't eat too much."

"Yeah, that's right. That's why I don't feel so bloated like you and mama."

Charlie gets up to turn the TV on. Just as Charlie takes his first step, Karen reaches over and pinches Charlie on his buttocks again.

"Ouch! You little rascal, you! Ma, did you see that?"

Karen mocks Charlie, "Ma! Did you see that? Tee, hee, hee."

"Karen! You should act more ladylike."

"Yeah, you should do as your mama says."

Karen mocks Charlie again. "Yeah, you should do as your mama says. Cry baby!" Karen sticks out her tongue again at Charlie.

Mrs. Thomas gets loud. "Young lady! You know better than that."

"I think I will go outside and play with my puppy."

Charlie gets an idea. "Oh, no, you're not! Not until you apologize to your mother."

"Are you crazy? I ain't gonna do no such thing!"

Charlie grabs Karen and begins to tickle her. Soon Charlie has her on the floor, tickling her more and more.

Karen laughs. "Stop it! Stop it!"

"Not until you apologize." Charlie continues to tickle her sides.

Karen then cries out, "Mama! Mama, make him stop!"

Mrs. Thomas smiles gladly as she watches the two lovebirds playing with each other on the floor. Their innocent teasing gives Mrs. Thomas great pleasure.

"Mama! Mama, tell Charlie to stop!"

"Why would I want to do that?"

Charlie continues to tickle Karen until she submits.

"Okay, okay! I give in! I give in! I apologize!"

Charlie rolls over on top of her and says, "That's what you get for being disobedient to your mother, young lady. Tee, hee, hee."

Karen looks up at Charlie, her face red. "Let me up! You let me up right now, or I will—"

"Or you will, what?" Charlie playfully replies.

"You had better let me up."

"Nope. Not until you say please."

"I ain't!"

"There is no such word as *ain't.*"

"Let me up right now!"

Karen's face is extremely red now. She is getting very angry. Charlie's playful antics no longer amuse her. The more Karen yells for him to stop, the more Charlie likes it. Her feisty look brings pleasure to Charlie, and to Mrs. Thomas. She loves to see them play.

Charlie smiles contentedly at Karen as he says, "Say, 'Please, master, let me up.'"

"Be damn! I ain't gonna do no such thing."

Karen tries to break Charlie's powerful grip, but to no avail.

Charlie laughs at Karen as she weakly attempts to break his mighty hold. Charlie sees the feisty look in Karen's face plainly now.

He laughs now, in a deep, low tone. "Ha, ha, ha! I have you now, my pretty. Ha, ha, ha!" The sound is fiendish.

Charlie laughs again in this deep, low tone, “Ha, ha, ha! You are in my power. Submit to me, or I will feed you to the crocodiles.”

“Like hell you will! You better let me up right now, young man, or else. I am tired of playing.”

This gives Charlie more reason not to let her up.

Charlie goes back to his normal voice. “Say it! Say, ‘Please let me up, master.’ Then I will release you. I promise.”

Karen again struggles pitifully to get loose. The attempt is quite useless.

Charlie takes great delight in seeing Karen struggle so futilely. He laughs the high-pitched laugh every time Karen tries to get free. Karen’s face is completely red now.

“I hope this goes on all afternoon!” he says.

Karen stops struggling. She looks up at Charlie, exhausted.

With a mean look, Karen says, “Okay! I submit! Will you please let me up, master!”

After Charlie hears this, he releases her. Karen gets up from off the floor and walks away as Charlie smiles contently at his accomplishment.

Karen goes outside and brings in her little basset hound puppy dog. She gives Charlie a pissed-off look and then quickly turns her head away. Karen lies down on the floor and begins to play with Little Charlie. Mrs. Thomas walks over, plays with the little pup for a while, and then disappears upstairs.

Charlie walks over and sits down on the floor.

“Oh no, you can’t play with Little Charlie. You have pissed me off.”

“I was only playing with you.”

“I am not a toy to be played with.”

Charlie rolls over and kisses Karen on her neck.

“I know … I guess I play too rough sometimes. I’m sorry …”

Karen turns around and looks at Charlie’s sympathetic expression. She picks up the little puppy.

“You see this puppy, Charlie?”

“Yes.”

“This puppy looks just like you.”

Charlie rolls over, close to Karen. He kisses her lightly on her soft lips.

"I love you, Cubby. I love you so much. Do you love me?"

Karen's eyes are luminous and aroused. She leans over and kisses Charlie passionately on his masculine mouth.

"Yes, Charlie, I love you. I love you. I love you."

The two sweethearts lie there, absorbing each other's affection as the puppy tries to steal some affection for himself.

As the innocent petting goes on, Charlie's sexual feelings begin to overwhelm him. He knows better than to touch Karen in a seductive manner. Boy, does he know! Although his erection is stimulated by the seductive gleam in Karen's eyes, Charlie tries to suppress his urge by getting up. He walks over and sits down on the sofa.

Karen turns her head sideways, looks confused by his behavior. She gets up, walks over to Charlie, and sits down on his lap.

The little puppy follows right behind, barking away as hard as he can.

Karen looks at Charlie with wonder as she says in a soft, virtuous way, "What's the matter, Charlie?"

After a long pause, Charlie says, "Karen?"

"Yes, Charlie."

"Why don't we … I mean … why don't we just … why don't we go to church tonight?"

Karen's disappointment is revealed by her sad expression. She thought he was going to ask her the big question. She looks very stunned for a few seconds.

"Charlie, is that really what you wanted to ask me?"

"Well … no. I mean, yes … I mean, no … well … let's go to church tonight. Do you want to go?"

"Charlie, I don't want to go to church tonight. The reverend scared me with what he said in that sermon this morning. Let's not go tonight, Charlie."

"I want to go," Charlie quickly declares.

Karen gives Charlie a silent stare as Mrs. Thomas comes walking down the stairs and into the living room.

When Charlie sees Mrs. Thomas his eyes light up. "I was wondering where you have been all this time, Ma."

"I thought I would put on something a little more comfortable."

Nodding his head, Charlie says, “I think I will do the same.”

Karen gives Charlie a stern look before saying, “I thought we might go to a movie tonight, Charlie.”

“No, not tonight, Karen. I am going to church to hear the reverend’s sermon, ‘John 3:3.’”

Mrs. Thomas gazes at Charlie as an eerie silence fills the room.

“Why don’t I fix us all supper tonight, Charlie? Then the three of us could go see a movie.”

“That will be just fine. I second the motion. Why don’t you rush home and change, Charlie? Be back by six so that we can all—”

“I am going to church tonight. I want to hear what Reverend Heath has got to say. What he said this morning has aroused my curiosity.”

“Charlie, I am glad you want to go to church, but why don’t you go some other time?”

“Yeah, why don’t you listen to my mama? Stay here and entertain us tonight.”

Charlie is reluctant to argue with both of the persistent females. He hesitates for a moment and then quickly gets up.

“I will be back for supper, Ma, around five-thirty. Then, I will have time to make the sermon at seven. Well, I have got to go! Bye now!”

“Hey! You wait one minute, Charlie Delaney.”

But Charlie doesn’t stay around to argue. He hurries out the door and to his truck.

Karen runs after him. She catches up to him, with fury and anger showing in her eyes. Karen runs over and hops into Charlie’s truck.

“Where the hell do you think you’re going?”

Charlie looks at Karen with anger. “You know better than to talk to me in that manner, young lady.”

“Well, you know better than to just get up and leave while my mama is talking to you. I am disappointed in you too, Charlie Delaney.”

Karen’s mean look evolves into a sad, enticing one.

“You know better than to use words like that. I don’t like hearing you curse like—”

“Okay, okay. I’m sorry for talking to you like that. You know I have a hot temper that I’m trying to control. I’m sorry, Charlie. You forgive me?”

"Well ... I guess I could overlook it this time."

Karen snuggles up to Charlie with love and affection.

"Why don't you come back in the house? Mama is really upset that you left so abruptly."

"I will be back at five-thirty, and then we will eat supper."

Karen kisses Charlie on the hand as she rubs her head on his shoulder.

"Come on back in, Charlie. I don't want you to leave now."

"I have this itch to leave, so I'm leaving. Tell Ma that I love her and I will be back at five-thirty. She'll understand."

"She might, but I won't. Why do you have to be so stubborn?"

"I guess I learned it from you. Tee, hee, hee."

"That's not funny, Charlie."

"I really have to go now, Karen."

"What happened to Cubby?"

"Okay, Cubby. I have got to leave now, so will you please let me go?"

"Okay! If that's the way you want it, Charlie! I know when you don't want me around! I guess you would rather be with your other girlfriend!"

Charlie's face erupts angrily. "You always have to throw that up in my face. Every time you get mad or don't get your way, you throw that up in my face. You ought to be ashamed of yourself. You know damn well I ain't going to see her!"

Karen's face is filled with guilt. She is sorry about what she just said, but she's too angry to admit it to Charlie. Without saying another word, Karen gets out of Charlie's truck and slams the door shut. She walks back into the house angrily.

Karen storms in as her mother says, "Why did you go out there, Karen? What did you say to Charlie?"

Karen's angry face begins to crumble into a river of tears. Her sad face and feminine sounds of melancholy hurt her mother's heart.

"Dear, what is the matter?"

"Charlie and I had a fight. I had to open my big mouth again."

"Do you want to tell me about it?"

"No, mama, I don't want to talk about it."

Karen walks over, picks up Little Charlie, and lies down on the couch. Karen hugs the little puppy lovingly as she lies on the couch in a sad state. She feels the agony of her own doing. After an hour or so, she gets an idea. She gets up from the couch and takes Little Charlie out to his doghouse. She runs upstairs, puts on some blue jeans and a T-shirt, and hurries back downstairs.

"Mama, I am going over to Charlie's to apologize. I can't sit here feeling sorry for myself any longer. I had no right to talk to Charlie the way I did."

Mrs. Thomas smiles gladly at her daughter. "Try to get him to still come over for dinner. I will be having fried chicken."

"Okay, mama, I will try. Bye-e-e-e."

Karen eagerly drives over to Charlie's house.

When she pulls into his driveway, she sees Charlie riding his lawn mower.

He sees her and drives it over to where she is standing. He looks at her, ticked off as he turns off the lawn mower.

Karen puts her arms around Charlie's neck and says, "Hey, Charlie."

She kisses his cheek several times as she says, "I'm sorry about the way I acted. I am so sorry. I know you weren't going to see anybody else. Will you please forgive me for acting so childish?"

Charlie's ticked-off expression disappears, turning into a happy smile.

"Yes, Cubby, I guess I could forgive you once more."

Karen kisses Charlie on the mouth passionately, several times.

"I love you so much, Charlie. I don't know why I act the way I do."

"Neither do I," Charlie says with a wry smile. "I have got to finish mowing now. Go on inside. I will be in shortly."

"Okay." Karen kisses Charlie once more and then walks inside the house.

While Karen is in Charlie's house, she begins to straighten up a few things. First, she gathers up all the clothes lying around the house and takes them to the laundry room. She just throws them all together in the washing machine, and then she goes into the kitchen and looks out the window. She sees Charlie riding along on his lawn mower. She gazes at him for a few moments until the phone rings.

Karen walks over to the phone and picks it up. "Hello. This is Charlie Delaney's residence."

There is silence on the other end of the line. Karen then hears a female voice that sounds vaguely familiar.

"Hello, I would like to speak to Charlie."

Karen feels fear rush through her body. It's *her!*

"Who is this?" Karen says.

"You know who this is. My name is Dee Swanson. You know, Charlie's lover."

Karen moves toward a chair and collapses into it. Her hand begins to tremble. "Listen here, Charlie and I are back together now, and I want you to quit bothering him."

Dee's voice becomes more determined. "Is that so? Well, I just want you to know something, little girl: I happen to be in love with Charlie. I have known him most of my life, and for your information, Charlie loves me too."

Karen begins to get very upset.

"Your lies aren't going to work! Charlie loves me, and me only, and I'd wish you would leave us alone! Now don't call here anymore!" Karen gets up and slams the phone down.

Tears begin to flow from Karen's eyes. She is shaking tremendously now. She walks over to the counter and gets a tissue to dry her sad eyes. She walks into the living room and falls on the couch in a state of self-pity. Before long, Karen's self-pity calls on his two friends, self-pride and jealousy, the green demon. Once again, they all join hands and begin to dance a jig in Karen's mind. They begin to trick and deceive Karen into thinking false thoughts about Charlie. She lies on the couch as the three demons poison her mind with these false thoughts. She doesn't move until Charlie comes inside the house.

"Hello, Cubby. I am sure glad that grass is mowed now."

Karen gives Charlie a strange look.

Charlie looks at her and sees that there is something wrong. "Cubby, why are you looking at me like that? I thought you weren't mad at me anymore."

"I'm not mad at you, Charlie. What makes you think that?" Karen's face is filled with mischief. "So have you decided what you are going to do tonight?"

Charlie gives Karen a disappointed look. "I thought we have already decided that. I am … I am … thirsty. Just a minute, Karen."

Charlie walks into the kitchen to get a soda. He calls out, "Do you want a soda, Cubby?"

Charlie doesn't get a response, so he walks back into the living room. "Do you want a soda, Cubby?"

Karen takes her time before answering. "No, Charlie, I don't care for one."

Charlie decides that there is definitely something wrong. He walks over and sits down on the end of the couch. He puts Karen's feet in his lap. "I am sure glad you came back, Cubby," he says, looking into Karen's eyes. "I don't like leaving when you are angry with me. You aren't angry with me, are you?"

"Me? How could I be mad at you?"

"Okay, Karen! What's the matter?"

"There's nothing the matter with me!"

Charlie gives Karen a very stern look.

"Something is bothering you, and I want to know what."

With that, the telephone rings. Charlie walks over to it.

Icy fear runs up Karen's spine.

Charlie picks the phone up and sits back down on the couch.

"Hello, Charlie. It's me … Dee."

Charlie's heart begins to beat fast. "I thought I told you not to call me anymore."

Karen rises from her comfortable position, listening eagerly.

"I know you did, Charlie, but I had to call you to apologize for the way I acted last night. I was drunk and lonely. I feel awful about the way I talked to you. Can you ever forgive me for the way I acted?"

Charlie glances over and sees Karen looking anxiously at him.

"Did you call a while ago?" he says into the phone.

"Well, yeah. I talked to what's-her-name. Did you know she was so rude that she hung up on me?"

"Oh, she did, huh? Well, that explains it. If you don't stop calling me, I am going to start hanging up on you too."

"How can you talk to me like that, Charlie? This is Dee. I love you."

Charlie takes the phone away from his ear.

He looks over at Karen and says, "I see why you are acting so strangely now. I hope you don't blame me for this."

Karen doesn't say anything. She just looks at Charlie sympathetically and nervously.

Charlie puts the phone up to his ear again and says, "Okay. Now you listen here. You have upset my girlfriend! I don't take it lightly when someone hurts her feelings. Don't you say anything to hurt her again, or I will excommunicate you! Do you understand? I will excommunicate you!"

"Charlie, please don't be angry with me. I was only trying to help."

"Oh boy, trying to help! I told you before that I love Karen."

Dee begins to get angry and very upset. "Then tell me you don't love me anymore! Tell me, and I will leave you alone!"

Charlie pauses for a moment before saying, "Now you know I can never say that, and I won't say it now. So please, just leave us alone! Please."

"You can't say it, because you do love me. I know you do. You showed me the night we made love. I can't live without you, Charlie. I love you so much. I have always loved you. Please don't treat me like this! Please don't."

Charlie doesn't know what to do. He is looking at Karen while listening to Dee. The only two loves of his life, and he doesn't know what to do with either one of them.

As Charlie thinks to himself in his confused state, Karen cries out, "Hang up on the whore!"

"Don't call her that! She is not a … just don't call her that!"

"Oh, so you are taking up for her now."

"I am not taking up for anybody. A good Christian girl isn't supposed to talk like that."

"So now I ain't a good Christian girl?"

"Will you quit confusing the issue? I just don't like hearing you talk like that."

Charlie hears Dee's voice over the phone. "Charlie! Charlie, are you still there? Talk to me, Charlie. Please talk to me."

Dee's crying voice hurts Charlie from within. He has never been in such a confused state.

What am I going to do now? What am I going to do? he wonders.

After a few seconds, Charlie decides to give Karen the phone. "Dee, Karen wants to talk to you, and if you hurt her feelings, I will do what I said I'd do a while ago."

Charlie looks at Karen and says, "If you call her that name or say anything like that word, I will have to punish you also."

Karen gives Charlie a confused look as she puts the phone up to her ear.

Karen says, "Well ..."

Dee answers, "Well ..."

Charlie gets up, turns on the TV, and then walks back over to his seat.

Dee breaks the stalemate. "Put Charlie back on the phone!"

Karen extends the phone to Charlie, saying, "She wants to talk to you."

"You mean, you are going to give me the phone so I can talk to her?"

Karen's timid look turns into a stern one. "Hell, no, I ain't." She puts the phone back up to her ear.

"Be kind. Remember—you are a good Christian girl."

"I will not put Charlie back on the phone! You have a lot of nerve calling Charlie here. What do you think Jesus would think of you right now?"

"Do what! What are you talking about?"

"I am talking about Jesus. What do you think Jesus would think of you being a saloon girl, seducing Charlie, practicing fornication, trying to break up what Charlie and I have? Are you sure your name isn't Jezebel?"

Karen then hears a click, followed by a dial tone. "Hello? Is anybody there? I guess she hung up."

Charlie applauds as Karen smiles gladly at him.

"Now that's how a good Christian girl should conduct herself. I am so proud of you, Cubby."

Karen runs over to Charlie, and the three little demons in her mind head for the door and vanish from the love-filled house.

Karen hops into Charlie's lap. They neck for a while, until Charlie's masculine urges begin to be aroused.

"Let me lie down on the couch," Charlie says.

He lies down and puts his head on Karen's lap. As Charlie lies there, Karen brushes her soft white hands through his hair. Charlie realizes that he can't continue to suppress his sexual feelings much longer. They remain on the couch until five o'clock.

Charlie glances at the wall clock and then quickly jumps up.

"Hey! We have got to go. I told Ma that I would be back by five-thirty. I have got to get dressed."

Karen still doesn't want Charlie to go to church tonight, but she sits there while he goes upstairs to put his suit back on.

He comes back down in fifteen minutes.

"Come on, let's go!"

Karen slowly gets up from the couch as Charlie impatiently waits for her at the door. Charlie and Karen each quickly walk to their vehicles.

"See ya later, sweetheart." Charlie kisses Karen one more time.

They drive to the Thomas's house. After they arrive, Charlie eagerly walks into the house, without waiting for Karen.

As Karen watches Charlie enter the house, she gets a devious idea. She takes a fingernail file out of her purse and uses it to let out the air in one of Charlie's tires. It only takes a minute to accomplish the deed. She smiles a devious grin as she joyfully walks into the house.

Charlie, Karen, and Mrs. Thomas enjoy a fabulous dinner.

Fried chicken is one of Charlie's favorite meals. He eats with gusto but keeps an eye on his watch.

After dinner, Charlie kisses Mrs. Thomas on the cheek about a half dozen times and then gives her a big loving hug.

"What was all that for, Charlie?"

"It was for cooking that wonderful dinner, for bringing my beautiful girlfriend into the world, and because I love you."

"Oh, Charlie!" Mrs. Thomas says, blushing.

Karen just sits quietly as the time reaches six-thirty.

Mrs. Thomas says, "Charlie, by the way you're dressed, I guess you are going to church again tonight."

"That's right, Ma. Are you sure you two don't want to go?"

Karen snickers as she takes the dishes into the kitchen. Nobody sees her grinning face, but when she comes back into the room her face is full of deviousness.

Charlie sits down beside Karen for a while.

At six-forty, Mrs. Thomas says, "Charlie. If you are going to church, you had better leave now. It starts at seven, you know. That's only twenty minutes from now."

"Okay. Thank you again for dinner, Ma."

Charlie kisses Karen quickly and then says, "See you both later. I will be back after the service, and then we can go to that movie you two want to see."

"Okay, Charlie, I will be waiting."

Just as Charlie walks out the door, Karen bursts out laughing.

This gets her mother's attention. "Young lady, what have you got on your mind?"

"Charlie ain't going nowhere. I want to go to the movies at seven-thirty, not nine-thirty."

Mrs. Thomas gives her daughter an angry look. "What did you do?"

"Oh, nothing … nothing but let the air out of one of Charlie's tires, that is."

"You did what!"

"Now don't get bent out of shape, mama. You would rather go to the seven-thirty movie than the nine-thirty one, wouldn't you?"

Mrs. Thomas pauses for a moment before saying, "Well … yes, I would, but letting the air out of Charlie's tires just so he would miss church, well … I don't know if that was the right thing to do, dear."

"Don't worry about it, mama. I know what I am doing."

So the two women go to the window and peep out, watching Charlie with excitement and anticipation.

When Charlie gets to his truck, he jumps in and begins to back out of the driveway. He feels the flat tire go up and down, so he jumps out to investigate the problem, noticing the left rear tire.

"Oh boy, a flat. I must have picked up a nail," Charlie mutters as he pulls back the driver's side backseat.

Charlie grabs the can of Fix-A-Flat stowed behind the backseat. He takes off the tire-stem cover, screws the end of the can to it, and presses the container. Miraculously, the tire inflates to its regular size. Charlie throws the empty container in his truck and drives away.

As Charlie disappears from sight, Mrs. Thomas laughs. "Goody, goody! I hope you are happy with yourself, young lady."

Karen turns her head sideways, a look of wonder and amazement filling her face. "How did Charlie fix that tire so quickly?"

"I don't know, but you should be ashamed of yourself for doing what you did. Sometimes I just don't understand you, Karen."

Karen's face is red with shame and guilt. "I just can't understand how he fixed that tire so quickly."

When Charlie arrives at the church, the evening service is just beginning. The choir begins to sing its first hymn. Charlie looks around and notices that the church is only one-third filled. The atmosphere is quiet. There are no people in the balcony; as a result, Charlie decides to sit up front. Something tells him to sit up close so that he'll be able to clearly hear the reverend's message tonight. Some powerful force in Charlie's spirit directs him to the very front row. He looks there and notices that there is nobody sitting in the first or second row. Charlie looks around and then sits down in the first row, right up front. He then eagerly and nervously waits for the sermon to begin.

Charlie looks at the reverend with great anticipation.

The reverend looks as if his mind is occupied by something. He doesn't look at the choir as they are singing; instead, he stares at the floor. He seems to be thinking of something very demanding and troubling.

As the choir finishes the hymn, they calmly sit down and wait for the reverend to speak.

The reverend remains sitting as the church grows quiet. The congregation is small in number tonight. The people sit quietly, beginning to wonder why the reverend is still sitting in his chair. The once-tranquil atmosphere begins to become intense as they wait for Reverend Heath to deliver his message. The reverend looks out at his congregation, showing them a tormented expression. He turns his head to his choir, flashing them a quick grin. The distraught expression returns to his face when he turns back toward the congregation.

Finally, the reverend slowly gets up and walks up to the podium.

The congregation looks on in complete silence. The intense anticipation is palpable in the room.

Charlie stares at the reverend with fascination and wonder.

The reverend begins to shuffle a few papers, and then he clears his throat, ready to present his sermon.

"There will be no more singing tonight, because after what I have to say to you, singing will not be an appropriate thing to do. I hope you all had a good day today. I didn't. I mean, thinking about this sermon has been troubling for me all day long. I can be finally rid myself of the mental anguish of thinking about this sermon, for now I can deliver it to you all."

Charlie barely breathes as he listens carefully to the message.

Reverend Heath says, "I want you all to turn in your Bibles to John, chapter 3, verse 3."

As everyone turns to this passage, the reverend begins to walk around the stage. He studies the people of his congregation as he walks. He studies them like a book.

"Before I read you this, I want to tell you something; something that is going on in this country and all over the world." The reverend pauses until the atmosphere is at a fever pitch. "On average, nearly four thousand children are destroyed every day of the year! One and a half million American children will be annihilated this year, and that figure is just in this country alone."

The church is still and quiet as the reverend pauses.

Reverend Heath continues. "Now, there are a lot of people in this world who don't think there is anything wrong with this wicked act. That is only because of the deceptions that plague this evil world of ours. Because of deception, millions and millions of little children have been murdered in this world!" The reverend pauses. "But that is not the main focus of my sermon tonight. No. There is something more sinister beneath the surface of this atrocity. My friends, what I am about to tell you is going to shock the living daylights out of you! The wickedness that the devil has ever deceived mankind into doing is being practiced today."

The reverend's face is stern and scary as he gazes out at the small congregation. "A few years ago, I had the privilege to meet with Billy

Graham. This topic of abortion came up, and he tried to explain his belief. He told me that these children who were being aborted would all go to heaven. Mr. Billy Graham himself said that! I didn't want to argue with Billy Graham, so I remained silent."

The reverend begins to get loud. "Well, I'm not going to remain silent anymore!"

The congregation becomes agitated by the reverend's tone.

Waiting until everyone is settled, Reverend Heath continues. "There is another minister I want to mention. Has anybody ever seen Pat Robertson? He is the founder of the TV show *The 700 Club.* One of the finest ministers I have ever heard. He has got to be one of the best TV evangelists today, but ..."

The reverend's voice trails off. He pauses for a long time.

After several moments, he resumes speaking, his voice filled with fury. "*But!* ... He also thinks that all these children who are being destroyed in these abortion death factories will also go to heaven! Oh, how convenient! I guess the devil would walk up to both of them, pat them on the back, and say, 'Fine work, fine work! You keep telling everybody that those children will go to heaven. You just keep telling them that. Then nobody will stop me from destroying their souls!!!'"

The reverend looks out at the terrified congregation, a strong, determined look blazing from his eyes. "Two of the smartest men in the entire world, and they too have been deceived! They think they have all the right answers! They think they know all there is to know about the life after this world. They think children who haven't been born into this world will go straight to heaven. Well, friends, there is something in the Bible that will shed a different light on this subject! Yes, it will shed a new light, indeed."

The reverend gazes out into the audience, noticing Charlie sitting in the front row all by himself. He rivets Charlie with his eyes as he stares directly at him.

Looking at the entire congregation, the reverend says, "Does everyone notice that there is only one man sitting in the front row tonight?"

Charlie looks around and sees everyone focusing their attention on him.

"That seems to be how the world deals with this sinister problem." The reverend gets louder as he continues to speak. "It seems like everyone's afraid of this subject."

The reverend looks right at Charlie once again, giving him an intriguing smile as he says softly, "Well, maybe not everyone."

The reverend walks back to the podium and begins to gesture vigorously with his hands in an attempt to better explain the meaning of his sermon. His arms move like those of an orchestra conductor. He transmits energy throughout the church, as if his words generate a surge of power. His presence becomes a spectacle of excitement.

"This world is afraid! This world has been deceived!" Reverend Heath thunders. "This world is destroying something far more precious than just the human lives of these innocent children."

Taking his Bible, the reverend speaks in clear, modulated voice. "Let us read from John, chapter 3, verse 3."

Everyone looks down at their Bibles, which are already open to this passage.

The weary reverend declares, "Jesus is talking with a man named Nicodemus, so let us first read about him."

The reverend begins to read from his Bible: "'*There was a man of the Pharisees, named Nicodemus, a ruler of the Jews: The same came to Jesus by night, and said unto him, Rabbi, we know that thou art a teacher come from God: for no man can do these miracles that thous doest, except God be with him.*'" The reverend's voice gets loud and blaring. "*Jesus answered and said unto him, VERILY, VERILY, I SAY UNTO THEE, EXCEPT A MAN BE BORN AGAIN, HE CANNOT SEE THE KINGDOM OF GOD.*'"

Reverend Heath looks deep into his audience, with a very stern and determined stare.

An expression of marvel on his face, Charlie gazes at the reverend with great admiration, listening very carefully.

The reverend says, "Let me repeat those words: '*EXCEPT A MAN BE BORN AGAIN, HE CANNOT SEE THE KINGDOM OF GOD.*' I hope everyone heard the words 'born again.' How can someone be born again if he has never been born in the first place! The scripture plainly says '*born again.*'"

In a loud voice the reverend spells the word. "B-o-r-n. The word *born* must be made known. You must be born into this world before you can be born again!"

Everyone looks at the reverend with fright and alarm; even Charlie's face is filled with dismay.

The reverend wipes his forehead and then continues. "Maybe some of you need more proof! Let me move down to the fifth verse. Yes. Here it is. Jesus answered, *'VERILY, VERILY, I SAY UNTO THEE, EXCEPT A MAN BE BORN OF WATER AND OF THE SPIRIT, HE CANNOT ENTER INTO THE KINGDOM OF GOD.'* Does everyone hear this? You must be born—b-o-r-n—of water and of the spirit before you can enter into the kingdom of God! The words plainly state the facts. You must be born into this world of water and of the spirit! It is very important to make this fact known!"

Once again, the reverend gazes out into the congregation with extreme emotion and feeling. His stern look is magnetic.

The reverend starts to speak again. This time, his voice is soft. "I just want you all to know that the words I have spoken to you tonight have a very special meaning. I can't begin to imagine the horrendous, wicked acts that will be performed tomorrow. You see, we live in a world controlled by forces over which we as individuals have little control. We must live by the laws that we have, and abide by them. Even when the laws are wrong, we still must abide by them."

As the reverend gazes wearily at the congregation, Charlie looks at the reverend with compassion.

The reverend seems to get strength and encouragement from Charlie's expression. He begins to walk around the stage. As he walks, a feeling of power rushes through his body. The burning fire of determination begins to build in his face. He finally gazes out at his congregation, showing them a strong, fiery expression of invincibility.

The reverend points his finger into the center of his distressed congregation, and with a strong, firm voice announces, "I just want you all to know that every time a little child is aborted, he or she dies twice! That's right! That child dies the life he or she would have lived on this planet; that is the first death. The child then dies the second death, which is the destruction of the life of eternity that he or she would have inherited. Abortion destroys the eternal soul of an individual, not just the physical body!"

The people of the church react to this profoundly. They begin to move around and talk amongst themselves, with horrified expressions showing on their faces.

Charlie looks around and sees how upset the people are. Some cry softly to themselves. Others cling to one another, their faces showing horror and grief.

The reverend walks back to the podium. All faces look directly at him as soon as he begins to speak. "It all begins with the act of fornication! Then, the pride of the expectant woman enters. She is tricked and deceived into having one of those wicked procedures performed on her unborn child."

The reverend raises his hands and begins to speak boldly. "There will be a day of reckoning for the ones who perform these diabolical acts! What kind of monster will destroy the souls of little children, just to receive a certain amount of money! What kind of creatures are they! Judgment Day! Judgment Day! The shame of this wicked sin will burn like fire!"

The entire congregation stirs with consternation at hearing these words.

The reverend waits until the church has settled down before he begins again. "I guess you all now have heard about this new sexual disease that is out there in the world today."

The reverend pauses for a moment and then says, "People have come up to me and asked, 'Why would God allow these killer viruses to come into the world? Is it here to punish the homosexuals?' I don't know if punishment is the reason, but I do feel it is in this world for some practical reason."

Charlie listens intently to the reverend's words, focusing with his complete attention.

"Just think for a moment," the reverend says. He begins to walk around as the congregation listens intently. "As long as people practice the act of fornication without any regard for the fact that this act is wrong, then it would seem to me that God would establish some type of substance to serve as a discouragement for engaging in this sinful act.

People who practice the act of fornication for a period of time alienate themselves from God."

Charlie's eyes light up. He understands now why his mother asked him to promise her that he would refrain from practicing fornication.

Reverend Heath continues. "Fornication drives a wedge between God and mankind! The pleasure is more important to the participants than a meaningful relationship with their maker. Once people begin to practice something—anything, for that matter—they get used to it, and then they think there is nothing wrong in doing it. Then the devil can deceive you into doing something else that you won't think is wrong, either. He knows you will one day answer for these abominations. He will wait for you to willingly join his army of rebellious sinners. Let me try to explain to you how the devil recruits souls for his army."

The entire congregation is mesmerized by the reverend's words.

"He must win you over," the reverend declares. "The devil will tempt you, trick you, or deceive you into doing something bad. Something so bad you will never acknowledge it, even when you stand before the great white throne and see for yourself what things you have done."

Charlie holds his breath.

The reverend holds the congregation in his gaze. "Then you will have to make a decision: to admit these things, or turn away from God. How many women will rebel against God because they can't admit they paid to have their children's souls destroyed!"

Every face turns toward the reverend in awe. Everyone has a very serious expression.

The reverend pauses for a moment and then continues. "The only way the devil can gain your soul is if you willingly give it to him. And you do this when you rebel against God and fail to admit your sins before Jesus. He is the only way to remove these sins from your soul."

A hum of voices arises from the congregation as people begin talking to one another.

Ignoring the sound, the reverend begins to walk around the stage. "People have been tricked and deceived to practice wrong acts throughout the centuries. Take slavery, for instance." The congregation grows quiet, and the atmosphere in the church becomes still and tranquil.

"Look at slavery. There were people who would buy slaves, make them work long hours out in the hot fields, day after day, for nothing but their meals and a place to sleep. It is hard to accept that anybody would do such a thing! But the ones who did were the same ones who would come to church and pretend to be good Christians. You see what I am saying? They didn't think there was anything wrong with making other humans their slaves. They were brought up thinking it was 'okay' to do this. Just like the people who practice the act of fornication. They tell themselves, 'Hey, I'm not doing anything wrong.' They don't even think about it until something happens that they aren't ready for, and then they have to make some decisions!"

Charlie studies the reverend, looking at him with profound understanding.

The reverend continues. "These diseases and viruses of today are out there for a reason. I believe, and I may be wrong, but I believe they are out there to get people to refrain from practicing the acts of fornication and sodomy. I truly believe that! I don't have any scripture to read to you, but I believe people need to have something to make them refrain from acting irresponsibly."

The reverend gazes into the congregation with an intriguing stare. "You folks might think I'm crazy, but ask yourselves something." The reverend begins to walk around the stage, keeping his eyes on his congregation the entire time. "Would you rather catch one of these diseases and suffer an agonizing death? Or …"

As the reverend lets his voice trail off intriguingly, he stops right in his tracks. He points his finger directly into the center of his audience, and in a loud voice says, "*Or,* would you rather practice fornication and not catch a disease, but then end up paying to have your own child destroyed twice by means of an abortion?"

The church grows quiet and still as the reverend looks at his congregation with great curiosity.

The reverend breaks the silence. "What would be worse, to suffer an agonizing physical death, or to live with yourself throughout eternity, knowing that you had the soul of your own child destroyed?"

The church once again becomes agitated, filled with intense emotion.

Reverend Heath persists. "What would be worse?"

He lets the congregation ponder the question as he walks around the stage, his fiery eyes glaring at them.

"We will all die one day!" says the reverend. "That is a fact. But it is not until *after* we die that we must begin to answer for what we have done with our lives!"

The reverend walks back to the podium. He says in a clear voice, "I don't want to give the impression that I am judging or condemning anyone."

He turns to his Bible. "It is just like Jesus said in John chapter 3, verse 17: '*FOR GOD SENT NOT HIS SON INTO THE WORLD TO CONDEMN THE WORLD; BUT THAT THE WORLD THROUGH HIM MIGHT BE SAVED.*' Condemning someone doesn't make the situation any better. Instead, it makes the one condemned rebel even more."

Charlie takes notice when he hears the word *rebel.*

"God doesn't hate the sinner; he hates the sin! God knows that we can easily be deceived by sin. So, when we sin, we don't think we are doing anything wrong; or, we don't care if we are. That's when the rebelling starts. People who won't admit their sins will rebel against God, and in doing so, they willingly create a hell for themselves. There will be a time when everything will be shown to us! We must prepare ourselves for that day, that Day of Judgment."

The tone of the reverend's voice gets deep and enticing. "One day, we will be shown exactly what we did with our lives: everything we said, everything we did, everything! And then, will we will be forced to admit those sins, or deny them—and rebel against God!"

The reverend begins to walk around the stage, with his hands behind his back. He focuses his attention directly at his congregation.

Some of the people start looking at their watches. Seeing this, Charlie looks at his. It is eight-thirty.

The reverend, observing the congregation, says, "I know I am running this service over tonight. If any of you have to be somewhere, you are welcome to leave."

He raises his hands and stares out into his audience. His face is compellingly stern, and his voice becomes powerful and demanding. "But this sermon will be given in its entirety, even if it takes all night!"

The entire congregation begins to applaud with excitement and jubilation.

The reverend waits until the church is quiet and still. His determined look draws the attention of everyone, keeping them fascinated and intrigued.

The reverend starts out in a soft tone. "I think about those slave owners who didn't think they were doing anything wrong. They would go to church, ask for forgiveness of their sins, and then march right back home to make their slaves work once again. I think about all those women who will have abortions performed on their innocent children. I think about the ones who will perform those awful murders in those clinics. They don't think they are doing anything wrong, either."

The reverend looks sternly at his audience, and his voice grows louder. "But there will be a day of reckoning!"

The congregation once again applauds the reverend with a robust amount of enthusiasm.

Reverend Heath continues. "No matter what you repent of in this life, you will one day be shown exactly what you have really and truly done! Then, and then only, will you come to know what wrong you have committed. Then, after you see your actions before your eyes, the shame will burn like fire!"

Charlie's eyes are full of excitement as his soul is flooded with a religious experience.

The reverend clears his throat and says, "Self-pride will pull you away from God so that you won't feel the burning shame of your sins. Remember what Jesus said, '*VERILY, VERILY, I SAY UNTO THEE, EXCEPT A MAN BE BORN AGAIN, HE CANNOT SEE THE KINGDOM OF GOD.'* So the next time someone tries to convince you that there is nothing wrong with the act of fornication, just tell that person about the four thousand little children who will be murdered that day. And think about the four thousand children who will be murdered the next day. And think about the four thousand children who will be murdered the day after that. And think about the four thousand children that who be murdered every single day of the year! And then think about the millions of little children who will be murdered worldwide!"

The reverend pauses, and his stern look evolves into a sad, depressed one. He speaks in a very soft manner, just above a whisper. "And then, finally, think about all those millions of children who will never see the kingdom of heaven."

The reverend pauses before softly saying, "Think of all those souls lost because of the deception and the self-pride of those ignorant individuals."

The reverend closes his Bible. He looks at his congregation, with a very disturbed expression on his face, and he says, "I hope you all have learned something tonight. I want you all to pray to God this week that someone will come into this deceived world of ours and stop this holocaust that is going on. Pray that someone will stop this unseen madness! Pray until you can't pray any more. Pray that the destruction of the souls of these unborn children will stop! The devil has this world in his grip!"

The reverend looks up toward the ceiling and prays out loud. "Dear God in heaven, please send someone into this mean world who will stop this tragic conflagration. Show the world what is really going on. Give him the wisdom not to be deceived by the things of this world. All these things I pray in Jesus' name, amen."

Reverend Heath slowly walks down from the stage, and without saying another word, he continues to walk down the aisle until he exits the church.

Everyone looks around, wondering what to do next.

The choir director finally walks up to the podium and says, "Everyone can go home now. These services are finished for the evening. Good night."

Everyone gets up and solemnly leaves the church.

That is, everyone but Charlie. He remains seated until everyone else has left. He then makes himself get up, walk down the aisle of the empty church, and go out to his truck. He gets in and drives away, filled with regret.

Back at the Thomas's house, Karen and her mother are worried that Charlie hasn't arrived yet.

Karen sits next to the window, looking out and hoping Charlie will soon drive up.

With a puzzled look, Mrs. Thomas says, "I wonder why Charlie hasn't gotten here yet. It's already past nine o'clock. The movie will already have started by the time we get there, even if we leave now."

"You don't think he has had a wreck, do you, mama?"

"I don't know, dear, I don't know. It's not like Charlie to be late like this. Church should have let out over an hour ago. I'm sure Charlie would have called if something came up."

Karen, with a panic-stricken face, says, "He's had a wreck! I just know it! He had a wreck because I let the air out of his tire. He probably had a blowout, and it's all because of me! It's all my fault!"

Karen begins to cry, and her mother tries to comfort her.

"Now, Karen, let's not jump to conclusions. He probably just went home and forgot about taking us to the movie tonight."

"No way, mama! Charlie would never forget about that."

Mrs. Thomas knows this. Her face is also full of worry.

They both wait eagerly near the window, until they see the lights of a vehicle that has pulled into their driveway.

Karen yells, "Yippee!"

Mrs. Thomas is also relieved to see Charlie's truck drive up.

Karen hurries to the door and runs outside. She throws her arms around Charlie and begins to kiss him profoundly.

"Oh, Charlie! Are you all right? I was so worried about you ..."

After Karen sees that Charlie is fine, she says, "Where the hell have you been! I have been worried sick over you!"

Charlie, still disturbed and bewildered by the sermon, says to Karen, "I have been at church. It took a little longer tonight."

Karen hugs Charlie with all her strength.

"I am sorry about something, Charlie. First, I am sorry for talking to you that way. Second, I did something to your truck before you left."

"Oh really? What did you do, young lady?"

Tears run down Karen's cheeks as she speaks. "I kinda wanted you to take us to the seven-thirty movie, so I let the air out of your tire to keep you from leaving. I'm sorry, Charlie."

Charlie looks at Karen's sad face, and then he says, "Oh, so that's why my tire was flat."

"Yes, Charlie. Will you please forgive me?"

"Not so fast, young lady! I am very disappointed in you." Charlie gives Karen a stern look as he says, "You will have to do something for me before I can forgive you."

"Anything, Charlie! I will do anything."

Karen is quiet, thinking about what it might be.

Charlie gets down on one knee, and with a single tear in his eye, he says, "Karen, will you marry me?"

Karen is dumbfounded. She looks down at Charlie, her face utterly surprised. "Do what!"

"What kind of answer is that? I am asking you to marry me! Is that all you have to say?"

"Yes."

"Yes, to which question?"

"I mean, *yes!* Why, heck yes, Charlie Delaney! I will marry you. Yes! Yes! Yes!"

Charlie gets to his feet, and Karen throws her arms around his neck. She begins to kiss his face all over as she says, "I love you! I love you! I love you!"

"I love you too, Cubby. I love you more than I love anybody in the whole world."

Just then, Mrs. Thomas walks outside. "What is all the racket out here?"

"Mama! Mama! Charlie proposed to me! He asked me to marry him! He did! He did! He really did!"

Mrs. Thomas gets excited and runs over to hug Charlie and Karen. All three stand there, embracing each other with happiness, love, and joy. After they all celebrate with hugs and kisses, they all go back inside the house.

Mrs. Thomas says, "That must have been some sermon Reverend Heath preached tonight."

"It was the best sermon I have ever heard in my entire life, Ma."

"So when do you want me to marry you, Charlie? Tee, hee, hee."

Charlie looks over at the calendar hanging on the wall. Karen and her mother walk over to it with Charlie. He points his finger to a day on the calendar.

Karen says, "That day is Saturday, June 6. I will be a June bride!"

"Okay, it's settled! We will be married June 6, at six o'clock, at the church."

"I will call Reverend Heath and make the necessary arrangements," Mrs. Thomas adds.

Karen asks, "Why six o'clock at night?"

Charlie tickles her before saying, "Because that was the same date and time my mother and father got married. Does that explain it, little girl?"

"Okay, okay. Six o'clock in the evening will be fine with me."

Charlie doesn't stay long after that. He leans over and gives Karen a gentle good-night kiss. And then he walks over to Mrs. Thomas, gives her a big hug, and kisses her good night also.

After Charlie leaves, Karen and Mrs. Thomas embrace each other lovingly. They begin to make plans for the wedding.

The next day, Charlie doesn't waste any time going to the mall after work. He walks into the same jewelry shop and sees the same lady who showed him the $31,000 ring.

"Hello again! Would you believe I am still looking for an engagement ring?"

"Well, good! I still have the one you looked at last time."

"I think I will want something a little less expensive."

The lady laughs a little laugh as she begins to show Charlie several other rings. "Have you asked her yet?"

"Yes, ma'am. I asked her last night."

"Maybe you would like her to come in and decide on what ring she would like."

"No. It takes her three hours to decide on what she wants to wear when we go out. I think it would be better if I pick out the ring."

"That will be fine. If you don't mind me asking, when are you supposed to get married?"

Charlie studies the rings over and casually says, "June 6, at six o'clock."

The lady pauses for a moment, and then her face fills with fear.

Charlie looks up and sees the disturbed look on the lady's face.

"What's the matter, ma'am? Did I say something wrong?"

The lady sits down and says, "Oh no. Did you say you are going to get married on June 6?"

"Yes, ma'am, at six o'clock."

"That's what I was afraid you said. Do you know that happens to be the sixth month, the sixth day, and the sixth hour?"

"What's wrong with that?"

"That is 666! That's the dev—" The lady stops before she finishes, seeming to change her mind about what she wants to say. "Why don't you get married on the June 16 or 26?"

Charlie doesn't like the lady's advice.

"No. We are going to get married on June 6, at six o'clock. We have decided on the date and time!"

The lady detects some hostility coming from Charlie, so she doesn't say any more about it.

Charlie finds a nice half-carat diamond ring. Even though it is a small one, it is of high quality. He pays the lady and receives his change.

"If the ring doesn't fit, take it to this address and show him the receipt. He will resize it for you for free." The lady puts the address and the receipt in a bag, along with the ring, which she has put in a nice box.

Charlie thanks the lady, takes the bag, and then happily leaves the mall.

Charlie drives to Karen's house. He walks up to the front door. Just as he gets there, Karen opens the door and wraps her loving arms around him. They both go inside. Just as they sit down on the couch, Charlie pulls out the box.

Karen's eyes begin to tear. "What's in the box, Charlie?"

Charlie doesn't say anything. He just opens the box.

Karen's eyes light up when she sees the sparkling diamond.

Charlie takes the ring out of the box and says, "My love, your hand, please."

Karen places her left hand in his. Charlie takes the ring and slips it on her third finger.

"The ring is too big," Charlie disappointedly declares.

Karen smiles at Charlie and says, "That's okay, Charlie, I will grow into it."

Karen leans over and kisses Charlie sweetly.

Charlie takes the ring off her finger and says, "Be back in a little bit."

Karen looks dazed as she sees Charlie get up and leave the house without saying another word.

She runs out to Charlie's truck and says, "Hey! You come back here with my ring!"

Charlie sticks out his tongue at her. "I will bring it back just as soon as I have it sized down. See ya later."

Charlie sticks out his tongue once again as he begins to drive off.

Karen is left standing there, with a somewhat angry, confused, and disoriented expression on her face.

Charlie looks at the address the lady gave him, and then he journeys to the establishment. He soon finds it and then parks his truck outside. He walks into the little store and finds a man behind the counter.

"Hello. I bought this ring at the mall today. The lady I bought it from said that if it didn't fit, you would resize it for free."

Charlie shows the man the receipt.

"No problem. Is it too small or too big?"

"It is too big. I believe one size too big."

The man takes the ring from Charlie and says, "I was about to close up. Could you bring it in tomorrow?"

"My girlfriend might not be my girlfriend if I keep her waiting another day. You see, I just gave it to her about twenty minutes ago. I saw that it was too big, so I yanked it off her finger, hopped into my truck, and here I am. I wish you could fix it now."

The man laughs as he hears Charlie's story.

"I guess I'd better fix it now, then! I wouldn't want her to be angry with you."

"Don't worry about that. She was angry with me when I took it off her finger. But you know how women are: the angrier they get, the more they enjoy loving up to you later."

The man roars with laughter as he begins to size down the ring.

About forty minutes later, Charlie is presented with the ring.

"Yeah, I believe that will work! I can hardly tell you did anything."

The man smiles at Charlie. "So when is the big day?"

"June 6, at six o'clock."

The man's smile fades, and his happy expression turns sour. "Did you say, June 6, at six o'clock?"

"Yes, that's right. June 6, at six o'clock."

Charlie notices a disturbed look on the man's face.

The man shakes his head and says, "You know that is the sixth month, the sixth day, and the sixth hour! That's three sixes. Young man, are you completely set on that exact day?"

Charlie gives the man a look of curiosity that quickly becomes stern. "Yes, I am! My girlfriend and I have already set the date."

"Okay, young man, I didn't mean to get you riled up. It's just that the date you are planning your wedding is 666. The sixth month, the sixth day, and the sixth hour. That is 666. That's the devil's number."

Charlie listens to the man, amazed and indignant at the same time. "You are the second person to tell me that today. I don't care if it's the devil's birthday. We set the date and time last night, and that's when it's going to be!"

Charlie takes the ring and leaves.

Charlie drives back to Karen's house. He walks in and finds Karen playing with Little Charlie in the living room.

"Hello, Cubby. Did you miss me?"

Karen gives Charlie a peeved look and says, "I beg your pardon. Who are you? Do I know you from somewhere?"

"You'd better know me. You are supposed to marry me in two weeks."

Charlie brings the bag holding the ring with him as he sits down beside her on the couch.

"Oh yeah, I know you. You are the one who took my engagement ring away."

Karen takes a pillow and hits Charlie with it. Charlie smiles at her as he takes the box out of the bag. This gets her attention.

"I had your ring sized down," he says. "Just one size."

"Oh, is that so! What makes you think I want it now?"

"Well, if you don't want it, I could always take it back. Maybe I could exchange it for an iron or a vacuum cleaner."

Karen reaches for the box as she says, "You ain't gonna exchange it for anything, you shit ass. Give me my ring!"

Charlie teases Karen a little bit.

"Oh no, you have been a bad girl. Bad girls don't get diamond rings."

"Oh, come on, Charlie, let me have my ring. I was only kidding. Please …"

Charlie sees how badly Karen wants the ring, so he teases her a little longer.

"No. I don't know if I should give it to you now. You have been a bad girl."

"You give me my ring, or I will—"

"Or you will, what?"

"Charlie Delaney!"

"Okay, okay. Just say, 'I'm sorry, master, for being a bad girl.'"

Karen gives Charlie a mean look as she says, "I'm sorry, master, for being a bad girl. Now give me my damn ring."

Karen's face lights up as Charlie takes the ring out of the box and gently places it on the third finger of her left hand.

Charlie announces, "It's a perfect fit!"

Now that Charlie has placed the ring on her finger, Karen begins to cry tears of love, showing intense emotion.

"It's so beautiful! I just don't know what to say."

Karen melts into Charlie's arms. Her eyes shed tears of happiness and joy. Charlie holds her lovingly.

"I love you so much, Cubby. I will try as hard as I can to make you happy."

Karen snuggles close to Charlie.

"Charlie, you make me so happy now, I can't stand it. I love you so much! Oh, how I love you."

So Charlie and Karen continue to embrace each other until Mrs. Thomas comes home.

When Mrs. Thomas walks in, she sees the engagement ring from clear across the room. She eagerly walks over to both of them and gazes down at the gleaming diamond.

"Wow! That sure is a pretty ring. Where's mine?"

Charlie and Karen laugh at Mrs. Thomas's remark.

"I didn't have the money to buy two, so … here." Charlie leans over and kisses Mrs. Thomas on the cheek.

"Thank you, Ma, for bringing the girl who has made me so happy into the world."

"Oh, Charlie, you are welcome."

"Mama, isn't it the most beautiful ring you have ever seen?"

"Yes, dear, it certainly is. I am so happy for both of you."

So Charlie, Karen, and Mrs. Thomas sit on the couch, admiring the engagement ring and each other. After a few moments go by, Mrs. Thomas looks at Charlie with a little bit of apprehension.

She finally works up her courage and says, "Charlie, why don't you two get married on Sunday instead of Saturday?"

Karen quickly reacts. "No! We have already set the date: June 6, at six o'clock, and that's that!"

"I will have to agree with Karen, Ma. Why don't you like Saturday?"

"It's not that I don't like Saturday, it's just that, well …"

Karen and Charlie look curiously at Mrs. Thomas.

Charlie gets that same feeling he has already felt twice today.

"Well … you see, June 6 is the sixth month and the sixth day, and since you are getting married at six o'clock … well … that means you are getting married on the sixth month and the sixth day, at the sixth hour. That is three sixes! You know what that represents?"

Charlie looks at Karen with sincerity, and Karen looks at Charlie with confusion.

"You are the third person who has told me that today, Ma. Maybe we should get married on Sunday, June 7. What do you think, Karen?"

Karen gives off a very disappointed expression. Her angry look makes the atmosphere very tense.

"No! I don't care what it represents! We set the date last night, and that's the way it's going to be! I want everything to stay the same as what we planned. I don't want to make any changes now! Well … is that agreed?"

Charlie leans over and kisses her on her soft lips, and then he says, "Yes, ma'am, that is okay with me."

Karen says, "Fine! It is official now. We will be married on June 6, at six o'clock."

Mrs. Thomas doesn't want to make any waves, so she agrees to their decision without saying anything further.

On Friday evening, the night before that all-important day, Charlie sits home alone. Mrs. Thomas won't let him come over to see Karen before the wedding. But his desire to hold her in his arms is all he can think of. His passion to be near her consumes his mind and heart. As his thoughts continue to flood into his heart he hears the phone ring.

Charlie walks over to the phone and picks it up.

"Hello. This is Charlie Delaney's residence."

Charlie hears a woman crying. He then gets a scary fright. "Hello! Who is this?"

"Hello, Charlie. This is Dee. Remember me?"

With that, Charlie sits down in a chair and begins to talk to his old flame. "Hello, Dee. I have some news to tell you."

"First, Charlie, there is something I want to tell you."

"Okay, you go first."

"First of all, I got fired from my job this week."

"What!"

"Yeah, Charlie, I got fired. I just don't know what to do. I am still living in my mobile home, but my little boy is living with my mama now. I told her that I am seeing you again and—"

"Dee, I wish you wouldn't phrase it like that," Charlie interjects.

"But it's true, Charlie! I have talked to you almost every week now since—"

Charlie interrupts again. "Even though I've asked you not to call me, I have talked to you every time because you are an old friend. That's what we are Dee: old friends."

"Charlie, you mean more to me than that. I think about you all the time."

"I think about you too but …" Charlie's voice trails off.

"But, what, Charlie?"

Charlie tries to change the subject. "So why did you get fired from your job?"

Dee pauses for a moment before saying, "I couldn't make myself get to work on time. I was late several times because I was crying over you."

"Dee, please don't."

"After I got fired, I told mama about us. She was furious about me losing my job."

Charlie, showing a worried look, says, "I wish you had not told your mama about me. She never liked me."

"Well, Charlie, your name came up in one of our conversations. I just can't seem to function without you. I miss you so much, Charlie."

"Dee, there is something I need to tell you."

Charlie pauses before telling Dee about his and Karen's wedding.

"You see, Dee, Karen and I are going to get married. Tomorrow."

Charlie hears Dee crying in the background. He listens it the sound, with pain burning in his heart.

After a few painful moments, Dee says, "I can't believe you would do that to me."

Dee begins to cry profusely. Through her tears, she says, "No, Charlie. No! Don't marry that girl! Don't you know that I love you?!"

"Of course I do, Dee, of course I do. But I can't help it. I love Karen. She is the girl I want to spend the rest of my life with. I want her to be the mother of my children. Karen is the most important person in my—"

Dee's shrill voice interrupts him. "I will kill myself if you do! I will, Charlie! I will kill myself! You love me, not her! How can you marry someone else if you love me!"

Charlie rubs his forehead as he tries to figure out what to say next.

"Listen, Dee, sure I love you. Part of me will always love you. But I love Karen in a different way. I want her to be my wife. I want her to share my life with me. I don't want to hurt you, Dee. I care a great deal about you. I always will, but there is someone else I want to be with."

Charlie hears Dee's ragged breathing over the phone. She continues to cry uncontrollably. The sounds cut deep into Charlie's conscience.

Charlie waits patiently, saying nothing.

Finally, Dee says, "All of our lives something or someone has tried to pull us apart, Charlie. Then we get thrown together with the force of a hurricane. We finally get to love each other. Now something else—someone else—is pulling us apart. I can't take being pulled away from you anymore! I can't." Dee's tears overwhelm her words, preventing her from saying anything else.

Charlie pauses and takes a deep breath before saying, "Dee, listen here. I can't help the situation any. I am to be married tomorrow to the girl I want to be my wife. I am truly sorry for the pain I have caused you. I really am! Everything will be all right. Please try to pull yourself together. I can't talk to you anymore now. I have to get ready for the wedding tomorrow. You need to accept that, Dee."

"I will never accept that, Charlie! I will never accept it!"

"You are going to have to, Dee. By tomorrow this time, I will already be married."

There is a short pause.

"Where are you going to get married?"

"I'm not going to tell you, Dee. You don't need to know that. Please try to understand."

Charlie hears Dee's crying again.

"Understand! How can I understand! You are going to get married to someone else tomorrow! How can I understand that! How can I accept that? I love you, Charlie. I love you."

Dee begins to cry awfully now. The sound would make all the angels in heaven cry.

Tears begin to run down Charlie's face also. The pain is so bad Charlie just puts the phone down. He picks it up after twenty seconds. Hearing a dial tone, he decides to leave it off the hook.

Charlie sits back and thinks painfully about Dee. His heart aches with sadness. He gets up and takes his lithium. The lithium removes all of Charlie's depression, but it doesn't faze the sadness he feels about Dee.

He goes upstairs to his bedroom, turns the lights out, and goes to bed.

Before long, that all-important day comes: Saturday, June 6.

Around 2 p.m. Charlie sits alone in his living room still wearing his pajamas. His worried, anxious look covers his face. His eyes are blood shot for he didn't sleep much last night thinking of Dee and her sad situation. Charlie wants to hurry up and married Karen before Dee does something to mess up things.

As he sits there on the couch he thinks about what Karen is doing. All he wants is to hold her in his arms right now. The thoughts he is thinking about her overwhelms his whole person. Then a knock is heard. Charlie jumps up and runs to the door to see who it is. It is Wayne

Scott, Charlie's best man at the wedding. Charlie welcomes him in and is relieved it isn't Dee.

Wayne speaks, "Man you look terrible. You need to get dressed and fix yourself up. You are getting married today. Have you forgot that?"

"No I haven't forgot. How could I forget that? I wish it would hurry up and be done with it. I feel anxious that something bad is going to happen and mess things up."

"You are just nervous. That happens to all men who are fixing to give away their freedom forever and become a slave to a woman's body forever. Tee hee hee."

"Oh very funny. And stop using my laugh. I have a patient on that laugh." Charlie grins to his good buddy as he speaks these words.

"Oh by the way, I need to have to ring." You know the engagement ring. I need to have it so I can give it to you at the ceremony."

"The ring! The ring! Karen still has it. I have to go over there and get it, now!" I need to call Karen.

So Charlie runs over the phone, thinks about what he wants to say, then dials her number.

Karen answers, "Hello Thomas's residence".

"Hello gorgeous. Just wondering if you still want to marry me today"?

"Charlie. Mama told me not to talk to you until the ceremony. You know that."

"Can't do that. I must meet you, my love. I got to get the ring back so I can put it on your finger. I can't talk any more. I will be over in ten minutes. Try to get Ma to leave the house. Ask her to go buy you something, anything to get her out of the house. I will come over get the ring and then leave. Bye."

Charlie hangs the phone up before Karen has time to say anything. She doesn't tell her mama that he called. She persuades her to go and buy a bottle of perfume, a special type.

Fifteen minutes go by since Charlie called. Mrs. Thomas gets into her car and drives way. Just as she turns on another street she sees Charlie's truck pull into her driveway. She angrily begins to turn he car around.

Charlie mumbles to himself, '*I didn't think she would ever leave.*'

He gets out of his truck and walks fast and determined to the house, opens the door and walks in unannounced. He doesn't take three steps until he sees Karen. She is standing around ten feet away and wearing her pure white wedding gown. Their eyes meet. Her innocent eyes are glassy. They are as blue as sapphires glimmering in the sunlight. Her temptation eyes makes Charlie want her right now! Her milky white complexion, long red hair, and innocent youthful smile gives her a vision of and angel. She stirs Charlie's heart like never before. She is the most beautiful woman Charlie Delaney has ever seen. His mouth falls open as he witnesses her captivating beauty. He is truly mesmerized by her glory.

He walks over to her, and without saying a word, locks his mouth to hers. Their passionate kiss is only broken by Karen's playful push.

"You are not supposed to be here. Mama told me not to see you before..."

Charlie interrupts, "I can't stand to be away from you. I love you more now than I ever had in my life. I don't ever want to be away from you ever again."

Charlie once again pushes his mouth wildly against Karen's. She welcomes his seductive kiss and her passion pulls Charlie closer. The passionate kiss last several minutes.

Then a loud, scary voice is heard, "Stay away from my daughter!!!" It is familiar voice Charlie has heard in a nightmare he had months ago. The loving couple turn and see Mrs. Thomas with a face full of anger standing at the doorway. She continues. "It is bad luck to see the bride on her wedding day. So get away from her, right now!"

Charlie holding Karen's hand grins at Mrs. Thomas and playfully says, "Hey Ma. I see you forgot to take your PMS pills today. Tee hee hee. I understand why you are so cranky right now. Tee hee hee."

Mrs. Thomas not amused bellows, "Get! Get from here right now!"

Ma, don't be so angry at me. I came over because I need to get the ring back. So you see, I had good reason to come over here." Charlie takes the ring off Karen's finger and shows it to Mrs. Thomas.

"OK, you got the ring. Now get! Get moving buster!"

Charlie wanting to have a little fun with Mrs. Thomas reaches over and kisses Karen on the mouth with vigor. Then sticks his tongue out at Mrs. Thomas. Mrs. Thomas responds by grabbing a broom siting in a corner and starts to hit Charlie with it as she chases him out the house.

"Get! Get I say! Move it! Out of my house! Move it!" She says this while she hits Charlie with the broom. She continues until Charlie is no longer in the house. Charlie laughs all the way out the door until he gets into his truck. Right before he drives off he looks at the hysterical female and says, "I love you Ma. I love you as much as I love Karen." He blows her a kiss then drives off.

The church begins to fill up by five-thirty. Some of Charlie's friends, acting as ushers, escort the guests to their seats.

Wayne Scott, Charlie's best man is smiling from ear to ear. Everyone is happy and cheerful. The ushers greet the guests and direct them to which side they should sit.

As the time gets closer to six o'clock, there is someone staring at the church across the street. No! It can't be! He's back! The Old Man is back! He is looking toward the church, with a frown on his face. His long curly blond hair dangles down below his shoulders. His beady blue eyes have mischief in them. He gazes at the church, with an evil scowl on his face. He stares at the white church for a few minutes and then turns and walks away, disappearing into the woods.

At six o'clock, the services begin. Charlie, wearing a tuxedo, waits at the altar. When the organist plays the processional of the Wedding March, Karen comes walking down the aisle, wearing a long gown of white silk. A lacy white veil covers her face. When Karen finally reaches the front, Charlie lifts the veil. He sees her innocent, nervous expression glowing out toward him. He smiles at her as he sees a tear run down her happy, nervous face.

Reverend Heath performs the ceremony without a hitch.

Charlie then says his personal vows to his virgin: "Karen, I promise to be faithful to you all the days of our lives. I will do all I can for you. I will try to make you happy in every way I can. I will protect you from all danger. I will love you every day of my life. I will always be there for you and will always remain there for you. I love you with all my heart."

Karen's eyes begin to water with tears of joy.

Reverend Heath asks in a soft voice, "Are there any vows you want to say to Charlie?"

Karen nervously answers, "Yes, there are."

Her hands shake, and her voice cracks as she says, "Charlie, I love you so. I promise to be faithful to you all the days of our lives. I promise to be a good wife and to always be there for you. I promise, above all, to be yours and yours only for all of eternity."

Charlie smiles contentedly as he reaches over and clasps Karen's shaking hand, holding it tight in his.

Charlie and Karen have exchanged rings and spoken their vows, so Reverend Heath announces, "With the powers vested in me, I now I pronounce you man and wife! You may kiss the bride."

Charlie leans over and kisses his wife as all the people in the church begin to applaud loudly. The organist begins to play the recessional of the Wedding March. A covey of white doves begins to fly around the church as the organist plays. Charlie, still holding Karen's hand, leads her back up the aisle. The two run out of the church, full of joy and happiness.

Mrs. Thomas cries like a baby. She is so happy to see her only child married. She greets the guests with joy and jubilation. Soon the church is empty.

Charlie and Karen go back inside the church to sign some papers. Charlie slides a hundred-dollar bill to the reverend as he shakes his hand. There are a few pictures taken and a few kisses given away.

Mrs. Thomas says, "Okay. You two have to go up and leave the church one more time so everyone can throw the rice on you."

So Charlie and Karen quickly go upstairs and depart the church one more time. All the people throw rice on the happy couple. Some of Charlie's friends throw handfuls of flour! Charlie just shakes his head as the guys laugh profusely.

Everyone goes to the reception hall adjacent to the church. Charlie and Karen cut the cake and feed each other as Mrs. Thomas looks on with joy and happiness. Just as Charlie puts the piece of cake near Karen's open mouth, he pushes in the entire piece. Karen's eyes widen at this unexpected move. Everyone laughs wholeheartedly at Charlie's mischievous deed. Karen gives him an I'm-going-to-get-you-for-that look. As Karen keeps her eyes on Charlie, she thrusts her hand into the wedding cake and pulls out a handful. She pushes the whole amount of the cake into Charlie's face. The people roar with laughter, happy and jubilant. The entire reception is full of laughter, joy, and happiness. Even Little Charlie seems to enjoy running around the place. The table across from the cake is filled with presents.

Someone says, "Come on, Charlie, Karen, open your presents!"

The rest of the guests join in.

After Charlie gets everyone's attention, he announces, "We won't have time to open the presents. We have to catch a plane in less than an hour. I just want to thank each and every one of you for bringing them."

Someone calls out, "Hey, Charlie, where are you going on your honeymoon?"

Charlie takes Karen by the hand and says, "We are going to Niagara Falls. We are going to be there for two weeks."

The faces of the people erupt with excitement as they all applaud vigorously.

At seven o'clock sharp, Charlie makes another announcement: "Everyone! Everyone! I am glad you all came today, but my wife and I are preparing to leave now. You all can stay here as long as you want, but I have other avenues to explore now."

Everyone laughs as Karen hits Charlie playfully on the arm.

Mrs. Thomas hugs and then kisses her daughter and Charlie.

Most of the people go outside to see the happy couple leave the scene. Charlie helps Karen into his truck. It has been baptized with shaving cream and toilet paper by some of Charlie's buddies. Karen kisses Charlie one more time, and then he runs around to the other side of the truck. He turns and waves good-bye to all the spectators. Charlie gets in and starts up his truck.

He looks over at his bride and says, "The first place we will go is to the car wash to wash all this crap off. Then it's straight to the airport, where our plane awaits our arrival. We can change clothes there. Wayne will follow us there and take our wedding clothes back home with him. I'm glad I married you, Cubby!"

Karen smiles and says, "I'm glad you did too! Let's go!"

Charlie puts the gear in first, and then he pulls out of the church parking lot.

As Charlie approaches the first stoplight, he sees it turn green. He's moving slow, so he puts it in a higher gear and steps on the gas. Just as Charlie gets under the light, he glances over and sees a car coming at them on Karen's side! The car is moving at an incredibly fast speed! There is no time to react! The car slams into Karen's door!

The sound of the two vehicles colliding is horrifying—metal hitting metal, glass shattering.

Mrs. Thomas sees the accident happen, as do most of the others there at the church. It sends a wave of shock and panic through all those present.

People begin to run to the scene. The sound of sirens fills the air.

Inside the truck, Charlie looks over at Karen and says in a panic-stricken voice, "Karen! Karen! Are you all right!"

Karen's white gown has been turn into a horrific vision of red.

Rolling her eyes toward Charlie, Karen says, "Charlie! Oh, Charlie! I love you …"

Charlie and Karen both lose consciousness.

The sirens get closer and closer.

Just around the corner from where the wreck took place, there is someone standing and observing the catastrophe in silence. It is he: the Old Man. He glares at the paramedics taking Charlie and Karen out of the demolished truck. He smiles a hideous smile! He jumps up and down with great jubilation. He rubs his hands together as he sees the red stains on Charlie's and Karen's clothes. The Old Man starts to dance a jig as he sees the panic-stricken faces of the people. The loud crying and heartbreaking moaning of Mrs. Thomas and the other people there puts the Old Man into an erotic frenzy! After the ambulance comes and goes, the Old Man smiles proudly and then disappears into the woods.

At the hospital, Mrs. Thomas and all the others wait nervously in the waiting room for news about Charlie and Karen. Mrs. Thomas's hands are shaking feverishly. She paces the floor, panicked. As she walks up and down the hallway, a doctor comes out of a room.

He looks at all the people there and asks, "Is there a Mrs. Thomas present?"

"Yes! I am she! Is my daughter all right?!"

The doctor looks at Mrs. Thomas sadly. "Please come with me."

Mrs. Thomas follows the doctor into another room.

When the doctor and Mrs. Thomas are alone, he says to her, "First of all, I understand that Mr. Delaney has no immediate family."

Mrs. Thomas gets control of herself and says, "That's right, doctor. His mother and father have both passed away. Is Charlie all right?!"

"I am glad to tell you that he will be fine. He has a bruised right shoulder, and his right hand is sprained; he has lots of other cuts and bruises. The worst of his injuries is a nasty concussion, but it's nothing too serious. Mr. Delaney should be out of here in a week or two."

Mrs. Thomas expresses relief when she hears about Charlie's condition.

The doctor pauses, and then he gives Mrs. Thomas a look of grave concern.

"So how's my daughter! Is she going to be all right!"

The silence is deafening, and then the doctor says, "Mrs. Thomas, the car rammed into the truck on the passenger side, where your daughter was sitting." The doctor pauses as Mrs. Thomas begins to panic. The doctor then continues in a very gentle tone. "Mrs. Thomas, I regret to inform you that your daughter, Karen, died about ten minutes ago. I am sorry."

"No! No! It can't be! She was just married! She can't die now! She just can't! It isn't fair!"

Mrs. Thomas begins to cry profusely. Her face is full of misery. She falls to the floor in a hysterical state. She cries as she rolls across the floor and into a corner. She makes sounds that show her heart is breaking. Her moans and pain-filled sounds of sheer misery are felt by the doctor tremendously. He slowly leaves the room, with tears flowing from his eyes.

Karen was only nineteen years old when she married the man she loved. The last day of her life was also the happiest day of her life. She was full of kindness and sweetness. The love she gave Charlie and her mother will never be replaced. Her youthful smile brought joy to everyone she encountered.

And yet, even though she married the man she loved, it must be said, Karen Thomas Delaney died a virgin.

THE END

Printed in the United States
By Bookmasters